SCARED TO DEATH

Also by Kate Medina

The Jessie Flynn series
Fire Damage

Standalone novels
White Crocodile

KATE MEDINA

Scared to Death

HarperCollins*Publishers*

HarperCollins*Publishers*
1 London Bridge Street
London SE1 9GF

www.harpercollins.co.uk

Published by HarperCollins*Publishers* 2017
1

A catalogue record for this book
is available from the British Library

ISBN: 978-0-00-813233-0

This novel is entirely a work of fiction.
The names, characters and incidents portrayed in it are
the work of the author's imagination. Any resemblance to
actual persons, living or dead, events or localities is
entirely coincidental.

Typeset by Palimpsest Book Production Ltd, Falkirk, Stirlingshire

Printed and bound in Great Britain by
Clays Ltd, St Ives plc

MIX
Paper from
responsible sources
FSC˚ C007454

FSC™ is a non-profit international organisation established to promote
the responsible management of the world's forests. Products carrying the
FSC label are independently certified to assure consumers that they come
from forests that are managed to meet the social, economic and
ecological needs of present and future generations,
and other controlled sources.

Find out more about HarperCollins and the environment at
www.harpercollins.co.uk/green

For my mother, Pamela Taylor, with love

The Story of the Three Bears

ONCE upon a time there were Three Bears, who lived together in a house of their own in a wood. One of them was a Little, Small, Wee Bear, and one was a Middle-Sized Bear, and the other was a Great, Huge Bear.

Robert Southey, 1774–1843

1

Eleven Years Ago

The eighteen-year-old boy in the smart uniform made his way along the path that skirted the woods bordering the school's extensive playing fields. He walked quickly, one hand in his pocket, the other holding the handle of the cricket bat that rested over his shoulder, like the umbrella of some city gent. Gene Kelly in *Singin' in the Rain*. For the first time in a very long time he felt nimble and light on his feet, as if he could dance. And he felt even lighter in his heart, as though the weight that had saddled him for five long years was finally lifting. Light, but at the same time keyed-up and jittery with anticipation. Thoughts of what was to come drove the corners of his mouth to twitch upwards.

He used to smile all the time when he was younger, but he had almost forgotten how. All the fun in his life, the beauty that he had seen in the world, had been destroyed five years ago. Destroyed once, and then again and again, until he no longer saw joyfulness in anything. He had thought that, in time, his hatred and anger would recede. But instead it had festered and grown black and rabid inside him, the only thing that held any substance or meaning for him.

He had reached the hole in the fence. By the time they moved into the sixth form, boys from the school were routinely slipping through the boundary fence to jog into the local village to buy cigarettes and alcohol, and the rusty nails holding the bottom of the vertical wooden slats had been eased out years before, the slats held in place only at their tops, easy to slide apart. Nye was small for his age and slipped through the gap without leaving splinters or a trace of lichen on his grey woollen trousers or bottle green blazer, or threads of his clothing on the fence.

The hut he reached a few minutes later was small and dilapidated, a corrugated iron roof and weathered plank walls. It used to be a woodman's shed, Nye had been told, and it still held stacks of dried logs in one corner. Sixth formers were the only ones who used it now, to meet up and smoke; the odd one who'd got lucky with one of the girls from the day school down the road used it for sex.

Nye had detoured here first thing this morning before class to clean it out, slipping on his leather winter gloves to pick up the couple of used condoms and toss them into the woods. *Disgusting.* He hadn't worried about his footprints – there would be nothing left of the hut by the time this day was over.

Now, he sprayed a circular trail of lighter fuel around the inside edge of the hut, scattered more on the pile of dry logs and woodchips in the corner, ran a dripping line around the door frame and another around the one small wire-mesh-covered window. Tossing the bottle of lighter fuel on to the stack of logs, he moved quietly into a dark corner of the shed where he would be shielded from immediate view by the door when it opened, and waited. He was patient. He had learned patience the hard way and today his patience would pay off.

Footsteps outside suddenly, footsteps whose pattern, regularity and weight were seared into his brain. Squeezing himself into the corner, Nye held his breath as the rickety wooden door creaked open. The man who stepped into the hut closed the door behind him, pressing it tightly into its frame as Nye knew he would. He stood for a moment, letting his vision adjust to the dimness before he looked around. Nye saw the man's eyes widen in surprise when he noticed him standing in the shadows, when he saw that it wasn't the person he had been expecting to meet. His face twisted in anger – an anger Nye knew well.

Swinging the bat in a swift, neat arc as his sports masters had taught him, Nye connected the bat's flat face, dented from contact with countless cricket balls on the school's pitches, with the man's temple. A sickening crunch, wood on bone, and the man dropped to his knees. Blood pulsed from split skin and reddened the side of his face. Nye was tempted to hit him again. Beat him until his head was pulp, but he restrained himself. The first strike had done its job and he wanted the man conscious, wanted him sentient for what was to come.

Dropping the cricket bat on to the floor next to the crumpled man, Nye pulled open the shed door. Stepping into the dusk of the woods outside, he closed it behind him. There was a rusty latch on the gnarled door frame, the padlock long since disappeared. Flipping the latch over the metal loop on the door, he stooped and collected the thick stick he'd tested for size and left there earlier, and jammed it through the loop.

Moving around to the window, too small for the man to fit through – he'd checked that too; he'd checked and double-checked everything – he struck a match and pushed his fingers through the wire. He caught sight of the man's pale face looking up at him, legs like those of a newborn calf as he tried to struggle to his feet. His eyes were huge and very black in the darkness of the shed. Nye held the man's gaze, his mouth twisting into a smile. He saw the man's eyes flick from his face to the lit match in his fingers, recognized that moment where the nugget of hope segued into doubt and then into naked fear. He had experienced that moment himself so many times.

He let the lit match fall from his fingers.

Stepping away from the window, melting a few metres into the woods, Nye stood and watched the glow build inside the hut, listened to the man's screams, his pleas for help as he himself had pleaded, also in vain, watched and listened until he was sure that the fire had caught a vicious hold. Then he turned and made his way back through the woods, walking quickly, staying off the paths.

It was 13 July, his last day in this godforsaken shithole.

He had waited five long years for this moment.

Thirteen. Unlucky for some, but not for me. Not any more.

2

Twelve Months Ago

He had thought, when the time came, that he would be brave. That he would be able to bear his death with dignity. But his desperation for oxygen was so overwhelming that he would have ripped his own head off for the opportunity to draw breath. He sucked against the tape, but he had done the job well and there were no gaps, no spaces for oxygen to seep through. Wrapping his hands around the metal pipe that was fixed to the tiled wall, digging his nails into the flaking paint, he held on, willing himself to endure the pain, knowing, whatever he felt, that he had no choice now anyway.

Closing his eyes, he tried to draw a picture to mind, a picture of his son, of his face, but the image was lost in the screaming of blood in his ears, the throbbing inside his skull as his brain, his lungs, his whole being ballooned and burst with its frenzied need for oxygen. He felt fingers clawing at his temples. But he had wrapped the gaffer tape tight, layer upon layer of it round and round his head, and his own fingernails, chewed and ragged, couldn't get purchase.

His lungs were burning and tearing, rupturing with the agony of denied breath.

The room was fading, the feel of his scrabbling fingers numbing. His brain fogged, his limbs were leaden and the pain receded. Danny's eyes drifted closed and he felt calm, calm and euphoric, just for a moment. Then, nothing.

3

Nobody noticed the pram tucked against the wall inside the entrance to Accident and Emergency at Royal Surrey County Hospital, until the baby inside woke and began to cry. It was another ten minutes before the sound of the crying child registered in the stultified brain of the A & E receptionist who had been working since 11 p.m. the previous night and was now wholly focused on watching the hands of her countertop clock creep towards 7 a.m. and the end of her shift. The 'zombie shift', nights were dubbed, both for their obliterating effect on the employee and in reference to the motley stream of patients who shuffled in through the sliding doors. The past eight hours had been the busiest she could remember. Dampness she expected in April, but constant downpours combined with unseasonal heat were a gift to unsavoury bugs. Back-to-back registrations all night, not enough time even to grab a second coffee, and now her nerves, not to mention her temper, were snapping. At fifty-five she was too old for this kind of job, should have taken her sister's advice and become a PA to a nice lazy managing director in some small business years ago.

She had noticed the pram – she *had* – she would tell the police when they interviewed her later, but she had assumed that it had been parked there, empty, by one of the parents who had taken their baby into Paediatrics. It had been a reasonable assumption, she insisted to the odd-looking detective inspector, who had made her feel as if she was responsible for mass murder with that cynical rolling of his disconcertingly mismatched eyes. The wait in Paediatric A & E on a busy night was five hours, so it was entirely reasonable that an empty pram could be parked in the entrance for that long. *God*, at least she didn't turn up for work looking as if she'd spent the night snorting cocaine, which was more than could be said for him.

Skirting around the desk, she approached the pram, the soles of her Dr Scholl's sighing as they grasped and released the rain-damp lino. Her stomach knotted tightly as she neared it, recent staff lectures stressing the importance of vigilance in this age of extremism suddenly a deafening alarm bell at the forefront of her mind. But when she peeped inside the pram, she felt ridiculous for that moment of intense apprehension. She breathed out, her heart rate slowing as the tense balloon of air emptied from her lungs.

A baby boy, eighteen months or so he must be, dressed in a white envelope-neck T-shirt and sky-blue corduroy dungarees, was looking up at her, his blue eyes wide open and shiny with tears. Wet tracks cut through the dirt on his cheeks. His mouth gaped, lips a trembling oval, as if he was uncertain whether to smile or cry, four white tombstone teeth visible in the wet pink cavity.

Reaching into the pram, Janet gently scooped him into

her arms. Nestling him against her bosom, she felt the chick's fluff of his hair, smelt the slightly stale, milky smell of him, felt the bulge of his full nappy, straining heavy in her fingers as she slid her hand under his bottom to support his weight. The child gave a sigh and Janet felt his warm body relax into hers.

'Now who on earth would leave a little chap like you alone for so long?' she cooed softly. 'Who on earth?'

How long since she'd held a baby? Years, she realized, with a sharp twinge of sadness. Her youngest nephew fifteen now and already on to his fourth girlfriend in as many months, her own son, nearing thirty, had fled the nest years ago.

She turned back to the reception desk, all efficiency now. 'Robin, get on the tannoy would you and make an announcement. Some irresponsible fool has left their baby out here and he's woken up. Probably needs feeding.' She looked down at the baby. 'Don't you worry, sweetheart. We'll find your mummy and get you fed.' She tickled his cheek with the tip of her index finger. 'We will. Yes, we will, gorgeous boy.' Glancing up, she met Robin's amused gaze. 'What? What on earth are you smirking about?'

4

Jessie woke with a start and opened her eyes. The room was dark, the air dusty and stale, a room that hadn't been aired in months. She felt dizzy and nauseous, as if her brain was slopping untethered inside her skull, her tongue a numb wad of cotton filling her mouth. Once again, the man's voice that had woken her spoke from close by. For a brief moment, caught in that twilight zone between sleep and wakefulness, she had no idea where she was. Which country. Which time zone.

'Some folk tales – or fairy tales as we like to call them nowadays – originated to help people pass on survival tips to the next generation. Many of the stories that we now tell our children at bedtime were based on gruesome real events and would have served as warnings to young children not to stray too far from their parents' protection.'

The radio. Of course. She had left it on when she went to bed last night, used now to being lulled to sleep by noise. The groan of metal flexing on waves, footsteps pacing down corridors, machines humming in distant rooms.

Home. She was home, she realized as cognizance overtook her. Back in England, waking in her own bed for the first time in three months.

'Over the years these stories have changed, evolved to suit the modern world. Even though humans are as violent nowadays as they were in 600 BC, we don't like to terrify our children in the same way that our ancestors did, so we sugar-coat fairy tales. But their horrific origins and the messages behind them are deadly serious.'

She had flown into RAF Brize Norton airbase late last night, arrived home at 2 a.m. – 5 a.m. Syrian, Persian Gulf, time – and collapsed into bed, exhausted, jet-lagged, struggling to adjust not only her body clock but her brain from Royal Navy Destroyer to eighteenth-century farmworker's cottage in the Surrey Hills, a juxtaposition so complete that she had felt as if she was tripping on acid. Washed out from months of shuttling between RAF Akrotiri in Cyprus and the HMS *Daring*, counselling fighter jet and helicopter pilots flying sorties over ISIS-held territory in Syria and Iraq, working with PsyOps to see how they could win hearts and influence minds in the region. Unused to the impenetrable darkness and graveyard silence of the countryside, she had, for the first time in her life, flipped the radio on, volume turned low, background noise, and fallen asleep to its soft warble.

On the radio, the man's voice was rising. *'Snow White and the Seven Dwarves is based on the life of a sixteenth-century Bavarian noblewoman, whose brother used small children to work in his copper mines. Severely deformed because of the physical hardships, they were referred to as dwarves. 'We know that Little Red Riding Hood is about violation, a young girl allowing herself to be charmed by*

11

a stranger. The contemporary French idiom for a girl having lost her virginity is "Elle avoit vu le coup", which translates literally as "She has seen the wolf".'

Reaching an arm out, Jessie jammed her finger on the 'off' switch. Silence. Not even birdsong; too early yet for the dawn chorus. Curling on to her side, she closed her eyes and tugged the duvet up around her ears, trying to tilt back into sleep. But she was awake now, her mind a buzz of jetlag-fuelled, pent-up energy. *May as well get up and face the day.*

Throwing off the duvet, she padded into the bathroom to have a shower, catching her reflection in the huge mirror above the sink that she had erroneously thought it a good idea to install after reading a home décor magazine at the dentist that had waxed lyrical about mirrors opening up small spaces. The harsh electric ceiling lights, another poor idea – same magazine – washed the face looking back at her ghostly grey-white, blue eyes so pale they were nearly translucent, black hair limp and unkempt, a cartoon version of Snow White with a stinking hangover. *Jesus, Jessie, only you could spend twelve weeks in the Middle East and still come back looking as if you've been bleached.* Coffee was the answer, and lots of it.

Downstairs, her cottage's sitting room was show-home spotless, exactly as she had left it: a cream sofa and two matching chairs separated by a reclaimed oak coffee table bare of clutter, fitted white-painted shelves empty of books and ornaments, the sole splash of colour, a vase of fresh daffodils that Ahmose must have left on the coffee table to welcome her home. Herself, by a long way, the messiest thing in the room.

Her gaze found the two framed photographs on the mantelpiece. Looking at Jamie, at his smiley face, all teeth and gums, lips ringed by a smear of chocolate ice cream, she felt the familiar emptiness in her chest, as if under her ribcage was nothing but air. Pushing away thoughts of him, of her past, she padded into the kitchen and made herself a coffee – strong, topped up with lots of full-fat milk, straight from the farm, that Ahmose must have put in her fridge yesterday, along with the bread and butter, lined side by side on the top shelf, an identical space between each item, Ahmose trained now to defer to her extreme sense of order.

She put the kettle back on its stand, straightened the handle flush with the wall, and then deliberately gave it a nudge, knocking it off-kilter. No hiss from the electric suit. No immediate urge to realign it. Not yet. Baby steps, she knew, but progress all the same. Progress she had worked hard, before leaving for her foreign tour, to achieve. Progress that she was determined to maintain, now, coming home.

Unlocking the back door, she stepped out into the garden, glancing up at Ahmose's bedroom window as she did so. Lights off, curtains closed, still asleep as any sensible person who wasn't a shift worker or in the Army should be at this pre-dawn hour. Moving slowly across the dark lawn, she inhaled deeply. The air was cool and clean, carrying a faint scent of water on cut grass, the lawn crisp and damp beneath her bare soles. At the bottom of the garden, she settled herself on to the wooden fence and gazed across the farmer's field. The sunrise was still only a narrow strip of fire on the horizon, the sky above inky blue-black, the somnolent sheep in the field hummocks of barely visible grey, the spring lambs, cleaner, brighter, lying tight against their mothers' stomachs for warmth.

Little Bo Peep has lost her sheep . . .

A peaceful pre-dawn, bearing the promise of a beautiful morning.

Home. She was home. Home safe. So why did she still have this odd sensation of emptiness in her chest? Jamie, yes – but something else too. What did she have to worry about? Nothing. She had nothing, or did she?

5

'Midnight?' Detective Inspector Bobby 'Marilyn' Simmons snapped. 'You first noticed the pram at midnight?' Tugging up his suit jacket sleeve, he tapped his watch with a nicotine-stained index finger. 'As in midnight eight hours ago?' His eyes blazed as he looked at the prim, mousy-haired woman in front of him who was clutching a mug of coffee emblazoned with the words *Fill with coffee and nobody gets hurt* and staring at him as if he was the devil. At least she had the good grace to blush.

'The baby was asleep.' She folded her arms defensively across her bust and tipped back on her heels. It was obvious that she was uncomfortable with his proximity, but he was in no mood to take a step back, out of her personal space, and make it easier for her. 'I thought that the pram was empty.'

Marilyn – a nickname he had acquired on his first day with Surrey and Sussex Major Crimes, the bi-county joint command serious crimes investigation team, thanks to an uncanny resemblance to the ageing American rocker Marilyn

Manson – sighed and rubbed a hand over his mismatched eyes. He had a persistent, throbbing headache, which he knew was well-deserved payback for last night's 2 a.m.'er, knowledge that didn't make dealing with it any easier. He could murder a cup of that coffee she was clutching. He was also fully aware that he was being an arsehole, could feel disapproval bleeding off Detective Sergeant Sarah Workman standing next to him, her lips pursed, he could tell even without looking. But he wasn't feeling generous enough to give anyone a break this morning.

The Accident and Emergency waiting room was standing-room only: rows of blue vinyl-upholstered seats, every one of them occupied, a tidal wave of groans, coughs, hawks and the occasional deep-throated retch submerging their conversation. A vending machine was jammed against the wall the other side of the entrance door from the chairs, dispensing fizzy drinks, crisps and chocolate bars to the sick. *The great unwashed.* The last time he had set foot in a hospital, Southampton General, was four months ago, to collect Dr Jessie Flynn – who he'd worked with on a murder case late last year and fished out of Chichester Harbour, hypothermic and with a gunshot wound to the thigh – and drive her home. That had been a serene experience compared to this one. This A & E department made the rave he'd been at last night feel positively Zen.

'As you can see, we're an extremely busy Accident and Emergency department, Detective Inspector,' the receptionist – Janet, her plastic name badge read – informed him. 'And occasionally things get missed.'

Marilyn pulled a face. 'Remind me not to come here when I'm sick. If you can't spot a bloody baby, you've got no chance diagnosing disease.'

'That day may come sooner than you think.' Her voice rose in pitch, wobbled. 'Cancer, I'd say.'

Marilyn raised an eyebrow. 'Excuse me?'

'The smell. Smoke. You reek of it.' She waved a hand in front of her face. 'You'd be doing yourself, and us, a good turn if you gave up. Now if that's all, Detective Inspector, I'll be getting back to work. We are one the best-performing A & E departments in the country with one of the lowest mortality rates and I'd like to do my bit to keep it that way.' Turning on the sole of one squealing Dr Scholl, she slap-slapped her way down the corridor.

Marilyn glanced at Workman. 'That went well, Sergeant.'

DS Workman sighed. 'Shall I get forensics in here, sir?'

'It's a baby, Workman, not a corpse. We just need to find the next of kin, pronto.'

'I've been calling the parents. The father left his wallet under the pram. No joy on his home or mobile numbers.'

The air was getting to Marilyn: a stifling smorgasbord of antiseptic, body odour, vomit and the rusty smell of dried blood, all cooked to perfection in the unseasonally warm spring sunlight he could feel cutting through the glass sliding doors behind him. The temperature must be hitting seventy, he thought, despite the best efforts of the air-conditioning unit groaning in the ceiling above him. Although he had chosen to specialize in major crimes, he didn't have an iron stomach and twenty years of dealing with violent assaults, rapes and murders across Surrey and Sussex, had failed to strengthen it. But, he consoled himself, feeling a pang of guilt at his attitude towards the overworked receptionist, at least he didn't have to deal with the walking dead who inhabited A & E. The dead he dealt with were certifiably dead, door-nail dead, laid out on metal gurneys, swabbed,

17

wiped down, sexless and personality-less, more akin to shop dummies than recently living, breathing people with hopes and dreams, the single-digit temperatures in the autopsy suite keeping a lid on the most visceral of smells.

'I'll be back in a minute, Workman. Keep trying the dad and if we can't get next of kin by midday, call Children's Services. We'll get the kid into a temporary foster home.'

Exiting the hospital building, he crossed the service road, skirting around an ambulance that was disgorging a gargantuan man on a stretcher, the ambulance crew scarlet with strain. Grateful for the fresh air, he leant back against the brick wall and rolled a cigarette. The sky was a relentless clear blue, wispy cotton wool streaks of cirrus lacing it, the sun a hot yellow ball which, even with his dark glasses on, made his one azure eye tear up. Shuffling sideways, he hunkered down in the patch of shade thrown by a bus shelter and lit his roll-up. Back across the service road, patients in hospital gowns crowded next to the A & E doorway, sucking on cigarettes, a few clutching the stem of wheeled metal drip stands, tubes running, via needles, into their bandaged arms. The cloud of smoke partially obscured the sign behind them that read, *Strictly a Smoke-Free Zone*. Jesus! Janet was right. He needed to give up smoking, drinking, drugs, the works and pronto. Put a stop to the relentless downward slide that was his health before he ended up swelling their ranks in a flapping, backless hospital gown.

DS Workman was crossing the service road towards him. In her beige flats, matching beige shift dress, the hem skimming her solid calves, brown hair cut into a low-maintenance chin-length bob, she could have come straight from the hospital admin department. She looked as diligent and

18

efficient as she was, but her appearance also belied a quiet, cynical sense of humour that ensured their minds connected on a level beyond the mundane, and, anyway, where the hell would he be without her to back him up, dot the i's, cross the t's?

'I managed to reach the little boy's grandmother. She'll be here in an hour or so.'

'An hour? Can't she get here more quickly than that?'

'She lives in Farnborough and doesn't have a car.'

'Can't she jump in a cab?'

'I got the sense that taxis were out of her price range, sir.' Flipping open her notebook, she ploughed on before he could make any more facetious remarks. 'She said that the baby, Harry, he's called, lives with his father, her son. She said that he, the father, Malcolm, has been off work for a year with depression.'

Marilyn nodded.

'She sounded upset, very upset. I tried to reassure her, but she's convinced that something terrible has happened to him.'

'Where's the baby's mum?'

'I gather she's no longer in the picture.'

'Surname?'

'Lawson.'

'Lawson?' Flicking his roll-up into the gutter, Marilyn looked across and met Workman's gaze, his forehead creasing in query. 'Is it a coincidence that his name rings a bell?'

Workman shook her head. 'Daniel Lawson, sir.'

He racked his brains. Nothing.

'Danny,' she prompted. 'Private Danny Lawson.'

It still took him a moment. *Private Danny Lawson.* 'Oh

God, of course.' Tugging off his sunglasses, Marilyn rubbed a hand across his eyes. *Christ, Malcolm Lawson. That was all he needed.* He'd had considerably more than he could stomach of the man six months ago.

'I think we should have a counsellor here when Harry's grandmother arrives, sir.'

'With Malcolm Lawson in the picture, I need a bloody counsellor, Workman,' Marilyn muttered.

With an upwards roll of her eyes that he wasn't supposed to have noticed, Workman pressed on: 'Doctor Butter is on annual leave and time is obviously too short to find a counsellor from a neighbouring force.'

Marilyn sighed. Why was he being so obnoxious? No explanation, except for the fact that everything about this hospital was putting him in a bad mood. The detritus of human life washed up on its shores. Something about his own mortality staring him square in the face.

And the baby?

When DS Workman had first telephoned him about a baby abandoned at Royal Surrey County Hospital, he'd acidly asked her if she had a couple of lost puppies he could reunite with their owners or a kitten stuck in a tree he could shin up and rescue. But now, something about this abandoned baby – Harry Lawson – and the history attached to that child's surname, was giving him a creeping sense of unease.

'Leave it with me, Sergeant. We do have a tenuous Army connection, so I'll call Doctor Flynn. I'm sure she's back from the Middle East this week.'

Malcolm Lawson.

He thought he'd well and truly buried that name six months ago. Buried that family. Buried the whole sorry saga. He forced a laugh, full of fake cheer.

'Those Army types spend ninety per cent of their time sitting around with their thumbs up their arses, so I'm sure Jessie could spare an hour. Find us a nice quiet room where we can chat to Granny.'

6

The sun was a blinding ball in an unseasonally cloudless, royal-blue sky when Jessie gunned her daffodil-yellow Mini to life, pleasantly surprised that, after so long un-driven, it started first time. She'd popped in to see Ahmose, had been persuaded to stay for a cup of kahwa, strong Egyptian coffee – a terrible idea in retrospect, layered on top of the two cups she'd already downed at home, the time zone change and the jet lag. She felt as if a hive of hyperactive bees had set up residence in her head. Negotiating a slow three-point turn in the narrow lane, she pressed her foot gingerly on the accelerator, the speedo sliding slowly, jerkily – *God, have I forgotten how to change gears?* – to twenty, no higher. She'd had a near miss with the farmer and his herd of prize milking Friesians last summer while speeding down the lane towards home after a long day at Bradley Court, windows down, James Blunt full volume, and his threats of death and destruction to her prized Mini at the hands of his tractor had been an effective speed limiter ever since.

Fifteen minutes later, she slowed and turned off the public road into Bradley Court Army Rehabilitation Centre. Holding her pass out to the gate guards, she waited, engine idling, while the ornate metal gates were swung open. The last time she had driven along this drive, in the opposite direction, the stately brick-and-stone outline of Bradley Court receding in her rear-view mirror, it had been mid-December, mind-numbingly cold, slushy sleet invading the sweep of manicured lawns like wedding confetti, the trees bleak skeletons puncturing a slate-grey sky. Early April, and the lawn on either side of the quarter-mile drive was littered with red and blue crocuses, the copper beeches that lined the tarmac ribbon unfurling new leaves, hot-yellow daffodils clustered around their bases. Someone had set a table and chairs out on the lawn in front of an open patio door and a group of young men were sitting around it playing cards. Two others on crutches, each with a thigh-high amputation, were making their way along a gravel path towards the lake, both coatless, their shirt sleeves rolled up.

Parking, she made her way up to the first floor where the Defence Psychology Service was located, sticking her head into office doors as she passed, saying her hellos.

'The nomad returns. Welcome back, Doctor Flynn.'

Gideon Duursema, head of the Defence Psychology Service and Jessie's boss, half-rose from behind his desk and held out his hand. It felt strange, to Jessie, shaking it. She couldn't recall ever shaking Gideon's hand, with the exception of during her job interview and on her first morning at Bradley Court two and a half years ago, when he had formally welcomed her to the department. Gideon must have felt the same sense of oddness, because he dropped her hand suddenly, skirted around his desk and pulled her into a brief, slightly awkward hug.

'We've missed you,' he muttered, retreating to safety afforded by the physical barrier of his oak desk, lowering himself into his chair. 'How was the tour?' he asked, when she had settled herself into the chair opposite.

'Now I know what living in prison feels like, except that prisoners get better food and their own television set.'

Gideon laughed. 'Did they chain you up in the bowels of the boat 24/7?'

'Ship.' She half-smiled. 'Ship is the technical naval term. Type 45 Destroyer, if I'm being really pedantic.'

'Pedantic is good in this job. I like pedantic, but not when it's directed at me. Type 45 Destroyer. Did they chain you up in the bowels of the destroyer 24/7?'

'I must have been away from other lunatic psychologists for too long – you've lost me completely.'

Holding up a paint brochure, squares of bland off-whites, insipid greys and beiges lined down the page, he squinted at her through one eye.

'Farrow and Ball colour trends, 2016. Tallow – a perfect match, I'd say. You mustn't have seen the light of day. Certainly not the light of any Middle Eastern sun, anyway.'

Jessie rolled her eyes. 'My skin colour is on trend, if nothing else.' She waved a hand back over her shoulder towards the door. 'Should we try this again, perhaps? I'll go out, come back in and you can attempt to avoid the insults. We don't all have the benefit of a year-round tan.'

Gideon smiled. 'I'm sorry. I've missed you. It's been dull around here without your chippy attitude to keep me on my toes.'

Originally from Zimbabwe, these days he was almost

more English than the English with his tweed jackets, faux Tudor semi-detached on the outskirts of Farnham, Land Rover Discovery, solid middle-class wife and two boys. Jessie had met his sons once, had felt gauche and awkward beside them even though she was five years older than the eldest – both boys a stunning, olive-skinned mix of their black father and English rose mother, both following their father to Oxford.

'Has Mrs D roped you into doing some DIY?'

'Sadly, yes, as my pitiful government salary doesn't run to the eye-watering sums charged by Home Counties building firms.' Flipping over the brochure, he read in a desiccated monotone: '"Is your kitchen looking tired and dated? We can simply resurface your current cabinets in a colour and finish of your choice."' He tossed the brochure on the desktop. 'Various shades of battleship, sorry, *destroyer* grey are all the rage these days, evidently, though why Fiona can't continue residing with the browns we have lived with happily for the past twenty years, I have no idea. Never mind the damn kitchen, it's me who's tired and dated. Maybe Farrow and Ball can resurface me while they're at it, two for the price of one.' Reaching for his bifocals, sliding them on to the bridge of his nose, he fixed Jessie with a searching gaze. 'Ready to get back to work?'

'I assume from your tone that my answer needs to be an emphatic "yes".'

Gideon patted a stack of files on the corner of his desk, ten centimetres high. 'Preferably accompanied with a beatific smile and boundless energy.' Sliding a thin cardboard file from the top of the stack, he held it out to her. 'Here's your number one. Ryan Jones: sixteen-year-old male trainee, Royal Logistic Corps, Blackdown Barracks. Referred by

Blackdown's commanding officer, Colonel Philip Wallace.'

Jessie flipped open the file. One typed sheet inside. 'Why was he referred?'

Gideon shrugged. 'An open-ended "we're concerned with his mental state".'

'Isn't the CO a bit high up to be referring trainees?'

Another shrug. 'From what I know of Philip Wallace, he likes to have his finger in every pie on that base.'

Jessie nodded, taking a moment, eyes grazing down the first page to digest the key details of the referral. Gideon was right – there was little more information than he had just told her. The referral was a triumph of saying nothing in one page of tight black type.

Ryan Thomas Jones

Sixteen and five months

Joined the Army on 2 November last year, the day of his sixteenth birthday

Keen.

Keen or running away from something. In Jessie's experience, people joined the Army for one of three reasons: patriotism, financial necessity, or to escape. There was a fourth, she privately suspected, though had never voiced: the opportunity to kill people legally. That last one was reserved for the nutters. Which one was Ryan Jones? Probably not the fourth, as Loggies weren't frontline fighting troops.

Looking up, she met Gideon's gaze. 'When is he coming in?'

'Two p.m.'

'Oh, OK. So I get the morning to organize my office, drink coffee, chillax. That's unexpectedly generous of you—' She broke off, catching his expression. 'No . . . I don't get the morning to chillax. Instead, I get to . . . ' She let the sentence hang.

'You get to go to Royal Surrey County Hospital.'

'And why would I want to do that?'

'I got a call from Detective Inspector Simmons ten minutes ago. He needs your help.'

'Since when did we provide psychologists to Surrey and Sussex Major Crimes?'

'Since DI Simmons asked me nicely. It seems austerity is pinching them as hard as it's pinching us.'

'Why does he need a psychologist's help at the hospital?'

'He'll fill you in.'

'Cryptic.'

'Not deliberately so. There is an Army connection, he said.'

Jessie's eyebrows rose in query, but Gideon didn't provide her with any more information. Stretching his arms above his head, waving one hand vaguely towards the window as he did so, he added, 'I was in a meeting when Simmons called, so our conversation was brief. You'd better get going. He's there now, waiting for you at the entrance to A & E, and I have another meeting starting' – he glanced at his watch – 'five minutes ago.' He began searching around under the piles of files, books and papers on his desk, continuing to talk as he did so. 'Welcome back, Jessie. As I said, I've missed you.' A fleeting, wry smile. 'And so, as you can see, has my desk. It has felt your absence most keenly. You can't see my mobile anywhere, can you?'

Ducking down, she retrieved Gideon's mobile from the floor and handed it to him. 'Here.'

'Ah. Thank you.'

'But that's it. No more Mrs Doubtfire from me.' Rising, she tucked Ryan Thomas Jones's file under her arm. 'Your desk is going to have to make its own way in the big wide world without my help. Sink or swim. Eat or be eaten.'

Gideon's eyebrow rose, but he didn't reply. As she left the room, Jessie glanced back. He was still watching her, the expression on his face conflicted: a part of him hoping that she was right; the other part knowing, from thirty years' experience as a clinical psychologist, that such deep-seated psychological disorders as hers were far from simple to cure. Jessie hoped that she was right too. She had navigated this morning without so much as a tingle from the electric suit; had navigated her time abroad with only three mild episodes. She'd even managed to leave the house with the kettle handle crooked and an unwashed coffee cup in the sink. Progress. Real progress.

She hoped that settling back into her normal routine would do nothing to disturb the delicate balance of her recovery.

7

Lieutenant Gold was already at the crime scene when Captain Ben Callan, Royal Military Police Special Investigation Branch, parked his red Golf GTI in the car park at Blackdown Barracks. Climbing out of the driver's seat, he stood – too quickly – swayed and grabbed the top of the door to steady himself. *Fuck*. He still felt sick and shaky, as if he was coming down off a drinking spree, which he wasn't. A hangover would, though, provide a plausible excuse for his wrecked physical and mental state. Nothing unexpected in soldiers getting drunk off-duty; it was virtually compulsory.

He'd had some warning of the fit this time: the car in front of him in the fast lane on the A3 starting to jump around as if it was on springs, the central reservation fuzzy, as though his windscreen was suddenly frosted glass. Swerving straight across both lanes, he cut on to the hard shoulder, narrowly missing an elderly couple in an ancient Nissan Micra; the glimpse he'd had of the driver's whitened face and wide eyes in his rear-view mirror still etched in his mind.

The ground fell away steeply from the hard shoulder into a deep ditch of tangled undergrowth and he slithered down it, making it only halfway before his knees buckled. Falling, rolling, he reached blindly for something to slow his descent, felt reed grass slice through his fingers. His body was writhing, slamming from side to side, legs cycling in the muddy soil and he was freezing cold, shaking uncontrollably, his brain feeling as if it would explode from the pressure inside his skull. Slowly, the fit receded. He lay on the damp ground, sweating and shaking, feeling the muddy ditch water seeping through his clothing, chilling his skin. Pushing himself on to his knees, he reached for the trunk of a sapling, hauled himself to his feet, wincing as the cuts on his fingers met the rough bark. On unsteady legs, he made his way slowly back up the embankment. A Surrey Police patrol car was parked behind his Golf, flashing blue lights washing the uniformed traffic officer standing in front of it neon blue.

'You do know that it is illegal to stop on the hard shoulder for any reason other than an emergency, don't you, sir?'

Sir. The policeman's tone entirely at odds with his words. *Just what I need right now.* Reaching into his back pocket, Callan fished out his military police ID, held it up. The traffic cop studied it, his gaze narrowing.

'What were you doing, sir?'

Which story was the more convincing? Having a piss? Answering a vital phone call? The truth, not an option. As an epileptic, he shouldn't hold a driving licence, but if his condition was made public, losing his licence would be the least of his problems. He would lose his job, his livelihood, his future. His tenuous clutch on normality.

'I was answering a call on my mobile. There's been a

suspicious death at an Army training base near Camberley. I'm on my way there now.'

The policeman's gaze tracked from Callan's face to his feet, taking in the sweaty, greyish-pale complexion, the hands jammed in his pockets to stop them from trembling, the mud caked on his white shirt and jeans.

'If you weren't an MP, I'd breathalyse you.'

'I'm not over the limit, Constable.'

'You don't look great, sir.'

'I don't feel great, but it's not alcohol. It's lack of sleep, too much work . . . You know how it is.' Callan lifted his shoulders, looking the constable straight in the eye, the lie sliding smoothly off his tongue.

Silence, which Callan had the confidence not to break. He maintained eye contact, an easy smile on his face, posture relaxed, hoping the constable didn't notice that his legs were shaking.

'Drive slowly, mate. My shift ends in two hours and I don't fancy spending it scraping anybody off the central reservation. Even a bloody MP.'

Callan held out his hand; the constable didn't take it.

'You've had your one favour,' he muttered. 'Next time, I throw the book at you.'

Callan stood by his Golf and watched the patrol car pull back into the flow of traffic and accelerate away. Twisting sideways, he retched on the grass. Retched and retched until only his stomach lining remained.

8

Squeezing her Mini on to the grass verge, the only spare inch of space available in the hospital car park, ignoring the dirty looks thrown her way by people in huge four-by-fours who were still circling, trying to find a space, Jessie jogged down the stone stairs and across the service road to A & E. Holding her breath as she ducked through the cigarette smoke fogging the entrance, she found Marilyn waiting for her inside. He was propping up the wall by the reception desk, one sole tapping impatiently against the skirting, thumbs skipping across the keys of his mobile. At the sound of her footsteps, he glanced up, his lined face creasing into a smile.

'Thank you for coming, Jessie.' A glance towards the packed A & E waiting room. 'To the asylum.'

'I won't say that it's a pleasure, but Gideon didn't leave me much choice. For some reason your request shot straight to the top of my day's admittedly short to-do list.'

'I must have forgotten to tell you that Gideon and I play golf together every Sunday.'

Her gaze tracked from the black bed-hair to the sallow, ravaged face that made Mick Jagger look a picture of clean living, to those disconcerting eyes hiding the sharp, enquiring mind she'd got to know. He had bowed to pressure from above and replaced his beloved black biker jacket with a black suit which hung from his scarecrow frame, only the suit's drainpipe trousers hinting that he was anything more than a straight-off-the-production-line policeman.

'Funnily enough, I don't see you in checked plus-fours.'

He grinned. 'Masons?'

'Ditto.

'Yacht club?'

Jessie rolled her eyes. 'Shall we get started? I need to be back at Bradley Court by lunchtime. I have work to do. *Proper* work.'

As they walked side by side down the corridor that cut from A & E to the main hospital, their rubber soles whispering in unison as they gripped and released the lino, Marilyn brought her up to date.

'We're not sure how long the baby has been here, but we know that he was left some time before midnight.'

'Midnight? As in midnight ten hours—'

He held up a hand, cutting her off. 'Don't get me started.'

'He was left by his father?'

'That's our working theory. DS Workman and a couple of constables are going through last night's CCTV footage of the A & E entrance to confirm.'

'Why would a father abandon his baby?'

'He abandoned him in a hospital, safe.'

Jessie frowned. 'A busy A & E department, all sorts coming and going? It's hardly secure. The fact that the

33

poor kid wasn't noticed for . . . what . . . ' She glanced at her watch, mentally calculating. 'Seven hours minimum suggests to me that it's not the first place a caring parent in their right mind would look to deposit their baby for safekeeping.'

'Right. So the rest of our working theory is that he wasn't entirely compos mentis at the time.'

Jessie glanced over. 'Why do you think that?'

They swung left into another corridor, identical to the first. Laying a hand on Jessie's arm, Marilyn pulled her to a stop outside a door labelled 'Family Room'. Tilting towards her, he lowered his voice.

'There's some history that you need to understand before we meet Granny.'

Jessie caught his tone and raised an eyebrow. 'And I presume the history is why you wanted me here.'

Marilyn sighed. 'The history and the story that I suspect may have played itself out last night, and what I fear might be the story going forward.' He cocked his head towards the family room door. 'The story that we need to break, as gently as possible, to Granny.'

'Which is?'

'The little boy is Harry Lawson. He lives with his father, Malcolm. Malcolm Lawson is also the father of Daniel Lawson.' He paused. 'Private Danny Lawson. Ring a bell?'

She shook her head. 'Should it?'

'Danny Lawson committed suicide at an Army training base near Camberley a year or so ago. He'd only been in the Army five months. He was sixteen.'

'I was in Afghanistan with PsyOps around that time. Nothing was on my radar except for that. What happened?'

'He went AWOL one night while his dorm mates were

sleeping. He was found in the showers early the next morning.'

'And?'

'And – he had committed suicide.'

'So you said. How?'

'The how isn't important.'

Jessie stared hard at him. 'If it's part of the backstory, it is important.'

'Method isn't relevant—'

'Marilyn,' Jessie cut in.

Marilyn shoved his hands into his pockets and hunched his shoulders. 'He suffocated himself.'

'With a pillow?'

'Tape.'

A shadow crossed Jessie's face. 'Tape?'

'Gaffer tape,' Marilyn said in a low voice. 'He wrapped it around his head, covered his mouth and nose with the stuff.'

'Bloody hell, poor kid,' she murmured, her eyes sliding from his, finding a crack in the lino at her feet, tracking its rambling progress to the wall, the image that Marilyn's words had etched into her mind – how desperate sixteen-year-old Danny must have been, to end his life that way – filling her mind with memories. Memories she struggled, at the best of times, to suppress. A little boy hanging by his school tie from a curtain rail, his gorgeous face bloated and purple. This boy, older, but not by so much, making a mask of his face with black gaffer tape. She felt Marilyn's eyes burning a hole in the top of her skull.

'He wouldn't have had unsupervised access to a gun,' he said.

'No.'

35

'The tape was what he had to hand.'

Biting her lip, Jessie nodded. Gaffer tape – what he had to hand. *A school tie and a curtain rail – what Jamie had had to hand.*

'You OK?' he asked gently.

Looking up, meeting those odd eyes, she forced a smile, sure that it must look twisted and horrible. 'What, apart from the dodgy hospital smell and the fact that it's five hundred degrees centigrade in here? Of course, I'm fine.'

She had formed a friendship of sorts with Marilyn since he had pulled her from the freezing sea in Chichester Harbour four months ago; a comfortable relationship that was characterized by his occasional calls for advice when he felt his own force's psychologist's recommendations were way off the mark, the odd cheery email to her whilst she was serving on HMS *Daring*, emails that had transported her straight back from featureless sea to rolling hills with their description of evenings spent drinking Old Speckled Hen in country pubs, sometimes with Captain Ben Callan. But her own history was something that she didn't choose to share with anyone besides Ahmose and, once only, in a weak moment, with Callan. She wondered if he knew though, anyway. If Callan had told him. She suspected, from Marilyn's unease, that he had.

'So what was Surrey and Sussex Major Crimes' involvement if Danny Lawson was Army?' she asked, breaking the laden silence.

'The Military Police conducted the initial investigation and came to the conclusion that Danny's death was suicide. But Danny's dad, Malcolm, refused to accept the verdict. He wrote to his MP, the Defence Secretary, the Armed Forces Minister, even the bloody Prime Minister, anyone

36

and everyone he could think of, calling for the investigation to be reopened by the civvy police. Police without prejudice, I remember he called it. He claimed that the Redcaps were covering up murder. That the Army had so many problems dealing with the Middle East that they didn't want to admit kids were being murdered on their home turf. I got a call from the Surrey County Coroner telling me that we were to do another investigation.'

'And?'

Marilyn sighed and shrugged. 'We reviewed all the evidence and found the same. Suicide.'

'Cut and dried.'

'Cut and dried. There was no evidence to suggest murder – and I promise you, I did look for it.'

'But Malcolm didn't accept your findings either,' Jessie murmured.

'No. No, he didn't.' His voice slipped to a monotone. 'He kept on and on and *on*. Wrote back to the same cast of politicians, wrote to all the papers, tried to whip up a media storm, but there was nothing there, no story, so none of them bit.'

'Why was he so determined?'

'I don't know. I just remember how mad he was with grief. Grief and anger. I was surprised that he was so damn angry. Grief, I expected, sadness, loss, guilt even, but not anger.'

Jessie was looking at the floor, her arms folded across her chest, defensive body language, she recognized, but too tense to unwrap. 'Anger is often the go-to emotion that masks others. Sadness, grief, loss – they can all morph into anger, particularly if they're mixed with frustration or perceived helplessness. It's hard for family members to accept . . . suicide.' She swallowed, eased the word out around the wad that had formed in her throat. 'Because where there's suicide, there is a deep, debilitating hopelessness that the victim can't see a way around. The family often blame themselves because they didn't notice, or didn't realize the depth of despair. Guilt, blame, self-recrimination, self-blame – they can eat you up. It's always easier to look somewhere else to lay that blame.' She glanced up, met Marilyn's gaze for a fraction of a second, couldn't hold it. 'Children shouldn't die before their parents,' she murmured, tracing the meandering crack in the grey lino with the toe of her ballet pump. 'It flips the law of nature on its head. A parent is programmed to protect their child at all costs, to do anything to keep that child safe, however old the child is.'

A child. A son. Committing suicide.

Jessie had held on to her own grief, dealing with the pain the only way a fourteen-year-old knew: internalizing it, taking the blame for her brother's suicide squarely on her own shoulders. She had the psychological scars to prove it. Danny Lawson's father sounded to have done the opposite and looked for someone else to blame. *Anyone* else to blame. Either way, she knew exactly what he had been going through.

She felt the weight of Marilyn's hand on her arm. 'We should go in now, Jessie.'

She nodded. 'Yes. Yes, of course.'

9

Slipping on his Oakley's, Callan walked slowly, collecting his thoughts with each step following the line of Blackdown's chain-link, razor-wire-topped boundary fence, towards the thick wooded area where he could see Lieutenant Ed Gold and the scenes of crime boys.

Although he was still two hundred metres away, Callan could see the arrogant rigidity of Gold's stance, recognize the disproportionate command in the staccato arcs of his gestures, hear each word of his barked orders clear as a bell. Gold was in his element, enjoying the control, even though the scenes of crime technicians were consummate professionals who needed no guidance. Callan would take pleasure in rescuing them, bursting Gold's bubble.

Callan glanced at his watch. It was a quarter past ten. He was late to the scene, very late. He had received the call notifying him of a suspicious death at Blackdown training base sixty minutes ago, while he'd been sitting in his neurologist's office, digesting bad news. He only hoped that Gold hadn't fucked up the crime scene already, though the presence of Sergeant Glyn Morgan, his lead SOCO, a forest ghoul moving silently through the trees in his white overalls, gave him a modicum of confidence that some integrity may have been preserved.

Gold glanced over, caught sight of Callan and the next order died on his lips.

'What have we got, Gold?' Callan asked as he reached him.

'A dead soldier,' Gold muttered, his navy-flecked, royal-blue gaze meeting Callan's insouciantly. A beat later, he added a reluctant 'sir' and followed it with a disinclined salute.

Callan returned the salute smartly, though he was more tempted to use his right hand to smack Gold around the head. He knew that it would take all his willpower not to wring the jumped-up little shit's neck on this case, suspected that Colonel Holden-Hough, Officer Commanding Southern Region, Special Investigation Branch, knew the same, which is why he had been given Gold as his detachment second-in-command in the first place.

'Who?' Callan snapped.

'A trainee, Stephen Foster.' Gold flipped open his notebook. 'Aged sixteen.'

'What was he doing out here?'

'Guard duty.'

'Alone?'

Gold shook his head. 'With a female. Martha Wonsag.'

'So where the hell was she when he died?'

Gold shrugged. 'I haven't got that far yet, sir.'

'Where is the rest of the guard detachment?'

'They're back on normal duties.' He held up the notebook. 'I have their names.'

'What?' Callan stared at him, incredulous. 'This is most likely a murder inquiry and the victim's guard detachment will be top of our list of suspects. Secure a suite of rooms and get the guard rounded up and isolated now. Do not leave them alone for a second, and do not let them talk to each other. I'll start interviews when I've looked at the crime scene.'

His jaw tight with anger, Gold nodded. 'Right, sir.'

Turning away, feeling the heat of Gold's fury burning into his back, biting down on his own anger – anger at himself for having been unavailable when the call about a suspicious death came through, at Gold for his incompetence, knowing that a significant part of his anger was fuelled by dislike – Callan climbed into a set of overalls and ducked under the crime scene cordon. Morgan's SOCOs fell silent as he approached, and he knew what they were thinking. He was famous, or more accurately infamous, in the Special Investigation Branch. Only thirty, eight years in, and he had already taken two bullets whilst on duty. The first a gift from the Taliban eighteen months ago in Afghanistan, still lodged in his brain; the fallout, permanent seizures, manageable at the moment with drugs, his neurologist had told him this morning, but likely to worsen with time. The second, a bullet in the abdomen from a fellow soldier four months ago, in woods not unlike these. He'd only been back on duty for two weeks. He knew that he was well respected in the Branch for being brave and professional, and found it unnerving. How opinions would change if his colleagues found out about his epilepsy and the demons that infested his mind at night. What he was feeling now, walking into this dense, shadowy copse of trees. *Déjà vu.*

'Sir.' Morgan straightened as Callan reached him. At five foot eight the top of his head barely grazed Callan's shoulder.

'I'm glad you're here, Morgan.'

'I'm glad you're here, too, Captain.' A gentle Welsh valleys accent, unmellowed by his decades-long absence from the Rhondda. He was the son of a coal miner, had faced only three life choices: unemployment, life down a pit, or the Army. He had chosen the Army and escape and was a career soldier, experienced and capable, with a degree of cynicism gained over twenty-five years in the Redcaps, that meant he was no longer surprised by any crime that the dark side of human nature could conjure up. 'My patience was wearing thin with Little Lord Fauntleroy over there.'

With his stocky frame, steel-grey hair and clipped moustache, he reminded Callan of a solid grey pit pony.

'May I take the liberty of saying that you look like shit, sir,' Morgan continued. 'Big night?'

'Thanks for your honesty, Sergeant. I feel like shit too.' Scratching a hand through his dirty blond stubble, he stifled a yawn. Branch detectives wore plain clothes most of the time and though he had changed out of his muddy shirt and jeans into a navy-blue suit he kept in the boot of his car for emergencies, he hadn't been able to do anything about his pasty complexion or his bloodshot eyes.

'Well, you're going to need a strong stomach for this one.'

Callan looked where Morgan indicated, taking in the salient details quickly, freeze-framing each segment of the tableau in turn, acclimatizing himself mental snapshot by mental snapshot. In a few moments, he knew that he would have to pick over the scene, the corpse of the kid in forensic detail with Morgan and he wasn't sure that his mind or his stomach were up to it.

'He hasn't been moved?'

Morgan raised an eyebrow.

'Sorry. Stupid question.' Callan squatted, taking care not to step too close to avoid contaminating the scene. He could feel his heart beginning to race, took a couple of deep breaths to slow it. The boy was slumped at the foot of a huge oak tree, tilted sideways, like a rag doll that had been propped in place, then slid off centre. His head was lolling on to his chest, dark brown eyes open, staring, and already showing the milky film of death, the tree's leaves making a dappled jigsaw of his bloodless face. He had been handsome in life, and young – fuck, he was young. He looked like a fresh-faced schoolboy who'd been playing soldiers – *you play dead now* – except that this victim wasn't the product of any game. The bloody puncture wound in his throat and the tacky claret bib coating the front of his combat jacket told Callan that this crime scene was all too real.

'Stab wound to the throat?'

'Yes, sir.'

'Weapon?'

'A screwdriver.'

'Where is it?'

'I've bagged it.'

'Was it still in his throat?'

'No, it was eight metres away. Here.' He indicated one of the numbered markers. 'The tip was dug into the ground, the handle sticking up at forty-five degrees.'

'Thrown?'

Morgan nodded. 'Without doubt.'

Shifting closer, Callan studied the stab wound in the boy's throat.

'It doesn't appear to be a vicious blow,' he heard Morgan say.

'No.'

There didn't appear to be any trauma around the wound, no damaged skin or bruising. It was as if the screwdriver had slid in gently, finding the pliable gap between two cartilaginous ridges in the trachea, nothing unduly violent, no loss of control or wild ferocity about this death. Even the expression on the kid's face showed no fear, merely an odd, chilling sense of calm.

A camera's flash and Callan straightened, shielding his eyes from the blinding white light. The last thing he needed was another epileptic fit.

'You OK, sir?'

'Sure. I just need a coffee and ten hours' sleep. I'll leave you to it, Morgan.'

He suddenly wanted out of this wood. There was something about the denseness of the trees, the constant shifting of shadows as the wind moved the branches, and the smell – damp bark and leaf mulch – that catapulted him back to Sandhurst, back to that night in the woods when Major Nicholas Scott, the father of Jessie Flynn's deeply traumatized four-year-old patient, Sami, had shot him in the back, when he had nearly died for the second time in his life. *Jesus, Ben* – he took a breath, trying to ease the pressure in his chest – *focus on the fucking case.* Stephen Foster, a sixteen-year-old kid, five months in the Army and already dead. There'd be hell to pay for this one.

10

The room Jessie and Marilyn entered was small and airless. Scuffed baby-pink walls, a burgundy cotton sofa backed against one wall, two matching chairs facing it, a brightly coloured foam alphabet jigsaw mat laid in the middle of the vinyl floor, each letter fashioned from an animal contorting itself into the appropriate shape – an ape for 'A', a beetle for 'B', a cat for 'C'. The air stiflingly hot, even though someone had made an effort to ease the pressure-cooker atmosphere by opening the window as far as its 'safety-first' mechanism would allow. A fly, seeking escape, circled by the window, cracking its fragile carapace against the glass with each turn.

A chubby, blond-haired baby boy in a white T-shirt and pale blue dungarees was sitting in the middle of the mat, smacking the handset of a Bob the Builder telephone against its base. An elderly lady – late seventies, Jessie guessed – tiny and reed thin, was perched on the edge of the sofa watching the baby. Her hands, clamped on her knees, were threaded with thick blue veins, her skin diaphanous and liver-spotted with age. She had dressed for a formal occasion in a grey woollen tweed skirt, grey tights and a smart white shirt, the shirt's short sleeves her only visible concession to the day's unforeseen heat. Her brown lace-ups were highly polished, but the stitching had unravelled from the inside sole of one, the sole cleaving away from its upper.

Starting at the sound of the door, she looked over, her face lighting briefly with a sentiment that Jessie recognized as hope, half rising to her feet before collapsing back, the light dimming, when she realized that it was no one she knew.

'Mrs Lawson, I'm Detective Inspector Bobby Simmons and this is my colleague, Doctor Jessica Flynn.'

From beneath her silver hair, the old lady's dull gaze moved from Marilyn to Jessie and back. She made no move to take Marilyn's outstretched hand.

'Have you found Malcolm?'

'Not yet, Mrs Lawson. We need some details from you to help in our search.'

She nodded, murmured, 'Of course. Whatever you need.'

While Jessie sat down in one of the chairs opposite the sofa, Marilyn moved to stand by the window, reaching behind him to give it a quick upwards heave to see if it would budge, which it didn't. Clearing his throat, he glanced down at the notes written in the notebook that DS Workman had thrust into his hand a few moments before Jessie had arrived at the hospital.

'Malcolm's car? He drives a dark grey Toyota Corolla, registration number LP 52 YBB? Is that correct?'

Mrs Lawson's gaze found the ceiling as she tried to summon a picture to mind. 'The colour is right, yes, and the make. I'm pretty sure that the make is right.' She paused. 'The registration number . . . I'm sorry, but would you repeat it.'

'LP 52 YBB.'

Her eyes rose again. 'The 52, yes, but the rest . . . I'm sorry, but I really can't remember.'

'We've got this information from the DVLA, so it should be accurate.'

'The car has a baby seat in the back seat, of course, for Harry. Red and black it is. A red and black baby seat.'

Marilyn made a note. 'Does Malcolm own or have access to any other vehicles?'

She shook her head.

'Do you have any idea where he could have gone. Any special places that he likes to go? Friends who he could have gone to visit?'

'He had a few friends, but he lost touch with them after . . . after Daniel died. He spends all his time looking after Harry.'

'Pubs? Clubs?'

'No.'

'A girlfriend, perhaps?'

'No. Really, no.' Her nose wrinkled. 'He wouldn't stay out all night and he wouldn't leave Harry like that.'

Jessie leaned forward. 'Where is Harry's mother, Mrs Lawson?'

'She's . . . she's in a home, Doc—' Her voice faltered. 'Doctor.'

'Jessie. Please call me Jessie.'

'She's in a home.'

'A home? A hospital?' Jessie probed. 'Is she in a psychiatric hospital?'

Breaking eye contact, the old lady gave an almost imperceptible nod, as if she was embarrassed by the information she'd shared.

'She couldn't cope when Danny died. She was always fragile and she broke down completely when Danny took his own life.'

'Where is the home?' Marilyn asked.

'It's . . . it's up in Maidenhead somewhere. I remember Maidenhead . . . ' A pause. 'I . . . I can't remember the name. I'm sorry, I never visited.'

'Don't worry, Mrs Lawson,' Jessie cut in. 'The police can find out if they need to talk to her.'

'You won't get any sense from her.' The words rushed out. 'She hasn't spoken a word of sense since she was admitted six months ago. Malcolm goes to see her, takes Harry along sometimes, but she says nothing to him. Nothing to Harry either.'

'Thank you, Mrs Lawson. You've been very helpful.' Marilyn cleared his throat again, the sound grating in the claustrophobic space. 'We are, uh, we're working on the assumption that Malcolm left Harry here deliberately, because he believed that the hospital was a safe place at that hour of the night, and then went on somewhere else, to a location that we have yet to determine.'

'To commit suicide?' Her voice rose and cracked.

Marilyn shuffled his feet awkwardly against the tacky lino, the sound like the squealing of a trapped mouse.

Jessie nodded. 'It is our working theory at the moment, Mrs Lawson.'

The old lady raised a hand to her mouth, stifling a sob. Jessie's heart went out to her. She could be sitting facing her own mother: decades older, but with the same raw grief etched on to her face.

'Something must have happened to him. He wouldn't have left Harry.'

'He left Harry in a hospital, Mrs Lawson,' Jessie said gently. 'Somewhere safe.'

'He wouldn't have left him. Not here. Not anywhere.' Jamming her eyes shut, she shook her head. 'And he would never kill himself, not after Danny.'

'Mrs Lawson, you told DS Workman that Malcolm has suffered from severe depression since Danny's death,' Marilyn said. He looked intensely uncomfortable faced with the mixture of defiance and raw grief pulsing from this proud old lady. Jessie wondered if he usually left Workman to deal with families of the bereaved. From his reaction, she concluded that he did, couldn't blame him.

'Malcolm believes in God, Detective Inspector. Suicide is a sin in God's eyes.'

'Mrs Lawson.' Jessie waited until the woman's tear-filled eyes had found hers. 'Depression is complex and the symptoms vary wildly between people, but it is very often characterized by a debilitating sadness, hopelessness and a total loss of interest in things that the sufferer used to enjoy.'

'Your own baby?' Her voice cracked. 'A loss of interest in your own baby?'

'A sufferer can feel exhausted – utterly exhausted, mentally and physically, by everything. Little children are tiring enough for someone who is healthy. For someone with depression, having to take care of a young child, however much they love that child, would be incredibly hard, a Mount Everest to climb each and every day. Depression also affects decision-making because the rational brain can't function properly . . . ' Jessie paused. 'And a person suffering from depression can believe that the people they leave behind are better off without them.'

Another sob, quickly stifled. His face wrinkling with concern at the sound, the little boy on the mat looked from his Bob the Builder phone to his grandmother.

'You're wrong, Doctor.'

'Mrs Lawson.' Moving to sit next to her on the sofa, Jessie laid a hand on her arm. Her skin was papery, chilled, despite the heat in the room. Jessie took a breath, fighting to suppress her own memories. 'Mrs Lawson.'

'No. *No.* You're wrong.' Tears were running unchecked down her cheeks. Unclipping her handbag, she fumbled inside and pulled out a crumpled tissue. 'You're both wrong. He would never leave Harry, not after Danny. He's already lost one child, he'd never risk losing another. You need to find him.' Her voice broke. 'What are you doing to find him? Why are you sitting here? You need to find Malcolm now.'

11

Head down, Jessie walked swiftly down the corridor, forcing herself not to break into a full-on sprint. The heat and that ubiquitous hospital smell of antiseptic struggling to mask an odorous cocktail of bodily fluids felt almost physical, a claustrophobic weight pressing in on her from all sides. And the suit. The electric suit – she'd barely felt it while she'd been abroad – was tightening around her throat, making it hard to breathe.

'Jessie.'

She took a few more steps, pretending that she hadn't heard Marilyn's call. The corner was an arm's length away. If she swung around it, she could run down the next corridor, cut through A & E and disappear outside before he caught up with her. *Escape.*

'Jessie, I know that you can hear me,' Marilyn called, louder. 'I don't do jogging, so wait.'

She stopped, turned slowly to face him.

'Jesus Christ, I need a drink after that,' he muttered, catching up with her.

'It wasn't the best.'

'So what do you think?'

Jessie focused on a patch of dried damp on the wall opposite, the result of a historic leak long since repaired but not repainted, avoiding meeting his eyes. 'I think that you need to find Malcolm Lawson quickly.'

'Isn't it likely that he's already dead?'

'You can't make that assumption. He has all sorts of conflicting emotions careering around in his head. Depression, exhaustion, hopelessness sure, but Mrs Lawson is right when she says that he also has a lot of positive emotions, pushing against those negative drivers. He believes in God, and suicide *is* a sin in the eyes of any Christian church. His older son committed suicide and he was horrified by that. And he has Harry, and for the past year that baby has been the centre of his world—' She broke off with a shake of her head. 'Mrs Lawson was adamant that he wouldn't commit suicide.'

'And you believe her?' Marilyn asked gently.

Jessie sighed. 'No . . . yes . . . no. I think that there is a lot of wishing and hoping that's fuelling her belief. But I also know that suicide won't be an easy choice for him. You can't assume that he's already dead.'

'So we should be out looking for him?'

'You should. Now.'

Marilyn tipped back on his heels and blew air out of his nose. 'It would be a hell of a lot easier if I knew where to start.'

'There's no word on his car? If he left Harry here at around midnight, it makes sense to assume that he drove.'

'It does, but we've had no word so far and every squad car in the county has been told to keep an eye out for it.'

Marilyn held out an arm. 'Shall we get out of here, talk outside? This place is giving me hives.'

They walked towards the exit. Sweat was trickling down Jessie's spine, pasting her shirt to her back. Marilyn was carrying his suit jacket slung over his shoulder, his lined face gummy with perspiration.

'Why would Malcolm have decided now?' he asked.

Jessie shrugged. She had asked herself that question virtually every day of the fifteen years since her little brother's suicide and she still hadn't come up with an answer that satisfied her. It seemed to come down to opportunity. Opportunity because she had left him alone, gone to Wimbledon Common with her boyfriend, leaving Jamie to be dropped home to a dark, empty house by someone else's mother, while she had lied to her own, told her that she would be there to look after him.

'The straw that broke the camel's back.'

Marilyn smiled, a half-hearted attempt to lighten the moment. 'Is that a technical term?'

Jessie returned his smile with one equally lacklustre. 'You have to get all the way to PhD level before you can use it.'

'So what was the straw?'

'It could be any of a number of things. A significant date, the time of year, the weather. Despite what most people think, suicide rates peak in the spring and early summer – April, May, June.'

'I would have thought winter. Winter is depressing.'

'Yes, but everybody is depressed in winter. In spring, most people's mood lifts. Warmer weather, flowers and trees coming into bloom, baby animals being born, new life – it makes everyone happier. Those people who are clinically depressed suddenly realize that they're more alone, more isolated than they had thought. I know this isn't helpful, but it could be one of a thousand things. He could simply have had enough. Reached the end, the point that he couldn't go on fighting any more.'

They made it to the exit, stepped outside. Weaving through the crowd of smokers they surfaced into clear air and turned to face each other.

'I appreciate you coming here today, Jessie.'

'Find him, Marilyn. Find him quickly.'

Jessie was halfway to the car park when an April downpour came from nowhere and turned the tarmac into a boiling slick of bubbles within seconds. Breaking into a run, she reached her Mini, yanked open the driver's door and dived inside, already soaked. Starting the engine, she flipped the wipers to maximum, heard them groan against the weight of water, clearing visibility, losing it. Scrubbing the condensation from the inside of the windscreen with the sleeve of her shirt, she eased the Mini back off the grass verge and crawled at snail's pace to the exit. As she pulled out of the hospital car park on to the main road, the rain still sheeting, she saw Joan Lawson with Harry in his pushchair, waiting at the bus stop. There was no shelter and the old lady had obviously come out without an umbrella because she was standing, looking fixedly down the road in the direction of the oncoming traffic, rain flattening her silver hair to her head and pasting her white shirt to her body.

Passing the bus stop, Jessie flicked on her indicator and bumped two tyres on to the kerb. She couldn't leave them standing there, getting drenched.

But what else could she do? She didn't have a child seat and there was no way the pram would fit in her Mini. She didn't even have an umbrella, a coat, anything to offer. Cursing her uselessness, she waited for a space in the traffic and eased back into its flow, watched them recede in the oval of her rear-view mirror, blurring under the downpour until they were toy people, the old lady still staring down the road, the bus nowhere in sight.

12

'Captain Callan?'

The man who had manoeuvred himself in front of Callan in the doorway, who was now holding out his hand and fixing Callan with a limpid green gaze, was as Irish as Guinness and leprechauns. He was around Callan's own age, but there the similarity stopped. Fine ginger hair feathered his head, freckles peppered his pallid face and the skin on his bare, extended forearm looked as if it would burn to a crisp in mid-winter. His body was soft and paunchy, his features slightly feminine looking. But the expression on his face was steadfast. Callan's gaze found the purple pentagon bordering the black crown on his epaulettes, the purple band around the cap that he was holding in his left hand, and his heart sank. He took hold of the proffered hand firmly.

'Chaplain. What can I do for you?'

'I'm Michael O'Shaughnessy, the padre here at Blackdown. Could I have a quiet word please, Captain.' He glanced past Callan to where a group of shock-faced sixteen-year-olds, last night's guard detachment, fidgeted on chairs in the larger of the two rooms that Gold had secured for interviews. 'In private.'

The only Army officers who didn't carry standard ranks, chaplains could hail from any Christian religion or Judaism, but were expected to provide pastoral care to any soldier who needed it, irrespective of the soldier's faith – or lack of it. All very worthy, but O'Shaughnessy's presence in this room with Callan's witnesses, his suspects, made him deeply uneasy. The last thing he needed was God or his earthly representative getting in the way of his investigation.

They stepped outside and Callan turned to face O'Shaughnessy. Though shards of sunlight were knifing through the grey clouds, it had started to rain, a soft patter on the tarmac around them. The chaplain gazed blandly up at Callan.

'You're leading the investigation into this poor, unfortunate boy's death, I presume?' His tone was soft, the lilt southern Irish, nothing hurried about his diction, no urgency.

Callan nodded, feeling impatience rear its head already. He resisted the urge to glance at this watch.

'I would ask you to suspend your interviews for a few hours, send the boys and girls back to their accommodation blocks for a bit of downtime. You can resume later today, when they've rested. Perhaps even tomorrow morning.'

Callan frowned. 'These "boys and girls", as you call them, are witness to and potentially suspects in a suspicious death.'

'Is it definitely murder?'

'I won't know for sure until the autopsy, but it looks that way.' His tone was curt, deliberately so. He still felt like shit, didn't have the mental or physical energy to exchange niceties with the chaplain. He wanted this conversation over, wanted to get back to doing his job.

'This is a training base, Captain, for the Royal Logistic Corps, as you know. These are kids, sixteen- and seventeen-year-olds, for the most part. They are all tired and scared. You will get far more sense from them if you give them a chance to sleep, to get some rest.'

'This is an Army base, Chaplain. These *kids* joined voluntarily and were legally old enough to make that decision.'

A shadow crossed O'Shaughnessy's face. 'They're hardly Parachute Regiment or SAS, though, are they?'

'They're still Army, none of them conscripts.' *Still witnesses. Still suspects.*

The rain was getting heavier; Callan could feel cold water funnelling down the back of his neck. He flipped up his collar and hunched his shoulders in his navy suit. O'Shaughnessy appeared not to notice the burgeoning downpour. Coming from Ireland, he was no doubt used to it. 'Nobody is going anywhere, until I, or one of my team has spoken with them. Now, if you'll excuse me.' Callan turned to go inside.

'Captain.'

Callan paused, his hand on the door, but didn't turn. 'Chaplain.'

'I will be around, Captain Callan. The welfare of the living in this case is as important – more so, I would venture – than the welfare of the dead.'

Don't tell me. Your God will look after the dead.

'And it is my job to ensure that these teenagers' welfare is not compromised.'

Callan's hard gaze met the chaplain's insipid green one.

'Of course, Chaplain, I would expect nothing less. Just

as it's my job to find out what happened.' He paused. 'Did you know him, Chaplain?'

'The victim?'

'Stephen Foster. He was called Stephen Foster.'

'My conversations are entirely confidential, Captain, you know that.' His soft voice didn't rise. 'I cannot divulge the names of those that I give counsel to. I need to be indisputably trustworthy, above reproach. No names, no comebacks, as they say.'

Callan's jaw tightened. 'This is potentially a murder investigation.'

'Potentially.'

'Whichever way you look at it, Foster is dead. Surely your professional and ecclesiastical responsibility are discharged on death.'

'The dead leave behind families, they leave behind loved ones and they leave behind their reputations.'

'And they need justice,' Callan snapped. 'He needs justice.'

'If this is found to be murder, Captain Callan, unequivocally murder, feel free to come and speak with me again.' His gaze slid from Callan's and found the low cloud ceiling above them, his brow creasing into a frown as if he had finally noticed that he was getting wet.

Callan gave a grim nod. 'The autopsy will be tomorrow morning. Don't go anywhere, Chaplain, and don't discuss this case with anyone. I will see you again soon, no doubt.'

'No doubt.'

Yanking the door open, Callan pushed through, leaving the chaplain standing outside in the rain, his mouth puckered into a moue of distaste. At the rain? At him? Callan couldn't tell and couldn't care less either way.

13

From her office window, Jessie watched the opaque curtain of another spring storm barrel across the lake at the bottom of the wide sweep of Bradley Court's lawn, turning the glassy water to froth. The leaves on the copper beech trees lining the pathway by the manor house twisted and bowed before they were engulfed, flattened under the weight of the downpour, and suddenly her view was misted, the glass opaque.

A knock on the door. The blond teenager standing in the corridor was barely taller than Jessie's five foot six, narrow-shouldered and thin. His soft hazel eyes looked huge in a pale face, framed as they were by the dark rings of insomnia. He looked very young.

'Private Jones, I'm Doctor Jessie Flynn.' She held out her hand. 'Please come in.'

Ryan Jones slid through the door, glancing sideways at her, a look of suspicion etched on his face. He didn't move to take her proffered hand. Jessie recognized that reaction, had come across it before with young soldiers a few months in who spent every day being drilled: woken up at first light and run for miles in their platoons, publicly belittled for every minor misdemeanour, their rooms swept with eagle eyes for dust specks, clothes checked for razor-sharp creases, even the shine on their boots studied forensically for signs that they weren't measuring up. And even if they were, imaginary holes picked in order to break down their confidence. Everything about Army basic training was designed to remove individuality and mould a team in its place. These recruits often found their initial visit to Bradley Court a destabilizing experience, no longer accustomed to being treated as an equal, a unique individual.

Closing the door behind him, Jessie indicated one of the two leather bucket chairs, separated only by a low coffee table that she used for her sessions. The chairs were deliberately placed underneath one of her office's two sash windows so that patients could relieve the pressure, if only momentarily, by looking at the view of nature beyond the glass. Ryan sat down, crossing his legs and folding his arms across his chest, nothing open or accommodating about his posture.

'Would you like a drink? Tea, coffee, water?'

Without making eye contact, he shook his head. Jessie grabbed his file and a pen from her desk and took the seat opposite. She had re-read the single typed sheet the file contained shortly before he arrived.

Ryan Thomas Jones

Sixteen and five months

Joined the Army on 2 November last year, the day of his sixteenth birthday

Phase 2 trainee, Royal Logistic Corps

Referred by Blackdown's commanding officer, Colonel Philip Wallace, because of concerns about his mental health

Nothing more than that: a vague, unspecific brief. She looked up from the file. It felt strange to be back in her consulting room, facing another patient who, from his body language and the shuttered look on his face, would give a lot to be somewhere else.

'Can I call you Ryan?'

A tiny lift of his shoulders, which Jessie translated as a teenager's 'Yes.'

'Thank you for coming in to see me.'

Another weary shrug. 'I wasn't given a choice.' A soft regional accent that Jessie couldn't place. She ploughed on. 'You've been in the Army five months?'

'Yes.'

'With the Royal Logistic Corps?'

'Yes.'

'How is it going?'

'OK.'

'Are you enjoying it?'

'It's not an exciting choice, is it, logistics? Not brave.' There was sneer in his voice.

'Don't knock it. An Army runs on good logistics.' Jessie racked her brains for the famous quote – something about wars being won or lost on the contents of soldiers' stomachs

– but try as she might she couldn't summon it, or its author, to mind. She still felt vague and headachy, half her brain mid-flight somewhere over the Persian Gulf, the other half in that small, depressing hospital room, hoping with all her heart that Joan Lawson was right when she said her son would never commit suicide, all her professional knowledge, her gut feeling, telling her that the old lady was wrong, the parallels with her own past deeply unsettling.

'An Army marches on its stomach, Napoleon Bonaparte.'

Ryan's face remained impassive.

'Logistics. The importance of logistics. Napoleon Bonaparte?' *Logistics, catering, near enough.* 'Military general, the first Emperor of France, Battle of Waterloo?'

Still no reaction.

'Never mind. So why did you choose the Logistic Corps then?'

He shrugged, a careless movement that brought to Jessie's mind a teenaged schoolboy sitting at the back of the class, thinking about smoking behind the bike shed and sticking his hand up girls' skirts rather than whatever subject the teacher was wittering on about at the front of the classroom.

'Do you want to be brave, Ryan?' Jessie asked softly, tilting forward, trying, and failing, to catch his eye.

Kids of this age *should* be still at school. She didn't believe that they had the emotional maturity, the mental robustness to handle rigid institutions like the Army, even in relatively soft options like logistics. The Army could be tough and isolating, the necessity of fitting in, of being accepted as one of the lads, stressful, particularly for people who were not natural team players. She suspected that Ryan was not a natural team player.

'Ryan.'

He had started to fidget, fingers picking at a thread that had come loose from the stitching of his navy-blue beret. His nails had been bitten to the quick, the cuticles raw, Jessie noticed.

'No.' His voice so low that it was almost inaudible. 'Not particularly.'

'So why the Army? Why did you join?'

He sighed, like a teenager whose mother was hassling him. 'Because people like me don't have choices. The Army seemed like a good way of getting out.'

'Getting out from where? Where did you grow up?'

'Birmingham.' The soft accent. Midlands – of course. She should have recognized it.

'Do you have family?'

'A mother.'

'Father?'

'He died when I was three.'

'I'm sorry.'

'It didn't affect me. I never really knew him.'

Jessie knew that wasn't true. Abandonment always affected children, however it happened. She knew that well enough from her own childhood.

'Does your mother still live in Birmingham?'

'Yes.'

'Are you close to her?'

The first sign of warmth and light that Jessie had seen in his soft hazel eyes, but the words thrown out insouciantly, entirely at odds with his expression. 'What's that got to do with you?'

She felt as if she was butting her head up against a wall. A smooth, featureless, wall, plain white, no finger-holds, nothing to get a grip on. Her office felt oppressive suddenly, a room shut up for too long over winter, which it had been. The shower had passed, sunlight breaking through the bank of grey clouds outside. Standing, Jessie unlocked the window and hauled up the lower sash. Cool, damp air eddied through the gap.

'Can I go now?' Ryan asked, narrowing his gaze against the sunlight.

'Not yet.'

'Why not?' he hissed.

The sudden flare of aggression surprised Jessie, gone almost as soon as she'd registered it. He had seemed too distant, too closed down for aggression. She made a mental note.

'Don't I get a choice?' he finished.

'Unfortunately you gave up your right to choose when you joined the Army.'

His mouth tightened as if she had unwittingly put her finger on a nerve.

'Ryan, Blackdown's commanding officer, Colonel Philip Wallace, referred you to the Defence Psychology Service. As you can see, there's not much information in your file.' She held up the single page. 'So why don't you tell me why you think he sent you.'

Jaw muscles clenched under his skin.

'I've never even talked to him.' He stretched his arm straight above his head. 'He's God isn't he? And I'm down here somewhere.' The hand moved to graze the carpet. 'Pond life.'

If he'd had no verbal contact with Wallace, had he talked to someone else about his feelings, or had his behaviour been noticed? 'Did you talk to someone else at Blackdown about how you're feeling?'

65

'I'm not feeling anything.'

'There must be a reason that you're here, that you were referred.'

Ryan's arms tightened around his torso, but he didn't reply. Everything about his posture telegraphed intense feelings of discomfort at Jessie's questions.

'Who did you talk to, Ryan?'

'No one.' His gaze found the window. Jessie let him stare. After a moment, his gaze still fixed on the outside, he murmured, 'He approached me.'

'Who approached you?'

'The chaplain.'

That wasn't in the file. She made a mental note.

'What did he say?'

'He said that it's his job.'

'To keep an eye on new recruits?'

'Yeah. Their spiritual health, mental health, all that crap.'

'What did you talk to him about?'

Another shrug. 'Stuff.'

'Can you tell me?'

He shook his head. 'They're supposed to be confidential, aren't they? My discussions with him? I should have known not to talk to him.' Ryan slumped in the bucket chair, started kicking at the carpet with one of his combat boots, muttered under his breath. 'Fuckin' kiddie fiddler.'

Catholic. Kiddie fiddler. The chaplain must get that all the time – an occupational hazard. Jessie continued to look at Ryan, but he didn't add anything else. She waited, the silence growing heavier.

'Do you believe in God, *Doctor* Flynn?' he asked suddenly.

Jessie took a beat before answering. She had been raised

a Catholic, sent to a convent school, but she had never seen any evidence that the people around her lived by God's word. Had seen no evidence at all of the existence of a just and gentle God. The only God she had experienced persecuted and destroyed.

And God will use this persecution to show his justice and to make you worthy of his kingdom, for which you are suffering.

Persecution without justice.

'No, Ryan, I don't believe in God.'

Ryan looked up and their gazes met for a fraction of a second before he looked away again. Minute progress, but progress all the same.

'My mum spent time in a mental home, you know, when I was younger. Perhaps madness runs in the family.'

'No one is saying that you're mad.'

'But it does run in families, doesn't it?' he murmured. 'Madness?'

'There is no such thing as madness,' Jessie said quietly, her gaze finding the window. 'There are disorders, some caused by physical factors, chemical imbalances in people's brains, some caused by psychological factors, such as bad experiences in childhood.' She fought to keep her voice even, feeling the tension rise, the electric suit tingle against her skin. *Madness.* 'They can all be treated, but the patient needs to be willing.'

She thought that Ryan would have switched off, be picking at his beret or kicking at the carpet again, but when she looked back from the window, she saw that he was watching her intently.

'Well, perhaps I am.'

'Willing?'

'Mad.'

'Perhaps we all are.' Jessie smiled, a smile that didn't reach her eyes. 'We're all individuals, Ryan. Don't feel that you need to be the same as the others to fit in.'

A chill shook Jessie as she closed the door behind Ryan, and she realized that the window was still open. The cloud canopy was back, draping itself over Bradley Court, the leaves on the copper beeches outside lifting and twisting in the wind, rain speckling through the open window. Hauling down the sash, she stood looking out, awed by the ability of the weather to change so suddenly from darkness to light and back to darkness again.

What had she been doing when she was Ryan's age? She would have been back at school then, trying to get a grip on normality, work for her GCSEs, make up for the time that she had missed, prove to herself – to them – that she could, would, carve a normal life for herself. Closing her eyes, she tilted her head and rested it against the cool glass. The hiss and snap of the electric suit was intensifying with the memories.

She could feel the box of matches in her shaking hand, the rough strip on the side as her fingers felt to slide it open in the dark. It was important that she was quiet, vital that she didn't wake them. She just needed to show them. Show her.

Her eyes snapped open. The electric suit was tight around her throat.

She had been fourteen, younger even than Ryan. Old enough to face the consequences though. Old enough to pay.

14

Callan found Blackdown's commanding officer, Colonel Philip Wallace, in his office. He was in his fifties, a large man, square and solid, both facially and in his build, running to fat around the middle, as were many men of his age, used to spending too much time behind a desk.

'Come in, Captain Callan. You're the Senior Investigating Officer on this case?'

'Yes, sir.'

'So where have we got to?' A clipped, public school accent, the tone controlled but commanding.

'It's early days, sir. The autopsy is booked for tomorrow morning, so we should have confirmed cause of death by end of day tomorrow.' Callan tried to catch his eye, to form the crucial first impression of the man who would, no doubt, be breathing down his neck until the investigation was concluded. But sunlight was cutting obliquely through the window to Wallace's right, lighting his face, masking his eyes behind the reflection in his frameless square spectacle lenses. 'But I suspect it's murder.'

'Why?'

'Because of the nature of the victim's injuries. A throat wound. It couldn't have been accidental and it's a . . . ' he paused, searching for the right word ' . . . brave way to commit suicide. And also the weapon that was used was found eight metres from his body, the tip stabbed into the ground, at an angle. Thrown, my CSI sergeant said. Long way to throw it when you're bleeding from a throat wound.'

Sighing, Wallace dipped his head and rubbed his hands over his bald scalp, the sound of his palms grating through the sparse grey stubble, sandpaper on wood.

'I'm sure I don't need to remind you how sensitive this death will be. Sixteen-year-old, five months in.'

There was a brusqueness to Wallace's tone that Callan was well used to: men who were accustomed, over years, to silence and assent. Not conditions that Callan reacted well to, despite his chosen profession. This case was Military Police jurisdiction, but Wallace was commanding officer at Blackdown, and although far above the victim in the Army hierarchy, he was still Foster's direct superior, which gave him an unalienable right to be informed, involved, omnipresent.

'We need to get this sorted quickly, Captain.'

'That is my intention.'

'Keep a lid on the negative publicity.' Wallace cleared his throat. 'Can you do that for me?'

'That's not my first priority, sir.'

The sun must have gone behind a cloud, because he met Wallace's gaze behind his glasses now. His eyes were light grey and shone with an intense, uncompromising gleam.

'Nevertheless, it is an important one.' Wallace's eyes narrowed. 'Discretion is the better part of valour, as they say. I've heard that you know all about valour.' His gaze found the scar on Callan's temple. 'But discretion . . . ?' He let the sentence hang.

'I have no intention of speaking to the press,' Callan replied. 'And I will ensure that none of my team do either.'

'That was all I wanted to hear.'

A knock on the door. Wallace frowned. 'Yes?'

The door inched open and Lieutenant Gold stuck his head through the gap. His eyes flitted from Callan to Wallace and back to Callan.

'The guard are isolated and ready to be interviewed, Captain,' he said.

'Come on in, Gold,' Wallace barked.

'I need to get back, sir.' Gold addressed his comment to Callan.

'You've left someone guarding the interviewees?' Callan asked.

'Sergeant Kiddie.'

'Fine. So come in.'

Fingering the knot of his tie, the yellow-haired lieutenant stepped over the threshold. He came to attention facing Colonel Wallace, a salute that Wallace waved away.

'No need for that.' Wallace came out from behind his desk and laid a light hand on Gold's shoulder. 'So you're working on this case too? I didn't realize.'

Taking a step back, Gold disengaged his shoulder. 'Yes, sir.' His gaze swung away from Wallace's and Callan noticed a muscle above his eye twitch.

'Well, I'm pleased to hear that,' Wallace said gruffly, his face creasing into a frown, the expression at odds with his words. He glanced over to Callan. 'You may have heard that we share a relative.'

71

Callan gave a non-committal half-nod. He hadn't heard and the information was irrelevant to him. He wouldn't view or treat Gold any differently because of it.

Leaning back against his desk, legs crossed at the ankle, Wallace slid his hands into his pockets. 'So how are you finding the Special Investigation Branch, Gold?'

Gold's slender fingers moved to smooth the collar of his shirt, a collar that was already starched and ironed within an inch of its life.

'Good, sir, I'm enjoying it. I'm enjoying the autonomy, the freedom.' His voice was too loud for the small office, as if he was struggling to pitch his volume at the correct level.

Callan, leaning against the wall, arms crossed over his chest, watching intently, realized with surprise that Gold was tense, stressed. There was a prickliness, an antagonism to the atmosphere in the room that hadn't been present earlier, when it was him and Wallace.

'Yes, I'm sure that the Branch is an interesting place to be,' Wallace said. 'Make the most of it, eh. Spend as much time as you can with Captain Callan here. Learn from him.'

A brief nod and Gold's eyes swivelled to meet Callan's. 'If there's nothing else, I'll get back to the interviewees.'

Callan glanced at Wallace before replying, but Wallace wasn't looking at him. He was gazing down at the carpet, his face creased again into that frown.

'Yes, you go. I'll join you in a minute.'

Turning, Gold left the room without another word.

Callan straightened. 'If that's all, Colonel, I'll get back too.'

Tugging his glasses off, Wallace massaged the bridge of his nose with two blunt fingers and sighed irritably. 'Make sure that you involve Gold in every aspect of the case. Keep an eye on him for me, will you? It's important to pass on your expertise to junior officers and Gold is bright and talented.'

The request was no doubt motivated by family connection, perhaps a favour Wallace owed to that relative he had mentioned, and the entreaty needled Callan. He hailed from a long line of factory workers, was the first in his family not to have ended up on the shop floor purely because politicians hadn't yet got around to closing the local grammar school and he'd been smart enough to win a place. His father had died fourteen years ago; his mother lived in a modern terraced house in a secure gated development in a nice part of Aldershot that he paid for. He had made his own way in the world from the age of sixteen, reviled others who hadn't done the same, some of that feeling motivated, he recognized, by envy.

'Yes, sir,' he muttered, making his way to the door. *Jesus.* This investigation was going from bad to worse and it had hardly begun.

15

Marilyn stared at the snowstorm on the screen in front of him.

'Is this mid-winter in Alaska?'

Workman sighed. 'Old CCTV, sir.'

Tipping back on his heels, Marilyn blew air through his nose. 'You can say that again.' His gaze moved from the screen that covered the A & E reception desk, entrance hallway and sliding doors to the outside, roamed across the other screens in the bank of monitors, five screens wide, four high, twenty in all, each relaying a fragment of hospital turf, the top right-hand monitor blank, the camera feeding it presumably broken, searching for a good view of the service road outside Accident and Emergency. He couldn't see one. 'What about the camera outside, covering the service road?'

'Vandalized last week,' Workman said.

Ka-ching. One chance in twenty and he'd hit the jackpot. 'Great. So this is it. This is all we have to go on.'

'It's not their priority, sir.'

'No, don't tell me. Failing to notice babies and telling middle-aged men who are beyond help to give up smoking is, though,' he snapped, ignoring the sideways glance that the hospital security guard shot him.

Pulling his reading glasses from his pocket – a purchase he'd been forced to make last month when he'd found that his arms no longer extended far enough to hold his newspaper at a distance whereby he could read the text – Marilyn sat down and slid the chair, on its squeaky plastic wheels, closer to the screen.

'Play that segment again, please,' he said to the security guard.

'The bit where the man comes in pushing the baby?' the guard asked.

'Yes.'

Fuzz on the screen while the segment was rewound. Then an empty A & E foyer, the sliding doors closed, dark outside their glass panes. Suddenly the doors slid open. A pram appeared on the screen and right behind, the man pushing it, visible only from mid-chest down.

'He's carrying an umbrella,' Marilyn said.

'Which makes sense, considering it was pouring,' Workman murmured.

Marilyn nodded, focusing on the screen. 'Dark jumper, dark trousers, dark coat, sensible shoes.'

'Sensible shoes?'

'Pause, please.'

The grainy image froze. Marilyn pressed his finger to the screen.

'Clodhoppers.'

The shoes were thick-soled, the type of shoes that would be sold at Clarks as 'built for walking'.

'Malcolm Lawson was certainly the sensible-shoe type,' Workman said.

'He was that.'

'It could be him,' she said.

'It could be me.'

'You don't wear sensible shoes, sir,' Workman said, glancing down at his £300 Edward Hill pebble-grain leather brogues.

Fair point.

Marilyn turned to the guard. 'Play it until the man leaves the hospital, disappears from view, but the sliding doors are still open. Pause with the doors open, please.'

The guard's eyebrows rose in query.

'The background. He could have driven to the door.'

'Not allowed.'

'Midnight? In the rain? Who's out there objecting?'

They waited while the man dressed in dark clothing parked the pram, stooping to take one last long look at baby Harry before he straightened, turned and exited the building, walking right, diagonally across the service road, out of shot.

'Now,' Marilyn said.

The screen froze, sliding doors still open, revealing the service road beyond, the darkness illuminated by the circular misty disc of an overhead streetlamp. Marilyn pressed his finger to the far left-hand side of the screen.

'This? What's this?'

'The front of an ambulance,' the guard said. 'The bumper, a bit of the grille and bonnet.'

'You sure?'

'Absolutely. I've worked here for twenty years. Seen enough of those in my time to recognize one from a square inch.'

'OK,' Marilyn said. 'Fine.' He could tell that the security

guard was a pedant. A twenty-years-in-the-job pedant; good enough for him. 'So that's an ambulance.'

His gaze tracked right, across the bottom of the screen, up an inch, left, the CCTV equivalent of a fingertip search in mud. Double yellow lines, showing muted white on the black-and-white screen. Something bright white, inflated – a plastic bag? At the top of the screen, two wheels, separated by a pale, blotchy – most probably, dirty white – stripe of metal, a horizontal row of alternate dark and light-coloured blocks above.

'The lower half of a police car, sir,' Workman cut in.

Marilyn tilted forward, squinting through his glasses, picking out every detail. The vehicle was parked on the other side of the service road, half its wheels, a segment of chassis, the stripes and the blocks – navy blue and fluorescent yellow in real life – showing gunmetal grey and luminous white on the screen.

'Yes, you're right. It's a police car.'

He glanced over at the security guard, who concurred.

One ambulance, one police car: nothing unusual in either of those being parked on a hospital service road. Nothing else visible. *No leads. No breaks. No bloody luck.*

Tugging off his glasses, sliding them back into his pocket before Workman had time to comment on his new-found old man accoutrements, he leaned back in the chair and stretched his arms above his head. Focusing so hard on the screen had left his eyes feeling as if someone had tugged them five centimetres from his face on their optic nerves and then pinged them back into their sockets.

'So it could very possibly have been Malcolm Lawson who dropped the baby off,' he said.

Workman and the security guard both nodded.

'He was tender with Harry,' Workman said. 'He stopped to take a last look. A long look.'

Marilyn sighed. 'He did. He did indeed.'

His mood hadn't improved. He felt as if he'd spent the whole morning running in circles, chasing his tail. He had snuck out of the hospital a couple of times to join the unwashed throng outside for a sneaky cigarette, hoping, ridiculously, that Janet, that dumpy receptionist, wouldn't catch him in the act. Lord knows why her opinion mattered to him, but for some reason he felt strongly that he needed to prove her wrong. Prove to her that he could take control of his health, even if he was delaying the attempt until tomorrow. *Tomorrow never comes.* Every traffic cop and patrol car in Surrey and Sussex had been told to keep an eye out as a priority, but as yet there had been no sighting of Malcolm Lawson's car. DS Workman had already been telephoned three times by Granny Lawson for updates, even though she'd only left the hospital two hours ago, each call progressively more tearful. He hadn't given the old biddy his mobile number, small mercies.

'Get a copy of the original film to the tech boys, DS Workman, see if they can clean it up.'

'That'll take two or three days, sir.'

Pushing himself to his feet, he threw her a withering look. 'Better get on with it then.'

16

She obviously hadn't turned James Blunt up loud enough, because she heard her phone on the first ring, caught its jittering progress across the smooth black leather of her passenger seat out of the corner of her eye. Easing her foot on to the brake, pulling her Mini to the side of the lane until the dogwood hedge fingered her passenger window, Jessie reached over, checked the name flashing on the phone's face.

Gideon Duursema.

She was tempted to toss it back on the seat, wind down the windows and turn up the volume, step on the accelerator, plead ignorance to her boss in the morning. But she couldn't start off on the wrong foot with him so soon after her return. She was good at her job, intuitive and dedicated – most of the time – so he cut her slack, but even he had limits.

'Gideon.'

'Jessie.'

Silence, which she let hang.

'How was DI Simmons?'

A diversionary tactic, from his tone.

'Rough, as always.'

'How was the baby?'

'Small. Fat. Baby-like.'

His deep laugh echoed down the line. 'So maternal.'

'Well, at least you're not going to have to worry about me getting knocked up and taking months off work.'

'Small mercies, Doctor Flynn.'

Doctor Flynn. Ominous. Echoes of the occasions when her mother called for 'Jessica', as a child. Nothing good ever came out of those occasions.

'You're on your way home, I presume?'

'Yes,' she replied in a cautious voice.

'Then, I'm sorry.'

'You're apologizing before you've even asked me to do anything. Now that really makes me nervous.'

'You weren't also feeling tired were you? Jet-lagged?'

Jessie glanced quickly at the washed-out oval segment of her face in the rear-view mirror. 'Knackered. Why?'

'I've had another request.'

'Don't tell me. From your dry cleaner. Your suit is ready for collection. Of course, yes, no problem, give me the address.'

Another laugh, this one a cynical bark, cut off before it was finished. 'I was hoping that your stint on a boat might have made you more respectful of authority, but I seem to be sadly deluded.'

'Type 45 Destroyer.'

She heard his exasperated sigh down the phone, remained stubbornly silent.

'There's been a suspicious death at Blackdown. Early this morning. A sixteen-year-old.'

'Sounds like a PR disaster in the making.'

Headlights suddenly, even though it was still daylight, high up, lighting the interior of her Mini operating-theatre bright. She held her breath, hoping her Mini was doing the same, while a huge metallic black Range Rover Sport squeezed past on the narrow lane, the woman driving, a slim blonde, mobile clamped to her ear, the nose of a chubby-faced, blonde toddler pressed to the back window, her breath clouding the glass.

'So the Branch need to clear this one up quickly before the press get hold of it and turn it into a public relations nightmare for the Army. Holden-Hough has requested our help.'

'Why?'

'The victim, all the key suspects and witnesses are trainees. Sixteen-year-olds. They're young, vulnerable and frightened.'

'More babies. Sounds like a nightmare brief.'

'I'm sure that you can handle it, Doctor Poppins, after this morning's practice and the Sami Scott case.'

Her mind cast back to this morning, skirting around the baby boy playing on the floor-mat as if he was an explosive device; four months earlier to four-year-old Sami Scott. The death of Sami's mother, a bitter pill that she hadn't yet managed to swallow. Still believing that she could, *should*, have done something to predict and alter that outcome.

'It's a bit less Mary Poppins and a bit more Doctor Doolittle with new recruits.'

'Thank you, I appreciate it.'

'I haven't said yes, yet.' She paused, heard nothing but Gideon's measured breathing. 'Who's the Senior Investigating Officer?' Her own breath caught in her throat as she waited for Gideon's answer, waited to hear if it was Callan.

'Holden-Hough didn't say.'

And you didn't ask. But, of course, why would you?

'Is the SIO on board with the idea of a psychologist's help?'

'In the Special Investigation Branch what Holden-Hough says, goes.'

'I'll take that as a "no" then.'

'You can handle it.'

Jessie didn't answer, because her answer was irrelevant. She was going anyway, no choice. She glanced at her watch: 5 p.m. Relatively early, but she felt wiped out, knew that it wasn't jet lag. Something about today – Joan Lawson, Malcolm, baby Harry playing happily, unaware that his world was shattering, Ryan Jones, suicide, madness – had sucked her dry. The tingle from the electric suit that she had felt first at the hospital, a tingle that had intensified during her session with Ryan, refused to subside, a background itch coating her whole body, barely there, but omnipresent all the same.

'Can you go straight to Blackdown?'

'Is there no one else?'

'No one who has acres of time in their diary because they've come back from three months away.'

'Working. Away, *working*.'

A heavy sigh. 'You know what the government has done to our funding.'

She did – all too well. It was one of his hobby horses.

'We're all stretched to breaking, and you have experience of working with the Branch. What was that officer's name? Cooper?'

'Callan,' Jessie murmured. 'Captain Callan.'

'Right, Callan. He seemed like a good guy. It might be

him.' The clink of metal stiletto heels on a wooden floor suddenly, echoing down the line, and a woman's voice Jessie recognized as Jenny, the service's secretary. 'I need to go,' Gideon said.

A click. Silence. Only the sound of her own heartbeat, slightly elevated, beating in the hollow car.

17

The afternoon sun cast a feeble rectangle of pale yellow over the bare wooden desk in the room that Callan had hastily commandeered for his interviews.

'You were the Duty Staff Officer for last night's guard?' he asked, though his tone made it more of a statement than a question.

Corporal Jace Harris, wiry, dark-eyed and dark-haired, intense and on edge, facing him across the desk, gave a brief, fretful nod. Callan tilted back in his chair, crossing his legs, one ankle resting on the other knee, slid his hands into his pockets; a deliberately relaxed, matey posture. An obvious tactic, which always surprised him with how effective it was at breaking down defensive barriers.

'So talk me through what happened last night.' He fixed Harris with a steady gaze.

Harris shrugged. 'Nothing much, sir.'

'Nothing much?'

Harris lifted his shoulders again and his small brown eyes slid to the window.

'One of your guard duty *died*, Corporal.'

'Apart from that.'

Was this guy for real? He didn't seem overly concerned that a sixteen-year-old under his command had been found dead. Or was it an act?

'On your watch, Harris. Someone died on *your* watch.'

'It was personal. A mate.'

'Who told you that?'

'It's the word on the street.'

Gangsta rap in leafy Surrey.

'Who from?'

'Dunno.' Harris swallowed as if his mouth was suddenly dry. 'It's not going to be a random murder though, is it? A terrorist or nothing. Not down here in middle-of-fucking-nowhere Camberley.'

'Why not?'

Harris jerked his thumb towards the window. 'Because nothing ever happens out there.'

'Until last night.'

A reluctant nod of acquiescence. 'Yeah, right. Until last night.'

'Who found Stephen Foster?' Callan asked.

'Martha Wonsag.'

'Who is she?'

'One of the new recruits, joined the same time as Foster, five or six months ago. They were on guard duty together. She radioed it in.'

'Where were you when you received the call?'

'In the guard hut.'

'By the main gate?'

'Yeah.'

'Inside?'

'Yeah.'

'Why?'

'It was raining.'

'Are you made of sugar?'

'Wot?'

Callan looked at the sullen ferret face. *Sugar, spice and all things nice. Hardly.* 'Do you dissolve in the wet, Corporal?'

Harris didn't answer. He had retrieved a stainless steel Zippo lighter from his pocket and was rolling it in his fingers like a worry bead.

'Why weren't you outside checking on the guard detail, Harris?'

'Because, like I already said—'

'It was raining. And nothing ever happens out there,' Callan cut in.

Sitting forward, he planted his elbows on the desktop and steepled his fingers. *Was this guy for real?* 'Until last night.'

Flicking the lid of the Zippo lighter half open with his thumb a couple of times, the noise irritatingly tinny in the bare room, Harris sneered and curled his lip. 'Until last fucking night.'

'Were you alone?'

'I'm not sure exactly what time Foster died, sir, so I can't say.'

'Were you alone at any time during the night?'

'For a brief period, sir.'

'How long?'

'Five or ten minutes. Ten max.'

'Where were the gate guards?'

Harris frowned. 'They were around.'

'Around where? Around the gate?'

Harris didn't answer; his gaze had found the window again. Callan looked over. Two male pigeons had settled on the windowsill, were strutting back and forth, fluffing their feathers to beef up their size, preparing for a fight. He shared their sentiment.

'Where were the gate guards, Corporal Harris?'

Silence. Callan waited.

Eventually, Harris sighed. 'One of them's girlfriend turned up.'

Callan didn't even want to ask the question, knew what answer he'd get if he did. Instead, he let the silence hang, saw Harris's hands begin to churn around the Zippo.

'She's off travelling for six months.'

'And?' He twisted the knife.

'You know what – *and* – sir.'

'What about the other guard?'

'I sent him back to my accommodation block to get my fags. I'd run out.'

Callan rubbed his hands across his face, massaging his fingers right into his eye sockets. He felt knackered, would rather be anywhere than sitting in this featureless, white-walled box, facing this moron.

'So Martha Wonsag radioed that she'd found Stephen Foster dead,' he said.

'Yeah.'

'What time was that?'

'Three ten a.m., sir.'

A stake in the sand. *One stake, in quicksand. Infinitesimal progress.*

'So where the hell was she when Foster died?'

'She said that she was on a toilet break.'

'A toilet break? How long does a toilet break last?'

'Mine? Ten seconds. But I can piss up against a tree, can't I.' Harris clicked his tongue sarcastically. 'Hers? You'll need to ask her that question, sir.'

'Did *you* ask her?'

'No?'

'Why not?'

'Why do you think? I wasn't going to question a woman on her toilet habits, was I? Anyway, all hell broke loose when we found Foster. Utter fucking panic. My guard detachment were all new recruits, all sixteen, and they thought that the Islamic fuckin' State had invaded Blackdown. It was like trying to control a herd of chickens.'

'Flock.'

'Wot?' The corporal reached to scratch the back of his head – an action that brought to Callan's mind a cartoon character wrestling with a particularly knotty problem – and his sleeve rode up to reveal the tattoo of a girl on his forearm. She was artfully arranged on all fours, her bottom, clad only in a tiny red G-string, facing the viewer. She was looking back over her left shoulder; a waterfall of blonde hair cascaded over her right. The look on her face was pure suggestion, or as suggestive as could be achieved with the medium of tattoo ink on a canvas of hairy skin.

'Nice tat,' Callan muttered.

'Like it?' Harris hadn't clocked the irony in his voice.

Callan's gaze narrowed. 'What do you think about women, Corporal?'

A wolfish smile. 'I love women, Captain.'

'In the Army, Corporal?'

'I don't notice.'

'You don't notice women?'

'I don't notice women in green, sir.'

The sound of a rough diesel engine and a four-tonner drove past the window, scaring the warring pigeons into flight.

'What was Foster like?' Callan asked.

Harris shrugged. 'A bit of a wimp, I'd say.'

'Why?'

Another careless lift of his shoulders. 'He seemed to be, is all.'

'Did he shirk his duties?'

'No.'

'Did he complain?'

'No.'

'Did he take time off sick?'

'No.'

Callan was getting sick of the attitude. 'So what?' he snapped.

Dropping the Zippo with a clatter on to the table, Harris sighed. 'Look, I've heard about you, sir.' Callan noticed Harris's gaze flick to the scar on his temple. 'I've heard about you and I respect you. But who the hell would you want watching your back, somewhere like Afghanistan? When you've got some crazy jihadi comin' at you? When you're in the middle of a firefight? Do you really want some woman or some young wimp backing you up?' His dark gaze searched Callan's face from under his black, spiky fringe. 'Who would you want next to you, sir?'

'Someone who is brave and professional,' Callan said.

'Brave and professional. Right, yeah, me too. But they're not typical wimps' or female traits are they?'

'Aren't they?'

The corporal looked uncomfortable; he'd expected

89

Callan's matey support and hadn't got it. Callan glanced at his watch – 5.30 p.m. – a darker haze muddying the sky outside the window.

'What's Marley stand for?'

'Huh?'

Callan indicated Harris's other arm, where the words 'Marley' were visible tattooed in black on the inside of his wrist.

'It's my nickname.'

'Why Marley?'

'It's just a nickname, sir.' His tone cagey.

'After the dog?'

Harris frowned. 'Wot dog?'

'There was a film, wasn't there? *Marley and Me*. About a dog called Marley.'

'No,' Harris snapped. 'It's not after any fuckin' dog.'

'What then?' Callan pressed.

'I've had it for years.' He blinked and his eyes slid from Callan's. 'Can't even remember who gave it to me. Probably my parents.'

Callan sighed. He'd had enough. He wanted out. 'Thanks for your help, Harris. We're done.' He paused. 'For now.'

Harris's narrow lips cracked into a grin. 'Great.'

Callan pushed himself to his feet. 'You know that you've made yourself a suspect, don't you?'

The grin vanished. 'Wot? I was alone for five fucking minutes. Ten max.'

'Your accommodation block is on the other side of the base. It's going to take more than ten minutes for someone to get there, find your cigarettes and get back.'

Harris's eyes blazed. 'The other guard,' he spluttered.

Callan held up a hand, silencing him. 'If my girlfriend

was off travelling for six months, I'd want to spend more than ten minutes with her.' Callan smiled. 'Unless I had a hair-trigger. Does he have a hair-trigger, Harris, or should I ask him that question?'

The muscles along Harris's jaw bulged.

Callan walked to the door. 'Don't discuss this case with anyone, and don't go anywhere. I'm pretty sure that I'll need to speak to you again.'

As he pushed through the door, he glanced back, saw Harris still sitting, his head now in his hands.

18

She noticed the red Golf GTI as soon as she pulled under the raised barrier into Blackdown. *Callan*. So the SIO on the Stephen Foster case was Ben Callan. Pulling to the far side of the car park, tucking her Mini behind a Land Rover Defender, Jessie cut the engine. The claustrophobic electricity from the suit still tingled across her skin and now, added to it, a wave of light-headedness at the thought of seeing Callan again, the combination making her feel keyed-up and slightly nauseous. Tilting her head back, closing her eyes for a moment, she took a few deep breaths, fixing her mind on the innocuous image of the morning sun rising over the fields at the back of her cottage, trying to slow the beating of her heart. She had thought about Callan many times since she'd last seen him, had been tempted, almost as many times, to email him. But she had no experience with men beyond meaningless physical encounters and every missive she had composed had sounded trite and uninteresting. She had no idea what to say, what tone to strike, even. In the end, it had been easier not to email at all.

She recognized Callan immediately, though he was standing with his back to her. Broad-shouldered and athletic, a head taller than the grey-haired man he was talking with, he was slouching, hands shoved in his trouser pockets, perhaps to reduce the height disparity, to listen more easily. His posture, the slouch, should have said 'relaxed', but Jessie knew that there was nothing laid-back about the rigid set of his shoulders, the jitter of perpetual motion in his long legs. He must have sensed her approach – someone approach – because he turned suddenly and their eyes locked.

'Jessie—' Shock registered briefly on his face before his expression settled into one of cool unreadability. 'Doctor Flynn. You're back.'

'Yes, last night. Actually, early this morning, more accurately.'

The last time she had seen him, he had been unconscious in a hospital bed, bandaged and wired to every device in the room, touch and go whether he would live or die. He had lived, the second gunshot wound that he'd survived in as many years, but she knew that the wound to his abdomen had been devastating, that he'd lost nearly half the blood in his body before he'd reached the operating theatre. Though he was back at work, she couldn't believe that he was physically 100 per cent recovered. And mentally? He was wearing a smart navy-blue suit, uniform knife-creases bisecting each trouser leg, a crisp white shirt, open at the neck, black shoes shined mirror bright, nothing there to upset her sense of order. But beneath the window dressing, he looked wrecked, his eyes washed out and skittish, skin pale and damp with perspiration.

'How was the Persian Gulf?'

'Good.' She hunched her shoulders. 'Interesting.'

'Glad you enjoyed it.'

'Thanks.'

He gave her a tight smile. 'So why are you here at Blackdown?'

She had kept a picture of him in her mind whilst she had been away, had taken it out and examined it closely when she was alone in her bunk at night. Looking at him now, she realized that the picture had faded, blended with the faces of the men around her until it seemed ordinary. But there was nothing ordinary about him, nothing regular. He was arrestingly handsome and she felt what little confidence she possessed draining from her, trapped as she was under the unremitting gaze of those haunted amber eyes. Heat rose to her face.

'I'm, uh, here to help.'

'Help who?'

'You. With the investigation, the suspicious death.'

'I didn't request a psychologist's help.'

'Holden-Hough did.'

'What?' He looked incredulous.

'He called Gideon Duursema and I'm afraid that you're landed with me because my diary was the emptiest.'

His jaw tightened. 'Give me a minute.' Pulling his mobile from his pocket, he flicked through his contacts. After a moment, 'Colonel, it's Captain Callan.' His voice faded as he walked away. A pause. 'I don't need—' she heard. Another pause, his legs jittering impatiently as he listened. 'Right. Yes, sir.' Jamming his phone back into his pocket, he turned to face her. His expression was one of barely suppressed anger. 'It seems I don't have a choice.'

'I'm sorry.'

He pulled a face. 'Not your fault.'

He turned back to the grey-haired man in the forensic overalls he had been speaking with, who had tactfully distanced himself when Jessie approached.

'Morgan, I'm going to search Foster's accommodation block now. I'll take Doctor Flynn with me.' The inference: keep her out of trouble, out of your hair. 'Post a guard here when you're done. I'll call the dogs in tomorrow, see if there's anything we've missed.'

Morgan nodded. 'Right, sir.'

Striding past Jessie, Callan cast back over his shoulder. 'Are you coming, Doctor?'

He walked fast, making no allowances for the fact that she had started off five metres behind and was wearing heels. She had to jog to catch up and then trot in his wake to keep up with his long stride, like some subservient wife. She was tempted to grind to a standstill and tell him to stick his attitude, but she had been briefed to work on the case with him and the atmosphere between them was already frigid.

'So how have you been, Callan?'

'What?' He glanced across, surprised at her question. 'Me? I'm fine.' His eyes were hard.

Her gaze flicked to the rough knot of stitched skin on his temple. His suit jacket and shirt hid the second bullet wound, from Scott's gun. She had been his psychologist after the first shooting, an attack from 'friendly' Afghan policemen who Callan and his Military Police colleagues had been training, an attack in which his best friend, Tom, had died. He had spent five months fighting to reclaim his sanity, a hermit in his mother's house. Jessie had tried – and failed – to help him, the only patient she had treated since she joined the Defence Psychology Service, two years previously, whom she felt she had entirely failed. He had pulled himself together, eventually, but it looked as though Scott's attack had pushed him back to the edge. She noticed that his hands, now that they were out of his pockets, were shaking.

'I'm sorry that I didn't email—'

'We need to search the victim's belongings,' he cut in. 'See if anything stands out as being odd, or out of place. See if we can find a clue as to why he died. I'd also like to get an understanding of his personality. The interviews have been wholly unenlightening.'

Jessie nodded. Personal conversation terminated. 'Was it murder?' she asked instead.

'It's unclear, but the autopsy tomorrow morning should answer that question.'

'Who was he?'

'Stephen Foster. Sixteen. Been in the Army for five months.'

They had reached the privates' accommodation blocks, six identical three-storey, rectangular brown-brick buildings reminiscent of a sixties council estate. Everything about them seemed functional, built on a budget to fulfil a practical purpose, nothing fancy or decorative.

Jessie followed Callan into the third block on the left-hand side of the tarmac path and into a rectangular room on the ground floor. Inside, the same institutional feel: each recruit sharing a room with the nine other members of his or her section. Ten narrow single beds, the beds covered with a sheet and a slate-grey blanket, each blanket tucked in with hospital corners. A faux-pine plywood wardrobe stood against the wall to the right of every bed, a matching plywood bedside table to the left. An identical, utilitarian, uniquely soulless space for each teenaged child. Surveying the room, Jessie thanked heaven for her officer status, for the opportunity to live off base in her own cottage. She tried and failed to picture Ryan Jones here with his gentle hazel eyes and his sullen attitude, could understand why he was having problems adjusting, could understand how the change from a teenage life on the outside to this would be a huge shock to anyone's system.

A spotty-faced Military Police private was standing at the end of the fourth bed along from the door. He snapped to attention when he saw Callan.

'At ease, Private Bryant,' Callan said. 'I'll take it from here.'

When Bryant had left, Callan pulled two pairs of latex gloves from his jacket pocket and handed a pair to Jessie. Snapping on the gloves, he moved over to the cupboard. Jessie stood at the end of Stephen Foster's bed, her eyes grazing over his small patch of Ministry of Defence turf.

'It's hardly a celebration of the individual, is it?' she murmured.

'What did you expect?' Callan said. 'The Savoy?'

'A tiny bit of identity perhaps.'

With a shrug, Callan opened the cupboard doors. Its interior was no more individual than its exterior: the left half given over to hanging space, the right half to six shelves. Both halves were almost entirely taken up with Army-issue clothing: olive green jumpers folded, laid one on top of the other, shirts and combat jackets hung, green mess uniform – number two's – hung. The bottom shelf held matching footwear, the top matching headgear. Only the second from bottom held anything from Foster's civilian life: two pairs of jeans, a pair of black trousers, three white T-shirts and two fleeces, all neatly folded, and a black-and-white patterned wash bag. Three of the six shelves were empty. Same with the hanging space – he had only used half of it.

Callan surveyed the fastidious interior. 'Christ, this lad would give you a run for your money.'

'What?' Jessie moved to stand next to him. 'Oh no, look here – these jumpers are half a millimetre out of line.' She reached over, adjusted the top jumper on the stack of three, stepped back, head tilted, one eye closed. 'That's better. All squared away. Everything in its place and a place for everything.'

She saw the ghost of a smile cross Callan's face, gone almost before she'd registered it.

'Where's all the kid's stuff?' he muttered.

'Soldiers don't have stuff. No stuff that isn't olive green, at any rate,' Jessie said, reaching past him for the soap bag, accidentally brushing his elbow with her arm as she did so. He flinched as if she'd branded him and stepped sideways, expanding the space between them. She glanced across, but he wasn't looking at her. He was staring hard at Foster's shelves, as if there was something inherently fascinating about them.

Turning away, settling herself on the edge of the bed, Jessie unzipped the soap bag. A well-worn toothbrush, paste and mouthwash, shampoo and conditioner both virtually empty, a cake of soap in a damp black soap box, a box of plasters, unopened, aspirin, also unopened, in the main zip pocket.

'Well, he was into oral hygiene, he liked to keep clean, skin and hair, and he wasn't a hypochondriac.'

'And he has no personal possessions, nothing from his civvy life, apart from a few clothes,' Callan said, closing the cupboard. 'How about the bedside table?'

Reaching over, Jessie pulled open the top drawer. Boxer shorts, each pair folded into a perfect square, layered one behind the other on one side of the drawer, socks, each pair balled into a fluffy cotton ball of identical circumference, laid one behind the other on the opposite side.

'What the fuck was up with this guy?' Callan muttered.

Jessie ignored him. She pushed closed the top drawer and opened the bottom. Empty, save for a bible, dark red, the kind placed by the Gideons in every hotel room in Britain. But unlike 99 per cent of the hotel room bibles, which languished unopened in drawers, this one was well used, the cover worn, its top corner bent from repeated openings. She could tell from the slight bulge in the maroon plastic that there was something inside.

'I feel like a grave robber,' she murmured, holding the bible, unopened, in her lap.

'It's a job, nothing more.'

'Yes, but don't you find it hard to stay detached? Rifling through a dead boy's things like this?'

Callan shrugged carelessly, but she caught the look in his eyes; however nonchalant his reaction, he felt it as much as she did.

'Open it,' he muttered.

Inside was a scrap of silky red material about the size of her palm, roughly cut into the shape of a heart, its edges frayed, the fabric itself worn so thin in places that the light showed through.

'What is it?' he asked.

She held it out to him. 'Love.'

'What?'

'A heart. Love.'

Another ghost of a smile. 'Perceptive.'

Jessie raised an eyebrow. 'I'm not a doctor for nothing, Captain.'

Their gazes met for a fraction of a second before Callan dipped his, holding his gloved hand out for the heart. He slid it into an evidence bag.

'The bed,' he said.

'Huh?'

'The bed. I need to search the bed.'

'Oh, right, yes.' Hopping up, Jessie stepped aside.

She watched while he pulled back the grey blanket and sheet, revealing a bed that looked as if it had never been slept in. Rearranging the covers, Callan lifted Foster's pillow, causing a draught of air that sent something fluttering to the ground at Jessie's feet. Bending, she picked up the rectangular piece of paper by its corner and turned it over.

It was a photograph. A photograph of a big-boned blonde girl, stunning azure-blue eyes fixed on the camera's lens. She looked happy and relaxed, or would have done, if the photograph hadn't been doctored with black marker pen, the addition of a crudely drawn penis disappearing into her smiling mouth. Next to the penis, someone had written: *Stevie Fs – good lad.*

Jessie held the photograph out to Callan. 'Lovely. Do you know her?'

'No.' He took it from her and slid it into an evidence bag. 'I think we're done here.'

Jessie nodded but didn't move. 'Dead at sixteen. It's such a waste.'

Callan didn't answer. Walking to the door, he pulled it open.

'Give me a minute,' Jessie said.

'I'll wait for you outside.'

When Callan had left, Jessie moved to stand at the end of Foster's bed. She knew OCD far too well, had lived with the disorder for more than half of her life. It was as much a part of who she was now as her blue eyes or her pale Irish skin. This boy wasn't ODC. There was something else that explained the tidiness and economy with which he had laid out his possessions, the lack of possessions, the impersonal nature of this, the only personal space he had in this new life he'd entered. Entered and left so quickly and so brutally. But what was that something? She didn't know.

Darkness was falling when she joined Callan outside, the sun a fiery orange ball scraping the tops of the trees beyond the accommodation blocks. A wind had picked up, rippling the grass, sending plumes of dust curling from the tarmac path. The air felt heavy with trapped water, another rain shower brewing. Callan was talking on his mobile. He started walking when he saw her, and she fell into step beside him.

He finished his call as they reached the car park and they stopped walking in unison, turned to face each other. His height put her at a disadvantage. She had to crane her neck to make eye contact, felt like a small child gazing up at an emotionally distant adult. Silence for a moment, a silence that quickly became awkward.

'Callan . . . Ben, I'm, uh, I'm sorry that I didn't email from the Gulf to see how you were.'

He held her gaze, his face expressionless. 'I didn't expect you to.'

101

'Yes, but I should have done.'

A nonchalant lift of his shoulders. 'I got your card.'

Jessie raised an eyebrow, trying to lighten the moment. She didn't understand why, what she had done to precipitate it, but the atmosphere between them had felt as light as lead boots from the moment they'd set eyes on each other. 'The puppy. Yes. It was either that, bandaged teddy bears or bunches of embossed pink and yellow flowers. The puppy felt like the lesser of many evils.'

No smile, no encouragement. 'It was thoughtful. Thank you.'

Silence again, as awkward as the first. Jessie surprised even herself with the next question. 'Do you want to go for a quick drink?'

A faint smile on Callan's lips, a smile that didn't warm his eyes. 'I've got a couple more interviews to conduct, so no thanks.'

'Oh, OK, no worries.' She dipped her gaze, feeling like an idiot. 'I'll stay and help you.'

He shook his head. 'Thanks, but I think I can manage on my own. I'll give you a call if there's anything else I need.'

Jessie nodded. She could remind him that Holden-Hough had requested her involvement and that she could reasonably refuse to leave, but that wasn't her style. She had no intention of forcing her presence on him when he didn't want her here. He could explain his decision to his boss, if he was pulled up on it – it wasn't her call.

'I'll email you a summary of my thoughts on our search of Stephen Foster's things.'

Without meeting her gaze, he gave a curt nod.

'Take care then, Callan.' Turning, she walked away.

19

Callan felt the weight of the day bearing down on him as he watched Jessie walk stiffly across the deserted car park to her Mini, her shoulders tensely set, her step dispirited. He knew that he had been a shit, but it had felt necessary. He didn't want her help on this case or her presence in his life.

As much as he wanted to, he couldn't tell her that he had thought of little else but her over the past three months, had read and re-read the few sterile words she'd written in that daft puppy card so many times he'd lost count, spent way too long obsessing over what she was doing while he was shuffling around St George's Hospital like a crippled old man, hours lying in bed staring up at the blank ceiling, trying to summon to his mind every detail of her face, the intoxicating mix of humour and challenge in those extraordinary ice-blue eyes.

His scar was throbbing. Raising a hand to his temple, he ran his fingers over the rough stitched skin, thinking of the bullet lodged somewhere beneath, the damage that bullet had done to his brain. The uncertainty he lived with every day that his condition would worsen, that the next fit might happen at work, exposing his lies and deception, or that it might disturb the lodged bullet and be his last.

His mind followed his gaze as he watched the tail-lights of Jessie's Mini disappear across the car park, followed them home to that tiny farmworker's cottage with its ridiculously fastidious interior. He pictured her curled defensively on that spotless cream sofa, the last time he had been there, when, if it hadn't been for Marilyn's damn phone call, he would have kissed her, gone further perhaps.

Shaking his head, he turned away, back to the interviews, back to reality. He couldn't allow himself to get close to Jessie Flynn, to any woman. It wouldn't be fair on them. His job, his health, his life were too uncertain, as was the control he had over his unpredictable temper – courtesy of the medication that controlled his fits – just – and his fucked-up brain.

He knew that he would get shit from Holden-Hough if he found out he'd sidelined her so early in the case, but his boss's wrath was the least of his problems.

20

Eight p.m., and Jessie was physically and emotionally exhausted when she finally unlocked the front door to her cottage. Realizing that she hadn't eaten anything since breakfast at six that morning, she had stopped off at a Tesco Metro on the way home, bought herself a limp-looking lasagne ready meal and a bottle of Sauvignon, cold, straight from the fridge. Tossing the lasagne into the oven, twisting the dial to 250 degrees centigrade, nuke temperature, she retrieved a wine glass from the cupboard, the one with *Happy Birthday, Princess* embossed on it in pink glitter that her father had given her for her eighteenth birthday. She was only using it, for the first time ever, because it was huge, bucket-sized. She poured in a third of the bottle.

No sooner had she settled on the sofa than she heard a knock on the door. Ahmose was standing on her doorstep, clutching daffodils.

'To replace the last bunch,' he said. 'They'll all be gone soon, now that spring is here.'

The morning she had first moved into her cottage, Ahmose

had arrived on her doorstep proffering a miniature rose and her heart had plummeted. She had bought the cottage in the middle of a row of three, down a single-track lane surrounded by fields, eschewing Army accommodation or a flat in Aldershot, precisely to avoid unwanted human contact. But in their three years as neighbours she had grown to love this old Egyptian man almost more than her own parents – certainly more than her father. Standing on tiptoes, she kissed him on the cheek, stood back while he hobbled through the door.

'Tea?'

'When you're having wine?' He winked. 'I don't think so.'

'I'm afraid that I'm fresh out of Princess glasses.'

He smiled. 'Any old glass will do, as long as there is wine in it.'

She poured him a glass while he lowered himself on to the sofa.

'So, tell me about this day from hell of yours,' he said.

'Is it that obvious?'

He inclined his head towards her glass.

She smiled and sighed. 'An abandoned baby, a possible suicide, a seriously troubled young man and a suspicious death.'

'All in a day's work for you.'

'Yes, normally, but today I found it all too gruelling.' She smothered a yawn with her sleeve. She could still feel a faint tingle from the electric suit, fading now in the comfort of her own home and the uncomplicated companionship of this old man she loved.

'You're tired.' He looked pointedly at her glass. 'Not too much alcohol, and an early night, and you will be . . . '

He paused. 'How do you say? Right as rain in the morning.'

It was a moment before she nodded, giving him a weary smile. 'You're right, Ahmose, as always.'

A sudden shrill ring – her home phone. Jessie didn't move. No one she wanted to speak with would be calling at 10 p.m. It was bound to be a telesales person from India trying to sell her PPI protection or asking if she'd recently had an accident for which she could claim to have whiplash. The answerphone clicked on. A pause, then a man's voice. Southern Irish. The accent ludicrously pronounced even after thirty years of living in England, as if he was calling direct from the middle of a County Kerry potato field. Her father.

'Answer it,' Ahmose said gently.

'No.'

'It's your father?'

'Yes.'

'So answer it.'

The message warbled on. Jessie remained seated. *Dinner? Was she free for dinner on Thursday evening? He was at a conference in Guildford all day.*

'It's not dat far, is it, where you live? From Guildford? I'd love to see ye, darlin'.'

'Yuck.' Jessie raised the Princess glass to her lips, almost choking herself, the slug of wine she took from it was so large.

A click and the voice was replaced by the intermittent flash of the answering machine message light, washing her spotless white ceiling strip-joint red.

'You made peace with your mother.'

Another slug, and she rolled her eyes. 'This is different. He dumped us. Walked out and left us, right when we

107

needed him most. And for what? For a . . . ' *Fuck*. She bit her tongue. Ahmose was from the old school and hated to hear women swear. Respecting his sensibilities was good for her, like forcing an alcoholic to have one sober night a week. *One sober night*. Perhaps she should give that a try too. 'I spent this morning with a woman who fears that her child is dead. That child is forty-five and she was still terrified. Still *cared*. My father dumped me when I was twelve, dumped Jamie when he was only five, sick, *dying*. He dumped all of us for that . . . ' *Bitch. Fucking bitch cow evil bitch monster woman*. The words shrivelled on her tongue. 'Woman. Diane. That nasty, *nasty* woman.'

Slamming her glass on to the coffee table so fiercely that dregs of the Sauvignon splashed the spotless wood, she stalked across the room and jammed her finger on the delete button. The wash of red vanished. Back on the sofa, she met Ahmose's thoughtful dark gaze. She knew exactly what was going through his mind, knew that he thought she was making a mistake. He had come to England forty years ago to make a better life for himself, had married Alice, an English girl, the love of his life, who had died of a stroke five years ago, four months after they had moved into their dream retirement cottage. His sister, nieces and nephews still lived in Cairo and she knew that he missed being near them and worried constantly for their safety with the violent disaster that the Arab Spring had become. Reaching across, he took her hand and she felt the calluses on his fingers, rough against her soft palm. He squeezed and she felt tears well in her eyes. Thank God that she had one solid, dependable, uncomplicated relationship in her life.

'Go to bed now, Jessie, and sleep. Don't worry about anything. Just sleep.'

He was right. She needed to sleep. Find some perspective, get her head in order for tomorrow. A tomorrow that would doubtless be another difficult day.

They both stood and Jessie wrapped her arms around his neck. 'I love you, Ahmose.'

'I love you too, Jessie. Very, very much.' He kissed her forehead. 'Now sleep.'

21

The girl who saluted Callan in the doorway was only a few inches shorter than his six foot four, shoulders almost as broad, white-blonde hair and the most startling azure eyes he had ever seen. *Teutonic* was the word that immediately sprang to mind. Big-boned, blonde, blue-eyed, she could have walked right out of a tourism poster he remembered seeing when he'd trained with the Army in Bavaria, a solid, ruddy-faced milkmaid on a flower-studded mountainside, two tin buckets hanging from a wooden yoke across her shoulders, wearing a dirndl dress, black skirt and bodice, red apron, white puffed-sleeved blouse, meaty arms placed coquettishly on her hips. *Martha Wonsag,* the sixteen-year-old girl who had shared guard duty in the woods with Stephen Foster early this morning. His mind moved from that wholesome poster to the pornographically doctored photograph he'd found under Foster's pillow. The same blonde girl, he'd realized as soon as she walked into the room, a different impression entirely. Which of those impressions would prove to be the real girl, if either? His job to find out.

He must have been staring in silence for longer than he realized, because she suddenly moved her hands to her hips, tilted her head and met his gaze from under dipped eyelashes in a way that was disturbingly flirtatious. *Christ, I need to get a grip.* Retreating behind the desk, he indicated the chair across from his.

'I'm Captain Callan, Special Investigation Branch, Royal Military Police,' he said, his tone deliberately curt. 'Take a seat, Wonsag.'

The legs of Martha Wonsag's khaki cotton trousers grated against each other at the thigh, as she strode across the room and seated herself in the chair.

'Do I need legal representation?'

Do you need legal representation? Perhaps he should come straight out and ask the question.

'At this stage in the investigation, I'm trying to understand what happened this morning and to clarify a timeline. As you were with Foster on guard duty, I need your help to do that. If you become a suspect at a later date, you will be advised to appoint a solicitor to represent you. We can arrange that for you.' He waited while she digested what he had said. When she gave a nod of understanding, he continued: 'So, you were on guard duty with Foster, but you weren't with him when he died?'

'No.'

'Where were you?'

'I was . . . ummm . . . otherwise engaged.'

'Otherwise engaged?'

A nod.

'Otherwise engaged where?'

Eyes flicking up to meet his for a brief moment, she muttered something under her breath that he didn't catch.

111

'Again, please.'

'The facilities,' she murmured. 'I had to, uh, use the facilities.' Her cheeks had flushed red, he noticed. 'The toilet.'

Callan nodded. Courtesy of Corporal Jace Harris, he already knew where she had been – or where she had said she'd been – when Foster died, but he wanted to hear it from her, wanted the gap in timing filled. 'How long were you gone for?'

'Not long.'

He sat forward, steepling his fingers, trying to catch her eye and failing. 'Long enough for Stephen Foster to wind up dead.'

A shrug. 'Twenty minutes, maybe a little more.' Her voice was reed thin; again, entirely at odds with her appearance.

Callan pictured Jace Harris, clicking his tongue sarcastically. *Mine? Ten seconds. But I can piss up against a tree, can't I. Hers? You'll need to ask her that question, sir.* If he was doing his job properly, he would press the girl for more details, but he knew that he wouldn't, not tonight. All he wanted to do right now was to tick the minimum number of boxes that needed ticking from this interview and get out of here. Get home, get changed and go for a moonlit run along the river, clear his body of this morning's epileptic fit, all this sitting and talking, his mind of this death, Jace Harris, the chaplain, Gold and Colonel Wallace, and most of all, Jessie Flynn, the way she made him feel.

'How was Foster when you left him?'

'OK.'

'Did you notice anything strange about him?'

A barely there shake of her head.

112

'About his behaviour? Did he seem tense or nervous?'

'Not really.'

'Did he seem to be worried about anything?'

'No.'

'Are you sure that there was absolutely nothing about his manner, his behaviour, something he said that led you to believe that he was worried or concerned about anything?'

A brief upwards flick of her eyes, another barely there shake of her head.

'Did you see anyone else while you were on guard duty?'

'No.'

'Did you see anyone when you went on your toilet break? Anyone hanging around?'

'No.'

Callan sighed. He couldn't get a clear handle on this girl and the monosyllabic answers were beginning to piss him off. Her looks, her stance, the first impression he'd gained when she'd strode into the room told him that she wasn't the feminine, submissive type, but her behaviour, the failure to make any kind of eye contact, the read thin voice, told him a different story. Was there something about him? Something he was doing that was putting her on edge, driving her to behave abnormally? Though she hadn't met his gaze directly for more than a couple of seconds since the interview had started, he had sensed her casting long looks at him each time he dipped his gaze to her personnel file, each time she considered herself to be unobserved. He regretted not having taken Jessie Flynn up on her offer to help him with the interviews – however she made him feel. Served him right for his intransigence.

'How well did you know Foster?'

She hunched her shoulders. 'Not well.'

'How well is not well?'

'We were on guard duty together a couple of times, that was all.'

Retrieving the photograph he'd found under Foster's pillow from his suit jacket pocket, he slid it over the table, sat back and crossed his arms. 'Is that you?'

Her gaze dipped to the photograph and her eyes widened.

'Is this you?' Callan repeated.

The thin voice again. 'Yes.'

'So, I'll repeat that last question. How well did you know Foster? Because I assume that the alterations to this photograph were motivated by something other than a couple of shared guard duties?'

Her cheeks were flushed, he noticed, redder even than when he was asking her about her trip to the *facilities*.

'I slept with him, OK,' she muttered.

'When?'

'After a party.'

'When was the party?'

'About six weeks ago.'

'Who was there?'

'Most of the trainees.'

'So what happened?' *As if I need to ask.*

'We all got drunk. And . . . ' she tailed off with a shrug.

'And one thing led to another,' Callan finished for her.

Foster had been five foot eight, slightly built. The physics of a union between him and Wonsag was something Callan didn't even want to contemplate. That thought must have telegraphed itself straight to his face, because she met his gaze properly for the first time since she'd entered the room, the light in her eyes aggressive.

'It's not illegal, is it?' Aggression driven by embarrassment

114

and defensiveness, he realized. 'Having sex on an Army base?'

Reaching for the photograph, Callan slipped it back into his pocket. 'No, it's not illegal.'

He didn't give a shit what Martha Wonsag got up to in her free time. She could fuck every man at Blackdown for all he cared.

'Was that it?' he said.

'Apart from the fact that he told everyone. All the lads.'

'Hence the photograph.'

She nodded. Though her eyes were still narrowed aggressively, her square jaw clenched, underneath the posturing she looked as if she was about to cry. He felt sorry for her, recognized the pressure that new recruits felt to fit in, to be liked, to be one of the lads, even if they were female. Recognized how one drunken mistake could blow that right out of the water, make you a pariah, a target. How the lads loved a target. Hard at the age of sixteen to make sensible judgements.

'Was he popular?' Callan asked gently.

'No, he didn't seem to be. He was quiet, kept himself to himself.'

A male soldier exploiting a sexual conquest to gain popularity. It wouldn't be the first time and it certainly wouldn't be the last. And even in 2017, it was still the woman who was made to pay, particularly in such a male-dominated environment. Real sexual equality still a myth, a pipe dream.

'They made me pay,' she murmured, echoing his thoughts. *The lads.* Her gaze dropped to the photograph on the desktop. 'They still are.'

'They'll probably stop now,' Callan said, pushing himself to his feet. *Now that Foster is dead.* 'I will need to interview you again, but for the moment you are free to go. Do not speak to anyone about our discussion or about Stephen Foster.'

She nodded and stood unmoving, her gaze fixed firmly on the floor.

'It's, uh, it's a long game, this career of yours, Wonsag,' Callan muttered. 'Just—' He broke off. Who the hell was he to dispense career advice? 'Just . . . play it sensibly from now on, hey?'

Without raising her gaze from the floor, she nodded. As Callan watched her walk out of the interview room, he found himself wondering if he was the only person on this base not getting laid.

22

The high street was morning rush-hour bumper to bumper, the road a fog of exhaust fumes, pavements empty of walkers – too early for shops, with the exception of coffee bars, to be open. Only a lone woman pushing a pram a couple of hundred metres ahead. Jessie had detoured on her way to work, having discovered this morning that she'd both run out of coffee and was redlining petrol. She'd regretted her decision as soon as she'd jammed herself into the inching throng of cars, too late now to do a U-turn, limp into work on fumes and settle for instant Nescafé.

Her gaze found the woman and child again, nothing else to look at. She watched as the woman flicked on the pram's brake, taking a moment to speak to the child inside before moving to the edge of the pavement. Rummaging in her handbag, she pulled out an A4 sheet of paper and taped it to a lamp post at eye height. Unlatching the pram's brake, leaning heavily on its handle bar, she trudged to the next lamp post, her laboured steps reminding Jessie of a deep sea diver navigating the seabed. *Elderly lady, lost cat.* But as she inched closer, she realized the old woman was familiar: her grey wool tweed skirt too heavy for the spring sunshine, the solid brown lace-ups, polished to a shine, but worn, the leather upper of the right shoe cleaving away from its sole.

Joan Lawson and baby Harry.

Braking, ignoring the infuriated hoots from the man in the car behind, stressed before he'd even started his workday, she flicked on her hazards and nosed into a parking space by the kerb. Grabbing her handbag, she opened the door, then immediately pulled it closed again. She could jump out, chase them down the street, but what the hell was she going to say to Joan when she caught up with them?

Malcolm is still missing, but let me buy you a coffee and we can talk.

Talk about what?

Platitudes.

Everything that she had to say, empty, pointless, not enough.

For the second time in twenty-four hours, Jessie inched her Mini back into the flow of traffic, leaving Joan and Harry receding in her rear-view mirror, feeling impotent and frustrated, thanking God for small mercies that it wasn't raining.

23

'Parked neatly. Locked. Key nowhere in sight.' Bending at the waist, Marilyn peered through the driver's window, taking care not to touch the glass. 'No sign of a disturbance or violence inside the car.'

The seats were beige, showing signs of wear commensurate with their age, but nothing else, no stains, no blood. A maroon paper Costa Coffee cup nestled in the holder between the driver and passenger seats, a few coins – change for parking? – in the other cup holder; the baby seat, Harry's seat, still in place in the back. Straightening, he met DS Workman's gaze over the roof of the ancient Corolla.

'No visible damage. No blood.'

Nothing at all, in fact, to suggest foul play. Everything to suggest that it had been driven down this isolated lane by its owner, parked in the muddy lay-by, locked up and left. Stepping into the middle of the lane, Marilyn looked left and right. He and Workman had been standing here for fifteen minutes already and not one car had passed. Not one bicycle. Not even a dog walker. The lane was single-track, running north to south, linking two other quiet country lanes, Littleworth Road and Suffield Lane. This one, so small that it didn't merit a name – not on the map that Marilyn was holding, or on his satnav. To reach the lay-by, they had driven past fields on both sides for a kilometre and then woods thick and dark for another five hundred metres. The car had been found and called in by a patrol car, only because the driver had taken a detour to have an undisturbed comfort break. *Lucky.* The first piece of luck he'd had and hopefully a sign of better things to come.

'Fantastic place to commit suicide,' Marilyn muttered.

Workman nodded grimly. 'Shall I organize a search, sir?'

Marilyn didn't answer. He was gazing into the trees. There was only one track that cut off from the lay-by, apparently little used, as the path that the wooden *Public Footpath* arrow indicated was overgrown grass and weeds. There was a twin footpath sign on the other side of the lane, indicating a similarly grassed-over track leading in the opposite direction.

'Fifteen minutes, Workman. You go west, I'll go east. Stick to the track, but obviously look for him.' *Up. Look up. He might be hanging.* He knew that he didn't need to verbalize his thoughts – she was a pro. 'Look for any signs of disturbance to the bracken, footprints, you know the drill. It was raining heavily the night before last, it stopped at about 4 a.m. If someone came through here that night, the ground would have been soft and we will hopefully see their prints, though the grass on the track may obscure them.'

Workman glanced down at Marilyn's black suede Chelsea boots.

'Don't say anything,' he muttered. 'I'm trying not to think about them.'

Marilyn hefted himself over the wooden stile, wincing as he lowered his foot, fully expecting a squelch as the leather soles of his boots made contact with the ground, pleasantly surprised and relieved when there was none.

Even though it was only 10 a.m., the sun was shining from a cloudless sky. Marilyn could feel sweat pooling in the small of his back as he hiked across the field, the gradient rising steeply as he approached the treeline. He hadn't noticed any footprints, but that didn't mean much. The track was overgrown, and because of the gradient, the ground was far dryer than he had expected. The soil was sandy, he noticed, from the glimpses of bare earth around the entrance to the couple of rabbit burrows he had passed. Sandy and well drained.

As he left the field, the trees closed around him, dappled light and shade, the smell of fresh pine and damp mulch. It was beautiful up here, a montage of greens, cool and utterly silent. He was surprised to realize that if he were here for a less depressing purpose, he would be enjoying every minute, despite the foreign sensation of fresh air filling his smoker's lungs.

Fifteen minutes later, he retraced his steps and joined Workman by the car.

'Anything?'

'Nothing, sir. But the ground wasn't as soft as I'd expected. Someone could easily have walked along that track and left no footprints.'

Marilyn nodded. 'My side too.' He paused, looking back up the path he'd descended, to the woods beyond. *What had Malcolm Lawson been thinking?* Marilyn had understood his pain at his son Danny's suicide but, despite that, he had still struggled to understand how the man's mind worked. The refusal to accept that his son could have taken his own life, the dogged determination with which he had pursued a murder charge . . .

'Organize a search, Workman. Nothing too dramatic – a couple of PCs with time on their hands. I don't want to take too many resources off the Guildford rape. And call Forensics. Let's get this car back to the garage and they can sweep it for fingerprints on the off-chance that something is amiss. I want to tick all the boxes on this one, purely because it's Malcolm Lawson, but I'd bet a sizeable sum that he's in those woods somewhere.'

'Shall I call Joan Lawson and give her an update?'

'Christ, no,' Marilyn said. 'Let's stall until we have something concrete.'

Workman nodded. She looked tired and depressed. As the first point of contact between the force and Joan Lawson, she was right at the emotional coalface. She was also enabling him to stay one step removed from the next of kin, which he appreciated. He enjoyed the mental challenge of solving difficult cases, but the customer service angle of policing really wasn't his bag. He knew that he should show his appreciation of Workman's efforts more often, but again, that whole soft management business wasn't his bag either. He laid a hand on her shoulder; she virtually jumped out of her skin, so surprised was she at the unaccustomed contact.

'You get back to the office, Sarah, grab yourself a cup of tea. I'll stay here and wait for the tow-truck.'

24

It took Jessie half an hour, map spread out on the passenger seat, to find the lane that Marilyn had described. As she pulled in behind an aged Toyota Corolla and the police tow-truck that was reversing up to it, Marilyn appeared at her driver's window.

'What took you so long?' He noticed the map. 'Oh, for Christ's sake, you techno dinosaur. I'll buy you a satnav for your birthday.'

'I'm quite happy with my Ordnance Survey map, thank you.'

'Dinosaurs are extinct for a reason.'

Jessie smiled sweetly up at him as she climbed out. 'Why would I let some weird disembodied voice be in control of where I'm going? I'd far rather be in control myself, even if that means getting lost.'

'I don't want to think what that says about your personality.'

'Nothing good, believe me.'

He smelt of smoke and Jessie noticed a few cigarette butts ground into the muddy bank behind him.

'Is that Malcolm's car?' she asked.

'Yes.'

'And?'

'And – nothing. It was neatly parked, as you can see, locked, and there was no sign of a disturbance inside.'

The grind of a winch and the Corolla inched forward.

'How far have you searched?' Jessie asked.

Marilyn answered with a question of his own.

'How far would someone walk to commit suicide?'

Jessie shrugged, playing the same game. 'How long is a piece of string?'

'Can't you be more—'

'Specific than that?' she cut in. Her gaze moved from his to the treeline.

'I suppose it depends on how certain he was, how committed. If he was still having an internal debate, then it makes sense to assume that he would have walked further.'

'How much debate is left, if you've already abandoned your baby at the hospital and driven all the way out here?'

She continued to survey the treeline, avoiding his gaze, knowing exactly how someone would commit suicide in a wood, pushing back an image of her little brother Jamie hanging from the curtain rail by his red-and-grey striped school tie. 'I don't know the answer to that question, Marilyn, but what I'm sure of is that it's never going to be easy, is it? Taking your own life. Particularly with his family history – Danny – and Harry, who he obviously adores.'

'But can I now assume that he's dead? Somewhere out there in the trees.'

Jessie didn't answer. Her gaze was still caught by the treeline, her thoughts trapped in a bedroom fifteen years ago.

'You said at the hospital that I couldn't assume that he's already dead,' Marilyn said gently. 'Can I now?'

'Can you get the dogs out? Dogs can find people quickly, can't they?'

'There was a nasty stranger rape in Guildford last night. The rapist got away. The dogs are there.'

Jessie nodded. It was a beautiful spot, English countryside at its best, sunlight dappling through the trees to create a gently shifting pattern of light and shade. Only birdsong and the grinding whirr of the tow-truck's winch to disturb the peace.

'I saw Joan Lawson and Harry this morning in Aldershot. She was taping "Missing" posters to lamp posts. She looked so forlorn. What will happen to them? To Harry?'

'It's not your job to worry about what will happen to either of them.'

'None of this was my job,' she said bitterly. 'But I'm in it now and I can't block them from my mind.'

She sensed him shuffle his feet awkwardly.

'People break, Jessie. Even I know that and I'm a rank amateur at all this stuff.'

'I feel like a rank amateur too, most of the time.'

'Maybe he just broke.' A heavy sigh. 'His wife broke. She's in a psychiatric hospital near Maidenhead. He lasted for a year, with all that pressure. The pressure of fighting a lost cause, the pressure of living with the death of his oldest son, of having his beliefs dashed, of the baby, for Christ's sake, however cute he is.'

Jessie felt the light touch of his hand on her arm, looked back and met his gaze.

'I've . . . we've got an appointment to see her tomorrow morning,' he said.

'What? Who? Malcolm's wife?'

'Anne – yes.'

'No.'

'I need you there, Jessie.'

'No way.'

'Please.'

She shook her head. 'I really can't do it.'

'Why?'

'Because the last time I checked my CV I was working for the Defence Psychology Service and none of these people are in the military.'

'Look, Jessie, I'm not so stupid that I don't realize the last thing you want to do after yesterday, the hospital, Granny Lawson, is to come and talk to Anne with me, but I don't have the required skills and you do.'

Jessie remained mulishly silent.

'What is it? What's the matter?'

She threw up her hands. 'I told you. It's not my job.'

'There's something else, isn't there?'

'No, really, there's nothing else.' She fought to keep her voice even, feeling the tension rise, the electric suit hiss against her skin. Marilyn was looking hard at her, his brow furrowed; she felt as if those odd mismatched eyes of his could laser right through her denials, see the truth buried deep beneath them.

Callan may have told Marilyn that her brother committed suicide when he was seven, but he hadn't told him more, because he didn't know more. She'd never told him the rest. She had a very good reason for not wanting to go and see Malcolm's wife, and it had nothing to do with her job description.

25

Major Val Monks, Army pathologist, gazed down at the naked body of the young man on the dissecting table in front of her. Though she had performed autopsies on hundreds of corpses – thousands probably, given how long she'd been in this job – each time she was faced with a fresh corpse, a new death, she still felt that tugging reluctance to make a start, make the first cut. The incision that would suck the last trace of 'human' from the victim, turn them into a side of meat, purely evidence. Some of the autopsies she had performed stuck in her mind, most didn't, but each victim represented a private horror story, a life, a future, snuffed out before it should have been. Usually, once her scalpel had bitten into flesh, the clinical scientist within her took over and she became methodical, objective, dispassionate, everything that she needed to be to get her job done without it taking too much of an emotional toll. But now, as she slid on her latex gloves, reached for her scalpel and moved to hover over Stephen Foster's gentle face, she noticed that the hairs on her forearms were standing on end. Glancing up, she met Callan's watchful amber gaze, realized that he felt similarly on edge, could feel the tension pulsing from him like a living thing.

'If you stand any further away, you'll be in the corridor, Callan.' Her voice rose and cracked at the end of the sentence.

Callan cleared his throat. 'Just giving you space to perform your art, Val.'

'Always the gentleman.'

He forced a smile, though his heart wasn't in it. He took a step forward, his gaze still grazing around the featureless white-tiled walls, anywhere but at the boy's body.

'How are you, Callan?'

'I'm fine,' he murmured.

He hadn't seen Val Monks since the Scott case last November, when he'd had to bolt outside this same autopsy suite to succumb to an epileptic fit in the corridor. She was the only one of his colleagues who knew what lasting damage the Taliban bullet had done to his brain; but however much he liked, rated and trusted her to keep his secret, tea and sympathy made him feel distinctly uncomfortable.

'You don't look well, Callan.'

'Really, I'm fine.'

'It's not a problem if you need to step out at any point—'

'Jesus Christ,' he snapped. 'I'll let you do your job and you let me do mine.'

Silence. Callan dipped his head.

'Sorry. Sorry, Val. That was out of order.'

She held up latex-gloved hands. 'No, my fault. The mother in me, worming its way out at the most inappropriate times. It won't happen again.'

Their gazes met for a fraction of a second and Callan gave a grateful nod. Val switched on her digital recorder. 'Private Stephen Foster. Male. Aged sixteen . . . '

As she talked, Callan's gaze drifted down to the dissecting table. Though this boy was more intact than most of the dead soldiers he had seen, he was also younger than most, and the sight, the knowledge that death had come before life had truly begun hit Callan hard in the gut. He thought of the roughly cut red heart that Foster had hidden in his bible. Who had given it to him and why? Who loved him? Who would miss him? Would anyone?

Monks leaned over the dissecting table, her fingers finding the soft hollow above Foster's left collarbone. Callan noticed her bicep tense as she forced the tip of the blade through the layers of skin, subcutaneous fat and muscle. He looked at his feet, hummed a tune in his head to mute the sound of slicing, of skin being separated from the muscle layer beneath. However much he wanted to, there was no way that he was going to leave this autopsy now, not after having bitten Val's head off. He was in for the long haul.

'The screwdriver nicked the left jugular vein and pierced the trachea, but didn't damage any major arteries, which is odd,' he heard Val say.

'Why is it odd?'

'Because the throat is basically a channel that takes blood to and from the body's most important organ, the brain. In simple terms, two carotid arteries take blood up and four jugular veins bring it back. They run down the throat, either side of the trachea.' Raising her hands to her own neck, bloodied fingers hovering over her skin, she traced her index fingers down her throat. 'The throat tract divides

129

into two: the trachea, commonly known as the windpipe, which takes air to the lungs, and the oesophagus, which takes food from the mouth to the stomach. The trachea is here' – she moved her bloodied fingers to hover over the centre of her throat – 'right in the middle at the front, protected by the cricoid cartilage, the hard bumpy bit, if you run your finger down the centre of your throat.'

Callan nodded, left his hands in his pockets. He wasn't in the mood for audience participation.

'Then either side – just to the side – are the arteries and veins. One artery runs about here . . . ' Her fingers shifted outwards, half a centimetre. 'The other here. Same with the veins. I would have expected the left carotid artery to be sliced – nicked, at least.'

'And then he would have bled to death very quickly?'

'Right. With a lot of fanfare.'

Callan raised a questioning eyebrow.

'Spray. Lots of it.' Her hands flew from her throat, outwards. 'Bright red arterial spray, like in the movies.'

'There was none of that. The only blood that Morgan found was on the victim, some pooled on the ground around him. But a pool, not a spray pattern.' Callan shuffled his feet. The smell of opened cavities, of intestinal gasses and viscera was getting to him. 'So how did he die, Val? Blood loss?'

She shook her head. 'Blood loss would have killed him eventually, but slowly, really quite slowly, considering the limited nature of the wound. Slowly, as in a few minutes, of course, not hours. My money is on the fact that he drowned. There is pink-coloured aspirate at the top of his windpipe. I'll need to dissect his lungs to confirm, but I'm pretty certain that drowning will be the cause of death.'

Drowning? He hadn't expected that. 'There wasn't any water. It was raining, but—' He broke off. *Pink-coloured aspirate.* 'In his own blood? He drowned in his own blood?'

Val nodded. 'Blood from the punctured jugular vein would have poured out of the wound – the blood that you saw on his clothing – but blood would also have flowed down his trachea. Inhalation of fluid causes obstruction to the airways, so the victim can't breathe. Circulatory and respiratory failure would occur simultaneously, due to anoxia of both the myocardium and respiratory centre.'

'How long would it have taken for him to die?'

A shadow crossed Val's face. 'I'd estimate around three to five minutes.'

Jesus. A long time. A long time to bleed and cough, knowing – *knowing* – that you were dying.

'He wouldn't have been able to scream,' Val murmured. 'His airway was cut, was filling with blood, so the only sound that he would have been able to emit would have been a gurgle. He definitely wouldn't have been able to shout or scream, to speak even.'

They exchanged tense glances.

'No one heard anything,' Callan muttered. 'And he had a radio.'

Reaching for her scalpel, Monks drew another line down the centre of Foster's trachea. Laying the scalpel back on the stainless steel implement tray, she gently inserted her fingers into the new incision, inching back the skin and layers of subcutaneous fat below to expose the cream ridges of cartilage and the trachea wall, slippery and red.

'The stab wound looks . . . ' she paused, brow wrinkling, searching for the word ' . . . tentative.'

'Tentative?'

A preoccupied nod. 'The screwdriver was thin and flat-bladed, very sharp. But another reason that the cut missed the major arteries is because it was only stabbed in once, purposefully, but not with excessive force. There was enough pressure to force it between the trachea's c-rings of protective cartilage, but just enough. Then out again . . . ' she paused, eyes rising to the ceiling, as if searching for the right words ' . . . carefully. God, surgically even, without causing any more damage – which is unusual.'

'No anger, Val? Is that what you're saying?'

She straightened, rolling her shoulders, tilting back to stretch out the base of her spine. 'I'm not a psychologist, Callan. I can't speak to feelings.'

'In your medical opinion? As an expert pathologist.'

She raised an eyebrow. 'Flattery will get you everywhere, Captain, but you know that already. As I said, there was as little force as necessary to get the job done. So yes, I'd say there wasn't much anger. Certainly not a mad, passionate fury. If there was anger, it was cold, methodical, calculated.'

'Could a woman have done it?'

'Strength-wise? Absolutely.'

An image of Martha Wonsag filled his mind, her meaty hands placed coquettishly on her hips, and he shuddered inwardly.

'There's something else . . . ' Val Monks clasped her gloved hands together, steepling her fingers.

'What?'

'He was standing.'

Callan frowned. 'Standing?'

'Yes. He was upright. His body was upright while he was bleeding and drowning.'

'But he was found slumped against the tree. Sitting, tilted sideways, to the left.'

'No. From the pattern of bloodstains on his clothing, his combat jacket and trousers, I'm sure that his body was vertical while he was bleeding. Not sitting, definitely not sitting. And look here—' Reaching for one of Foster's hands, Monks levered his arm sideways to expose his armpit. Callan saw before she indicated.

'A bruise,' he muttered.

'Yes, right at the front edge of his armpit. The same under the other arm and one solid bruise across his chest.' She pointed and Callan saw. 'Here. I'd say that these bruises were from an arm, a forearm.' She held her forearm horizontally. 'Someone wedging a forearm against his chest, from armpit to armpit.'

Callan tried to bring an image to mind: Foster, a forearm jammed across his chest, pinned against that tree as he bled and fought for breath. He was small for a man, only five foot eight, and relatively light. Propping him up against that tree wouldn't have taken a bodybuilder's strength.

'If he was upright, he was most probably held against the tree that we found him under,' Callan said. 'There was no indication that he had been moved.'

'Right. I also found lichen and bark on the back of his combat jacket, plus some on his trousers, on his buttocks. In my opinion, someone held him up while he bled to death.'

The image made Callan deeply uneasy.

'Why? Why would someone do that? To make him bleed more quickly?'

'No. Upright, he would have bled more slowly. Gravity was working against him. His heart, which would have

133

been failing, would have had to work harder to pump the blood around his body, to pump it up and out of the throat wound.'

'So why would the killer do that? Take the risk of staying with him? He or she could have been disturbed at any time.' He met Val's gaze, expecting reassurance, an easy answer, but it wasn't there. Instead, she spread her hands and shook her head.

'As I've already said, Callan, I'm not a psychologist, but on this case I reckon you could use one.' Her eyes hung closed for a moment. 'It was a silent, drawn-out, traumatic death. Not nice, really not nice at all.'

As Callan walked back down the corridor, Val's words came back to him.

I'm not a psychologist, but on this case I reckon you could use one.

She was probably right, but there was no way that he was calling Jessie Flynn. He'd solve this one alone. He needed to. His pride, his self-respect – what precious little he had left – needed him to.

26

Back in her office, Jessie spent the afternoon in back-to-back sessions, chipping away at the backlog of cases that had stacked up with the Defence Psychology Service, the majority involving young men suffering from post-traumatic stress disorder as a result of combat. These were bread-and-butter cases, nothing to be complacent about, but something that the psychologists were well used to dealing with. Soldiers with PTSD were let down by the lack of available resources rather than the quality of those resources once they were lucky enough to receive treatment.

The last session affected her the most. A forty-five-year-old lieutenant colonel who had been in the Army for twenty-nine years, done multiple tours in Middle Eastern war zones, but, because of subsequent defence budget cuts and forced redundancies among his men, had begun to question the huge segment of his life that the Army had occupied. He had joined the Army at sixteen, straight from an orphanage, looking for a surrogate family and finding it. Increasingly, though, he felt as if the military ideal had been betrayed by politicians seeking political notoriety and lately, cost savings.

There was something about him that resonated with Jessie, the economy of his movements, the way that, even though he carried a coat, a briefcase, and another bag, when he settled himself into the bucket chair in Jessie's office, and put his possessions next to him, it was as if he occupied half the space that someone a similar size would occupy. He glanced appreciatively around her office.

'You like tidy.'

Jessie nodded, didn't elaborate. She never lifted the lid on her own demons in sessions with patients, knew that they expected her, mentally, to be whiter than white.

'In the children's home that I grew up in, I slept in a double-sized bedroom with six other boys. We each had a bed and a small chest of drawers. That was it. I learned to be incredibly tidy, to take up so little space.' He smiled, a distant smile that didn't reach his eyes. 'It's a habit I've been unable to train myself out of, even after thirty years.'

'The Army is not the best place to practise breaking habits of tidiness,' Jessie said gently.

Another sad smile. 'No. Perhaps you're right.'

Back at her desk after the session had finished, about to type up the notes, she stopped. *I learned to be incredibly tidy, to take up so little space.* Saving and closing the word document that she had barely started, she clicked on the Safari icon and Google appeared on the screen. Moving the mouse to click in the search bar, she typed: orphan.

The first in the list of returned searches was a *Time* article on how Sierra Leone's Ebola epidemic had left the country with an orphan crisis; the second, the obligatory Wikipedia entry: An orphan (from the Greek ὀρφανός Orfanos) is a child whose parents are dead or have abandoned them permanently. She scrolled down, scanning entries for orphaned orangutans in Borneo, elephants in Tanzania, various YouTube videos, not entirely sure what she was looking for, but with a strong sense that she would know when she found it. At the top of the second page was a title: 'Threads of Feeling – The Foundling Museum'. Clicking, she read.

On a winter's day in 1912 a shabby woman called Laura Wood made her way to the London Foundling Hospital. Under her arm was tucked her baby boy, Thomas. She was certain that surrendering him to their care would be a temporary arrangement. One day, she wasn't sure when or how, she was determined to return and claim her darling boy. Thousands of poor women, similarly at the end of their tethers, deposited their newborn babies at the hospital. A sign instructed them to leave some kind of identifying token pinned to the child, for example a scrap of coloured material, in the event they were one day in a position to take their baby home. The vast majority of mothers failed to heed the instruction to leave an identifying token, too beaten down by rotten lives to imagine a time when they would be able to provide a warm, clean home for their child.

Jessie sat back and rubbed her hands over her face. A story about a woman a hundred years ago, stirring her thoughts in the present. Perhaps the red heart in Stephen Foster's bible was a token from a friend or girlfriend, but Jessie had believed that the scrap of material, its edges frayed, the fabric worn almost transparent from touching, meant much more. She'd also known that Foster's obsessive tidiness had a root cause different to her own OCD. *I learned to be incredibly tidy, to take up so little space.* Could the red heart be a foundling token? Stephen Foster, abandoned as a baby by a mother who'd had no choice, but hoped one day to come back and claim her son. A hope that would never now be realized.

Reaching for her mobile, she flicked through the contacts until she found Callan's number. She felt her heart rate quicken, adrenalin pulsing, flight or fight for the second time today, as her thumb touched his name on the screen and the ringtone buzzed in her ear.

Relief surged through her when his voicemail clicked on. Far easier to talk to a machine after yesterday evening's humiliation in the car park at Blackdown, than to encounter him, even if separated by two mobile handsets and miles of ether.

'Captain Callan. It's Doctor Jessie Flynn . . . '

27

Tucking his mobile back into his pocket, Callan walked into the incident room. He'd listened to the message from Jessie and spent fifteen minutes making a few more calls, confirming her theory. So Stephen Foster had been an orphan. He had joined the Army on his sixteenth birthday, walked out of the children's home that he had grown up in, that had been his home virtually since birth, and straight into the Royal Logistic Corps. Five months later, he was dead. Why? And did his background have any relevance to his death? In many murder cases, Callan knew that the answer was yes, but in this case, how could it?

'Right. Listen up.' He thumped his fist on the wall next to the huge whiteboard on which were displayed photographs of the crime scene. The largest photo was a full-length shot of Foster's broken body slumped beneath the tree, speckled with a languorous mosaic of light and shade from the leaf canopy above him; it gave the impression he was snoozing in the shade on a sunny day, the whole effect a mind-screwing dichotomy between what the eye saw and what the brain knew. 'The autopsy showed that Stephen Foster drowned in his own blood. Val Monks estimated that it took him between three and five minutes to die, and all that time he must have been conscious and desperate. The autopsy also revealed that whoever killed Foster – and let me be very clear, this person could be either male or female' – a murmur rippled around the room – 'stayed with him, held him up against the tree underneath which he was found, while he was dying.'

His eyes roved across the assembled faces, noting the unease his words had etched across many of them.

'Held him up, sir?' Sergeant Kiddie asked, his brow furrowing. 'Why would he have done that?'

'He or *she*. And the answer to your question is that I don't know, but it's something that we need to find out as a priority. It's unusual behaviour. He or she could have been disturbed at any time, so the motivation to stay must have been strong. So far, we have a murder with no witnesses and virtually no forensic evidence. Lieutenant Gold and I have interviewed Stephen Foster's guard detachment and none of them admit to having heard or seen anything, or to know anything about his death. Morgan and his SOCO team are still analysing the crime scene, but so far they have turned up nothing useful. So we're going to have to dig deep on this one.' He paused to let his words sink in. 'We need to focus on researching the backgrounds of our short list of key suspects. And I mean researching, not having a quick flick through their Army personnel files.' He looked across at Gold, who was sitting cross-legged on a chair by the window, gazing down at his mobile phone.

'Gold.'

No response.

'*Gold.*'

Gold looked up. 'Yes, sir.'

'I want you to take the lead on researching our suspects' backgrounds. Our priorities are . . . ' Callan held up his right hand, raising a finger as he said each name in turn. 'Corporal Jace Harris. He was in charge of the guard that night, but there are parts of his statement that don't add up. He was alone for twenty minutes or more around the time that Foster was stabbed, so he definitely had opportunity. Whether he had motive is something that we need to establish. He also has the nickname Marley, which I found out is derived from the word animal. The nickname is fitting.'

Quiet laughter rippled around the room. He let them have their moment. Opportunities for humour were thin on the ground in cases like this and helped release tension.

'He also had a couple of choice tattoos. I won't bore you with the details. Our second suspect is Martha Wonsag. She and Foster were assigned to patrol the boundary fence west of the main gate, an area that included the wood where Foster's body was found. The pair had had drunken sex after a party, details of which Foster then shared with his mates. Suffice to say, Wonsag has suffered off the back of his generosity. She says that she took a toilet break, came back and found Foster dead, but again, that doesn't quite add up.' He glanced down at the scribbled notes he'd made. 'The other soldiers on guard duty were in pairs, were interviewed separately and their stories concurred to the minutest detail, so they can be put on the back burner, for the time being at least. The final name I'd like you to focus on for now is Michael O'Shaughnessy.'

A moment of silence.

'Hang on a second, sir.'

All heads turned to Gold.

'Yes, Lieutenant.'

'Did you say Michael O'Shaughnessy?'

'I did.'

'Isn't he the chaplain at Blackdown?'

'He is.'

'Can't we assume that he had nothing to do with this?'

Callan frowned. 'We can't assume that of anyone.'

'But he's . . . he's a man of God.'

'The Yorkshire Ripper was keen on God.'

The muscles in Gold's jaw bulged. 'That was unnecessary, sir.'

Callan sighed. He wasn't in the mood for a challenge and God had never done anything for him. But he also grudgingly had to concede that Gold was right – his comment had been out of order. From his experience, God and soldiers had a binary relationship. Many were atheist, seeing lack of belief as a macho badge of honour, but he also knew that many others had faith, even if they chose not to divulge that information to their mates. Perhaps it was only natural to turn to God when you were doing a job where there was a real risk of meeting your maker sooner rather than later.

'Just do it.'

Gold met his gaze coldly. 'Yes, sir.'

Turning back to the whiteboard, Callan continued: 'Foster's killer may, of course, not be one of our three key suspects. There are over six hundred soldiers stationed at Blackdown and many of them would have had opportunity. But before we start trawling the ocean, let's first shake down the people we know were around, who had clear opportunity, and who knew the victim. Any questions?'

Callan looked around the room. Everyone met his gaze steadily; no hands were raised.

'OK, you all have your brief, so let's get started. Next team meeting is 0700 hours tomorrow. And if anybody needs me this evening, I'll be up at Blackdown. I'm meeting the dog teams there in an hour.'

28

The red-brick block, windows grey and slick with grime from traffic fumes, loomed six storeys above a row of shops, the entrance doorway wedged between a William Hill book-makers on one side and an Oxfam charity shop on the other. The door was unlocked – someone had folded the corner of the doormat to keep it open, someone who was nowhere in sight – so after she had checked the names against the flat numbers on the wall by the door and found Malcolm Lawson's name, Jessie went inside, stamping the mat down and closing the door behind her. She didn't want to think of Joan being robbed by some degenerate who had taken the opportunity of the open door to slip inside, however wildly unlikely that scenario might be.

The lobby was windowless and dingy, nutmeg-coloured walls, beige vinyl-tiled floor, bare concrete stairs with a peeling brown painted metal banister curving away from her right-hand side to the upper floors. A black pram – Harry's pram – was parked in the nook under the stairs, the primary colours on the cardboard 'ABC' book hanging from its handle the only colour lighting up this unprepossessing space. There was a cramped single-person wooden lift behind a metal cage door to her left that looked as if it had been salvaged from the ark. Better to walk, she decided, than risk getting stuck in that vertical, mobile coffin.

Reaching the fifth floor, Jessie stopped for a moment to catch her breath and assemble her thoughts. After seeing Joan putting up posters this morning and meeting Marilyn in that quiet, wooded lane, she had decided to take a detour after work to check on Joan and Harry. But now that she was here, standing outside Malcolm Lawson's flat, she wasn't sure whether she'd made the right decision. She had no right to pass on information; that was the remit of Surrey and Sussex Major Crimes. But the image of the solitary figure trudging from lamp post to lamp post this morning had lodged a splinter in her chest. She knew all about loneliness, about the fallout from the death of a loved one. How friends, who had no idea what to say, felt that it was easier to distance themselves and say nothing. How others saw vulnerability as an invitation to persecute. She had experienced all that herself after Jamie's death, knew how psychologically damaging suicide could be on the family members left behind. Knew, too well, the gaping black hole left by a death. But more than that, the guilt of missed opportunities to save, the blame. And all those emotional pressures before the self-hatred at still being alive kicked in.

The flat was the middle doorway of three on this floor. Stepping across the stained brown carpet, Jessie tapped her knuckles lightly against the flaking cream paint. Taking a step back, she waited, feeling her nervousness manifest itself in clammy hands. As she rubbed her palms quickly down her trousers, streaking salty sweat into the black cotton, she became aware of movement to her left. Glancing across, she saw the vertical sepia sliver of a heavily powdered face before the door clicked shut. A nosy neighbour. Occupational hazard in built-up areas and one of the main reasons she'd chosen country isolation.

Light footsteps from inside Malcolm Lawson's flat, and the door flexed against its frame; Jessie realized that Joan must now be leaning her hands against the inside, eyeballing her through the spyglass. The sound of locks being drawn back, one, two, a chain, and the door inched open to reveal Joan's drained face, tired brown eyes cloudy with cataracts and underscored with black shadows, pale lips pressed into a tense line.

'Mrs Lawson, it's Doctor Jessie Flynn, from the hospital, yesterday morning.'

She was wearing the same clothes that Jessie had seen her in this morning, pale pink slippers in place of the worn leather shoes.

'Yes, Doctor Flynn, I remember you. Do you have news of Malcolm?'

Jessie shook her head; the old lady shrank visibly at the motion.

'I'm not involved in the police investigation, Mrs Lawson. But I'm sure that Detective Inspector Simmons will telephone you as soon as he has more information.'

She couldn't mention the abandoned Corolla, even though she was now wondering why, eight hours after they'd found it, Marilyn still hadn't called Joan with an update.

'I wanted to see how you and Harry are.'

Joan nodded. 'Please come in.'

146

Jessie followed her down a narrow hallway, catching a glimpse of a double bedroom to her right, a pair of grey woollen stockings abandoned in a pool of orange evening sunlight on a crumpled white duvet, the brown shoes side by side on the carpet beneath the bed, stacks of papers on both bedside tables, bifocals on top of one stack, a cot room opposite, in darkness, yellow stars from a night light peppering the ceiling, a closed door next to that.

She hadn't taken the time to form an impression of what Malcolm Lawson's flat might be like, but the rectangular kitchen, diner, sitting room – two grimy windows over-looking the main road, the cramped space filled with a navy-blue corduroy sofa and matching chairs to Jessie's right, a Formica table dividing them from a galley kitchen to her left, a jumble of files and papers on every surface – was pretty much what she would have expected. He had been off work for a year now with depression, had lost his job after the first six months. Money was tight; the will to keep the flat tidy, unsurprisingly, absent, though Jessie could see where Mrs Lawson had made an effort to instil some order in the wiped kitchen surfaces and stripes on the carpet indicating that it had been recently hoovered.

'Would you like a cup of tea, Doctor Flynn?'

'Yes, please.'

She waited until Joan had made her a cup and sat down at the kitchen table before taking the seat opposite. Tail-lights from the evening's queue of rush-hour traffic flashed crimson in the filmy glass windows, washed across the pale blue Formica surface and Joan's tightly clasped hands.

'Why aren't the police doing anything, Doctor Flynn?' she asked quietly.

'They are doing things, Mrs Lawson, I promise you.'

'Why haven't they been in touch?'

'They will soon, I'm sure.' *Platitudes*. She made a mental note to call Marilyn the second she was back outside, ask him to telephone Joan and feed her fluff, anything but this destabilizing vacuum of information.

'They still think that he has committed suicide, don't they? They didn't believe me . . . at the hospital.' Her eyes hung closed for a moment. 'That's the problem with getting old. People think that your brain is as broken down as your body.'

'I promise you that DI Simmons doesn't think that.'

'But he does think that I don't know my own child, doesn't he?'

'It's hard to know anyone properly, even your own child,' Jessie said gently. 'Often, even yourself.'

'But suicide?' Joan's voice rose. 'I'd know that? Surely, I'd know that?'

Jessie bit her lip. 'My brother committed suicide when I was fourteen.'

Joan's hands flew to her mouth. 'I'm so sorry, Doctor Flynn. I didn't mean—'

Jessie stared resolutely across the table at the old lady. 'Don't worry. It . . . it was a long time ago.'

'But it still hurts, doesn't it?' Joan murmured. 'I'm sure that it hurts every day.'

Jessie looked down at the worn Formica. She felt as if Joan had lifted a flap in her skull and peered, keen-eyed, straight into her brain. She took a breath. 'Why was Malcolm so sure that Danny's death wasn't suicide, Joan?'

It took her a moment to answer. 'Because of nothing specific and everything, I suppose,' she began. 'Because of the way he lived, most of all. He was a happy, easy-going kid. Handsome. Popular. Malcolm couldn't imagine why Danny would want to kill himself.'

'What did you think, Joan? Did you agree with Malcolm?'

The old lady sighed. 'Malcolm and Anne – Malcolm's wife – had a big argument with Danny.'

'When?'

'Two, two and a half years ago now.'

Jessie mentally calculated. He would only have been thirteen or fourteen then. A child. As she herself had been when Jamie had died and her parents had withdrawn from her into their own private nightmares.

'What did they argue about, Joan?'

'I don't know.' Joan's pale fingers touched her ear. 'They didn't tell me and I didn't like to pry. They lived down in Midhurst back then, further away, so I saw less of them. Malcolm only moved to this flat after Danny's death, after he lost his job. He couldn't afford to keep the old house on and wanted to be near me so that I could help with Harry.'

'Was it something to do with Harry? That would have been around the time that Anne found out she was pregnant. Perhaps Danny was jealous?'

Joan looked horrified. 'No, it was nothing like that. Nothing to do with Harry. Danny loved Harry.'

'I'm sure he loved him when he was born, but perhaps he didn't love the idea of him,' Jessie probed gently. She was treading on delicate ground, needed to choose her words carefully. 'He was a teenager – it's a tough time. Maybe he felt neglected, felt that his parents were trying to replace him?'

Mrs Lawson bowed her head. 'Harry was an accident. He wasn't planned. And Danny loved him, genuinely.'

Jessie nodded. 'So what happened with Danny after the argument?'

'He moved out,' Joan said quietly.

'Where did he go?'

'To an older friend's flat initially, a friend he'd met through church. And then the next thing I heard, he'd signed up to join the Army.'

'Why do you think he joined?'

'I don't know. To find stability, perhaps. I think that he was lonely. My son, Malcolm, is principled and very intransigent, and Anne was even worse. Once they made up their minds, they weren't going to shift. They were determined that Danny wasn't going to be accepted back into the family until he apologized. "Until he's changed his ways" was how Malcolm put it.'

Apologized for what? Changed what ways?

'They built a wall.' Joan's voice held a bitterness that surprised Jessie. 'Both of them. All three of them. A wall of silence and anger that none of them were going to break down. I tried to contact Danny, but . . . ' she tailed off. 'It's hard. I loved him, but I found him very difficult to deal with as a teenager. My generation and his are so different, poles and poles apart in terms of our experiences, the world in which we grew up, societal norms.'

A sudden, penetrating cry from the next room. *Harry.* Jessie stood. 'Thank you for speaking with me, Mrs Lawson.'

Joan gave a distracted nod, but didn't rise. 'It's my fault, Doctor Flynn.'

Jessie lowered herself back into the chair. 'What's your fault, Joan?'

'Malcolm asked me to look after Harry the night he left him at the hospital. He said that he needed to do something and could I stay the night. I got a migraine and let him down at the last minute.' Her pensive gaze drifted to the grimy window. 'He was angry with me. Really angry. He said that he needed to do something important and that he didn't want to take Harry.' She lifted her shoulders in a faint shrug. 'He never got angry with me. Not with me. If I hadn't let him down, perhaps he'd be sitting opposite me now instead of you.'

'None of this is your fault, Mrs Lawson.'

Joan's gaze moved back from the window to meet Jessie's. She looked bereft.

'My husband used to say that old age is not for the faint-hearted, Doctor Flynn. We're boring, old people. There's nothing attractive about us, nothing glamorous. Our skin is sagging, our bones ache, our vision is failing, we can't hear and we're lonely because all our friends are dead or dying.'

Another cry, louder than the first.

'Joan—' Jessie cut in.

Joan held up a hand to silence her. 'But the thing that disturbs me most about being an old lady is none of those things, Doctor Flynn. The thing that disturbs me the most is that everybody thinks I'm stupid. And yet, I know that I'm sharp as I ever was. I feel forty – thirty, even – in my mind, and then I look in the mirror and see a frail old lady and I don't blame people for treating me how they do. Like some helpless idiot. Like an infant. Whether this is my fault or not, I need you to take me seriously, Doctor Flynn, because I know that the police won't. You're my only hope. You're Malcolm's only hope.'

29

'As you would expect, Malcolm Lawson's fingerprints are all over the glass and plastic surfaces in this car, including the dashboard, the front and rear doors, inside and outside, and the windows, inside and out,' Tony Burrows, Marilyn's lead CSI said, smoothing a latex-gloved hand over his bald patch, fingers grazing the dark hair that ringed his scalp. In his blue forensic onesie overall, he reminded Marilyn of a tasteless Facebook joke he'd seen doing the rounds a few weeks ago: four middle-aged men photoshopped on to Teletubby bodies, one of the men, round-faced and balding, bearing an uncanny resemblance to Burrows. The whole effect had been alarming, to say the least, enough to give small children nightmares for weeks.

'And the bit I wouldn't expect?' Marilyn asked, reading Burrows' tone.

They were standing in one of Surrey Police's Vehicle Recovery and Examination Service garages in Guildford, where Malcolm Lawson's car had been towed and forensically examined. Pale grey aluminium fingerprint dust coated the beige plastic surfaces inside the car and clouded the windows.

'There are no fingerprints on the steering wheel.'

'Not unusual.'

'No. Not unusual,' Burrows conceded.

Steering wheels were difficult surfaces from which to lift decent fingerprints as drivers' hands were moving constantly, sliding backwards and forwards as they turned corners, leaving fingerprints and then smudging them.

'But the gearstick also returned no prints. Nor did the outside or inside handles on the driver's door, the rear passenger-side door, outside or inside, or the buckle on the baby seat.'

Marilyn's eyes hung closed for a moment. 'Unusual.'

Burrows nodded. 'Right.'

'So you're saying that those surfaces have been wiped clean of fingerprints?'

'Unless Malcolm Lawson wore gloves to drive, which is not borne out by the fact that his fingerprints are all over the rest of the car, that's exactly what I'm saying.'

'Damnit,' Marilyn said with feeling. There was only one inescapable conclusion from the fingerprint evidence and it directly contradicted everything he had surmised these past thirty hours. *Damnit.*

'There's something else, Marilyn.'

'I'm not sure that I want to hear it.'

Despite the relative warmth of the day, the air inside the garage was chill, as if they'd stepped into a gigantic cool box, and although the ground in the lay-by and footpaths up where they'd found Malcolm's car had been dryer than Marilyn could reasonably have hoped, some water must have seeped through the seams of his suede boots as his socks felt damp and cold and his toes were numb. Stamping his feet to get the circulation going, he watched Burrows massage the dome of his head, a nervous habit and a sure sign that he was debating how best to phrase bad news.

'The tyre iron was missing from the wheel-change kit in the boot.'

'Oh, Christ.' He met Burrows' pale blue gaze. 'Blood? Did you find any blood?'

'None. Not a trace.'

'And we have no signs of a struggle or any violence inside the car?' He posed the sentence as a question. Though he could see from a cursory look at the undisturbed Costa Coffee cup in the holder between the front seats, the maps stored carefully in the webbing holders behind them, the folded coat and wellingtons in the boot, that the interior of the car showed no signs of a struggle, the fingerprint evidence had destabilized him. He met Burrows' gaze, waiting for confirmation.

'Absolutely no signs of a struggle within the car.' Burrows held up a finger. 'But.'

Marilyn steeled himself.

'The baby seat is damp.' Beckoning Marilyn to the rear passenger-side door, he leaned into the car and pointed to the right-hand edge of the baby seat's padded headrest. 'Here. Right here.'

'It was raining last night,' Marilyn said, working out, the instant the words had left his lips that the evidence didn't feel right for rain damp. The car didn't have a sunroof and if the child seat was damp from rain it would surely have been on the left-hand side, the side closest to the window.

Burrows shimmied back out of the door and straightened. 'I've taken a sample for analysis, but I'll bet a week's wages that the liquid on the baby seat will have sodium and chloride in it.'

He looked expectantly at Marilyn, who shook his head. 'I'm still nowhere, Tony.'

'Tears,' Burrows said. 'I'd put good money on the fact that the little boy was crying.'

Marilyn's gaze dipped to the oil-stained concrete floor.

Surfaces that a driver would touch, wiped clean.

Tears.

A little boy's tears.

'How old is he?' Burrows asked.

'Nearly two.'

'Old enough to know if something bad had happened to his daddy and to be upset by that.'

Rubbing his hand over the back of his neck, Marilyn nodded silently.

He'd wasted thirty hours. Thirty hours, working on the assumption that Malcolm had left his baby son in the hospital and gone off to hang himself from a tree. Wasted that first vital day in a missing person's case, after which the trail would be that much colder. However insouciant he might appear to be, his own bad decisions infuriated him. He should have listened to Jessie Flynn this morning, should have kicked off a proper search with or without the dogs. Pulling out his mobile, he pressed redial. Sarah Workman answered on the first ring.

'Workman, have the dogs finished at that stranger rape?'

He waited, mobile clamped to his ear, sole tattooing an impatient rhythm on the concrete floor.

'Good. We need them at Halesmoor Wood as soon as possible – and as many spare PCs as we can muster. I'll meet you back there in half an hour.'

Sliding his phone into the inside pocket of his suit jacket, he laid a hand on Burrows' shoulder.

'Fancy an outing, Tony?' Belying the matey hand and flippant tone, his expression was tense.

Burrows sighed resignedly. 'A nice walk in the woods?'

'And a spot of crawling around in a muddy lay-by too, if you play your cards right.'

30

Though the day was inching to a close, the air was warm, the car park steaming from a combination of the unexpected evening sunshine and the brief cloudburst that had engulfed Callan's car as he drove the five miles from the Branch offices to Blackdown. The guards remained in the hut as he parked and climbed out of his Golf; the corporal who had checked his ID had scuttled inside again the moment the barrier returned to horizontal. They were unwilling, Callan knew, to get too close to a Branch detective now that death had cursed their turf, even though, from the cursory glance he threw in through the window, none of them had been on duty the night before last.

It was behaviour that he had come to accept, enjoy even, in the five years he'd been in the Branch. Despite his chosen profession, he wasn't a natural team player and found the whole process of building consensus to be tedious and time-wasting. Being the object of suspicion and mistrust made it easier to get on with the job undisturbed, which suited him fine.

Turning his back on the guardhouse, he walked towards the wooded area where Stephen Foster's body had been found. From a distance, the trees looked country park picturesque, their canopies glinting emerald as the low-slung sun reflected off their rain-damp leaves. But up close there was an Amazonian denseness and darkness to these woods that felt unnatural for the English countryside; he half expected to turn and see a man in a loincloth, clutching a spear, darting through the trees. It was a sense that catapulted him straight back to Scott's attack four months ago. He was recovered now, physically. But mentally? That was a whole other story. He took a couple of deep breaths, head dipped, hand resting on the back of his neck, waiting for the thumping in his chest to subside. The last thing he needed was an epileptic fit with the dog handlers due. Turning, he looked through the trees towards the gate and guardhouse. Where the hell were they anyway? If they didn't get here soon, they'd lose the light.

31

The moment that Joan Lawson's front door shut behind her, Jessie sensed movement. Glancing to her left, she saw the same vertical sliver of powdered sepia skin that had greeted her arrival, the sliver expanding this time to reveal narrow, downturned lips painted dark plum, heavily kohl-lined eyes, a choppy, pixie haircut dyed as jet black as her own natural Irish colour, a ruched purple blouse embellished with a thick gold necklace. The woman was probably only mid-forties, but the heavy make-up and the suspicious slant to her eyes made her look a decade older.

'You a social worker?' she asked in theatrically hushed tones, a gush of heavy perfume accompanying her as she stepped into the hallway.

'A psychologist.'

The dark plum mouth, which was already slightly twisted, as if she doubted everything that she was told, twisted further as she absorbed this new information. 'Isn't that the same thing?'

'Sometimes,' Jessie said plainly. 'But not this time.'

The woman nodded sagely. 'I used to hear him crying, you know,' she said, jerking her thumb towards Malcolm Lawson's door.

Jessie didn't reply, maintained an impassive expression, though she could already feel her hackles rising.

'Crying. Screaming and crying.' She tilted forward, right into Jessie's personal space and lowered her voice to a stage whisper. 'I wasn't prying, mind you. It's just that the walls are tissue-thin. There was no way that I couldn't hear.'

'Harry,' Jessie said calmly.

'Sorry?'

'The baby is called Harry. I assume that you're not close to the Lawsons or you would know that.'

The woman pulled a face, ignoring the inference behind Jessie's comment.

'Not the baby.' Plum polished fingernails gripped Jessie's forearm. '*Him.*'

Horns sounded suddenly from the street outside, and the noise of an engine revving into the red zone, tempers fraying as office workers fought to get home.

'The *father*. Every night it was. Two, three in the morning, screaming and crying like he was being murdered. And now he's disappeared and dumped the kiddie with that old woman. If you ask me, the kindest thing would be to put the poor little mite into care. I'm tempted to make the call myself.'

Jessie took a step back, disengaging her arm as she did so. 'The outcome for children in care is appalling.' She kept her voice measured, though it was an effort. 'They have significantly poorer educational outcomes and are over-represented in vulnerable groups such as teenage parents, young offenders, drug users and prisoners. Oh, and over

160

half have what us psychologists term "severe emotional and behavioural health". You really shouldn't wish care on any child, particularly one who has a grandmother as loving and capable as Joan Lawson.' She smiled. 'Have a good evening. I'll send your regards to Malcolm when I see him.'

Turning, she walked away, sensing the woman staring, open-mouthed, at her back.

32

Two Military Police Special Investigation Branch dog handlers were climbing into forensic overalls outside the crime scene cordon, their dogs, both German shepherds, one a huge black beast with wolf's eyes a similar colour to Callan's own, the other smaller, slighter, the traditional black and tan, sitting by their handlers' sides, ears pricked, muscles trembling with anticipation.

Callan glanced up through the leaf canopy. The sun was the colour of a blood orange, the sky above him laced with cotton wool bands of orange-infused grey. He needed the light to stick with them for another hour, the rain to hold off. Dogs' noses were so sensitive that they could smell dead bodies wedged under rocks at the bottom of streams and rivers, detect drugs contained in heat-sealed Mylar bags, floating in petrol – he'd seen it himself on a drugs bust a couple of years ago where a Royal Electrical and Mechanical Engineers sergeant had smuggled two kilos of pure opium back from Afghanistan in the petrol tank of a Land Rover. But their job was made harder if the elements didn't play ball, and on this case, he could do with all the help he could get.

'We have virtually no forensic evidence so far, no footprints, and no fingerprints on either the murder weapon or on Foster's clothing, his buttons, belt buckle or corps badge.' *In fact, we have pretty much fuck-all so far* – though he didn't say it. 'The only thing we know for sure is that the killer – he or she – stayed with him, with Foster, held him upright for a number of minutes after the stabbing.' Callan pointed. 'There, against that tree. But we don't know why.' He produced an evidence bag containing Stephen Foster's bloodied combat jacket and held it out to the sergeant, the more senior of the two handlers. 'This is from the victim. What I need from you—' He broke off. The larger of the two dogs had turned to face him, gums rolled back from her teeth. Callan looked her straight in the eye, a direct challenge that should have knocked her off-kilter, but she didn't flinch. She continued to eyeball him, looking straight into his amber eyes with her own, a low rumble emanating from deep in her throat. It was as if the animal was looking right through his pupils, a window into his brain, as if she knew exactly what he was feeling, could measure the raised, stressed pulse in his temple. Dipping his head, he rubbed a hand across his eyes.

'Right, uh, if the, uh, if the dogs can trace the killer, find out where he or she went after the murder, that could give us a proper lead.'

The sergeant nodded, tugged hard on the black shepherd's lead a couple of times, refocusing the animal on him. 'No problem, sir.'

Pulling her around to his side, he indicated to her the base of the tree where Foster had been found. The black and tan dog moved to search the perimeter of the crime scene. Callan's hopes rose as the dogs glued their noses to the ground, sniffed purposefully around the raised, knotted roots of trees, crawled under bushes. But the larger dog, the huge black animal, wouldn't focus. She seemed distracted, constantly turning her head towards Callan, dipping her nose back to the ground, lifting her head again, straining towards him, against her leash.

'Come on, girl.' The sergeant jerked the dog back to her task. 'Here.' He indicated the base of the tree. '*Here.*'

Callan stepped forward. 'Is there a problem, Sergeant?'

'No prob— *Jesus!*'

The shepherd lunged at Callan. He leapt back, but not fast enough, and the dog's razor-sharp incisors tore into his hand. He snatched his hand away, felt her teeth gouge twin tracks through his skin. Blood flowed from the gashes.

'Down, girl, down!' the sergeant yelled, hauling on her leash.

The dog lunged again, jaws clamping on to Callan's forearm like a vice. He tried to yank his arm away, but her teeth were fastened solid.

'Leave, girl. Leave.' The handler wrenched her collar tight around her throat. She growled and clung on. The handler wrenched again; her jaws released, for a second, and Callan yanked his arm away, a large chunk of material from his forensic overalls and suit jacket beneath ripping with her teeth.

'Jesus, I'm sorry, sir. I'm so sorry. She's never done that before.'

Callan held up his hands. He was shaking. His forearm felt as if it had been slammed in the door of a truck.

'No problem.'

'Really, sir. I'm sorry.'

164

'It's fine, Sergeant. I'll live.'

The sergeant's gaze found the teeth marks on Callan's hand, blood dripping from the twin gashes, the shreds of material hanging from his forearm.

'It might be something about your clothes, sir. Maybe because you came here straight from the autopsy. She can probably smell the victim, his blood.' The sergeant rubbed his nose and looked at his feet, embarrassed. 'She's usually a fantastic working dog, sir. Bullet-proof.'

Callan nodded. 'It's not a problem,' he muttered.

Maybe his clothes? Maybe something to do with the sweat he could feel oozing from his every pore. Dogs could smell illness, couldn't they? Could be trained to scent out tumours, warn diabetics that their blood sugar was running low, that they needed an injection of insulin. Sense if people were epileptics, warn of impending fits minutes before they happened. Could smell weakness, human frailty, decaying minds . . .

'Why don't I step away, leave you to it.'

The handler nodded gratefully. 'That might help, sir.'

Ducking under the crime scene tape, Callan walked further into the trees, staying close enough so that he could hear if he was called, far enough so that he was out of their immediate field of vision if he had an epileptic fit. Crouching down, he closed his eyes, took a few deep breaths, feeling the cool evening air funnel down his throat and into his lungs, letting his mind find the quiet place he went to when he felt that an attack was imminent. The triggers of his epilepsy, his neurologist had told him, were mainly lack of sleep and stress. Avoid those and you'll reduce their incidence substantially, he'd said. *Fantastic. Plenty of opportunities to do that in this job.*

Opening his eyes, he stood, walked slowly back through the trees towards the handlers, stopping and watching the dogs from a distance as they circled the tree underneath which Foster's body had been found. The smaller one, his tail on a spring, set off in a straight line towards the car park and the guardhouse, but the other dog, the huge black animal that had attacked him, was on a different track, lifting her head and turning in tight, fidgety circles.

'Come on, girl.' The handler pulled on her lead, trying to focus her on the scent trail that the other dog had followed, but she wouldn't be swayed.

Every square centimetre of the crime scene had been searched by Morgan and his SOCO team and, apart from the screwdriver, which was clean of fingerprints, they had found no useful forensic evidence. But there had to be something they had all missed, surely? Something that explained why the killer would have stayed with Foster, held him up? What was he failing to see? Val Monks' words came into his mind: *I'm not a psychologist, Callan. But on this case, I reckon that you could use one.*

'Let her go where she wants,' he called out to the handler.

The sergeant looked over, his face colouring, still embarrassed about the dog's aggressive lapse.

'Right, sir.' He let the lead go slack.

Immediately, the shepherd spun away from her handler, snagging the lead taut, nearly tripping him off his feet. Rearing up on to her hind legs, she planted her front paws firmly against the side of the tree, nose pointing straight up towards the leaves.

'Has she got something?' Callan shouted.

The handler looked over, uncertainty written on his face. 'I'm not sure, sir. I can't see anything. Bark, the tree trunk, nothing else.' He tried to jerk the dog back to the ground, but she resisted, head still cocked upwards, neck straining against the leash snagged tight around her throat.

Callan walked over. The dog sank to her haunches and the sergeant clamped her lead to his thigh, keeping her attention focused on him as Callan approached. He searched the bark, his gaze criss-crossing backwards and forwards, tracking slowly upwards from where the dog had placed her paws.

Nothing. There was nothing on this tree trunk, only the rough grooves and indentations of age-old bark, dusty olive-green lichen, a tiny red spider that skittered away as it sensed his proximity.

Nothing. There was nothing.

And then he saw it.

A stain. Virtually invisible to the naked eye against the dusty brown bark. A bloodstain. A handprint? Right up high. He hadn't noticed it, Morgan and his team hadn't, but the dog had. The dog with the sixth sense. The dog who had his measure.

33

It would be rush hour now, Marilyn realized, glancing at his watch, picturing cars paving both lanes of the A3, tempers fraying as commuters swore at each other from behind the safety of locked doors and sealed windows. But on this narrow lane that came from nowhere and led nowhere, not one car had approached in the two hours since he and Tony Burrows had cordoned it off, officially declaring the lay-by and the cracked tarmac that stretched fifty metres either side of it a crime scene.

Whatever the public thought from the TV programmes that showed hot American CSIs in their designer jeans and salmon pink Ralph Lauren polo shirts, trapping serial killers with no more than a microscopic flake of skin from under a victim's toenail, far more cases were solved by tip-offs than anything else. Unfortunately for Marilyn – and Malcolm – it was unlikely there would be any help from Joe Public on this case. Malcolm Lawson's attacker had chosen well, enticing Malcolm to meet him here. He was streetwise and cunning, if not an intellectual. A worthy opponent.

Shoving his mobile in his pocket, Marilyn walked back down the road to the lay-by. He'd just answered a call from Jessie Flynn, asking – or rather, demanding – that he instigate a proper search for Malcolm Lawson. He'd been only too pleased to tell her that it was already under way. He had also grudgingly conceded that he should have listened to her advice this morning and widened the search then and there, dogs or not. His obstinacy had wasted ten hours and significantly reduced the prospect of finding Malcolm alive. It was now over forty hours since Harry had been deposited at A & E and it had, to Marilyn's chagrin, taken him thirty-eight of those forty hours to twig that a crime had been committed. In failing to recognize this case for what it was, an abduction and possible murder, he had screwed up spectacularly.

The specialist search teams that had joined them an hour ago were already combing the heath and woodland that stretched away uphill from either side of the lane. It comprised hundreds of acres, clogged with new spring growth: oak and elm, broad sweeps of bracken and fern, stagnant ponds stewing with water weed and teeming with tadpoles, a few lone houses, a couple of clusters of farm buildings and a small industrial estate. Marilyn had discussed every inch with the search team commander, indicating key points on the 1:50,000 ordnance survey map he'd laid out on the bonnet of his beloved Z3. The search wouldn't go on for much longer tonight, he knew. As SIO he'd have to call it off when they lost the light. It was impossible to conduct an effective search in this terrain in the dark, like searching for a needle in a haystack blindfold.

'Marilyn.' Tony Burrows was calling to him, waving him

over. 'I've found a tyre track, a second one, definitely not Malcolm's.'

'In the lay-by?'

'No, and that's why I didn't see it at first. It's further down the lane.'

Signalling Marilyn to follow, he walked twenty metres down the potholed tarmac, to where a yellow cone numbered with a three had been placed.

'Here.' Burrows pointed to a small patch of flattened mud, a few centimetres from the edge of the muddy kerb. 'The car that left this tyre track was parked at the side of the lane, but not . . . *not* . . . ' He emphasized the word. 'On the muddy kerb . . . ' Burrows paused. 'So the driver – he or she—'

'He, if it's our target.' Marilyn interrupted. 'We know it's a "he", because we have the CCTV from the hospital at the time Harry was left. It was definitely a man.' *A man pushing a pram through a snowstorm in Alaska.*

'OK. So *he* parked carefully at the side of the lane, far enough over so that another car could get past if one happened to drive down here, but without either of his wheels touching the muddy kerb.'

'Forensically aware,' Marilyn muttered.

'Isn't everyone with a television forensically aware these days?' Burrows' mouth twisted irritably, as if the plethora of CSI programmes on TV were filmed and aired purely as a personal challenge to his professional zeal.

But Marilyn acknowledged that they had, without doubt, made life harder for the police: feeding tips on beating the CSI teams straight to criminals. The entertainment industry, for some reason, seemed to feel that it was their personal responsibility to undermine real-life detectives at every turn

170

and yet Marilyn was expected, by the powers that be, to keep them on side at all times, answering banal questions from scriptwriters, letting crime novelists nose around his offices and sit in on his team meetings, when most of the time he felt like giving them a kick up their smug, skinny-hazelnut-macchiato-swilling arses.

'However' – Burrows tapped the side of his nose with his forefinger – 'he didn't see this patch of mud, here. Right here. But I did.'

Pedantic to a fault. A crucial personality trait for a great CSI.

'From an animal, I'd say,' Burrows continued. 'A deer possibly, crossing the road with soil stuck to its hooves.' His moon face broke into a smile. 'So we have the imprint of a car tyre.'

'Enough to take a useable cast?'

Burrows nodded. 'Enough to take a useable cast. If you feel that it's relevant to the case. It could, of course, be a dog walker.'

Marilyn cocked an eyebrow. 'How many cars have you seen driving down here over the past two hours?'

'None.'

'Right. None. It was the same this morning. I was here for a couple of hours and again, no cars.'

'And if you're stopping here to walk the dog, you'd park in the lay-by,' Marilyn continued. 'It would make no sense to park on such a narrow lane, risk getting your car scraped by someone squeezing past.'

Burrows cast his gaze to the darkening sky; his view was blocked by the dense leaf canopy of an ancient ash.

'This patch of earth became damp after the tyre track was left. You can see a bit of water pooled in the grooves, but not enough to damage the integrity of the print.' He pointed with his index finger. 'It has rained since two nights ago, but only a brief cloudburst and I doubt that it would have penetrated the leaves of that ash enough to deposit this much water in the tyre track. That indicates to me that the car that left this print arrived either before or during the heavy rainstorm we had two nights ago, but no earlier. It rained pretty much constantly during the two days and nights preceding that night, so if it had been left earlier, I'd expect it to be awash and the integrity of the print to be water-damaged, regardless of the leaf canopy.'

Marilyn pushed himself to his feet, wincing as both his knees clicked in unison. It seemed it wasn't only his lungs that needed a refit.

'God was smiling on us for once.'

Burrows rolled his eyes. 'I think God gave up on you years ago, Marilyn.'

Marilyn smiled. 'Satan then, rewarding me for years of loyal service.' He smothered a yawn with his sleeve. He'd spent last night at the dog track in Reading, hadn't made it home until gone 1 a.m., convinced that he had no pressing cases on the go. *Wrong.* 'Let's get a cast of the tyre track made pronto and we can go from there.' He clapped a hand on Burrows' shoulder. 'Congrats, Tony. It looks like you may have given us our first break.'

34

One of the things that Jessie had missed most during her recent tour of duty was the total and utter blackness of the night sky above her cottage. No sodium city glow and no lights from the Royal Navy destroyer, a mini-floating city in itself, to flood the sky with a creamy haze and drown out the stars. Moving to the middle of the lane outside her cottage – knowing that she could stand here all night and not risk being hit by a car – she tilted her head back and looked straight up at the pitch-black sky above her, clear of clouds now, the stars appearing to ramble away for miles in all directions, thousands of them, each a perfect bright-white pinprick. The silence of the night, total and absolute. Lovely to be alone, surrounded by space after the claustrophobia of Malcolm Lawson's flat, the grind of constant traffic outside the window, the emotional intensity of her discussion with Joan. She didn't know much about the constellations, but there were a few that she recognized from her childhood: Ursa Major, the Great Bear, Ursa Minor, the Little Bear, and her birth sign, Gemini, the twins, two bright stars, Castor and Pollux forming their heads, fainter stars sketching out their bodies, easy to recognize because it was one of the few constellations that actually looked like the figure it represented.

Gemini. The twins. The split-personality. Yin and yang.

When her neck became sore and she felt the cold seeping through her thin waterproof mac, the air chill now that the spring sun had vanished, she went inside. As she opened her front door, she saw the intermittent wash of red lighting her ceiling. Another answerphone message. Ignoring the flashing light, she shrugged off her coat, hung it carelessly on the hook beside the door and kicked off her ballet pumps. She was halfway across the living room when she stopped. The message would be from her father. She knew that it would be her father because everyone else she knew used her mobile, with the exception of Ahmose, who ambled up the front path and knocked. She didn't need to press play to know that he had called again with his request for dinner on Thursday, only two days away now. With thoughts of her father's looming visit – a visit she would avoid at all costs – she felt tension rise, the electric suit hissing across her skin. She took another step towards the kitchen, felt the hiss and snap intensify.

Retracing her steps to the coat stand, she took hold of the sleeves of her coat and straightened them until they were level, to the millimetre; bent and lined up her ballet pumps side by side on the shoe rack, pressing her hand against their backs until toes and heels were precisely aligned. Walking over to the answer machine, she jammed her finger on to the 'Delete' button. But she must have pressed 'Play' by mistake in the dimly lit room, because the silence was filled by her father's jolly Irish lilt, forced, she sensed in the brief second before her finger found the 'Delete' button and he was cut off mid-sentence.

In the kitchen, she found the Princess wine glass, newly washed and right at the front of the cupboard, filled it to the brim and, grabbing a blanket from the sofa, went back outside, settling herself on to the old wooden bench the previous owners had left propped against the back wall of her cottage. Wrapping the blanket around her shoulders, she gazed up to the stars, trying to focus her mind on finding Gemini again – yin and yang – trying to push away the memories that her father's voice had dredged to the surface. But they came anyway, seeping through the cracks in her mind's fragile defences.

Yin and yang – night and day – heaven and earth – life and death.

When Jamie was four and a half, they had wrapped up in blankets on a clear spring night like this one and taken their mugs of hot chocolate outside, to lay on the grass in the middle of the garden and look up at the stars, a treat before his bedtime. She had pointed out the constellations that she knew, the same ones as now, knowledge gained for a school quiz team that she had been co-opted into joining by her teacher.

Ursa Major. The Great Bear.

'A bear,' Jamie had laughed, clutching Pandy, the adored stuffed panda bear that had been his constant companion since birth, that he took everywhere, his fist clutched tight around Pandy's neck, holding him like a wrung chicken. 'What is a bear doing up in the sky?'

'He lives there.'

A pause. Jessie could almost hear the cogs in his brain whirring.

'Isn't he lonely?' he murmured. 'Up in the sky all on his own?'

'No, he's not lonely at all, because he's got a friend up there with him. There are two bears in the sky: Ursa Major, the Great Bear, and Ursa Minor, the Little Bear.'

Shifting sideways, so that she was right next to him, so that he could look down the length of her arm, she pointed, sketching out the twenty-one stars making up the Great Bear constellation with her finger. But before she'd reached halfway, he'd lost interest.

'Does big bear take care of little bear?' he interrupted. 'Like in my story book.'

'Of course he does.'

'Like you take care of me.'

Jessie smiled. 'Like I take care of you.'

Jamie lifted his own arms, stretched them ramrod straight above him, holding Pandy – filthy, saggy Pandy, more black and grey than black and white – aloft to the sky.

'Do you want to live in the sky, Pandy?' he asked, twisting Pandy's head so that he was looking up to the stars.

'No,' said Jessie, putting on a tiny, squeaky voice. 'I want to live with you, Jamie.'

Jamie giggled. 'Whyyyyyy, Pandy?'

'Because I love you, Jamie.'

Jamie had twisted on to his side then, clambered on to her chest, rubbing Pandy over her face, making kissing noises.

'Pandy loves you too, Jessie.'

Six months after Jamie had committed suicide, Jessie had emptied his room, loading his clothes into bin bags, methodically emptying his drawers, one by one, carrying the bin bags down to the garden. Dawn still an hour away, she had piled the bin bags in the centre of the lawn, sprinkled them with cooking oil and burnt everything. The only things that she had left untouched were the Athena poster that he had loved (a litter of chocolate Labradors squashed into a wicker basket – she couldn't bring herself to take it down), and Pandy, his beloved Pandy, which she had carried back to her own bed and tucked under her duvet.

As soon as she had done it – burnt his things – as soon as she'd seen the look on her mother's face, the desperate scrabble to rescue any remnants that she could from the fire, Jessie knew that she had made a terrible mistake. But she had been drowning, and the only thing that made sense to her fourteen-year-old self was that she needed her mother back, needed to shock her out of the dark hole into which she had crawled since Jamie's death.

A week later, Jessie was sent to live with her father and his new wife, Diane. Her mother was unable to function, unable even to drag herself out of bed in the morning, let alone look after a teenage daughter; the weight of her sadness too heavy, nothing important enough to encroach on grief's all-consuming territory.

Her father and Diane lived in a tall, narrow house, in a terrace in fashionable Fulham; four floors, the top floor an attic converted into a guest bedroom. Lying in bed at night, Jessie could see the sky through the dormer window. But there was nothing up there, no stars, only a neon-orange wash cast by the sodium streetlights. Wimbledon was three miles down the road, but it felt like a different planet with the sound of birds, the wind in the trees. And stars. She could see the stars in Wimbledon.

It had been wrong from the start. Diane, fifteen years younger than her father and only fourteen years older than

Jessie, had no intention of adopting anyone's child. Particularly not a deeply disturbed teenaged girl. She hadn't married for that. She had broken up a family, she had won – and she wasn't about to start losing. Through two floors, Jessie heard Diane's voice at night, clear as a bell, audible even over the sound of the buses rumbling down Fulham Palace Road at the end of the street.

I didn't sign up for this when I married you. I didn't sign up for her.

For hours. It seemed to go on for hours. Night after night.

She's so quiet, so odd. It's not normal. She's not normal.

No other topic of conversation now. Only her.

If I'm being honest, she frightens me.

Everything that was wrong with her.

She pressed a pillow over her head, but she could still hear their voices, coming up the stairs. Diane shouting; her father appeasing.

She's disturbed, darling. She needs help. We can't provide her with the help that she needs.

She lay in bed, motionless, hardly daring to breathe. If she didn't move, if she was completely and utterly still, they would forget that she was here, forget that she existed and carry on as before. Before she came. Before she came and ruined everything. She knew that she was ruining everything, that she wasn't wanted here – Diane told her often, when her father was at work – but she didn't know what to do to make things better. All she could do was to make herself as small and still and silent as possible, as if she wasn't there.

I don't care where she goes. To a fucking foster home. To a fucking mental home. I don't care.

She was good at ruining everything. That was one thing

she was very good at. Her mother had told her so, too, after she had burnt Jamie's things.

Jessie lay still as a statue and her insides constricted in agony. Her life wasn't supposed to have been like this. Curling on to her side, she held Pandy tight to her face, pressing his ragged nose to her own like Jamie used to do, sucking in Jamie's smell, the only real sense that she had now of Jamie, his only reality, caught in Pandy's dirty fur.

Pandy loves you too, Jessie.

Everything else only memories that were already fading. Nine months since she had found him hanging from that curtain rail, and her brother's face, the detail of it, was blurring. The sound of his voice, the feel of his warm little hand in hers, his laugh, those uncontrollable fits of giggles that he would dissolve into when he found something funny, that would make her laugh out loud just listening.

I WANT HER GONE.

One afternoon, three months after she had moved in with her father and Diane, arguments a nightly torment, Diane barely speaking to her, she had arrived home from school, grabbed a drink of milk from the fridge and headed straight upstairs to her room as she always did now, avoiding contact, making herself invisible, *gone.*

She had been in her room for five minutes, setting her homework out on the desk, when she realized that something was amiss. Her bed was neatly made as always – her OCD well established now – but the space in the middle of the pillow, Pandy's space, was bare. She had left him, as she always did, tucked under her duvet, his ratty black-and-white head resting on her pillow. Pulling back the duvet and pillow, she shook them both out, waiting for Pandy to drop from the folds. He didn't.

Her room was spotless, the surfaces empty of clutter, only the day's homework on the desk, the efforts of a fourteen-year-old girl who had no order in her life, no control over anything other than the space boxed within these four white walls.

Panic rising in her throat, she wrenched open her wardrobe, yanked each of her drawers open in turn, knowing, *knowing* that he wouldn't be in any of them. Knowing that she had, as she always did, left him tucked under her duvet when she had left for school that morning.

Through a blur of tears, she sensed someone standing in the doorway – Diane.

'What have you done with him?' she croaked.

Diane tilted her head, a cruel smile on her lips. 'He was filthy. Totally unhygienic.'

'You've washed him?'

'Oh, no. He was far too old to be washed. He would have fallen apart.' There was a lightness to her tone that made Jessie shiver.

A car swished by on the wet road outside, tyres hissing, a dog barked, a small yappy toy dog, the only dogs that lived around here. Someone shouted in the street outside.

'No, I didn't wash him. I threw him in the dustbin.'

Shoving past Diane, Jessie charged down the stairs.

'It's too late,' a cool voice called down after her. 'They emptied the bins this morning. He's gone. Pandy has gone.'

35

The Special Investigation Branch's arc lights powered up, illuminating the tree against which the black German shepherd had signalled the bloody handprint, like a monolithic, Stone Age sculpture. Callan stood, hands in his pockets, his breath making vapour clouds. Next to him stood Lieutenant Gold, a thin cigarillo pinched between his pale lips. Smoke from the cigarillo drifted straight upwards into the darkness, no breeze to disturb its lazy ascent.

'You're asking a lot, here, so you are,' Sergeant Morgan said, in his soft Welsh accent, hitching an eyebrow at Callan.

Callan rubbed his nose and shrugged. It was still there, the tension he felt at being amongst these trees, a tight knot in the pit of his stomach, the unsettling sense that he, Gold and Morgan were being watched. Resisting the urge to spin around and search the dark spaces between the trunks for alien shapes, he forced a smile, trying to lighten the moment and his own negative sense of this place.

'Do the best you can, Morgan. But remember that you've

turned up no forensic evidence so far. Nothing. Nada. Dick shit.'

Morgan rolled his eyes. 'Thanks for the support, Captain.'

'Pleasure.'

'Shouldn't we wait until morning, sir? First light?' Gold interrupted, turning towards Callan, the cigarillo held out to his side, clasped between two slender fingers, as if he'd slipped out of a cocktail party to have a quick smoke in the garden. 'This looks like a pretty impossible job in the dark.'

'Nothing's impossible,' Callan snapped.

Breaking eye contact, Gold dipped his head and gave a silent nod. Callan sighed. Gold was trying, he realized. *Trying in more ways than one.* But at least, on this case, he *was* trying hard to follow orders, to be effective. They would never be comfortable in each other's company: Callan descended from generations of factory workers, Edward Gold, the product of landed gentry. But Gold was attempting to join in, to be one of the lads, and in refusing to reciprocate, Callan knew he was being unfair. Unfair and juvenile. This case was stressful enough without tension within the team; tension that he, as senior officer, should alleviate, not exacerbate.

'The forecast says heavy rain later tonight,' Callan said, turning to Gold. 'We'll be lucky if there's anything left on this trunk, apart from the blood which has soaked into the bark and which I'm pretty sure will be exclusively Foster's.'

'But even so, we're under heavy leaf canopy here. I'm sure the print would be preserved,' Gold argued.

'Foster was killed close to forty hours ago. Leaving it another night, with rain forecast, will probably blow our chance of lifting anything useful from it. We're unlikely to lift anything useful from it even now.'

Gold frowned. 'Right, OK, sir.'

They lapsed back into tense silence as they watched Morgan and his SOCO team, one clutching a camera, the intermittent flash illuminating the darkness in hot white bursts, Callan shielding his eyes as unobtrusively as possible each time. *Bright flashes, another trigger for epilepsy. Everyone thinking that he was being a bad-tempered arsehole by demanding the cameraman warn him before firing off a shot.*

'The blood is from a handprint, the killer's handprint, I would say, given the height. Foster was only five foot eight,' Morgan murmured. 'So our man must have killed Foster, got his hands covered in blood and, at some point, perhaps when he was holding Foster up, touched his hand up here, right up here. Maybe . . . ' He paused for a few moments, making shapes in front of the tree, moving his hands and feet into different positions. 'Maybe to stabilize himself while he was holding Foster up.'

'Dumb,' Gold said.

'Not really,' Morgan countered. 'The handprint is on bark, so we've no chance of lifting prints from it.'

'Fuck,' Callan muttered with feeling.

'Hold on, sir. I'm not defeated yet.' Morgan pulled a microscope from his bag.

Callan looked at his feet; Gold continued to smoke, humming a soft tune under his breath, something classical, a tune Callan was unsurprised that he didn't recognize. After maybe five minutes – five tense minutes that felt like fifty – Morgan spoke again.

'Luck, the gods, my goddam genius, whatever, smiling on us for once! I may have a partial.'

Callan and Gold both stepped forward. Morgan held up a gloved hand, stopping them in their tracks.

'Not so fast, gentlemen. It's a partial – and when I say partial, I mean a sliver. It's on a section of the tree where the bark is missing, probably from woodlice or something like that.'

'Can you lift it?' Callan asked.

Morgan didn't answer for a moment.

'A fingerprint powder has recently been developed by scientists at London University to retrieve poachers' finger-prints from elephant's tusks, of all things. The size of the powder grains is much reduced, so it sticks more easily to fingerprint residues than traditional powders, even on rough, irregular surfaces such as ivory.'

'Or wood,' Callan said.

'I hope so, Captain, I certainly hope so. I was sent a sample, so I'll try it and see.' Morgan smiled, a slight, hopeful smile that morphed into a yawn. 'Why don't you and Gold go and get some sleep, sir, and I'll report back in the morning.'

Callan nodded. 'Fine.' Morgan was a consummate profes-sional and he was happy to leave him to it.

'I'll stay,' Gold chipped in.

Morgan shook his head. 'Thanks for the offer, Gold, but I'm fine with my two SOCOs.'

'I'm happy to stay and help out,' Gold repeated.

Another shake of the head from Morgan. 'As I said – we're fine. You'd only be twiddling your thumbs.' His gaze met Callan's for a brief moment and he winked.

'Morgan is a miserable shit, Gold,' Callan said, suppressing a smile. 'You head home, get some kip.'

Callan knew that he needed a break too, to catch up on some much-needed sleep, approach tomorrow with a clear head. But something was bothering him.

'Why was there so much blood on the killer's hands?' he said. 'Enough to soak the bark and leave that print?'

Morgan frowned. 'Because he or she had just murdered someone?'

Callan didn't rise to the sarcastic tone. 'The screwdriver missed all the major arteries, so there was no arterial spray. The handle of the screwdriver wasn't bloody. Foster died from drowning – drowning in his own blood – so I don't see why the killer had so much blood on his or her hands.'

'The screwdriver nicked the jugular vein, sir,' Gold interjected. 'Blood from severed veins doesn't have the force of arterial blood, but the jugular is still a major vessel. Foster bled outward as well as inward. His clothes bore substantial bloodstains.'

A shadow crossed Callan's face. 'Sure. But doesn't the psychology of a murderer make him or her want to minimize the amount of blood they get on themselves? Unless they don't want to get away with it, which isn't the case here.'

His gaze tracked from Gold to Morgan and back. They were both looking at him dubiously. Callan rated Morgan: he was down-to-earth and experienced. The jury was still out on whether Gold would make a good Special Investigation Branch detective, but he was intelligent and analytical and by offering to stay with Morgan tonight, he was showing commitment. Despite the weight of their united doubt, there was still a nagging voice at the back of Callan's mind telling him he was missing something important. The murderer had stayed with Foster. Taken the risk that Martha Wonsag would return from her toilet break at any moment, that Corporal Jace Harris or one of the other soldiers on duty would radio Foster and come to investigate when they didn't get a response. He had no idea why the killer stayed. It didn't make sense.

Everything about this case, about this crime scene, was telling him that the facts didn't add up, but he couldn't see it, just couldn't see what he was missing.

I'm not a psychologist. But on this case, I reckon you could use one.

The more he saw of this case, the more he was coming to the conclusion that Val Monks was right. But was he going to do anything about it? Or was he going to plough on alone?

At this moment, the only thing he could say for sure was that he needed to crash.

36

Jessie had jammed her feet into sky-high black patent leather heels, added a black pencil skirt and white silk shirt, power-dressing medicine to fortify her for this meeting – yet more dubious advice from the women's magazines she read on her six-monthly visit to the hairdressers. Now, tottering across the gravel drive, her stiletto heels catching on the smooth stones and tipping her off balance with each step, she cursed herself for having eschewed her usual ballet pumps, felt more high-class hooker than power exec.

Marilyn glanced across. 'Would you like to hold my arm?'

Jessie cast him a withering look. 'No, thank you.'

As she reached the stone steps and followed Marilyn through Hartmoor Psychiatric Hospital's oak front door, the dose of relief she felt at having escaped the gravel was tempered by the electric suit tightening around her throat, the bare wires snapping across her skin. Nothing had changed in the fifteen years since she herself had been incarcerated between these stately walls. The oak-panelled entrance hall was almost as she remembered it, the ceiling lower, the space smaller and lighter, the sun cutting in through windows either side of the front door. Her overwhelming sense, back then, had been of hugeness and darkness: a gaping, black, malignant space. There was nothing malign about it now – nothing, beyond her memories. It was merely an entrance hall, a desk, a bored-looking blonde receptionist studying her shell-pink nails.

Marilyn held up his warrant card. 'Detective Inspector Simmons. I've arranged to see one of your adult patients: Anne Lawson. This is my colleague, Doctor Jessica Flynn.'

The receptionist's gaze switched from her nails to his ID, from that to the computer, typing with two index fingers, shellacs clicking against the keys.

'I'll call Pamela Brown, the head psychiatric nurse.'

They waited in silence, Marilyn studying his feet, Jessie's gaze tracking around the hallway, absorbing every detail, her brain lodged a decade and a half ago, a scared and traumatized girl back then. She remembered arriving in the police car, driving down the long gravel drive, watching as the huge white house grew to fill the windscreen. She had been to a family hotel in Cornwall one summer that looked similar to this building – *before*, when Jamie was five and she was twelve – and as the psychiatric hospital grew nearer, she tried to hold on to that memory to stop the fear from overwhelming her. She hadn't known it at the time, but that had been their last holiday as a family, her parents' futile attempt to mend their relationship; Diane, unbeknownst to her mother, already waiting in the wings. Cornwall was still in the United Kingdom, so if a heart became available for Jamie, an air ambulance could fly them to London within the hour. Her parents had spent most of the week sniping at each other, while she and Jamie had roamed like a couple of savages: through the country-side to lie in fields of cows, holding hands and giggling until the herd had surrounded them, looking down with their gentle brown eyes at these odd two-legged intruders; down to the beach to charge into the waves and fish for crabs and tiddlers in rock pools; to the shops in the local village for ice creams. She still remembered Jamie's delight at finding a sea anemone, at pressing his finger against its plump, wet body; laughing when it popped away from his touch, a shimmering raspberry jelly.

She had closed her eyes as Hartmoor House drew near, tried to keep hold of those images, of her happy twelve-year-old self, of Jamie, so close, so real that she could almost reach out and touch him. But sudden silence, the engine being switched off, the heavy breath of the policeman as he twisted in his seat to face her, drove those images from her mind and she felt as if she would be sick from fear. She was fourteen and she was alone. Neither her mother nor her father had come to see her incarcerated.

A firm hand on hers, stilling the movement of her fingers. 'Stop,' Marilyn mouthed.

She had straightened the visitor's book, replaced the cap on the pen, lined it up flush with the edge of the book, rearranged the roses in the vase of flowers so that each rose was an identical distance from the next. She hadn't even realized that she'd been doing it. She returned the receptionist's quizzical look with a smile, knew that it must look twisted and pained.

'Detective Inspector Simmons? I'm Pamela Brown, the head psychiatric nurse.'

The nurse was a middle-aged woman. Having shaken Marilyn's hand, her gaze moved to Jessie. Her eyes lingered longer than they had on Marilyn – people's reactions usually the opposite – something changing in her face as she studied Jessie. A dawning recognition? Maintaining eye contact, trying to exude nothing but professional confidence, despite her ludicrous hooker heels, Jessie held out her hand, tensing her arm muscles to stop her hand from shaking.

'Doctor Jessica Flynn, Clinical Psychologist with the Defence Psychology Service.'

Pamela Brown nodded, her head tilted slightly to one side. She had pale grey eyes, made prominent by the dark brown of her hair.

'Pamela Brown. Have I met you—'

'I doubt it,' Marilyn cut in, surprising Jessie by barking out a short, cheery laugh. 'She's usually to be found in camouflage gear, hiding in trees. Not my cup of tea or yours, I'd imagine.' He held out an arm. 'Shall we?'

As they followed Pamela Brown up the stairs, Marilyn glanced over and mouthed, 'Thank you for coming.'

Jessie nodded, realizing he knew that something was badly wrong beyond a simple visit to interview a psychiatric patient, and she was grateful that he hadn't quizzed her.

'Anne Lawson has been here for nearly half a year now,' Brown said, sliding her security pass down the card reader, holding the door open for them. 'Referred by the NHS after outpatient treatment failed.'

'What is her diagnosis?' Jessie asked, following her down the corridor, looking neither left nor right, knowing that beyond those blank wooden doors with their small shat-terproof windows were identical, soulless bedrooms where people lay awake at night, staring up at the ceiling, trapped alone with their own personal demons. Narrow cells, each carved from a much larger room in this draughty old house, containing a bed, a bolted-down desk and chair and a single cupboard for the few clothes patients brought with them, a blind that slid up and down at the touch of a button between two layers of unbreakable safety glass – no cords, no material, nothing with which a patient could hang themselves; no pictures on the walls, no ornaments, no glass or heavy objects, nothing that could be used as a weapon or to self-harm. This floor was for the adults; juveniles were downstairs. But the layout, the décor, the heavy sense of dread and hopelessness, was the same.

They had taken her watch when she arrived, she remembered, and the only way she could tell the time was to look at the sky, which was why, when she was here, she had left the blinds open at night. All there was to do was to lie in that blank room alone and listen to the boy next door snoring and muttering as he slept, the sounds of the nurses talking and phones ringing at the nurses' station along the corridor, until footsteps – morning checks – the sound that would signal her release from solitary confinement. Night after night she stared at the shadows of the leaves from the oak outside her window playing across the scuffed white walls. She hated this helplessness, hated being trapped in this place with only her thoughts for company. Because no matter how hard she had tried to concentrate on other things – the patterns made by the shadows, the dawn chorus that she could barely hear through the thick glass – fear and helplessness found the cracks in her defences and trickled like corrosive acid into her brain. The acid of fear and the helplessness of betrayal. She had been at Hartmoor Psychiatric Hospital for a month when she celebrated her fifteenth birthday. A meaningless date, just another day to be marked off in her head.

A month that had felt like a lifetime. A month that was only the first of many.

'Anne Lawson was diagnosed with severe clinical depression.' Pamela Brown's words jerked her back to the present. 'She hasn't spoken since she arrived. You know the history?'

Jessie nodded, unable to meet the nurse's direct gaze. 'What about when Malcolm visits?'

'She doesn't speak to him either. He used to come often, bringing the baby with him, but he's only been once in the past two months.' She cast a glance over her shoulder. 'I got the impression that he, too, was struggling mentally.'

'How does she react with baby Harry?'

'She holds Harry on her knee. She rocks him and croons to him sometimes. You can tell that she loves Harry, but she doesn't speak to him. Anne has disappeared inside.'

'Does she communicate at all?'

'She draws sometimes.'

'What? What does she draw?'

'There's no pattern. Sometimes it's animals. Sometimes letters.'

'Words? Sentences?'

Brown shook her head. 'Letters. A few words.'

'Which words?' Jessie pressed.

'Various. Nothing memorable.'

Brown stopped outside a door and turned her pale grey gaze on Jessie.

'I'm expecting you to be sensitive, Doctor Flynn.' Her eyes moved to Marilyn. 'Detective Inspector. Lynsey Curtis one of our psychiatric nurses, is in with Anne now and will remain with her during your visit. If she feels, at any time, that Anne is becoming stressed, she will ask you to leave immediately. Is that understood?'

Feeling like the teenage girl she had been when last here, Jessie nodded.

Anne Lawson was sitting at a table in a small, sunny room, looking out over the gardens. Beyond the expanse of green was a wide sweep of the River Thames, a ribbon of polished silver in the morning sunlight. A long way off, to the left, the outskirts of Maidenhead rose from the landscape, spoiling the sweep of woods and fields with its Lego-like grey blocks.

Anne was beautiful. Jessie hadn't expected her to be. She had expected her to look hunched and folded in on herself, a physical manifestation of her mental state, as Jessie had perceived herself to look when she had been incarcerated here at Hartmoor. Anne's blonde hair was shoulder-length, her eyes a stunning, contrasting deep brown.

Jessie nodded to the nurse and then sat down at the table opposite Anne.

'Anne, my name is Jessie Flynn.' She spoke slowly and quietly, no edge or challenge to her tone. 'I'm a psychologist working with the police.'

Anne showed no reaction. Not even the flicker of an eyelid or a slight shift in the fix of her mouth to show that she had heard.

'Harry is fine, Anne, but Malcolm is missing. He has been missing for three days now. The police are concerned about him and need to find him.'

Anne continued to look straight ahead, her dark eyes impenetrable pools. No light in them. No expression.

'We need your help, Anne. We need you to help us find Malcolm.'

Jessie glanced over at Marilyn. He shrugged – *your call.* Not that she blamed him. They were clutching at straws, coming here. It was always understood that she would take the lead – but lead where?

'The police think that Malcolm may have been abducted.' She maintained the calm, gentle tone, though her words were anything but. 'Can you think of anyone he may have had a disagreement with? Anyone he may have argued with?'

Anne's gaze remained fixed on the spread of garden beyond the window, looking but not seeing, Jessie realized, her eyes illuminated only by the sunlight shining in through the glass, no light from inside. Jessie took a breath. She was full of jittery tension, the electric suit still snapping against her skin. She shouldn't have come; they shouldn't have come. This was a futile visit. She tried again, choosing her words carefully, aiming to provoke this time.

'The police think that Malcolm's disappearance may be linked to Danny's death. They don't know how or why, but it's a lead that they need to pursue.'

Still no reaction. Just the crackle of the electric suit against her skin, her throat constricted, limbs on fire.

'After Danny died, Malcolm contacted a number of people about his death. Was there anyone he talked about more than the others? Anyone who he said he had had problems with?'

A barely perceptible rigidity appeared in Anne's posture; or was she imagining it?

Jessie sat forward. 'Anne, you need to help us. You need to help us find Malcolm. Harry needs him, he misses his father.'

Anne's hands, already clenched into fists, tightened minutely. Jessie hadn't imagined that, she was sure that she hadn't.

'And he misses you, too, Anne. He's only a baby and he misses you. He misses his mum.'

A tiny noise, almost a yelp, and Anne's eyes swivelled to find Jessie's.

'I think you should leave now,' Nurse Curtis said, her voice panicky.

Ignoring her, Jessie tilted closer to Anne, lowering her own voice. 'Why did you and Malcolm throw Danny out? Why did you ban him from seeing his baby brother? Why, Anne? What did he do? Why did you isolate him?'

Sudden movement: Anne's fingers snaked around Jessie's wrist. Jessie flinched; Anne's grip tightened. In her peripheral vision, Jessie saw Marilyn step forward, gave a quick, almost imperceptible shake of her head, saw him move in front of the nurse, blocking her view, holding up one finger. *A minute. Give her one more minute.* Jessie kept her eyes fixed on Anne's, on those blank, brown eyes. Windows on the soul. *Windows on emptiness.*

Anne's other hand stole across the table and the tip of her index finger stroked the pale skin of Jessie's forearm. Anne's finger looped up and down, across, the feeling barely there, a tickle that set the hairs on Jessie's arm on end. Again – Anne's finger tracing the same lines, her chewed nails scratching this time, like the beak of a little bird. Jessie bit her lip to stop herself from wrenching her arm away. She felt as if she would explode from the tension building inside her, but she sat still, feeling the maddening scratch of Anne's nail on her skin. Again. Again. The ragged nail tracing the now familiar lines, the same letters on her skin.

'You should have stopped her. You should have let *me* stop her,' said Marilyn.

195

They were back in the car park.

Jessie shook her head. 'We came for a reason.'

'Jesus Christ,' Marilyn muttered.

Jessie's arm shook as she held it out, tilting her forearm so that the sun lit her pale skin and the grazed word written there.

'D-a-d-d-y,' Marilyn murmured. 'It seems like Malcolm Lawson has a lot to answer for.'

37

Flipping her rear-view mirror down, Jessie stared at the drawn oval reflected back at her, the ice-blue eyes still rabbit wide with shock and wet with tears. The eyes of a warrior, an upholder of principles – her father had told her that, once. The eyes of a psychotic.

Some people claimed that you could see mental illness in a person's eyes. Perhaps she was missing a vital component, because in all the years that she had treated patients, she had never looked into anyone's eyes and been able to see what was going on in their heads, normal or abnormal. Immediate diagnosis was the stuff of fiction as far as she was concerned.

What was mental illness anyway? Her profession was still debating, the sands still shifting beneath them, the brain perhaps far too complex an organ ever to be fully understood. Was mental illness a medical disease or was it a problem of living within society's norms? Was it merely a label for behaviour that most people – but not all – considered deviant? In Anne Lawson's eyes, Jessie had seen nothing.

No light. No depth. Almost as if an impenetrable barrier had been inserted right behind her pupils.

She had wondered when she went back to school – *after* – whether her classmates could see in her own eyes the truth of where she had spent the past year. They had been told that she had been living abroad, had moved because of her father's job – the father who had long since left them and married someone else, married Diane. Dubai: the location chosen because she would have been educated in English, wouldn't be expected to come back with knowledge of a foreign language.

Her old friends treated her differently, probably, she realized now as an adult with the benefit of maturity and hindsight, because they had forged new friendships during her absence, constructed a teenage existence that didn't include her. But at the time she was terrified – terrified that they could see right through her pupils and into her brain, see the lies lodged there, the deception.

They emptied the bins this morning. He's gone. Pandy has gone.

She had prepared in advance, taken six bin bags off the roll in the utility room before she'd left for school that morning, tucked them under her duvet, right where Pandy would have spent the day, knowing that Diane had no reason to come into her room now that she had destroyed the only thing that Jessie loved and cherished.

She used her pocket money to buy lighter fuel at the mini-market across the road from the school on the way home, the man behind the counter hesitating for a fraction of a second, giving her a questioning look, but selling it to her anyway, used to slipping packets of cigarettes over the counter to girls he knew to be underage, even though they looked five years older than they were, with their A-cup push-up bras, top buttons undone and school skirts rolled up bottom-skimming short.

Ear pressed to her father and Diane's bedroom door, listening to the regular, sucking sound of their breathing as they slept, Jessie was infused with a sense of weightlessness, of unreality. How easy to turn back now, tiptoe upstairs to her room, climb under her duvet and lie there awake until morning, sleep eluding her as it often did these days, pretending that she had never had these thoughts or plans. Then an image of Jamie rose in her mind, lying in the garden, looking up at the stars. *Do you want to go and live in the sky, Pandy?*

She took a step forward, her foot flexing heel to toe on the soft carpet, ears tuned for any changes in the pattern of their breathing. It was important that she was quiet, vital that she didn't wake them. She needed to show them. Show *her*.

Diane's clothes filled her dressing room, rows of expensive blouses and dresses in a rainbow of colours, a flock of exotic birds: the silks, soft waterfalls of fabric between Jessie's fingers as she pushed them into the bin bag; the lace, intricate doilies; the thousand-pound beaded dress that Diane had worn to a charity dinner a couple of weeks ago, heavy in her hands as it slid off the hanger.

It took her what felt like an eternity to empty the hangers, hardly daring to breathe, her arms shaking with every minute movement. It took her another eternity to empty all of Diane's drawers, sliding each one open a millimetre at a time, her pulse pumping so loudly in her ears that she thought people halfway down the street would hear it. She piled the cashmere jumpers into one bin bag, trousers into another. The only thing that she didn't touch was Diane's underwear, recoiling from touching something that her father's hands had grappled with.

The garden was smaller than that of her childhood home in Wimbledon, a quarter the size, a neat rectangle of manicured lawn bordered by clipped box hedging, a patio area by the back wall of the house made of Yorkstone, Diane had told her proudly one day, still relishing the opportunity to spend that marrying a corporate lawyer had afforded her.

But it was big enough. Big enough for her purpose.

The night was windless, the air still hot and muggy, even though it was 3 a.m. Mid-summer, London sweltering during the day, lazy and somnolent at night. She made a neat pyramid of the bin bags right in the middle of the lawn, as far from the fences and the back of the house as was possible. By touch, she unscrewed the lid of the lighter fuel and poured the whole lot on to the pile of bin bags, tossed the empty bottle on top.

She felt the box of matches in her shaking hand, the rough strip on the side as her fingers felt to slide it open in the dark. Striking one match, she let it fall on to the black plastic pyre.

Flames sprung at once with a fierceness that shocked her, and she stumbled backwards. It was seconds before the pile of bags was engulfed. Now that the fire was burning, the garden felt minuscule, the fences either side of her closing in, the space between them a sealed vacuum. The flames were leaping higher than she remembered in Wimbledon, hot orange and scarlet and the heat from the bonfire was intense. She stepped backwards, her bare heel colliding with the edge of the Yorkstone. She couldn't breathe. The whole garden seemed to be filled with black smoke. Black smoke and heat so extreme that she felt as if she would melt from it.

She was frightened now. Really frightened.

She couldn't catch her breath and she couldn't see either with the black smoke and the tears that were clouding her eyes. Turning towards the house, she frantically searched for a hose, but they didn't have one, only a watering can painted dark green and adorned with red and yellow peasant flowers. Snatching it up, Jessie wrenched open the kitchen door and ran to the sink.

Outside again, the filled watering can in her hand, she saw that the flames had found one of the side fences, a blue ribbon of scampering fire. She tossed the water at the fence, heard the fire hiss, smoke – barely a puff – recede for a second, before bursting across the damp patch to lick at the side of the house. Pulling her pyjama top over her head, she ran to the fence and pressed her top to the flames, the hot fire tumbling in all directions. Her pyjama top was burning in her hands, the flames running up her arms. Screaming, she dropped the flaming top, flapping her scorched hands to ease the heat, the pain.

A gunfire crack behind her and the kitchen window shattered.

Yanking at the back-door handle, feeling the burnt skin on her hand stick to the metal and peel agonizingly from her palm, she tore a blind path through the kitchen to the bottom of the stairs, slammed straight into her father coming down, leaping them two at a time, Diane behind him, her face white and frightened.

'Call the fire brigade, Diane.' Her father yelled. 'Quickly. Do it quickly and then get outside. Out into the street.'

201

Dizziness. A huge wave of nausea swept over Jessie and she vomited.

The walls caved in, the floor came up to meet her and everything went dark. She felt distant hands grab her under the arms and haul her up, a puff of air as the front door was opened and she was carried out on to the street.

'Breathe, Jessie. Breathe.'

She drank in air. Another wave of nausea flooded through her and she vomited again, crouching on all fours in the street, vomited until there was nothing left inside her stomach. Curling up into a ball on the pavement, she pulled her arms over her head and jammed her eyes shut. *Pandy loves you too, Jessie.*

A voice echoed somewhere nearby. Her father's voice.

'What have you done, Jessie? *What the hell have you done?*'

38

Major Val Monks was in her office, an unprepossessing, small, square space with the ubiquitous military offices' grey vinyl-tiled floor and scuffed white walls, the fittings cheap and functional. The last time Callan had entered this room, in early November, he had been recovering from the epileptic attack he'd suffered during the last autopsy he'd attended with Val. Back then, the vase on her desk had been filled with hot-pink tulips. He remembered that detail, locking on to the buoyant colour in the sea of grey and white, his vision still clouded from the attack. Today, lemon yellow daffodils occupied the vase, lifting the atmosphere in the utilitarian space.

Sitting behind her computer, tortoiseshell reading glasses perched on the bridge of her nose, lick of peach lipstick that had run into the crow's feet radiating from the corners of her mouth, Callan could have taken Monks for a middle-aged secretary. Sexist and patronizing, he realized with a sense of shame, his brain naturally pursuing the old, familiar paths that he'd been taught by his father as a boy, that he'd spent most of his adult life trying to reprogramme. Attitudes that women in the Army, even women of Monks' age and professional stature, had to deal with every day of their working lives; attitudes that shifted from lechery to dismissiveness as the woman aged.

He rapped his knuckles against the door frame. Val looked up, finding his gaze over the rim of her glasses.

'You got a moment, Val?'

'For you? Of course, Callan.'

Dropping her glasses on the desk, she tipped back in her chair and rolled her shoulders. 'Coffee?'

'You're going to risk giving me caffeine after last time?'

Val laughed. 'Decaf only, in your case. I don't want to have to wheel out my decades-old medical school training and actually deal with a live patient. I'm not sure that I'd be able to tell one end from the other these days.'

Stepping into the room, Callan closed the door behind him.

'So what's up?' she asked.

'I was at Blackdown last night with the dogs. One of them signalled a bloody handprint on the tree under which Stephen Foster's corpse was found. Morgan confirmed that the blood was Foster's, but not the handprint. Most of the print was on bark, high up, around the side of the tree, virtually invisible to the naked eye, which is why Morgan didn't notice it the first time around.

'That's a step in the right direction.' Val held his gaze, raising one eyebrow in query. 'Isn't it?'

'It is,' he murmured.

'But?'

'But I don't believe that the handprint should have been there. Not if the scenario, Foster's death, played itself out in the way that we concluded it had during his autopsy.'

'You've lost me, Callan. I think that the conclusion we came to from the autopsy – a cold, methodical killer – was pretty robust.' There was an edge of defensiveness to her tone.

Flopping into a chair across the desk from her, Callan held up his hands. 'Hear me out, Val.'

'I'm happy to do that, Captain.'

'So, we have a stab wound to the throat, but a tentative stab wound. That was the word you used in the initial autopsy, wasn't it? Tentative.'

She nodded.

'So the stab wound was tentative, not much force behind it, and Foster bled slowly. He died by drowning in his own blood, rather than from blood loss.'

'Yes, but it's a matter of timing. Given the nature of the wound, blood loss would certainly have killed him without emergency medical treatment. He happened to drown first, poor kid.'

Callan sat forward, resting his forearms on Monks' desk. He noticed her gaze take in the dressing covering the dog bite on his hand, but she didn't say anything, wanting to avoid, no doubt, another accusation of mothering him. He had thoughts, ideas that were beginning to link together in his mind, making a thread – gossamer thin, but a thread all the same. A thread that he believed contradicted the conclusions they'd come to in the autopsy, the conclusions that he, based on experience from past murders he'd investigated, had automatically assumed were correct. He ploughed on, ignoring the cynicism written all over Val's face.

'There was definitely someone else with Foster, someone

who stayed with him, held him up against the tree for three or four minutes after the stab wound was inflicted.' He waited for another confirming nod before continuing. 'Morgan said there was no way Foster could have thrown the screwdriver as far as it was thrown, not with a stab wound in his throat. So we can assume that this second person pulled the screwdriver from Foster's throat – carefully – wiped it clean of prints and tossed it to where we found it.'

Eyes narrowing, Val gave a suspicious half-nod. 'Where are you going with this?'

Callan held up his hands again. 'Just bear with me.'

'I'm bearing. Just. But I'm still bearing.'

'The only way that I can see this unknown person, the person we've assumed is a murderer, getting that much blood on his or her hand is if they put that hand directly over Foster's throat wound for a period of time.'

Monks shifted dubiously in her seat.

'How else? Come on, Val, how else?'

Pinching the bridge of her nose between her thumb and index finger, Val massaged where her glasses had left two elliptical red marks. 'Why would a murderer do that, Callan?'

'If he or she was trying to save Foster.' Even as he said it, he realized how unconvincing his words sounded.

'Save him?' Monks clearly hadn't expected that. '*Save him?* Come on, Callan. I agree that the facts don't quite add up, but I've performed any number of autopsies where the facts don't *quite* add up. Pathology is a science, but it's not an exact one. We're trying to draw conclusions from the dead. Sometimes I feel that it's one up from reading the blinking tea leaves.'

Callan met and held her cynical gaze. 'What if it was

suicide? What if Foster committed suicide and that person, that second unknown person, tried to save him?'

'Suicide?' She looked at him sideways, scratching her head and frowning.

'The wound could have been self-inflicted, couldn't it?'

'Physically, yes. But mentally . . . really? A boy, a sixteen-year-old boy, stabbing himself in the throat with a screwdriver? I don't see that happening. And then this good Samaritan arrives out of nowhere, like Batman?'

'You're not a psychologist, Val. You said that yourself.'

Val threw up her hands. 'I don't need to be a bloody psychologist to recognize someone who's clutching at straws, Captain. I only need to be vaguely compos mentis – and I hope you'll agree I'm that.'

Callan scratched his fingers through his dirty blond stubble and sighed. 'I appreciate that it sounds fanciful.'

'Fanciful? You ever get bored of being in the Branch, I can see a great career for you in crime writing.'

Callan held up a hand, halting her flow. 'I appreciate that it sounds fanciful, but it also explains the facts. Explains the inconsistencies.'

'The murderer being a looney tune also explains the inconsistencies, which, considering he or she murdered a sixteen-year-old lad in a pretty gruesome way, is virtually a given, I'd say.'

Monks liked Callan, liked him and rated him. He was the most intuitive Special Investigation Branch detective she had ever worked with. But even she knew that being shot in the back by Scott had hit him hard, both physically and mentally. He might have been declared fit to return to duty, but he looked terrible. Pale and washed out, his eyes shot with red and flitting constantly, alert to everything, even sitting here in her office, the door shut firmly behind him.

'Call the Defence Psychology Service, Callan. That girl you worked with on the Starkey case. She was good.'

'I don't need help.'

Monks held up her hands, palms up, as if each was a weighing scale. 'The male ego versus solving the case.'

'It's got nothing to do with my ego,' Callan snapped.

'Then call her. Because I'm done with this case, Callan. From the autopsy, it could be suicide absolutely – but I don't buy it. I simply don't buy the psychology. I don't buy the fact that a sixteen-year-old, five months in the Army, would fall so far as to stab himself in the throat with a bloody screwdriver. And I don't buy Batman, or any other superhero, turning up in that wood at Blackdown in the nick of time.'

Wearily, Callan pushed himself to his feet. 'Thanks for your time, Val.' He pulled open the door.

'Call her, Callan.'

He lifted a hand, but didn't turn.

'*Call her.*'

39

Jessie had tidied her desk, aligning every article, her blotter, notebook, files, pens and pencils, so that their straight edges lined up perfectly with the straight sides of her desk; rearranged the furniture, shuffling the legs of the two battered leather bucket chairs back into the worn discs in the carpet they had lived in for the two and a half years she'd occupied this office – who had shifted them while she'd been away? – swept the imaginary dust that the office cleaners had missed from the windowsills. But still she felt as if she'd explode from the tension inside her; the urge to claw her hands down her face, her arms, tear the skin from her bones was almost overwhelming. Anything to rid herself of the intense snap and hiss of the electric suit.

A knock at the door. *Shit, Ryan Jones.* She'd been so occupied with tidying that she hadn't noticed the wall clock's hands creep to 12.00 p.m. She took a breath, a second, holding the air inside her lungs for longer this time, exhaling slowly through her nostrils, repeating the process as she crossed the room to the door, the deep yoga breathing doing nothing to calm the suit's heat.

'Come in, Ryan.' Her voice shook, but the boy didn't seem to notice. She held out her hand, which also shook. He didn't seem to notice that either. In their last session, two days ago, he had swerved away from her outstretched hand, his body rigid, hazel eyes fixed on some distant horizon. This time was no different. He was no more relaxed at the idea of this session than he had been the first one. Jessie responded to his stiff salute with a smile and a nod towards the bucket chairs.

'Take a seat. Either one.'

He chose the chair furthest from the window, the one in slightly more shadow, pressing himself right against its back, spine ramrod straight, as far away from Jessie as he could physically get without tipping the chair over backwards in his desire to escape her scrutiny. His bitten nails made claws on the chair's arms. He looked very young, the rash of acne peppering his jaw and neck stark against the washed-out white of his skin, deep black ringing his soft hazel eyes, their pupils devoid of light. Looking at him, Jessie wondered which of the two of them looked worse. She had deliberately not sought out a mirror since her visit to the Hartmoor Psychiatric Hospital this morning.

Sitting opposite Ryan, placing her hands on her own chair's arms exactly as he had done, planting her feet, in their black leather hooker heels, as close as equidistant to Ryan's as she could manage whilst maintaining a vague sense of decency in her tight pencil skirt, Jessie tried to catch his gaze. Developing rapport, a successful connection, with another person was only in small part about the words spoken. *Remember that your body has a really loud mouth,* one of her professors had told her. Mirroring another person's body position and language, the stiffness of their stance, the tilt of their head, the way they moved their hands, whether they held eye contact or not, helped connect with that person at a subconscious level, and Jessie used the technique in virtually every one of her sessions. Her patients wouldn't – shouldn't – consciously realize what she was doing, but their subconscious would tell them that she was on their wavelength, someone to be liked and, more importantly in her job, to be trusted. With Ryan Jones, animosity and mistrust pulsing from him like a living thing, Jessie needed to use every psychological trick in the book to try to crack a chink in that armoured carapace of his. In their first session, she'd failed spectacularly and she couldn't afford this second session to go the same way. She wouldn't stand a hope of successfully accessing his mind, of him allowing her to, without good rapport.

'Thank you for coming in again, Ryan.'

He continued to look at his feet.

'The last time we talked you told me about your mum.'

His gaze jumped from the floor to find hers briefly, before flicking away.

'The last time we talked, I said that I thought you should spend your time on people who need it,' he muttered. 'Men and women wounded in combat. People with post-traumatic stress disorder. People who *need* your help.'

You're deemed a suicide risk. She didn't say it. *You need my help.*

Because of her visit to Hartmoor this morning, she hadn't had the time or the inclination to give much thought as to how to play this session – unprofessional, she knew. But she had researched his background in the two days since their last meeting, accessed his Army personnel records, read his entrance application and interview notes. She knew that he had been taken into care at the age of eleven, placed, not into a children's home, but with a foster family. The placement hadn't worked out and he'd been bounced around other foster families, how many wasn't clear. All she knew was that the care system seemed to have done him few favours. She had memorized the key points in all those files and left them on her desk. The last thing he needed, after his hike around the care system as a young boy, was to be faced with yet another adult clutching a file of notes on him. His life depersonalized to lines of neat black type.

'You were taken into care at the age of eleven.'

His eyes raised and his jaw dropped. Jessie cut him off before he could verbalize the 'How the hell did you know?' growing on his lips.

'It's in your Army personnel files,' Jessie continued, her tone relaxed, unchallenging, face angled obliquely, as his was, so that he could look at her, but also easily break eye contact and find the window.

'Does everyone have access?'

'Everyone in your chain of command, on request. And us, of course, on request. Privacy isn't one of the Army's strong points. We're all supposed to live in each other's pockets and love it.'

His legs tensed and his feet pressed flat against the carpet, tipping the chair back slightly, shifting the front legs from their worn discs. Jessie resisted the sudden, intense urge to make him stand, slot the chair legs back into their discs, tell him to sit still and stop disturbing the balance, the order in her office.

Tearing her gaze from the carpet, she asked, 'Why were you taken into care?'

He lifted his shoulders. 'Because social services decided that it was the best thing for me.'

'Why?'

Another careless shrug. 'Because I skipped school once too often.'

'Why?'

'Is that all you say?' He sneered. 'Why? The "why" parrot.'

'It's as good a word as any and, as long as it works, I'll keep on saying it. As soon as it stops working, I'll try something else.'

He rolled his eyes and once again Jessie was reminded of a petulant schoolboy, sitting in the back row of class, watching the clock tick its way to the end of the school day.

'I don't have to talk to you.'

'No,' Jessie agreed. 'You don't. But talking to me might help. That's why you were referred.'

She wanted to help him – it was her job, and her responsibility to help him – but she knew that this boy must have heard the words 'I want to help you' or some variant of that theme more times than he'd had hot dinners, and each time it proved to be an empty promise from an adult who was more concerned with ticking boxes than understanding and meeting the emotional needs of a child. Most children who entered the care system were viewed as a stack of papers, not an individual with their own hopes and dreams. The system, madly overstretched since Baby P's death, no one wanting to be the next face on the cover of the *Sun* demonized under the headline 'Blood on Their Hands'. Ryan Jones's trust in adults would be in tatters; playing the distant adult, the professional psychologist, wasn't going to help her win his confidence. She needed to get closer to him than that, more on his level. She was twenty-nine, but she looked young enough, vulnerable enough, traumatized enough to be ten years younger. She looked as she felt – broken inside. Like him.

'How about I tell you about myself instead?'

Another careless shrug.

Jessie ploughed on. 'I was taken into care when I was fourteen. Actually, scratch that. It wasn't care—' She was taking a massive risk and she knew it. No one in the Army, not even Gideon, knew about her background, her eleven-month incarceration in Hartmoor Psychiatric Hospital. She should have declared it in her application, but she had buried that experience so deep in her psyche that, until this morning, she could almost have believed it had happened to another child, in another life. 'It was a psychiatric hospital.'

Ryan didn't say anything – he still wasn't going to allow himself to be visibly drawn in – but he hadn't expected that information because he looked up, eyebrows raised slightly in surprise. Instead of holding his gaze and smiling as she would with most other patients, after a brief second of eye contact, Jessie flicked her gaze to the window, circled it around the walls, a moment later, back to meet his, the movement deliberately flaky, teenaged. Matching his body language, his attitude.

'My brother committed suicide, after a long illness, when he was seven and I was fourteen. My father had left my mother, Jamie and me for another woman two years earlier. He couldn't deal with my brother's illness, he wasn't strong enough. I was sent to stay with my father and his new wife after my brother's death, because my mum couldn't cope any more. I burnt their house down. It was an accident. I was just trying to burn some of Diane's clothes, but the fire got out of hand, tore through their house and spread to two neighbouring houses . . . ' she tailed off with a shrug.

He still didn't say anything, but Jessie noticed a half-smile and a further, slight, widening of his eyes. 'Why did you burn her clothes?'

'Because I hated her.'

'And now?'

Jessie shrugged. 'I still hate her.'

Another slight smile. 'So what happened?'

'I was tried in a youth court. My stepmother insisted that I'd been trying to kill them, my father protested, but not very much. He was, still is, completely dominated by her. The court took my history into account . . . ' A pause while she swallowed the lump in her throat. ' . . . my brother. I was given a Youth Rehabilitation Order that required me to undertake an indefinite stay at a secure psychiatric hospital.'

'How long were you there?'

'Nearly a year.'

'If you'd been sent to a young offenders' institution, you'd probably only have got three or four months.'

The irony wasn't lost on her. It was one of the reasons that she had become a Clinical Psychologist. She waited, watching him; his thoughts, as he processed the information she'd shared, were reflected in minute changes of facial expression.

'Does all that appear in your Army personnel file?' he asked.

'None of it.'

'So if I tell them, you might lose your job.'

'Or perhaps they'll promote me. What do they say? Takes one to know one.'

'Takes a fuck-up to know a fuck-up.'

'So they say.'

A pause. She had been looking directly at him, he at the window. Now his gaze found hers.

'But you're not a fuck-up, Ryan,' she said softly.

'Aren't I?'

'I don't think that you are.'

They held each other's gaze. His eyes were a soft hazel. Gentle and kind. Too gentle for the Army. Too gentle for life.

'And you?' he asked.

If only you knew.

'You were your mother's carer? A child carer. That's why you missed school, wasn't it, Ryan?'

'Yes.'

Despite what she had told him, she could still feel animosity pulsing from him; animosity mixed with an intense dose of *I don't need your sympathy*. Tempered, though, with that thread of connection that her opening up to him had strung between them. His hands moved from their grip on the chair's arms and folded into his lap. A few moments later, Jessie followed, folding her hands also, settling them on to her skirt.

'My mother has motor neurone disease. She was diagnosed when I was five. We were fine for a few years, but it was getting worse. By the time I was ten, she couldn't do anything for herself. Couldn't eat, couldn't bath, couldn't get herself into bed.' His voice trembled. 'The powers that be decided that she'd be better off in a home for disabled adults and that I'd be better off in a foster home.'

'How many foster families did you have?'

'Eight.'

Eight. In five years from the age of eleven to sixteen. Christ, she hadn't expected the number to be that high.

'You're going to ask "Why?" again, aren't you?'

Jessie nodded. 'I am the "why" parrot, after all.'

'And what do you think I'm going to say?' His tone suddenly aggressive. Aggression mixed with vulnerability. 'That no one wanted me?'

'It's the care system that's broken, not you.'

'How would you—' He broke off, his eyes finding the window again. 'Why would anyone want a child who wasn't theirs?' he murmured. 'Adoption I can understand, but fostering?'

However much Jessie wanted to refute what he was saying, she had a feeling that he was right. Teenagers are a pain – she knew that well enough herself. Her own flesh and blood hadn't wanted her teenaged self.

A cloud passing across the sun cast Ryan's face in shadow. 'I had to change schools four times in the five years because some of the families lived in different towns. I couldn't keep in touch with any of my friends. I gave up trying to make new ones because I knew that they wouldn't last. I'd come back from school to find my stuff packed into boxes, stacked in the hall. The family would have called children's services while I was at school and told them they couldn't cope and then my social worker would turn up.' His voice shook. 'They didn't even let me pack my own things. By the eighth family, the last family, I started going to bed in my clothes. I'd lie underneath the duvet in my clothes every

217

night, so that I'd be prepared when they came to tell me that I had to move again. I left on the day of my sixteenth birthday. I got to choose for once, and I got to pack my own things.'

Jessie caught the clock on the wall above her desk. Two thirty; she was running out of time. 'Is that why you joined the Army? For security?'

He nodded.

'So what's not working now, Ryan?' she asked gently.

'Everything's working.'

'Ryan.'

Shaking his head, Ryan stood. 'It's two thirty. I need to be back at base for three.'

'Ryan.'

A shrug. 'It's hard adjusting, that's all. The discipline . . .'

It wasn't that; Jessie knew it wasn't that.

'Are you being bullied?'

'No. There's nothing, I told you.' He fiddled with the rim of his navy beret. 'Look, I . . . a bit, OK. The making friends thing. It's like I don't know how to any more.'

They walked together to the door.

'I'll see you again the day after tomorrow,' she said.

'No. I don't need to come again.'

'I'll see you anyway. Once more.'

'But I told you, I don't need to see you again.' He looked desperate. 'It was supposed to be confidential.'

'Our sessions? They are confidential. You have my word on that.'

'No.' He shook his head. 'Not our sessions.'

'What then?'

The sound of a telephone ringing down the hall, a moment

218

of silence, Jenny's warbled voice and then louder, as she called down the corridor to Jessie.

'Telephone call for you, Jessie. Shall I put it through to your office?'

'You have to go,' Ryan said.

'Whoever it is can wait.' Jessie raised her voice. 'Ask them to hold for a minute, please, Jenny. What was supposed to be confidential, Ryan?'

'The chaplain. I told you before that I spoke to the chaplain. He seemed trustworthy, seemed like he would give a shit.' A shadow crossed his face. 'It was supposed to be confidential. He said that our discussion would be confidential.'

'The Army has a duty of care to ensure that you are mentally fit to serve. The chaplain didn't believe that was the case.'

'Even so.'

Even so. He was right. His discussion with the chaplain should have been confidential.

'Why do adults always let you down?' His voice was bitter.

'They don't.' *Not always.*

'Like fucking hell they don't.'

Back in her office, Jessie picked up the telephone.

'Jenny, I'm here now.'

'Don't you want to know who it is before I put them through?'

Not really. She was beyond caring.

'It's a Mr Flynn. Irish.' A tone of amusement. 'Your father, I presume?'

'Tell him I'm not here.'

'I've already told him that you are here.'

Jessie sighed. 'Fine. Put him through.'

Her index finger poised a millimetre from the receiver, she waited until she had heard the transfer go through, breathing on the end of the line, then a tentative, 'Jessie.'

Jamming her finger on the receiver, she cut him off. Dropping the receiver into the cradle, grabbing her coat and handbag, she jogged down the corridor past Jenny, hearing the phone on her desk ringing again, knowing exactly who it would be, calling back. Her father having no idea, in his total and utter self-absorption, that his daughter would have deliberately cut him off.

Why do adults always let you down?

It was supposed to be confidential.

What had he discussed with the chaplain? And why had the chaplain broken his vow of confidentiality?

40

The garage was situated in a twee cul-de-sac of pastel-coloured houses near Guildford town centre, a few roads back from the historic cobbled high street. Marilyn parked his Z3 on double yellow lines and climbed out, shucking off his black suit jacket to reveal a short-sleeved dark grey shirt, the unseasonal lunchtime heat overcoming even his pathological reluctance to show his pasty white skin beyond the neck up.

In one of the mews houses towards the far end of the cul-de-sac someone was practising violin arpeggios, the lament competing with Coldplay's 'A Rush of Blood to the Head' issuing from the gaping doors and windows of Marshall and Sons, Automotive Repair Shop. Outwardly respectable, with its Farrow and Ball Chappell Green paint and sign written in Bookman Old Style proclaiming that Marshall and Sons were open for business six days a week, Marilyn knew Johnny Marshall of old and knew better.

A silver 2016 Range Rover Sport occupied one bay inside the garage, a black Audi Q5 the other, the Audi raised to head height on a four-post automotive lift. A woman in lemon-yellow Capri pants, sunglasses tucked into her auburn hair, was standing beside the Range Rover, giggling with Johnny Marshall. Marilyn rapped his knuckles on its rear window to attract Johnny's attention. Casting his gaze past the woman, Johnny's eyes widened as they found Marilyn's.

'Give me a minute, sir, while I finish serving this young lady.'

He was originally from Southend-on-Sea, Marilyn knew, had adopted a Surrey counties accent when he'd moved to Guildford and set up this garage twelve years ago, a direct appeal to the middle-class ladies who brought their family four-wheel drives here for reasonably priced MOTs, services and tyre refits and the chance to flirt with Johnny for half an hour while he was sorting out their motors. Late thirties and without a wife, let alone any sons – legitimate ones, at any rate – he was a significantly better-looking version of Sylvester Stallone, with the same gym-pumped physique, square jaw and brown puppy-dog eyes. Marilyn suspected that, for some of the housewives, it was more than their motor Johnny serviced, but with his own lifestyle and dubious taste in women, he was a man standing in a glass-house throwing stones, making any comment on that score.

'I'll wait in your office then, shall I, Johnny?'

'No . . . I . . . uh . . . why don't you wait outside, sir? It's a lovely sunny morning. I'll be finished in a second.'

Marilyn nodded, skirted around the back of the Range Rover and headed straight into Johnny's office. It was cramped, messy and oven hot, a small window behind the desk opening on to the cobbled mews, which afforded little breeze, a plate-glass window looking out over the garage workshop. A couple of nude pictures of women torn from a hard-core porn magazine were taped to the front of Johnny's desk drawers, so that he could appreciate them without any of his respectable lady clients realizing that they were there. Marilyn's gaze found the mini-fridge, tucked behind the filing cabinet. Pulling the door open, savouring for a brief moment the blast of cold air, he extracted a Carlsberg and settled himself on to the two-seater brown leather sofa opposite the desk. It exhaled a puff of warm, dusty air as he sank into it.

'Right, I'm—' Johnny broke off when he saw the beer in Marilyn's hand. 'For fuck's sake.' No need for fake Surrey accents when it was only him and Marilyn. 'Why don't you go on and 'elp yourself, DI Simmons.'

Marilyn smiled. 'Surely these are kept for visitors, because I don't imagine for a moment that you'd drink on the job, would you, Johnny? Not while operating heavy lifting equipment? Some of the stories I could tell you about mechanics being crushed to death under lifting equipment would make your hair curl. Not to mention being over the limit whilst driving.'

'Yeah, yeah. And what do you want?' Johnny snapped.

Marilyn held out the cast of the tyre print that Burrows had made. 'I need your help to identify the make of tyre and the make and model of vehicle these tyres are fitted to.'

Johnny rolled his eyes. 'You think my life is so narrow that I can tell you exactly what make of tyre it is and which cars use it just from lookin' at it? Go to freakin' Kwik Fit. They're keen as mustard. They'll 'elp you out.'

'Why would I need to go to Kwik Fit when I have you, Johnny? Doyen, as you are, of the automotive service sector.'

Last year, Marilyn had worked with the Metropolitan

Police to break up a stolen car racket, in which Johnny was involved. Luxury cars lifted from the streets of Mayfair and Belgravia, destined for a new life in Eastern Europe or Africa, dropping in on their way down the A3 to Portsmouth Docks to have their genuine number plates switched for fakes and to be furnished with forged DVLA ownership documents behind Marshall and Sons' Chappell Green garage doors. Johnny had turned police witness and got off with an eighteen-month sentence, suspended for two years, and two hundred hours' of unpaid community service. Marilyn had used him occasionally in the year since for advice on automotive-related cases and a cheap service for his Z3, visiting frequently enough to remind Johnny that he still owed him for his lenient sentence and that payback would be a long, drawn-out, unrelentingly painful process. Their relationship was one of comfortable contempt from both sides.

'OK, OK, give it 'ere.' Johnny grudgingly held out his hand and Marilyn passed the cast over. Johnny took a moment, holding the cast up to the light, rotating it in his hands. 'Well, it's not from a four-by-four,' he muttered. 'I've seen enough of them 'ere to know that.'

'So no farmer's vehicles, forestry commission vehicles or anything like that?'

'No.' Johnny smirked. 'And no Surrey ladies-who-lunch either.' His puppy-dog eyes met Marilyn's briefly, before sliding away. 'And it's not from any of them poxy little city cars, Micras and the like.'

There was a click-clack of heels on concrete and an attractive woman with long cinnamon hair pulled up into an untidy chignon poked her head in through the office door.

'I've got a slow puncture.' She glanced at her watch. 'But

224

I need the car fixed in time to get to my tennis lesson at two o'clock.'

Johnny smiled and held up a hand. 'Give me a minute, please, Mrs Barker, and I'll come and help you.' The Surrey accent firmly back in place.

When she had walked back to her car, he redirected his attention to Marilyn. 'Leave it with me, can you?'

'It's urgent.'

'Why?'

'Suspected abduction.'

'Well, it's going to take me time to search all the manu-facturers' brochures, innit? It's not a five-minute job.'

'You've got until four p.m., Johnny.'

'For Christ's sakes, when are you gonna get off my back?'

Marilyn drained the rest of his beer, lobbed the empty can into Johnny's bin and pushed himself to his feet. 'When you learn not to get caught.'

'Thanks for the tip, Detective Inspector.' Johnny sneered and rolled his eyes. 'I'll see what I can do about that then.'

41

Callan looked across his desk to where Gold was sitting, lowering his mobile phone from his ear. A deep furrow of concern had entrenched itself in his brow.

'You OK, Gold?'

A pensive nod. 'I've been on the phone to the Irish Garda.'

'Background checks?'

'Yes.'

'The chaplain?'

'How did you know, sir?'

'Lucky guess.'

A contemplative. 'Mmm.'

'So what did you find out?'

'Before joining the Army, Michael O'Shaughnessy was pastor at a church in a harbour town called Dungarvan, County Waterford, on the south coast of Ireland.'

'And?'

Gold balanced his mobile upright on one corner, and spun it around on the surface of his desk.

'Gold.'

'Sorry, yes. He, uh, he was accused of sexual assault by the fifteen-year-old daughter of one of his parishioners.'

'Jesus.' Callan slung his pen down with a clatter. 'What the hell is a man accused of sexual assault doing working on a training base full of sixteen- and seventeen-year-olds?'

'Hang on.'

'For fuck's sake, this reads like a low-budget TV series – the Catholic chaplain with a history of sexual misconduct. It doesn't get any more sickly stereotypical than that, does it?'

'Hang on, sir. Hang on.' Gold held up his hands. 'Let me finish.'

Callan nodded. 'OK, finish.'

'The girl accused him of raping her. Full penetrative—'

'Yes, all right, and . . . ?'

'And she was examined by a police doctor and found still to be a virgin. No sign of penetrative sexual activity. Nothing, nada.'

Callan subsided in his chair, embarrassed by his earlier flare of anger. 'So the girl lied and that was the end of it?'

Gold spun his mobile again and shook his head. 'Not quite. She changed her accusation to oral sex, said that he'd forced her to give him blow jobs.'

'Nice. What happened next?'

'Her testimony was discredited by then, so no charges were brought. She was seen by a psychologist after the second accusation and was found to have . . . ' He glanced down at the notes he'd made. 'Immature Personality Disorder.'

Callan rolled his eyes. 'Immature Personality Disorder? Is there really such a thing?'

Gold nodded, holding up one slender finger. 'The disorder usually develops in teenagers and is indicated by the absence of mature behaviour.'

'Immaturity indicated by the absence of mature behaviour. You don't say.'

Gold read on, putting on a bored monotone this time, enjoying this unexpected sojourn in Callan's good books. 'People with mature behaviour know the difference between maturity and childishness, but with this disorder there is no such distinction and the patient acts childishly at all times.'

'Who the hell was that written by? Noddy?'

Gold laughed. 'There's more, sir.'

Callan fiddled with a paperclip. 'Go on, surprise me.'

'Patients with this disorder live in a world of imagination. They do not think of the future and cannot take responsibility. They also do not understand the consequences of their actions.'

Callan broke the paperclip in two and threw the two halves into his waste-paper bin. 'So the chaplain is clean?'

'The Garda gave me nothing else, so it looks like he is.' Gold scanned his notes again, quickly. 'The girl was also said to have had a crush on the chaplain for a number of months before she made the accusation.'

Was she blind as well as immature? Callan didn't voice it, recognized sensitivities in the office regarding the Church.

'It's not unknown, sir.'

'What? The Catholic Church and dubious sexual allegations?'

'No. Hysterics. Teenage girls. Fantastical accusations. Focusing on a power or authority figure.'

Callan sighed and nodded. 'And the moral of this story is, never move to a small town in Ireland, Gold. There's not enough shit to do there and you'll lose your mind. Thanks, good work. I'm going to see Corporal Jace Harris again. Keep going with the background checks and I'll see you later.'

42

Sixteen years ago

Nye lay in his narrow single bed and listened to the sound of sleeping boys breathing all around him, to the snuffles, the soft, cottony rustle of a duvet as one of his dorm mates turned in his sleep.

He was the only one awake. He had tried to force himself to sleep for how many days now? He'd lost count. He had lain in his bunk bed, drifting between half-slumber and wakefulness, never feeling soothed enough to fall into a deep sleep, unused to sharing his space with so many others, wanting more than anything to be back in his own bed, in his own room, at home. He knew that his mother thought she was doing her best for him by sending him here, but there was still a part of him, small but insistent, that whispered, *Who wants a teenaged boy in their house? Not even your own mother.*

He heard another noise, this one irregular, a click, a creak; it sounded like the dormitory door opening. Holding his breath, his body frozen apart from the six extraocular muscles that he had learnt in biology controlled the movement of the eyeballs, Nye swivelled his gaze to where he judged the door to be. But he could see nothing but soupy blackness. He stared hard, his eyes accustoming themselves in increments to the darkness, but even when they had, he could make out nothing beyond vague shapes. The metal springs of the bunk bed above him – so close that he could reach out and bump his fingertips along them if he wanted to – but he didn't, didn't want to reach out from under his duvet, to surrender his hand to the cold and dark, didn't want to move or make a sound.

Had someone come into the room?

Someone. Or *something*?

Bending his arms, he inched the duvet higher, so that only his forehead and eyes showed, everything else covered, *protected*.

A shape had appeared in the darkness a couple of metres away, he could see that now. An unfamiliar shape, lumpy and unformed. Not one of the boys from his dorm – too big, too bulky. It was a broad, looming shape. Fearfully, his gaze tracked up a blackness fractionally blacker than the air surrounding it, his breath catching in his throat with each inch that his gaze rose.

On the top of that looming body, a face, a human face – he'd see a human face, wouldn't he? Because the thing in his room was human, wasn't it? One of the housemasters, come to check that all the boys were sleeping soundly?

He had expected to see a human face, but what met his gaze were the bright yellow eyes of an animal, the mouth beneath open and panting – it appeared to be panting – lined with teeth, jagged and razor sharp.

A wolf?

Nye jammed his eyes shut and opened his mouth to scream, but no sound emerged, only the hoarse sucking noise of the gaping vacuum that his insides had become.

A wolf. It was a wolf. He could see that now.

A huge, grey-black wolf, rearing up on its hind legs.

Tears welled in his eyes but he wouldn't cry, couldn't cry. He was thirteen, too old for crying, too old to be frightened of the dark and too old to believe that there was a wolf in his bedroom.

Nye jammed his eyes shut. It was a hallucination, wasn't it? It had to be, because his mind, his rational mind, knew that everything about what he was seeing was wrong. He used to hallucinate, back home, sometimes, a couple of times anyway. He'd imagined a rat running across his floor once and, another time, a butterfly on his pillow, so delicate and brightly coloured, so real, that he could have stroked its soft, velvety wings. He wasn't at home any more, but he was still hallucinating. Wasn't he?

Slowly he opened his eyes.

The wolf was still there, watching him with its bright yellow eyes. But it was closer now, he realized with horror. So close that if he hadn't been frozen with terror, he could have reached out and touched it.

Nye felt utterly desperate.

It's only a hallucination.

The wolf loomed over him.

'Who's afraid of the big bad wolf?' it whispered.

43

Sunlight glinted off the tarmac around Jessie as she tottered across the deserted parade ground to the Officers' Mess, where she had arranged to meet Michael O'Shaughnessy. She was still in her pencil skirt and hooker heels, had forgotten, leaving the house this morning in a fog of tension, to pack more sensible footwear and hadn't had time to duck home and change. Her feet were already griping and she felt like a naughty librarian, hair pulled into a tight ponytail at the back of her head, taking wobbly bird steps across the parade ground, her metal stilettos pecking at the tarmac. At least, she consoled herself, she was providing a valuable psychological service to Queen and Country beyond her day job: she'd been wolf-whistled at four times already in the two hundred metres she'd walked from the main gate.

She could hardly make out the chaplain in the shadows as she neared him, the dark lenses of her sunglasses mixing with the blanket of shade thrown by the porch he was sheltering under. As he stepped forward, holding out his hand, the sun lit his pale red hair, giving the impression that his peaked cap was rimmed with a red-gold halo. *God's messenger.*

'Michael O'Shaughnessy.' His voice was soft, the lilt strongly southern Irish, undiminished by the time he had spent – she had no idea, yet, how long – in England.

'Doctor Jessie Flynn. Thank you for taking the time to speak with me.'

He was younger than she had expected, thirty, if that. She had envisioned a grey-haired, bespectacled preacher man, realized that the image she nursed was anchored in Sacred Heart, the church she had whiled away Sundays in as a young girl, playing cat's cradle with the ties of her blue Sunday-best dress or tipping her head back to look at the kaleidoscope of colours cast on the walls by the huge stained-glass windows. Then, when Jamie had arrived – still a baby when they used to go as a family, before the grind of his illness wore down her parents' faith – tickling his tummy to make him giggle and disrupt the dreary monotone issuing from the pulpit.

'Flynn. Your husband or father must be a fellow Irishman with a surname like that.'

Jessie nodded. 'My father.'

'From where?'

'Killarney.'

'Ah, County Kerry. There can't be many places in the world more beautiful.'

Jessie smiled, playing along with the genial preamble. She had time. 'It is beautiful, if you can see through the fog and driving rain.'

'Ah, yes, it's not called the Emerald Isle for nothing.' He held an arm out. 'I've been sitting for hours. Do you mind if we walk while we talk?'

'Of course not.' She smiled again, cursing her heels for the millionth time. How did some women live in these things?

She could play this one of two ways, she realized, as they walked side by side along the edge of the parade ground: combative or conciliatory. Combative was a more natural response for her when faced with what she felt was injustice, but conciliatory would get her further – always got her further – got anyone who wanted answers further, unless they were in possession of chains and a waterboard. Pity that she didn't have the self-control to use 'conciliatory' more often, despite the window into the human mind that her profession afforded her.

'Where are you from, Padre?' Jessie asked, making her choice.

'County Offaly. Not the best name or the best location. It's slap-bang in the middle, miles from the sea, miles from a decent city, miles from anywhere remotely useful. Just green fields as far as the eye can see. Nothing but green.'

'Ireland's national colour.'

'So it is, for good reason. I hail from a village called Crinkill. It originally grew up around a British Army barracks, two hundred years or so ago. There's nothing left now but the ruins of the barracks and a memorial to the Prince of Wales, Leinster Regiment.'

'Is that why you joined the Army? The barracks?' She looked across, met his limpid green gaze and smiled. 'Some collateral influence?'

There was something soft and slightly feminine about him, something she couldn't quite put her finger on. Looks, some nuance of character, or perhaps both? But after weeks on a Royal Navy destroyer, the macho cult virtually infused

234

in the furniture, it felt nice to wander and chat with a man who could have almost have passed for a woman.

'I joined the Catholic Church because I have faith, and I joined the Army because . . . because I . . . ' He paused. After a moment, he gave a slight shrug. 'Perhaps because I wanted to escape.'

Patriotism. Financial necessity. Escape.

They had reached a huge oak that spread its canopy over the path.

'Escape what?' Jessie asked.

By tacit agreement, they both stopped walking, turned to face each other under the shifting jigsaw of light and shade. The chaplain's pink skin was shiny with perspiration.

'Oh, I don't know. Life. Mundanity.' A faint smile curled his lips. 'What do they say? Join the Army and travel the world.'

'What were you doing before?'

'I was clergy at a church in Dun— in Dublin.' Pulling a handkerchief from his pocket, he wiped it across his forehead, down over the rest of his face. 'I'm not constructed for the heat.' Folding the handkerchief back up into a neat square, briefly checking the alignment of the edges in a way that even she would feel proud to call her own, he slid it back into his pocket.

'Dublin is a great city,' Jessie said, re-engaging.

'Ryan Jones, you said on the phone, Doctor Flynn.' He looked not only hot, but also slightly harassed suddenly. 'You want to speak to me about Ryan Jones.'

The sudden switch from meandering chat to purpose surprised her.

'Ryan, yes. You know him?'

'I know most of the trainees on this base. It's my job to

keep tabs on them, from a distance of course, unless they request otherwise.'

'He told me that he'd spoken with you,' Jessie said softly. 'Can I ask you what you talked about?'

O'Shaughnessy frowned. 'You know I can't tell you that, Doctor Flynn. All my discussions are confidential, much as I assume yours are.' The tip of his tongue darted out and wet his cracked lips. 'Like you, I need to be entirely trustworthy, above reproach.'

'Ryan Jones didn't come to the Defence Psychology Service voluntarily. He was referred to us because of his discussions with you.' When O'Shaughnessy didn't answer, Jessie continued, 'Referred with a non-specific "personality disorder".'

'Did he ask you to come and speak with me, Doctor Flynn?'

The bonhomie they had established at the outset was fast eroding and she wasn't sure what had precipitated the switch. She smiled, a smile that she hoped didn't look as fake as it was, trying to re-establish the earlier positive atmosphere, her mind racing to work out how she could pose what were seriously antagonistic questions without antagonism.

'He asked me why you hadn't respected his right to confidentiality,' Jessie replied.

O'Shaughnessy met her gaze, his pale eyelashes blinking. 'That wasn't what I asked, Doctor Flynn.' The inference in his tone said: *And you know it.*

All bonhomie dissolved.

'*I* wanted to speak to you,' she said.

'And here you are.'

Yes – here I am.

'Why didn't you respect his right to confidentiality?' she repeated.

'I have. I am.'

236

'You must have told Colonel Wallace what Ryan said to you. Why else would he have referred Ryan Jones to us with that "non-specific personality disorder"?' She had abandoned all attempt at conciliatory. 'So either your conversations are confidential, or they aren't.'

O'Shaughnessy's eyes travelled back and forth across her face as if he was working something around in his head, and slowly his expression changed.

'It's not so simple,' he murmured.

'Isn't it? Why not?'

'Men of God create . . . ' He paused, casting his eyes to the leaf canopy above them, to heaven, Jessie supposed, as if searching for inspiration. Jigsaw pieces of light caught in his eyes, turning his limpid green irises so pale that they became virtually colourless. ' . . . hysteria. I have experienced it before. Been accused before – baselessly, I might add – and it nearly destroyed my life.'

Jessie's gaze narrowed. 'I don't understand what you're saying.'

'Much like people in positions of power can create hysteria.'

'Ryan Jones is a hysteric?'

'He has had a very tough, destabilizing childhood during which he was betrayed many times by adults, by people with power over him. I believe that Ryan Jones is not mentally robust enough to be in the Army and I am pretty sure that you will reach the same diagnosis. Now, if you will excuse me, Doctor Flynn, I am needed elsewhere.' Sidestepping her, he walked hurriedly back along the path towards the Officers' Mess.

44

Johnny was nowhere in evidence on the garage floor, so Marilyn strode across the oil-stained concrete to his office. The smelly space was as cluttered and claustrophobic as it had been this morning, but Marilyn was gratified to see that a Michelin brochure had been added to the jumble of oddments on Johnny's desk.

Johnny was lying on the leather sofa, a copy of the *Sun* spread across his face, a half-empty cup of black coffee on the floor next to him. The paper rose and fell in time with his breathing, as if operated by a miniature pair of bellows. Crossing the office in one stride, Marilyn pinched the paper between his thumb and index finger and whipped it from Johnny's face.

'Wot the f—' Johnny's eyes snapped open, blearily struggling to focus. When he saw who it was, he collapsed back, grinding the heels of his hands into his eye sockets. 'Fuckin' 'ell, it's you,' he muttered.

'Afternoon, Johnny,' Marilyn said brightly.

Yawning, Johnny swivelled his feet to the floor, navigated

around his desk and, clicking on the kettle that was stationed on top of his filing cabinet as he passed it, slumped down into his office chair.

'It was a lovely afternoon until a few moments ago.'

'It's five p.m., Johnny. I was feeling generous, so I gave you an extra hour.'

A groan. 'Leave it out, will you. Checking these damn tyres for you took me most of the afternoon.'

'Glad to hear it. So what do you have for me?'

Johnny reached for his laptop; a state-of-the-art MacBook Air that looked as if it was newly descended from outer space, so incongruous was it given the state of the rest of the office.

'Right, well the whole world of tyres really isn't that simple.'

Marilyn felt his heart sink. 'Make it simple for me, Johnny. Simple and quick.'

Johnny looked hurt. 'Did I mention that this took me hours. *Unpaid* hours.' He spun the computer, so that Marilyn could see the screen. 'Right, so most manufacturers recommend a tyre make and specification for every model of car that they manufacture. They sell the new cars with those tyres already fitted and recommend that, when the tyre's worn out, you go buy the same.'

Marilyn nodded.

'All the car manufacturers do deals with tyre manufacturers to get tyres cheap. Part of the deal is that they recommend them to customers – you scratch my back, I'll scratch yours and all that. But in reality you can pretty much buy any tyre you want for your car, as long as the width and the rim size matches. So you're playing a game of probabilities, Detective Inspector.' A smirk. 'Whatever information I give you, it probably ain't going to help that much.'

Bad comedy – all he needed. Marilyn's eyes hung closed for a moment. He sensed that this conversation was going to be neither quick nor painless. But since he had what could politely be termed as fuck-all other evidence to work with, there was little alternative but to hear Johnny out.

'Go on.'

'From the cast you gave me, that tyre wasn't hardly worn at all. Which means that it was from a new car – two or three months old, I'd say, depending, of course, on the mileage. Either that, or it was from an older car that had been refitted with new tyres, again a couple of months ago, depending on the mileage. These are high-performance, winter-specific tyres – not cheap.'

'Can we narrow it down to a make or model?'

'Well, we're back to probabilities.'

Jesus. 'You call this the *simple* explanation?'

Johnny grinned. 'I'm making it simple as I can for you, Detective Inspector. Them tyres you're looking for are Bridgestone Blizzak LM-32s. As I said, they're high-performance winter tyres.'

'High-performance as in . . . ?'

'As in sports cars, like yer Porsches and Astons, sport coupes and yer performance sedans.'

Marilyn shook his head. Somehow he didn't see a Porsche or an Aston Martin wending its way down that narrow country lane to meet with Malcolm Lawson. Everything he knew about Malcolm Lawson, about the life he led, the circles in which he moved, told him that he could strike drivers of those cars off his list.

'I think we can eliminate Porsches and Astons.'

240

'How so?'

'Call it a hunch.'

Johnny's lip curled. 'Aren't hunches another name for bad policing?'

'Get on with it, Marshall. I don't have all bloody evening,' Marilyn snapped.

'All right, all right, keep yer hair on.' Another grin. 'So, like I said, these tyres are also recommended for the high-performance variants of big family cars, salesmen's cars – yer Ford Mondeos, Vauxhall Vectras.'

A travelling salesman. Was that more likely?

'As I said, they're not cheap tyres and they're winter tyres. So if it's not a new car with tyres fitted by the manufacturer – which I'd say not, given that they're specific winter tyres an' all – then it's someone who likes their car.'

'Or someone who drives a lot?'

'Or someone who drives a lot. Someone who drives a lot in all weathers and needs good tyres, guaranteed road-holding, good performance. The tread compound of these tyres has some unique polymer technology in it to enhance cold-weather traction.' Johnny held up his hand, index finger pointed straight at Marilyn. 'And despite the high purchase price, these tyres last well, so you get a longer life for your money, reduced fuel consumption, all that guff.'

'OK.'

Johnny raised an eyebrow. 'Or it could be one of them pedantic types who dots the i's and crosses the t's. Someone who does what they're told. Winter tyres for the winter, summer tyres for the summer, even though they're only pootling around Surrey's leafy lanes.' Leaning back in his chair, Johnny knitted his fingers behind his head and smiled. 'Or it could be a rich bastard who likes the best of everything.

If I was buying a Mondeo, I probably wouldn't put them tyres on it, even with the guaranteed road-holding in winter, long life and all that, 'cause it's not like we live in the North Pole or nothing, is it?' He spun his computer back to face him, clicked a couple of keys and spun it back so that Marilyn could see the screen again. 'You'll be talking a thousand quid for a set, excluding fitting. Mad money. I'd go for something cheaper. Like Goodyear Eagles or Yokohama Advan Sport V105s. See, Yokohama, they're a Japanese make and though they're cheap as chips they're—'

Marilyn held up both hands to halt Johnny's flow. He could feel himself losing the will to live.

'The summary. Give me the summary.'

Johnny looked hurt. 'Right, so you're either looking for a banker type who's a bit bored with the office, like, uh, like in that film . . . what was it? Oh yeah, like in *American Psycho*. Or you're looking for a travelling salesman who likes a bit of kidnap on the side.' Another smirk. 'Good luck, Detective Inspector. Looks like you're going to need it.'

45

Jessie had given in to her feet's pleas and tugged off her hooker heels. The cold tiled floor of Blackdown's SPAR supermarket was bliss to her aching toes, and the odd looks cast at her bare feet, she could handle. Grabbing a bottle of cold water from the fridge, she joined the back of a queue of teenage girls in Army fatigues. The girl in front of her, a head taller than Jessie's five foot six, shoulders twice as wide, paid for a packet of crisps and a chocolate bar and turned. As she stepped out of the way, Jessie caught the name stitched on to the girl's jumper: Wonsag.

Wonsag. It took her a second: the girl who had been on guard duty with Stephen Foster. And now that she looked at the girl's face, though free of make-up and serious of expression, it was recognizable from the pornographically doctored photograph she and Callan had found under Foster's pillow.

The chatter receded as the girls left the store, the door wafting in warm air as it swung closed behind them. Jessie hurriedly paid for the bottle of water and jogged out behind them, squinting at the sinking sun, its rays brighter at this angle than when it was high in the sky. She retrieved her sunglasses from where she'd tucked them into her hair and slid them down over her eyes. Breaking into a barefoot jog, she called out:

'Private Wonsag.'

The girls stopped walking and all of them turned. Jessie directed her attention to the tall, solid girl in the middle, wisps of white-blonde hair escaping from the sides of her beret, angular jaw set into an intractable square, striking azure-blue eyes narrowed in suspicion. She should have been beautiful – her hair, the narrow, aquiline nose and those incredible eyes – but her size, her stance, feet apart, hands planted on her hips, the look of aggression and mistrust written into her clashing features made her anything but.

'V-onsag,' she said. 'It's pronounced Vonsag.'

'Sorry. German isn't my strong point. Your surname is German, isn't it?'

A curt nod.

'Can I speak to you for a minute please?'

'Why?'

'I want to talk to you about Stephen Foster.'

Wonsag looked sideways at her friends and gave an exaggerated sigh. 'I'll catch you up.'

She waited until they were alone together on the path before asking, 'Who are you?' Her tone no more friendly or accommodating than it had been at her first words.

'My name is Doctor Jessie Flynn. I'm a clinical psychologist with the Defence Psychology Service. I want to talk to you about the night that Foster was killed.'

A shadow crossed Wonsag's face. 'I'm not going to talk to you. I don't have to.'

Late afternoon on a tough day and Jessie's patience had run out. 'No, you're right, you don't. I can always call the Special Investigation Branch. Captain Callan said that you were intransigent, to say the least, when he interviewed you about Foster's death, so I'm sure he's getting ready for round two. I think this time he'll probe in far more detail about why it took you twenty minutes to have a wee. Either that or you can talk to me about your toilet habits.' Jessie smiled sweetly, feeling like a bitch, though not really caring. Everything about this girl was rubbing her up the wrong way. 'Up to you, V-onsag.'

The girl looked sullen. 'Are you working with the MPs?'

'I've been called in to advise.' She had briefly, so she consoled herself that her words were more half-truths – white lies – than blatant black ones. She probably shouldn't be talking to Martha Wonsag at all, but opportunity had presented itself, and she'd never been one to turn down opportunity.

'What reason would I have to kill him?'

'I don't know. What reason *would* you have to kill him?'

The girl's temper flared again. 'If you're going to accuse me, I'm leaving.'

'Leaving to go where, precisely?' Jessie snapped. 'Back to your accommodation block? To the mess? You're not a civilian. You can't simply disappear. Well, actually you can, but that's called going AWOL – absent without leave – and it's a criminal offence in the military.' She'd had enough of intransigence, avoidances, subtexts, half-truths and lies for one day, even if she'd just told one herself. 'Look. Make it easy on yourself and make it easy for me. You told Callan that you went to the toilet, but it doesn't take twenty minutes or more – long enough for a healthy,

245

fit young man who you claim to have left alive to wind up dead – to squat in the bushes. So what were you doing?'

Her blazing eyes flicked away from Jessie's. 'I had my period,' she said in a quiet voice. 'It started while I was on duty. I didn't have anything with me.'

'Couldn't you have made do?'

'*Made do*? What, with leaves or something?' Her voice was scornful.

Rightly so. It had been a facetious comment to make and the reality of Martha Wonsag 'making do' didn't bear thinking about.

'I still had three hours left on guard duty.'

'So what did you do?'

'I went back to my accommodation block to sort myself out. I told Stephen that I'd only be fifteen minutes, but it took longer than that. My accommodation block is the other side of the base. It's a hike and it was dark.'

Jessie raised an eyebrow.

'Look, my life wouldn't be worth living if the guys saw a bloodstain on my trousers,' Wonsag snapped. 'It's bad enough being a woman in the Army, but the guys can forgive you a bit' – she held up her right hand, thumb and index finger a millimetre apart – 'a tiny bit, if you're as macho as them or if you shag them.'

Jessie nodded. She didn't need to think too hard to know which of those boxes Wonsag fell into, despite the photograph underneath Foster's pillow.

'If they worked out that I was a woman with natural bodily functions? Fuck, I might as well move to Timbuktu . . . or kill myself.' She broke off, slapping a hand over her mouth. 'I'm sorry. I shouldn't have said that.'

Jessie shrugged. 'Semantics. Don't worry about it. How long were you away?'

'Thirty minutes or so.'

'What time did you leave Foster?'

'Two thirty-five a.m.'

'Did you radio in to the Guard Duty Staff Officer to say that you were going?'

'What? That I was going to get a tampon? To Marley? Funnily enough, no I didn't.'

'Who's Marley?'

'Corporal Jace Harris.'

'And he's a sleazebag?'

Wonsag half-smiled, the first time that Jessie had seen anything but open hostility on her face. 'How did you guess?'

'Your expression said it all. Did anyone see you?'

'It was nearly three o'clock in the morning.'

'You would have passed the main gate, the guardhouse, wouldn't you?'

'Marley hangs out in the guardhouse most guard duties. He can't be bothered to walk around and actually do his job. I didn't want him to see me, to have to explain. I snuck past and then jogged down Royal Way, the road that runs through the camp from the main gate, to my accommodation block.'

'Is Marley really that bad?'

'No.' Her mouth twisted. 'He's worse. You only need to see the tattoo on his arm to know what he thinks about women.'

Jessie rolled her eyes. 'I'll put that on my list of must-sees at Blackdown. The list isn't long.'

'Not that I'm his type. I'm not pretty enough, sweet enough, or stupid enough to be on his target list.'

Jessie nodded, only half-listening, her gaze rolling up to the sky while she brought the layout of the main gate to mind.

'There are CCTV cameras mounted on the gateposts, facing out and facing in. One of them faces down Royal Way. If you're telling me the truth, you'd be on it.'

Wonsag wrinkled her nose, shaking her head. 'Does anything get past you, Doctor?'

Lots, particularly over the past three days. It felt as if the world and his wife had got past her since the morning she had met Marilyn at Royal Surrey County Hospital. As if she'd been floundering around like a seal pup on ice, waiting to be clubbed over the head by something vital that she'd missed. Still was – waiting and floundering.

'And if I don't appear on the CCTV?'

'It's not up to me. It's up to the Military Police. Why didn't you tell this to Captain Callan?'

The girl threw up her hands. 'Why do you think?'

'He's not a sleazebag.'

'No, he's the other type. The super-hot type.' Her cheeks flushed. 'There's no way I'm discussing my period with a man who looks like that. Anyway, he interviewed me as a witness and I didn't witness anything. I wasn't a suspect then, was I? I presume that's now changed, has it?' The antagonism firmly back in her voice. 'I presume that I'm now a suspect, am I?'

Jessie shrugged. 'You had sex with Foster.'

'Once. Once, and I paid for it. He made me pay. The lads made me pay big time.'

Jessie nodded. She was pretty sure what payback would feel like for a woman on an Army base, and it wouldn't be pleasant. She had no idea how far Callan had got in his investigation, whether he had unearthed more unsavoury details about Wonsag that she wasn't privy to, but was this girl really a suspect?

248

She had a motive, she was aggressive and she had low impulse control – both personality traits overrepresented in violent criminals. But murder? The more time she spent at Blackdown, the more she felt that there was a huge malevolent elephant in the room that they were all missing.

Seal pup. Ice. Club.

A suicide a year ago that a father refused to believe.

A murder now that felt . . . odd. There was no other word to describe it.

'No, you're not a suspect.' She had no right to utter those words. Only the Special Investigation Branch – Callan, to be precise, as he was SIO – had that right, but she no longer cared. Gaining this girl's cooperation, seeing if she could shed any light on Foster's personality, was more important than lining her up as a suspect.

'Even though you didn't see anything, you're still a witness. A witness to Foster's personality if nothing else. Did you know him well?'

Wonsag's hands were still on her hips, feet planted shoulder-width apart in her black combat boots, eyes glazed with suspicion.

'I don't think anyone knew him well,' she muttered.

'Why's that?

'He kept himself to himself.'

'Did he fit in?'

She hunched her wide shoulders again. 'He was private. He definitely wasn't one of the cool gang.'

Jessie nodded. 'Anything else? Any behaviour that you thought was strange or out of character?'

'Look, I really didn't know his character that well, despite what you might have heard, so I wouldn't know what was out of character. We had sex once, and we were on guard duty together a couple of times because Marley thought it was funny to put us together after—' She broke off, then opened her mouth again, as if she was about to add something else.

'What?' Jessie prompted, when she didn't speak.

'It's probably nothing, but right at the beginning of guard duty, before Marley had split us into pairs and allocated our patrol areas, Stephen received a text. He pulled his phone out to check it and one of the other guys snatched it from him. He was teasing Stephen, asking if it was a girlfriend or his mum. *Mummy* was the word he used.'

'And?'

'Stephen went mental. I mean really mental. He jumped on Leo, punched him in the stomach and snatched his phone back.' She shrugged. 'It was a massive overreaction. We were all surprised, because it wasn't like him. He wasn't aggressive, wasn't that type.'

Jessie nodded. Did Callan have Foster's phone, she wondered. Had he accessed the texts?

'Thank you.' She paused. 'Anything else?'

'Look, as I already said, I hardly knew him.'

Jessie didn't believe that there was any more to be had from this conversation. She held out her hand. After a moment, Wonsag took it.

'Thanks for your help,' Jessie said, watching her walk away, her muscular thighs chafing against each other with each step.

Wonsag easily had the strength to slide a screwdriver into a boy's throat, but Jessie doubted that she had reason to. But then, who did have a reason to want Stephen Foster dead?

Perhaps the answer was, no one. Not directly, anyway.

46

Callan's mobile went straight to voicemail, so Jessie cut off the call and tried the SIB offices. An unfamiliar male voice answered.

'Can I speak to Captain Callan, please?' she asked.

'He's out of the office at the moment.' The voice was cut-glass, assured, each syllable crisply enunciated. 'I can pass on a message. Who shall I say is calling?'

'It's Doctor Jessie Flynn from the Defence Psychology Service.'

'Captain Callan has mentioned you. You were helping us with the Stephen Foster case.'

'I . . . ' *I was. Whether I am now, officially is anybody's guess.* 'Yes. That's why I'm calling.'

'I'm Lieutenant Ed Gold. I'm working for . . . with Callan. Can I help?'

'It's about Martha Wonsag, the girl who was on guard duty with Foster.'

'The girl who has twenty or thirty critical minutes unaccounted for?'

'Yes.'

'Have you spoken with her?' he asked sharply.

'Yes.'

'Unofficially? That's not procedure.' His tone was disdainful. 'I'll have to speak to Captain Callan about that. We can't have random people interviewing witnesses whenever they feel like it.'

Go ahead. Speak to Callan. I couldn't care less. She could hear his measured breathing coming down the line, but he didn't add anything further. She suspected that he was employing the interrogation technique of 'letting silence hang'. If he expected her to roll over and capitulate, he was wasting his time. It was a technique she used herself with patients and the silence didn't bother her. She let it stretch until he felt compelled to fill it.

'Please do not make that mistake again.'

Jessie still didn't speak. What she felt like saying wasn't polite enough for public consumption.

'Did she account for the missing time?' he asked finally.

'She did.'

'And?'

'And – she had personal issues to deal with.'

'Personal issues?' His tone even more disdainful.

Jessie smiled inwardly. 'Women's issues. Women's *biological* issues.'

'Oh.' He cleared his throat. 'Right.'

'Would you like me to elaborate? I'd be happy to.'

'Uh . . . no, that's, uh, that's enough information, thank you.'

I bet it is. She would have given a lot to be having this conversation face to face.

'She had to go back to her accommodation block. She

went down Royal Way, the road that cuts directly north from the main gate. If she's telling the truth, she'll be on CCTV.'

'Are you still at Blackdown?'

'Yes.'

'Can you wait for me there? I'll be ten minutes.'

Jessie cast her face to the warm evening sun. 'Sure. I'll walk back to the main gate and meet you there.'

The phone clicked off.

47

Corporal Jace Harris was back in the guardhouse, his Guard
Duty Staff Officer role having cycled around again, seventy-
two hours after the last stint, business as usual at Blackdown
despite the chilled, eviscerated body of a sixteen-year-old
in Val Monks' morgue. Callan rapped his knuckles on the
glass door and entered without waiting to be invited. Jace
Harris and the young private next to him, who had raised
the barrier to Callan's Golf a couple of minutes before,
both looked up. The private leapt to his feet and saluted.
Harris took a moment longer, the look on his ferret face
pure mistrust.

'Private Perkins, leave us, will you,' Callan said, returning
their salutes, stepping sideways from the door. Perkins
almost tripped over the toes of Callan's boots in his hurry
to leave, the presence of a Branch detective having the
same effect as an exploding stink bomb in the small space.
An effect that had served Callan well many times, and
suited him now.

He had stopped in at a newsagent's in Camberley on the

way here, bouncing his Golf on to the kerb, ignoring the 'What the fuck?' looks and hand gestures of other drivers searching for legitimate parking spaces, jogged in and bought a packet of cigarettes, Super Kings Blue. Settling himself on to one of the desks, he pulled the packet from his jacket pocket.

'Cigarette?'

Harris's eyes narrowed with suspicion. *Rightly so.*

'We're not allowed to smoke in the guardhouse.'

Leaning across the desk, Callan flicked the window open. 'Suit yourself, Harris.'

He tapped a cigarette from the packet and stuck it in the corner of his mouth. Patting his pockets in a show of searching for matches, he caught Harris, out of the corner of his eye, watching the charade.

'OK, sir, I will 'ave a cigarette if you don't mind. I left mine back at my accommodation block.'

Again? Callan tossed the packet over to him. Shaking one out, Harris dug the smooth, stainless steel Zippo lighter that he'd been fiddling with the last time Callan had interviewed him from his trouser pocket, lit the cigarette and sucked the smoke deep into his lungs. His small, dark eyes hung closed for a moment while he savoured the sensation, his expression that of a free diver taking his first breath of air after surfacing from a hundred feet under.

'Can I borrow your lighter, Harris?'

Pinching the proffered lighter in the tips of his fingers, touching as little of its smooth surface as possible, Callan lit his cigarette and dropped the Zippo on the desk next to him. Except for a few cigarettes years ago, when he was fifteen or sixteen, drinking, having sex for the first time, he'd never smoked. It was not a vice that had ever appealed to him. Drink and sex, yes. Smoking? It had felt like a fool's game, even back then. As the smoke grated down his throat, he felt like a kid again, hiding behind the school bike sheds trying to look cool, trying not to splutter.

'You said when I first interviewed you, that you thought Foster's death might be personal, Harris. Why?'

'Like I said before, it was the word on the street.'

'Who from, so soon after his body had been found?'

Harris shrugged. In silence, Callan watched him haul another draught of smoke deep into his lungs, funnel it out through the side of his mouth. Despite the open window, a blue fug had formed in the air between them. Harris was waiting for Callan to speak and when he didn't, he let the vacuum of silence pressure him into filling it: 'You know what Army bases are like, sir, gossip and shit. Nothing stays private for five minutes.'

'So what else did you hear?'

Harris pulled a face. 'He was a bit of a wimp, that's all.'

Harris's lips around the cigarette had pressed into a thin line and he was staring at his feet.

'Is that why you put him on guard duty with a girl? What was her name? Martha? Martha Wonsag? And sent them to patrol the most isolated part of the base, the woods? Because you hate women and you hate wimps?'

The corporal looked up, a lopsided, sick smile on his face. 'I don't hate women, Captain.'

Callan's eyes were drawn for a second to the tattoo on his forearm, the blonde on all fours, waiting for some scumbag like Harris to take her from behind.

'But you do hate wimps?'

The questions that he was posing were irrelevant; mining character when he already had a pretty solid handle on

256

Harris's character. He hadn't come to ask questions, but Harris would be suspicious if he didn't play the detective, didn't probe.

'If you can't patrol a patch of woods in England without getting scared, what hope have you got against the Islamic fuckin' State? I mean, for pity's sake, I'm supposed to be making soldiers of these kids and most of them are so wet behind the bloody ears that they make Cinderella look like a hard-arse—'

Harris had stopped talking, was looking expectantly at Callan. *What had he said?* Callan had switched off halfway through, his attention caught by a bright yellow Mini parked on the far side of the car park.

The male ego versus solving the case.

It's got nothing to do with my ego.

Hadn't it? So what the hell had it go to do with? The fact that he felt as if his epilepsy was spinning out of control? That if he didn't let anyone get close enough to read his feelings, access his mind, see the instability lodged there, he'd be able to carry on, clinging to normality by his fingernails, just enough hold to stop himself from hurtling into the abyss.

Harris was clearly expecting him to pose another question, but he'd lost his thread. Pinching the lit end of his cigarette between his thumb and forefinger, extinguishing it, he tossed the butt into the bin under the desk.

'How did you come to be nicknamed "Animal", Harris?'

Harris's eyes widened.

'You said your parents gave you the nickname. They must have a sense of humour.'

Harris shuffled his feet, eyes fixed on some distant point past Callan's shoulder. 'Nah, it wasn't my parents. I got the name when I was a new recruit. The lads. You know how it is, sir.'

He did know how it was. Army lads loved nicknames. The mildest were derivatives of surnames: Heathie, Jonesy. Others, less politically correct. But Harris was the first soldier he'd come across nicknamed Animal, and he was pretty sure that it wasn't after the cute furry variety.

'Why did you lie to me?'

'I was nervous, like. The murder an' all.'

'Nervous? What? Of a few questions?' Callan raised an eyebrow. 'If you're nervous of a few questions, what hope have you got against the Islamic State?'

Harris's mouth opened, but no words came out.

Callan pushed himself to his feet; he'd got what he came for. 'Thanks for your help, Corporal. If anything else occurs, you know where to find me.'

As Callan walked away from the guardhouse, the weight of Jace Harris's Zippo in an evidence bag in his trouser pocket, he glanced back, saw Harris patting his pockets, scanning the desk, the floor underneath it, a confused frown etched into his brow.

48

Workman was sitting at her desk by the window in the incident room, quietly warming her face in the evening sun. As Malcolm's disappearance had been elevated to the status of kidnapping, she was not alone. Telephones rang, stacks of papers were read, leads followed, coffee mainlined and crisps and doughnuts consumed in obscene quantities by officers and civilian staff dressed in short-sleeved shirts in deference to the unexpectedly hot spring day. The air in the room felt as dense as liquid, a strong smell of stale body odour elbowing out what would have been the more pleasant scent of brewing coffee. Helping himself to a tea, which probably should have been cold water, given the temperature, but he'd always regarded water as unappealingly tasteless and alarmingly healthy, Marilyn made his way over to the window.

A manual bearing the Sussex Police logo, entitled *Kidnap Threat to Life Policy*, rested on Workman's desk. Sliding it over, Marilyn perched one skinny buttock on the corner of the desk.

'Good to see you're still here, Workman.'

Workman rolled her eyes. 'I live for this job, sir.'

'You will be rewarded in heaven.'

Picking up her empty mug, she held it out to him. 'I'd prefer to be rewarded with another cup of tea.'

Grabbing the mug, Marilyn leaned back and dropped it on to the desk of DC Darren Cara, a keen newbie who'd transferred from Traffic.

'Sergeant Workman would like a cup of tea, prease,' he said, in a ludicrous approximation of a Chinese accent. 'Milk and one sugar and make it quick, lackey-person.' He turned back to Workman and winked. '*Kung Fu Panda*, my favourite film.'

Workman shook her head, all faux shock, but there was a hint of a smile on her face. 'Isn't that called abuse of status?'

'Good for his soul, making tea for superior officers. It means that he'll propagate the same hierarchical divisions when he's a DI, which is fantastic. Every solid profession thrives on metaphorically beating juniors to within an inch of their lives so that when they get the opportunity, having crawled up the ranks by their broken fingernails, they'll work their juniors into the ground and treat them like shite. We can't have standards dropping when I'm gone to my bath chair.' Marilyn tossed the list he had drawn up with Johnny Marshall on Workman's desk.

Reaching for her glasses, she slid them on to her nose. 'What's this, sir?'

'The fruits of my labour.' Marilyn tapped his finger on the kidnap manual. 'Something to save you from reading this fun tome. Here' – he shifted his finger to the list – 'is the brand and code of tyre that left the prints we found on the mud patch near Malcolm's car, and below is a list of the makes and models of car that are likely to use that tyre.'

'Johnny M?'

'Yes. I'm pleased to say that the little shit is still making himself useful. Not with good grace, but that I can live with.'

Workman read down the list: 'Porsche 911, Aston Martin DB9, Mercedes S class, BMW 5 series. Why have you put a question mark next to these?'

'Because we need to narrow our search parameters, or we'll be looking for this car long past the point where I should be in that bath chair playing bridge, picking my nose and chatting up the nurses in the old people's home.'

'I don't see you playing bridge, sir.'

'Stranger things have happened.'

'Really?'

'Perhaps not.' Marilyn pulled a face. 'We need to make the assumption that Malcolm's disappearance wasn't random. Random happens to teenagers, drug addicts, your unlucky homeless person – people who routinely put themselves in danger, either knowingly or unknowingly. So we're looking for someone who moved in Malcolm's circle.'

'From what Joan Lawson said, very few people moved in his circle.'

'His social circle, yes. But I think that his disappearance must have something to do with the suicide of his son. He created a whole new circle based on his obsessive refusal to accept that his son's death was suicide. I believe that someone in that new circle is responsible for his disappearance.'

'Why, sir?'

261

'Purely and simply because I haven't come up with any better ideas.'

Workman nodded. Marilyn's reasoning sounded simplistic and random, but she knew that his thought processes were anything but. That ravaged Ronnie Wood excuse for a face and those odd mismatched eyes hid a sharp, enquiring mind and though he had many faults, lack of intelligence and insight weren't among them. His team had already interviewed everyone with whom Malcolm had had contact on a regular basis in what could be called 'social situations', a woefully short list made up of local shopkeepers, staff at his GP's surgery, the petrol station where he filled his car and all employees of Davey-Davenport, the small firm of accountants in Guildford town centre where he had worked up until ten months ago when he was signed off long-term sick with depression. His disappearance had been a source of amazement to all these acquaintances, anything outside the mundane being considered 'out of character' for Malcolm.

Marilyn sighed. 'Malcolm Lawson is' – he deliberately used the present tense – 'a harmless, Home Counties, mid-forties, mid-level white-collar worker – until he left work due to depression. By any metric, he seems to have been staid, pedestrian, content with the status quo, *until* his son committed suicide.'

He massaged the bridge of his nose with his fingertips. He was tired now, weary right through to the marrow of his bones. After his failure to listen to Granny Lawson and commit proper resources to the search for Malcolm from the get-go, he had allowed himself virtually no sleep in penance and it was now hitting him with a vengeance.

'How did he do it, sir?'

'How did who do what?'

'Danny Lawson. How did he take his own life?'

'He suffocated himself by wrapping duct tape around his head – his nose and mouth – wrapping and wrapping it until he'd covered all his airways, until he couldn't breathe. Obviously, I didn't see the body as it was discovered, because it was Military Police jurisdiction, but I did see the crime scene photos.' A shadow crossed his face. 'It was one of the grimmest things I've ever seen. A sixteen-year-old kid with this black shit wrapped around his face like a . . . Christ, like he was wearing a ski mask except it was tape. His face was bloated and the whites of his eyes were bright red, like the Devil's. All the blood vessels in them had burst from his body's utter desperation for oxygen. It was sickening.'

'What would lead a child to do that to themselves?' she asked quietly.

Marilyn shrugged. 'That wasn't our brief.'

'Even so.'

'Right. Even so.'

She regarded him carefully. 'Is there no chance at all that Malcolm Lawson had a point?'

'What do you mean, "had a point"?'

Workman sighed. 'I don't know, really. I've never met the man. But he seemed to be so furious with the Army. He must have had some reason to believe that Danny's case hadn't been properly looked into. What did the autopsy conclude?'

'There wasn't an autopsy.'

'Why not?'

'Because the Surrey County Coroner decided that an autopsy wasn't necessary. It was clear how the poor kid

263

died and that he had taken his own life. The Branch forensics boys went over that shower room with a fine toothcomb. Danny's were the only fingerprints on the tape and there was no trace evidence at all that anyone else had been near his body. He was discovered in the morning by one of his dorm mates, who had the good sense to keep his distance, so there wasn't any contamination. The Branch decided that it was pretty clear-cut and the coroner concurred.'

'They didn't think it odd that a sixteen-year-old embarking on a new chapter in his life would suddenly commit suicide? What if he was trying to escape from something?'

Marilyn hunched his shoulders. 'It's still suicide. And aren't all suicides escaping from something?'

'Yes, but . . . but what if someone drove him to it?'

Grasping the corner of the sopping teabag in the tips of his fingers, Marilyn dragged Workman's waste-paper basket out from under her desk with the toe of his boot and dropped the bag in. It landed with a soggy splat, spraying brown drops over the discarded papers at the bottom of the bin. 'It's still suicide.'

The tea in his mug was over-stewed, a wholly unappealing sludge brown. He took a sip, wincing at the tannin tang on his tongue, then put the cup down.

Workman nodded. 'And there was nothing that you thought was odd,' she persisted.

'What, apart from a sixteen-year-old covering his face with gaffer tape?'

'You know what I mean, sir,' she said in a quiet voice.

Marilyn sighed. 'Yes, of course I know what you mean.' He paused. 'No, Workman there was nothing – and believe me, I looked for it.' His gaze found the window, his mind searching the space outside for the right way to phrase what he was thinking. 'In the end, our findings concurred with the Special Investigation Branch: suicide, plain and simple.'

Workman nodded. 'I'm sure you were right, sir. But was there nothing that struck you as out of the ordinary?'

His gaze wandered to the window again. 'I'm not immune, Workman. It did get to me.'

'Tell me, sir.'

He shook his head and sighed. 'It was the commitment. It felt like an incredibly desperate and committed way for someone so young to take their own life. And perhaps that's what Malcolm struggled to come to terms with. That his own son was *so* desperate to die.' He tapped his finger on the list he'd dropped on to Workman's desk. 'Let's focus on the job at hand, eh? These tyres. We can't have Johnny M's hard work going to waste now, can we?'

He was seemingly back to his jokey self, but Workman knew different. The image of that poor kid with his head wrapped in gaffer tape would stay with him for hours.

'The tyres were new, high-performance winter tyres, Marshall said. So let's check out people who have replaced these tyres in the past three months. Start with Surrey; contact all the chain tyre stores such as Kwik Fit, and all the little guys, the Johnny M type outfits. We also need to look at your keen home mechanics, so contact auto-parts stores who sell these tyres to the public for self-fitting – Halfords and the like. And don't forget, Mondeos and Vectras are typical fleet vehicles. These are expensive tyres but they perform well in winter and wear well, so some companies may favour them for top-end sales reps during the winter months. Hopefully there can't be that many, not with tyres this expensive. Once we've got a list of all the cars which have had these tyres fitted in the past three months, we sift through the results and prioritize. The Porsches are right at the bottom of the list.'

'A lot of wealthy people live around here . . . ' She let the rest of the sentence hang, the inference clear.

'Right. But we're in the Home Counties – four-by-four heaven.' He raised his eyes to the ceiling, gave a slight, silent nod. 'And thankfully these tyres aren't fitted to those beasts.'

'Even so, sir. It's a big job.'

Sliding off the corner of Workman's desk, retrieving his virtually untouched and now cold mug of tea, Marilyn nodded. 'It is, so you'd best get on with it.' He tilted his head towards the desk behind. 'Delegate, Workman, delegate. There's a keen lad somewhere around here who used to be in Traffic. All about cars and tyres isn't it, Traffic?'

49

'Doctor Jessie Flynn?' His navy-flecked, royal-blue eyes grazed from her face quickly down her body. Not quick enough, though, to be subtle. When his gaze found its way back to hers, she held it directly, without smiling, cursing for the umpteenth time her slutty 'power dressing'.

'Yes.'

'I'm Lieutenant Gold.'

He shook her extended hand, holding it for a few seconds longer than was necessary for a formal handshake, before Jessie slid her fingers from his grip.

'Talk to me,' he said.

He was wearing a pristine dark grey suit with a pale yellow silk paisley tie, the knot, unlike Callan's, straight – nothing there to knock her sense of order off-kilter – everything about him meticulous, from the knife creases down each leg to the matching yellow silk paisley hand-kerchief poking, in a perfect triangle, from his top pocket. From the brief moments she had spent in Ed Gold's company, and from their conversation on the telephone, she could imagine him slotting comfortably into the Army's rigid hierarchy – preferably at the top, if he had his way.

Jessie indicated the CCTV cameras perched either side of the main gate.

'As you can see, the camera on the left-hand side is angled straight down Royal Way.' She twisted back to face him. 'Martha Wonsag said that she walked from the woods, where Foster's body was found, to her accommodation via that road. She would have come on to the screen when she cut around the corner of the NCOs' Mess.' Again she indicated. 'And been on film all the way down the road.'

'It was dark.'

'Yes, but the main road is lit.' She thought of Martha Wonsag, six feet tall with that white-blonde hair. 'I'd say that she's pretty recognizable, even from the back and in the dark.'

'What time was that?'

'Around two thirty-five a.m., she said.'

'Jace Harris didn't mention one of his guards leaving their post for half an hour.'

Jessie didn't mince her words. 'He's a sexist scumbag, evidently, so she didn't want him to know.'

Gold's eyes widened. 'Right.'

'Marley, I think she said?'

'Yes, I've interviewed him.'

'And is her description accurate?'

Beginning to relax, if only slightly, into the conversation, he gave a brief half-smile. 'Very accurate.'

'I can't wait to meet him.'

'I wouldn't rush, if I were you.' His narrow lips stretched into a fuller smile this time. 'I'll put in a request for the CCTV first thing tomorrow. Colonel Philip Wallace,

Blackdown's commanding officer, is a personal friend so I'm sure that my request will be expedited.' Sliding up his sleeve, he revealed a slim, gold Bulgari on his wrist. 'It's getting late. Time for a drink, I'd say. Would you join me, Doctor?'

The suggestion, backed up by the raise of one eyebrow, almost made Jessie laugh out loud it was so unexpected.

'We could grab a bite to eat too. There's a great new steak restaurant in Farnham, if you're a red meat lover.'

'Look, I, uh, I'm sorry, but I need to get back to the office.' She smiled and shrugged, the lie sliding smoothly off her tongue. 'I've still got a couple more hours of admin to do. Writing up today's sessions. Unexciting, but necessary.'

Titling his head, he met her gaze with navy-flecked, royal blue eyes. 'All work and no play makes Jill a dull girl.'

'Perhaps Jill likes being a dull girl.'

'Jill is far too beautiful to be a dull girl.' Reaching out, he laid a light hand on her arm. 'Come on.'

Taking a step back, she gently disengaged her arm. 'Look, I'm sorry, but I don't date soldiers.'

'Gold.'

A voice she'd recognize anywhere. Heat rose to her cheeks as she and Gold both swung around to face Callan.

'Hello, Captain.' Her tone was deliberately chilly.

'Doctor Flynn. Nice to see you again.' His eyes moved from her to Gold and back, a frown flitting across his face.

Gold had straightened, rigidity gripping his body, Jessie noticed, as soon as he realized that the voice belonged to his superior officer. From both his and Callan's body language, it was obvious that they didn't have a comfortable working relationship. Pulling a clear evidence bag containing a Zippo lighter from his pocket, Callan held it out to Gold.

'Get this to Morgan now, will you. I want it fingerprinted tonight.'

'I was heading out to dinner,' Gold said, casting a sideways glance at Jessie.

Callan followed his gaze, another, deeper frown etched into his brow. Jessie was tempted to contradict Gold, make it clear to Callan that his subordinate's dinner plans didn't include her, but there had been nothing explicit in the statement, merely intimation. She couldn't believe that she still cared what Callan thought, still had feelings for him, after so many months away, feelings that had knotted her stomach the moment she'd heard his voice.

'I want it fingerprinted tonight.' His tone was curt. 'Now.'

Gold took the bag, but didn't move. 'Whose is it?'

Callan cast a glance at Jessie. Raising appeasing hands, she stepped away, to leave them to talk in private, though she thought the unvoiced request was unnecessary, purely weight throwing. Callan obviously wasn't in a good mood.

She heard him say, 'Jace Harris.'

Then Gold's response: 'Marley?'

'Yes.'

Gold raised his voice, turning his head slightly, broadcasting in Jessie's direction. 'Surely the lighter won't be admissible as evidence because of the way you acquired it.'

'Thanks for the 101 in basic police work,' Callan snapped. 'I want to know if the fingerprints match. If they do, I'll get his prints officially, legally. So go.' A moment of silence, then a growled, 'Now.'

'Right, sir.'

Gold stepped towards Jessie, his pale face tight with anger.

'Nice to meet you, Doctor Flynn.' He held out a slender hand, which Jessie took, feeling the cool of his skin against her own. Again, he held it a fraction longer than for a formal handshake, longer even than before, a move Jessie sensed was entirely deliberate, to provoke Callan. 'That restaurant I mentioned. I'll look forward to taking you there.'

Jessie smiled, but didn't reply. She felt like a doe caught between two stags locking antlers during mating season. Even so, she wasn't about to cut Gold dead in front of Callan, however tempted she might be to do so.

When Gold was out of earshot, she turned to Callan.

'Are you done with the macho bullshit, Captain?'

'What?' His voice was incredulous.

'You and your colleague. You didn't need to be quite so rude to him.'

'Rude? It was work. I was asking him to do his job properly, nothing more.'

'It was posturing.'

Raising a hand, Callan rubbed it across his eyes. He looked tired and stressed. 'He annoys me.'

'Really? I didn't notice.'

Callan sighed. 'I'll try and be more . . . collegial next time, Doctor. Now, have you got a minute? Time for a drink? I need a beer and I need to discuss something with you.'

'What?'

'The case.'

'Stephen Foster?'

He nodded.

'I thought I'd been fired.'

'Temporarily sidelined.' The corners of his mouth lifted. 'I sense bruised professional pride, Doctor.'

271

She was tempted to tell him that she was busy – or more accurately to go fuck himself – but then she thought of Joan Lawson in that cramped flat with nothing but her hope, Malcolm's abandoned Corolla, the baby seat damp with tears, a boy wrapping gaffer tape around his head and suffocating himself. And Ryan Jones. Callan needed her help and she could do with his.

'I'm surprised that you can sense anything beyond the all-encompassing aura of your own ego.'

'Ouch.'

She turned towards the car park, cast coolly back over her shoulder: 'Shall we, Captain?'

50

There were only two cars parked on the narrow country lane outside the pub: a Land Rover Defender, so covered in mud that neither registration plate was visible, and a sleek pillar-box-red convertible BMW, its roof down in deference to the evening sun. Callan pulled his Golf on to the kerb in front of the BMW and Jessie parked opposite, tucking her Mini against the pub's low flint-stone wall. The pub was rural picture-postcard: whitewashed walls and clay-tiled roof, hanging baskets of scarlet geraniums and orange nasturtiums complementing its red-painted front door and window frames.

The only previous time they had been here together, last November, when Jessie had scraped Callan out of the gutter after he'd suffered an epileptic fit, a log fire had been roaring in the grate at the far end of the narrow, low-ceilinged room, curtains half-drawn across windows to keep in the heat. This evening, windows were ajar to let in the fresh spring air, the back door was open and through it Jessie glimpsed a walled garden, laid out with a few wooden tables and chairs.

'Grab a table and I'll get you a glass of wine.'

Ducking, so that he wouldn't bang his head on the gnarled wooden ceiling beams, Callan crossed to the bar. In the garden, Jessie chose a table by the back wall, the only one that was still bathed in evening sunlight. Digging her sunglasses from her bag, she slipped them on.

'Here.'

Setting a glass in front of her, he pulled a pair of Oakley's from his pocket and sat opposite, pulling the chair back from the table so that he could arrange his long legs in comfort. They looked at each other across the table in silence for a few moments. Jessie was pleased that they were both wearing sunglasses; it diluted the pressure, the two of them alone in the walled garden.

'So, the case,' she began, all efficiency. 'Stephen Foster? Something's bothering you, Callan?'

Back in November, facing each other across a table inside, he had smiled, an easy, familiar smile and said, *Perhaps you should call me Ben, as we're having dinner together, Jessie.* She had hoped that, this evening, he would be more relaxed in her company than when they had searched Foster's room two days ago, but she was wrong. There was nothing relaxed about him, nothing easy-going or personal; a force field of tension surrounded him.

'Virtually everything is bothering me,' he muttered.

'What specifically?'

'The supposed killer's MO. The autopsy. The evidence the dogs found at the crime scene.'

'You don't think that Foster was murdered, do you? You suspect that he committed suicide.'

Callan's brow furrowed. 'How did you know?'

'Call it an educated guess.'

274

He spread his hands. 'We know for certain that someone else was with him when he died. Our first assumption . . . *my* first assumption was that that person killed him.'

'And now?'

'Now, I don't know. But the whole scenario – the scenario we've developed on the basis of the autopsy, doesn't feel right to me. You kill someone and then you hang around. Why? No killer in his or her right mind would do that. It doesn't make sense.'

'Does Val Monks agree with you?'

'No. She thinks that pathology isn't an exact science, and she's right. It's not.'

'But it's not the physical evidence that's bothering you. It's the psychology.'

'Whoever was there at the scene held Foster up. We know that from the blood patterns and bruises. Holding someone upright when they're bleeding from a throat wound reduces the flow of blood to that wound, because the failing heart has to pump harder to fight gravity. I also now believe that that person pressed his or her hand against Foster's wound to further stem the flow of blood. I went back to the crime scene yesterday with the dogs and one of them found a bloody handprint on the tree underneath which Foster was found.'

'Not his.'

'The blood was his, but not the print. He was five foot eight. The print was too high.' He gave a wry half-smile. 'Though Val also doesn't buy the hero-arriving-out-of-nowhere-like-Batman theory.'

Twisting the stem of the glass in her fingers, Jessie looked down at the pale liquid, at the pattern she'd made in its surface, concentric circles lit orange by the evening sun.

'There was a death twelve months ago on the same base. Male, sixteen – Danny Lawson,' she said.

'At Blackdown?'

She nodded. 'The Branch investigated and concluded that Danny's death was suicide, but Lawson's father didn't accept the findings. He created a huge fuss. Marilyn was asked to reinvestigate.'

'And?'

'He found the same.'

'Suicide. Definitely?'

'Yes.' Jessie sat forward. 'But there's more. Malcolm Lawson, Danny's father, disappeared three nights ago. His car was found abandoned on a quiet lane that runs through woods near Aldershot. And his son, Harry, Danny's little brother, was left in A&E at Royal Surrey County Hospital at around midnight that same night.'

'The night that Stephen Foster died?'

'Yes. Stephen died a few hours later – at about three a.m., is that right?'

Callan gave a brief nod. 'Why don't I know about Danny Lawson?'

'I presume you don't know because you were recovering from the injury you sustained in Afghanistan at the time. Also, more serving soldiers die of suicide every year than die in combat.'

'Still, Blackdown's CO should have mentioned other deaths on the base.'

Jessie bit her lip, thinking about the reasons that people join the Army. *Patriotism. Financial necessity. Escape.* She would bet good money that both Stephen Foster and Danny Lawson had joined to escape.

And then she thought of Ryan Jones. Ryan who was also escaping.

Ryan Jones. A disabled mother. Eight foster homes in five years. *Escape.*

'There's someone else.'

'Who?'

'A kid called Ryan Jones, also from Blackdown. I've seen him twice now.'

'Why have you seen him?'

'He was referred by the base's commanding officer, a Colonel Wallace, because of "concerns about his mental health".'

Callan nodded. 'Wallace. Yes, I've met him. And?'

'And, I got nowhere.' She paused. 'The boy was unforthcoming. But he's the same as the other two.'

Callan frowned. 'The same?'

'The same surface profile – gender, age, been in the Army around six months. But the most important thing is that I think he joined the Army to escape, same as the other two. And he's isolated, same as the other two.'

'What do you mean by isolated?'

'Danny Lawson's parents had thrown him out of the house. I haven't yet found out why. He joined the Army on his sixteenth birthday. Stephen Foster was an orphan. He, too, joined the Army on his sixteenth birthday. Ryan Jones's mother has motor neurone disease. He was forcibly taken away from her when he was eleven and bounced around eight foster homes until he joined the Army on his sixteenth birthday.'

As she reached for her glass, the sleeve of her shirt slid up her forearm. She felt the sudden grip of Callan's fingers on her wrist.

'What the hell is that?'

Looking up, she met his questioning gaze. 'What? Oh.'

The fingers of his other hand had found the cuff of her shirt, unbuttoned and slid it up to her elbow. She twisted her arm to free herself, but his grip was firm.

'Daddy?' He looked horrified. 'You? You did—'

'What? No. *No*. I'm not quite that mad!'

Colour had risen to her cheeks at his touch; she hoped that he hadn't noticed through the tinted lens of his sunglasses.

'So, who?' he snapped, releasing her arm.

She told him about her visit to Anne Lawson with Marilyn, about Anne's nail scratching its repetitive, maddening course across her skin.

'Why the fuck didn't Marilyn stop her?'

'Because I didn't want him to.'

'For Christ's sake, Jessie.' The concern in his voice surprised her. *Why the hell would he care?*

'Marilyn has nothing. We had nothing. We need to find Malcolm.'

Callan sat back, shaking his head. 'Marilyn needs to find Malcolm. It has nothing to do with you.'

Her wrist felt cold from the sudden absence of his fingers.

'So what does it mean?' he asked.

'Daddy – Malcolm.'

'Is that what Marilyn thought?'

'Yes.'

'You too?'

Jessie shrugged. 'It seems to make sense, given the context, the person writing it—' She broke off, her mind starting to race. Back to earlier in the day, walking in her hooker heels along a sunlit path, the pale face of the man with her,

278

framed by a glowing red-gold halo. 'Daddy,' she murmured. 'Dad. Father.' *Father.*

Their gazes locked.

'Father?' Callan echoed. 'Michael O'Shaughnessy? You know him?'

Jessie nodded. 'I spoke with him briefly today.'

'Why?'

'To ask him about Ryan.'

'Stephen Foster spoke with him.'

'About what?'

Callan gave a sarcastic half-smile, put on an Irish accent. 'You know that my discussions with people are entirely confidential, Captain.'

'I got pretty much the same reaction when I asked what he'd discussed with Ryan.'

Removing his sunglasses, Callan sat forward, steepling his fingers. His eyes were bright. Even through her dark lenses, Jessie couldn't hold them.

'Did he see Danny Lawson?' he asked.

'I don't know, but the Lawsons are Catholic.'

'What else did O'Shaughnessy say to you?'

'Nothing much. We bonded over Ireland, then I started asking awkward questions and our bonhomie suddenly evaporated. He told me that he comes from a village in the middle of Ireland, that he worked in Dublin before joining the Army, that he—'

'Dublin?'

'Yes.'

'You're sure?'

'Yes, why?'

Shaking his head, Callan sat back and rubbed a hand over his eyes. The light in them was gone. He just looked

279

tired now: wound up spring-tight and knackered. Reaching for his beer, he drained his glass.

'I'll pay the chaplain a visit tomorrow morning, see if I can get him to open up a bit about his discussions with these kids, but if he doesn't want to speak to me, he doesn't have to. And if Stephen Foster's death is suicide, as with Danny Lawson, there is no crime.'

'What?' She stared back at him, incredulous.

'Suicide is not a crime, Jessie.'

'But something drove them to it, Callan. Something drove Stephen and Danny to commit suicide.'

'That's irrelevant.'

'Why? Why is it irrelevant?'

'Because it's my job to investigate crimes and suicide is *not* a crime.'

'Isn't it important to find out what that something is? Who the other person with Stephen Foster was? Even if that other person was trying to save his life?'

Callan sighed. 'I suspect that "someone" is the chaplain. and as I've already said, I'll have a chat with him tomorrow. And yes, from a moral perspective, it might be important to find out what drove those kids to suicide, but from a criminal perspective it isn't. I'm a detective, Jessie.'

'Oh, for God's sake, Callan. You yourself admit that from a moral perspective—'

'I've got enough shit to do without being some kid's moral guardian.'

Angrily, Jessie slid her chair back. 'I didn't have you down as a jobsworth.'

'Hey, hold on, I'm only being practical.' Reaching across the table, he took hold of her wrist again, below the grazed words written there. 'Look, Jessie, I know what you went through when you were a kid, with your brother, but you can't let that cloud your judgem—'

'Don't.' Jessie snatched her arm away. 'Don't you fucking dare do that, Callan. This has nothing to do with my brother.'

51

Nine p.m. and the Special Investigation Branch offices were deserted. Lieutenant Gold had delivered the bagged Zippo lighter to Morgan, returned to his desk and dipped his head, pretending to be engaged in investigative work. In reality, he was biding his time, seething with impotent fury, until the last of his colleagues had called it a night and left.

Moving over to the ajar door, treading softly, he listened. He could hear the occasional voice echoing in some other part of the building – presumably non-SIB Military Police soldiers, working late. A phone rang in a room along the corridor, its shrill tone unanswered, and a car engine fired to life outside in the car park, puttered into the distance. When he was satisfied that he was truly alone, he pushed the door closed, and walked, on soft feet, to Callan's desk. His slender hands were shaking slightly as he pulled the 'Easy Pickings' lock-picking set from his pocket. He'd acquired it from Amazon for the princely sum of £9.99 fifteen months ago, when he had first joined the Special Investigation Branch, excited about the direction his Army career was taking, wanting to be prepared for every eventuality, as was his nature. He had not yet had the chance to use it.

There was only one lock, set into the face of the top drawer, which served to lock all three in the stack. Most Branch staff left their desk drawers unlocked, trust amongst the team implicit. But not Callan, and Gold knew precisely why.

It took him a couple of minutes to pick the lock, feeling for the row of pins against the roof of the cylinder, nudging them gently into position, eyes flicking to the door as he worked, ears straining for any sound, the excuse he had formulated if caught at Callan's desk written on the Post-it Note stuck to the back of his hand: *Zippo delivered to Morgan as requested, Gold.*

The lock's cylinders clicked into place. His heart beating faster now, a combination of anticipation and a lingering tension, he eased open the top drawer and scanned the contents. Callan was untidy, a trait that Gold abhorred, and the drawer was a jumble of pens, pencils, erasers, a couple of rulers, a spare pay-as-you-go mobile phone, some loose change, together with accumulated dust and lint that Callan hadn't bothered to clean away.

Tucked right at the back, secreted behind a box of drawing pins, Gold found what he was looking for. An opaque brown plastic tub with a white screw-on lid. Swivelling the tub in his fingers, he read the label: *Trileptal (Oxcarbazepine)*. Underneath, a long list of possible side effects: dizziness, blurred/double vision, clumsiness or unsteadiness, irritability, agitation, mental depression. With a brief, smug nod, he slipped the pills into his pocket, slid the drawer carefully back into place and locked it.

Peeling the Post-it Note from the back of his hand, he scrunched it up, pulled out Callan's bin, then checked himself. *No way.* He was too clever to make that schoolboy error. Instead he returned to his own desk, tore the note into eight pieces and dropped them into his own bin. Then he collected his coat, pulled the door open, flicked off the light and walked down the corridor towards the car park, no longer bothering to muffle his footsteps.

I don't date soldiers.

He'd seen her with Callan, recognized the subtext beneath that awkward exchange this afternoon, and he knew that what she had told him, her brush-off, was bullshit. So it was him then, him specifically that she had rejected. Why? What was wrong with him? Anger twisted in his gut. There was nothing wrong with him, was there?

And Callan? *I want it fingerprinted tonight. Now.*

No one made a fool out of him.

No one.

And anyway, he was doing the Army a favour. If Callan had any integrity, he'd have resigned his Commission long ago.

52

Ahmose must have been sitting by his window, watching the lane, because his front door opened, casting a rectangle of light on to his front garden, before she'd even switched off her engine. Walking up her path, leaning over the low flint wall dividing their gardens, she gave him a kiss on the cheek.

'Fancy a drink?'

'You already have a visitor.'

For a second Jessie thought that her visitor might be Callan, that he had driven here from the pub instead of back home, and her stomach constricted.

'Your father,' Ahmose said.

'*What?*'

He lifted his hands defensively. 'I couldn't leave him standing in the road.'

'Why not?'

'Because I have manners.'

'I don't.'

Ahmose smiled benignly. 'You weren't here, so I had to make the decision for you.'

Jessie groaned. 'Couldn't you have told him that I was away. That I'd gone back to the Middle East? For the rest of my life.'

'He is your father.'

'Therein lies the problem.'

'Just be polite.'

'I'm not going out to dinner with him.'

'Jessie.'

'I'm *not.*'

Ahmose took her hand, held it until she had stopped jittering, until the tension had subsided slightly from her limbs.

'You're busy and you have to get up early. It's already nine. A glass of wine, an hour's talking, a couple of well-placed yawns and the evening is over.'

Jessie rolled her eyes. 'Sadly, my father was never one for taking hints.'

'Ah, here's my beautiful baby girl.'

He rose from the sofa, arms outstretched, bright blue eyes glinting, caught not by any sun or electric light, but lit from within by the force of his personality. Jessie had forgotten how attractive he was, not a thought that sat comfortably when the man in question was her father. The jet-black-haired, blue-eyed Irish good looks and easy, familiar, hard-to-resist charm. Looking at him was like looking in a fairground mirror, one that replaced an X chromosome with a Y. Or looking at a grown Jamie, the man her little brother would have become, in looks at least. The thought made her heart harden again.

'Hi.' Her voice was cool. She stood stiff and unyielding while he wrapped her in a bear hug and kissed the top of her head.

'How are you, darlin'? It's been donkey's years. Far too long. I've missed my little girl.'

She disengaged herself from his arms, but not before she caught the look of hurt that flashed in his eyes at her rigid refusal to mould her body into his hug. For all his bravado, he wasn't entirely immune to the atmosphere between them. *Good.*

'Would you like a drink?' She was tempted to call him by his Christian name, Aiden. 'Dad?'

He grinned. 'Have you ever known me to turn down a drink?'

'White wine?'

'Don't you have anything stronger? I've had a long day. Listening to corporate litigators talk about the latest developments in our industry can hardly be described as scintillating.'

Did she have anything stronger? Probably not. A woman after her father's heart in that one dimension only, she would doubtless already have drunk it if she had anything stronger in the house.

'Sorry. Sauvignon or nothing.'

'Sauvignon it is then.'

Pulling the Princess glass out of the cupboard for herself, she retrieved another, smaller, for her father and filled them both to within a few millimetres of the brim.

'You're still using the glass. It's lasted well, hasn't it?' He winked. 'You're not drinking enough.'

'The Princess bucket is reserved for spectacularly shitty days. Run-of-the-mill shitty days, I use a normal glass.'

If he picked up on her snide aside, he didn't show it.

'Shall we sit outside, Dad? It's a lovely evening.'

'I've been in a stuffy conference room all day, so outside sounds grand, darlin'.'

They sat at her garden table, the wooden slats of the table and chairs laced with cobwebs, the wood slippery with moss, she hadn't used them since last summer. The sun had gone down, but it was still warm enough to sit outside with a coat on and the smell of rapeseed on the breeze was sweet and pleasant. She could almost feel Ahmose's eyes drilling into her back from next door, felt, for him, if not for her father, that she should be polite, give her father a chance. She raised a hand slightly to signal that she had listened to his doorstep advice, had no idea if he saw.

Her father lifted his glass. 'May the road rise to meet you, darlin'.'

'You too, Dad.'

They clinked glasses and drunk, both staring off down the length of the dark garden, eye contact fleeting and awkward.

'So how long is it since we last saw each other?' he asked, after a moment. 'What, a year, is it now? A little over that?'

'Two and a half.'

'Two and a half? Surely not. It can't be that long.'

'It is. Twenty-seventh of October 2014. We went out to dinner the day before your birthday.'

Silence, while he cast his mind back.

'Christ, you're right.' He looked momentarily embarrassed, an embarrassment that he smoothed over with another drink and another broad smile. 'So what have you been up to, sweetheart?'

She told him about her job, her tour of duty in the Middle East, leaving out the monotony, adding spice to turn it into good old Irish craic. He responded with craic of his own, leaving out all mentions of Diane, knowing how much of a red rag her name was to the Jessie bull, even now.

'So do you have a boyfriend?'

'No.'

'Why not?'

Because I only fancy one and he's not interested. 'I don't have time.'

'Of course you have time. All work and no play makes . . . '

'Jill a dull girl. Funnily enough, someone else said that to me this afternoon.'

'A boy?'

'A man.'

Her dad laughed. 'A prospect?'

'Not remotely.'

'Surely there are loads of them in the Army, aren't there? A beautiful girl like you should be inundated.'

'What's with the desperation to get me set up? This isn't 1970s Ireland. I'm not over the hill at twenty-nine. Nearing the summit, Dad, but not quite over it yet.' She realized that her own voice had taken on an Irish tinge, speaking with him, subconsciously aping her childhood accent, the first five years of her life spent in Dublin before they had moved to London with her father's job, before Jamie had been born and their lives had hit that downward spiral. She also realized that she was quite enjoying speaking with him, that despite all he had done, the depth of his betrayal, he was still her father and they still had a connection, however hard she had tried to deny it, to sever it.

'Talking about over the hill, just give me a minute.' With a grin, he slid his chair back and disappeared inside. A minute later, he was back out, a package wrapped in silver paper resting in the palm of his hand, a shiny silver bow tied around it, the ends of the bow teased into curls. Sitting down, he placed the parcel in the middle the table, his smile faltering at the lack of expression on Jessie's face.

'For Saturday,' he said.

She frowned. 'Saturday?'

'Yes.' He cocked an eyebrow, an expression that morphed into a crease between his brows when she didn't react. 'Your birthday, sweetheart.' A hint of uncertainty now in his tone.

'It's April, Dad. Saturday is April sixth. My birthday is in May. May twenty sixth.'

A tentative smile. 'Are you sure?'

'I don't know many things, but I do know my own birthday.' *As my father should know my birthday.*

He winced, put his head in his hands. 'Shit. I'm an idiot. I'm such an idiot.'

Jessie reached across and took the present, laid her other hand on his arm.

'Don't worry. I'm sure you've got a lot on your mind. Shall I open it now, anyway, or save it?'

But he looked, suddenly, as if he wasn't listening to her, as if he hadn't heard a word she'd said.

'Even so. It, uh . . . Lord, I'm an idiot. I'm a hopeless idiot.' Pulling his arm from her grasp, he sat back, biting his lip in the same way that she did when she was stressed. She didn't know if it was a trick of the moonlight, but his face looked pale. 'I did the same with, uh, with Jamie,' he murmured. 'With Jamie's birthday.'

Jessie frowned. Why had he suddenly mentioned Jamie? They hadn't talked about Jamie for years, all mentions of him tacitly off limits, the subject of his son, her little brother, way too raw and inflammatory between them.

'When? Which birthday?' she asked quietly.

Her father sighed and shrugged. 'The day, he—' He broke off, rubbing a hand over his eyes. 'That last day. I met him at the school gate with a present. He wasn't with you or your mum. He was with some other woman and her son. They looked like they were giving him a lift home. I went over and tried to give him the birthday present I'd bought him. They walked on a bit, the woman and her son, to give us space to talk.'

Jessie was staring hard at him now. *That last day?* Was he joking? He had never mentioned this before; never mentioned that he'd seen Jamie on that last day.

She fought to keep her voice even. 'What happened?'

'He was standing by the tree. You know that horse chestnut tree that grows out of a square of dirt on the pavement, right outside the school gate. I remember that he looked so small. So small and so skinny next to the tree trunk. It really struck me then, how . . . how little he was, how young.' He ground the heels of his palms into his eyes, raked his fingers down his cheeks. 'And he looked sick, you know. I remember looking at him then and thinking how sick he looked. God, I think I'd kind of blinded myself to the fact of how ill he actually was.'

That's because you weren't there that last year, because you never saw him, Jessie wanted to scream. Instead, she gave a silent nod, hardly daring to breathe, feeling the electric suit tingle against her skin.

'When I think of Jamie now, I always think of him that day. Of seeing him standing by that tree, looking so small and lost and ill.' Shadows had filled his eyes. 'I wanted to hug him. I wanted to take him into my arms and wrap him up and keep him safe. Keep him safe from that fucking thing, from that . . . that illness. I would have

291

done anything then. I would have done anything to make him well again.'

Anything except stay with us. The electric suit was hissing and snapping, so tight around her throat that breathing was a struggle.

'What happened?' she croaked.

He reached for his glass of wine and drained it, three-quarters of a glass in two big gulps. Twisting the stem of the empty glass in his fingers, he stared down at the patterns of refracted moonlight it made on the gnarled wood.

'I'd got Jamie a present for his birthday. That's why I went to meet him at the school that day, to give him his birthday present. I couldn't bring it to the house, with your mother there.' He chewed his lip again. 'When Jamie saw me with the present, he bent down, grabbed a handful of stones from the base of the tree and threw them at me. Threw them right in my face – hard in my face. Then he ran off.' He closed his eyes and shook his head. 'Look, I know that I've been a shitty dad, and that you both hated me for leaving your mum for Diane, but it . . . you have no idea how hard it was. How hard it was dealing with Jamie's illness, with your mother, with you, for Christ's sake, an angry, unhappy teenager. I couldn't do it any more. I couldn't take it. I might be fuckin' soft, but I just couldn't take it.' Dipping his head to his hands, he buried his face in his palms. 'And you were both too young to understand.'

'Jamie died in June. June thirteenth.'

Tuesday, 13 June 2000.

Thirteen – unlucky for some – baker's dozen – the Devil's number.

The stinging electricity from the suit hummed over her limbs, so intense now that she felt as if she would explode

292

from the tension. 'His birthday was in July. July thirtieth. We always had his party a week early, before school broke up for the summer holidays, so that his friends could come.'

Her father's gaze rose from his hands to meet hers.

'You didn't remember?'

The movement barely there, he shook his head.

'Why not? Why didn't you remember?' She was aware that her voice had risen, become high-pitched – high-pitched and desperate. 'Why didn't you remember, Dad? It wasn't his birthday when you met him outside school. That last day wasn't his birthday. It wasn't even close to his birthday.'

The straw.

She had always blamed herself for Jamie's death, because she had left him alone that day, gone to Wimbledon Common with her boyfriend and let him be dropped home by a friend's mother to an empty house. *The only thing I keep coming back to is that he felt abandoned. Abandoned and alone – because I left him alone.*

'I know that now. But at the time, I forgot. I fuckin' forgot, OK.' Even across the table, in the darkness, she could see that her father's pale face had lost all of its colour. 'I'm an idiot and I forgot.'

The straw. Her father.

'I went to Berkshire today,' she said quietly.

'Berkshire?' His voice was barely a whisper.

She nodded.

'Is that supposed to mean something to me?'

'Berkshire. Hartmoor.'

Still no recognition. 'Hartm—' He broke off. 'What the hell were you doing there?' A surge of aggression in his voice. Aggression and defensiveness, a whole depth of self-hatred, hurt, anger, regret, guilt and more anger.

293

'I'm a psychologist. I had to go there for my job.'

'You nearly killed us, Jessie. I had no choice. It was there or juvenile detention.'

'You let her win. You let Diane beat me. I'm your daughter and you still helped her to win.' Her limbs felt on fire, the electric suit burning.

'It wasn't about winning and losing.'

'Wasn't it? Really? Wasn't it?' Tears welled in her eyes and she blinked to push them back. She wasn't going to cry in front of him. 'I lost my father, then I lost my brother, and then that bitch threw Pandy away – the last thing I had of Jamie's – and then I lost a year of my life, locked up in that shithole, because of her.' She felt a single tear run down her cheek. Wiping it roughly away with the back of her hand, she met his gaze defiantly. 'Because of her and because of *you*.'

'It wasn't a shithole.'

'FUCK YOU.'

His jaw tightened. 'You nearly killed us, Jessie.'

'I was fourteen. It was an accident.'

'You still nearly killed us.'

'And you killed me, Dad. I was dying inside and you killed me stone dead.'

53

'Daddy.'

Michael O'Shaughnessy's eyelashes blinked against the few shafts of thin morning sunlight that had carved their way through the dense grey clouds overhead.

'Excuse me?' he said.

Callan had found the chaplain climbing out of his car in Blackdown's main car park, a cup of takeaway coffee in a polystyrene cup in his hand. He looked tired, his face pinched and creased with tension, a good ten years older than his thirty years.

'Daddy. Father. It took me a while.'

Callan had nothing concrete, only five letters the deeply damaged mother of a dead boy had scratched in skin, and conjecture, theories, cooked up in the pub last night with Jessie Flynn. Only conjecture and the will to bullshit.

'What on earth are you talking about, Captain?'

'Danny Lawson. You counselled him, didn't you? A year or so ago?'

O'Shaughnessy shut his car door, ducking his gaze to

fiddle with the key fob. The locks on his car clicked shut.

'Danny Lawson? Yes, I spoke with him a couple of times.'

'What about?'

'Captain, you know that—'

'Isn't there a rule, morally, if nothing else, that says if you suspect a person's life is at risk you are allowed to break confidentiality?'

'Danny Lawson's life is not at risk, Captain.'

'No. He's dead. But I suspect that you knew he was a suicide risk when you were counselling him.'

'Suicide is never obvious—'

'And you did nothing.'

'Captain—'

'What did he tell you, Chaplain?'

'Captain Callan—'

'*What did he tell you?*'

Placing his coffee cup on the roof of his car, O'Shaughnessy sighed. 'He told me that he'd joined the Army because his parents threw him out and he didn't know what else to do, where else to go.'

'Why did they throw him out?'

O'Shaughnessy laid his car keys on the roof, next to the coffee cup. He spent a moment arranging them so that they wouldn't slide off.

'Chaplain,' Callan pressed.

'They threw him out because he got a girl pregnant. A girl from his church. They were both thirteen. The girl's parents wouldn't countenance abortion, but wanted nothing to do with the baby when he was born, so Danny's parents took him in, raised him as their own son.'

Harry – the baby Jessie Flynn had mentioned last night. The baby who she thought was Danny's little brother.

296

'Because abortion is a sin in the eyes of the Catholic Church, as is having a child out of wedlock.' Callan shook his head bitterly. 'Between a rock and a hard place.'

The frown line between O'Shaughnessy's brows deepened. 'We are modernizing. The Pope has made it clear that children born outside wedlock should no longer be denied Baptism.'

'That's heart-warming to hear.' His voice was cold, his eyes hard. 'Did you suspect that there was more? Other things that Danny Lawson was worried about?'

'There's always more, Captain. But as I have already told you, I saw Danny only twice. We didn't get further than baby Harry.' He collected the cup from the roof of his car, gathered up his keys. 'Now, if you'll excuse me.'

'I believe that Stephen Foster's death is suicide and that it is linked to Danny's. I also believe that Ryan Jones is a suicide risk.'

'Surely it is your job as a Military Policeman to solve *crimes*, Captain.'

Callan ignored his comment. 'What is happening on this base, Chaplain?'

'Ryan Jones has been referred to the Defence Psychology Service. They can help him better than I can.'

He moved to step past; Callan stretched out his arm, boxing him against the side of the car.

'Dublin.'

O'Shaughnessy sighed irritably. 'You've lost me again, Captain. Now I really must—'

'You told Doctor Flynn that you were a parish priest in Dublin before you joined the Army.'

'I really don't recall saying—'

'Dungarvan. County Waterford. It's a fair way from Dublin.'

'As I said, I don't recall—'

'We tracked your records down with the Garda. You have an interesting past.'

O'Shaughnessy stiffened.

'How did you get into the Army, Chaplain, with a past that interesting? And why is there no mention of it in your personnel file?'

'There was no substance to those allegations, Captain. The girl was proven to be a hysteric – a liar, to put it bluntly. I don't doubt that the Garda would have told you that.'

'You're not averse to a few lies yourself, are you, Chaplain? And aren't lies a sin – or is that what confession is for?'

Callan noticed that, for the first time since he'd met the chaplain, O'Shaughnessy couldn't look him in the eye.

'You obviously don't like God, Captain.'

'Wrong. I'm fine with God. My problem is that I don't like you. When I spoke to you three days ago, you said that the welfare of the living was more important than the welfare of the dead. Who are you protecting? Or are you protecting yourself?'

O'Shaughnessy didn't reply, but Callan could tell that he was rattled. Dropping his arm, Callan stepped back, giving the padre space to leave. As O'Shaughnessy stepped past him, eyes on the ground, Callan spoke again, his tone pure provocation.

'One more thing, Chaplain. How did you know that Stephen was going to kill himself – or was it pure luck that you arrived in the woods just in time to try and save him.'

O'Shaughnessy stopped in his tracks and turned, forehead wrinkling with confusion.

'You failed and he drowned in his own blood,' Callan continued. 'But I suppose at least you tried. What I don't understand is how you knew what he was going to do, where and when.'

O'Shaughnessy stepped forward, right into Callan's personal space, craning his neck to hold Callan's gaze, fury etched into his soft features.

'Enough, Captain. *Enough* now. I have no idea what you're talking about – and if you want to go and fetch a bible I'd be happy to swear on it to that effect. I spoke to Stephen, as I spoke to Danny and Ryan. All three were troubled young men. In answer to your question, "Was there more?" – I'm positive that there was, with all three of them, but I never got to the bottom of it. It's my job to listen, not to pry.' His pale face was red. 'I'm sick of your accusations. I've done nothing wrong, and I'm sick of you hounding me.'

A grim smile on his face, Callan nodded. He had achieved what he had set out to achieve, and he was sure now that O'Shaughnessy hadn't been in that wood, holding Stephen Foster up, trying to stop him drowning in his own blood. Those five letters etched into the skin of Jessie's forearm – *Daddy* – didn't refer to him. He had no idea who or what they did refer to, but he was certain, holding the chaplain's insipid gaze, burning now with an intense anger, that it wasn't O'Shaughnessy.

'Thank you for your honesty, Chaplain. Have a nice day.'

As he watched O'Shaughnessy walk away, he pulled his mobile from his pocket, dialled Jessie Flynn's mobile and when it went to voicemail, left a message.

54

As soon as Joan pulled open the door, Jessie could tell that something was wrong. A woman shrunken and faded had usurped the neat, proud old lady she had begun to know. Unwashed hair curled over her head like steel wool, pink scalp visible where patches had thinned, patches that Jessie hadn't noticed before when her hair was clean, brushed and secured in place with hairpins. An old navy-blue towelling dressing gown, Malcolm's from the size, hung off her coat-hanger shoulders and swallowed her feet, the collar frayed and cracked with what looked like drying egg yolk. Jessie could tell from the shadowed bags underlining each eye that she hadn't slept.

The old lady regarded her, grey-faced and unsmiling. 'Have the police found Malcolm yet?'

Jessie shook her head. 'I'm afraid not.'

'What do you want then?'

'I came to see how you are.'

'I'm not some aged relative of yours, so you don't need to check on me.'

Jessie winced at the frostiness in her voice. 'I'm sorry.' She waved her hand in the direction of the main road, somewhere beyond Joan's shoulder. 'I was passing.'

It was a white lie, yet another lie – she'd told too many recently – but fuelled by her discussion in the pub yesterday evening with Callan, she had come for a reason other than to check on Joan and Harry and she needed to rescue the situation, so that she could see the purpose of her visit through.

'Was that all, Doctor Flynn?'

'No.' She held Joan's hostile gaze. 'I'd like to look in Danny's room to see if I can find anything that might give us a clue to Malcolm's whereabouts.' *And to see if I can find out why he was driven to suicide.*

'Shouldn't the police be doing that?'

Probably. 'The police are out there, searching for Malcolm, Joan.'

The old lady pursed her pale lips to stop them from trembling. 'The police have given up on us, haven't they, Doctor Flynn?'

Jessie's heart went out to her: another mother, like her mother, the same heartbreak, all too achingly familiar.

'No, they haven't, I can promise you that. I haven't told DI Simmons that I'm here and it will probably lead to nothing, but I might find something useful. I'd like to try.'

They regarded each other across the threshold for a silent moment.

'Oh, do whatever the hell you want,' Joan snapped bitterly. 'Here.' Pulling a bunch of keys from a hook beside the front door, she thrust them into Jessie's hand. 'It's locked. Malcolm keeps it locked. The key is on this bunch. I haven't been in there since Danny's death, so I have no idea what you'll find. Hang the keys back up there and leave when you're done.'

Without another word, she turned from the doorway and disappeared down the dark corridor, head bent, shoulders slumped, her slippered feet scuffing the worn carpet with each dragging step. Disappearing into the lounge-kitchen, she shut the door firmly behind her.

Pulling the front door closed, Jessie followed a few steps behind, giving Joan space. Past Malcolm's bedroom to her right, Joan's worn brown lace-ups still tucked side by side on the floor at the end of the bed, but the duvet and pillows crumpled, the bed unmade; Harry's room to her left, the door ajar also, the cot empty, a couple of drawers in his dresser hanging open, clothes spilling from them. She stopped outside Danny's room. The door, as before, the only one that was firmly closed. It took her a couple of attempts to find the right key.

She hadn't thought in advance what she might find inside, and as she unlocked the door and cracked it open, she realized, with a flash of clarity, that her lack of pre-analysis had been subconscious but entirely deliberate, her brain protecting her heart, shying away from thinking through the reality of a long-dead boy's room frozen in time by a parent who couldn't move on.

As she stepped into the darkened room and fumbled her hand up the wall to find the light switch, she felt the hairs on the back of her neck stand straight on end.

'Danny,' she murmured.

No reply – of course not. *I didn't expect there to be, did I?* She knew that this room was empty, that she was alone, but still she stood frozen on the threshold of the small, dark space, not wanting to step forward, not wanting to shut the door behind her, close herself in with the haunting memories – the Lawsons and her own.

The air was hot and musty, thick blackout curtains drawn over the one window, vertical bands of grey dust caught in their folds. Finding the light switch finally, she clicked it on and the bulb flickered before the room flooded with dull yellow electric light. She removed her other hand from the door handle and the door swung closed, the click as it shut making her flinch. *Get a grip, Jessie.*

The room felt as dead and soulless as Jamie's had felt in the years succeeding his suicide: a museum, a dedication to a boy, a life that was no longer being lived, an existence frozen in time. But where her mother had dusted and polished, made Jamie's bed, kept folded pyjamas tucked under his pillow, as if he might one day walk back in, toss his school bag on the floor and flop on to the bed, reaching for Pandy with one hand, his Walkman with the other, Malcolm Lawson had locked the door on his son's room, if not, mentally, on his life.

Jessie positioned herself in the middle of the room and let her gaze drift around the walls, taking in a pine desk and chair to her right, the poster of a blonde girl in a red bikini sitting astride a motorbike tacked above the desk, a single pine-framed bed pushed against the far wall under the window, navy-blue duvet and pillow case, the curtains a matching blue – Danny, unlike Jamie, too old for Batman curtains or football duvet covers – to her left a pine cupboard and chest of drawers, a cricket ball and bat and a tennis racquet tucked underneath the chest, every item in the room as if she was looking at it through grey-tinted lenses, everything layered with a uniform coating of thick grey dust. The room of a long-dead boy and there were GCSE revision books on the desk, a jumper hooked over the back of the chair and sports equipment shoved under the chest. The life Danny Lawson had led before he became a Loggie. Everything so normal, a million other teenaged boys' rooms like it, but so disconcertingly abnormal at the same time.

Walking to the desk, she scanned its surface, not knowing what she was looking for, but hoping that she would know when she found it. With the exception of Stephen Foster's sterile barrack-room space, she had never searched a room before, had never needed to. But she had searched many people's minds and she was pretty sure that the same process would apply: *empty your mind of expectation – look, don't search – find the abnormal behind the normal.*

Pulling the chair out, she squatted down in front of the desk, not wanting to sit on his chair, disturb too much, feeling as if every touch left a permanent print, desecrated this grave, Danny's memory, a bit more. Hooking her index finger into its handle, she pulled open the top desk drawer and looked quickly through the contents: a pencil case, more revision books, a notepad, only the first page written on, a list of things that he needed to remember to bring to school that day. The second and third drawers more of the same, the detritus of a teenager with exams to focus on.

She moved over to the cupboard; his clothes, those he hadn't taken with him, hung in a neat row from the single rail, shirts, trousers, one smart jacket and one formal looking dark-grey suit that she could imagine a teenage boy being made to wear once a year for a smart dinner out or, knowing what she knew about this family, for a formal visit to church. Or perhaps he had bought it himself for his Army entrance interviews? The chest of drawers was similarly half-empty: boxer shorts and socks in each of the small top two drawers, T-shirts in the middle, jumpers and fleeces in the bottom.

Moving over to the curtains, she checked the windowsill behind them, feeling the gritty particles of dust coating her fingers – nothing – squatted and looked under the bed – a sports bag, empty – a suitcase – she pulled it out; empty, also – and then, far in the back corner, a cardboard box. Slithering on her stomach, the tickle of carpet dust in her nostrils, she hooked her hands around the box and, snaking awkwardly backwards, hauled it out.

The first thing she saw when she eased open the flaps was Danny's navy-blue Royal Logistic Corps beret, the gold cap badge catching what little light the dim overhead bulb cast. The memory it brought to her mind immediately: berets laid on the coffins of dead soldiers returning from Afghanistan as they were unloaded from Hercules transporters. With a shudder, she put it back, feeling as if she was handling something too personal.

What else was in this box, apart from the beret and folded uniform underneath it, sent back to his family by the MOD upon his death? She delved her hand around the edge of the uniform, feeling, as she had when searching Stephen Foster's belongings with Callan, like a grave robber.

Tucked in the corner of the box was a black notebook, the Loggies' logo on its cover. Picking the notebook up by its corner, in pincer fingers, Jessie laid it on the carpet directly under the single hanging bulb. The first page was blank, the second, third and fourth too. Turning the book over, she opened the back cover.

Something was drawn on the last page. An amateur pencil sketch.

A bear. The kind of cartoon bear that featured in the stories she had read to Jamie when he was a toddler. Round-bodied, big-bellied and hairy, with dark button eyes. And underneath the picture, the scribbled words: *Somebody has been at my porridge, said Great, Huge Bear in his great gruff voice.* She leafed to the next page.

Another bear. This one's mouth gaping open, teeth bared. *Somebody has been sitting in my chair, said Great, Huge Bear in his great gruff voice.*

She flicked slowly through the other pages. There were several drawings, all of bears, each one slightly different, many of the pictures only a face. In one, the bear had the eyes of a human. In another, it looked as if the bear was wearing a mask – of a dog? A wolf?

In the last scribbled sketch, the bear was rearing up on its hind legs, its mouth gaping open, teeth bared, and there was a glimpse of something else – another smaller bear, a person? – Jessie couldn't quite tell, lying beneath. Cowering was the word that came into her mind. And underneath the sketch, was written: *Somebody has been sleeping in my bed, said Great, Huge Bear in his great gruff voice.*

Slipping the notebook into her handbag, not sure why, she closed the box and shoved it back under the bed, as far as she could without having to lie on the dusty carpet again, shuffle into that claustrophobic space under the dead boy's bed.

Her mouth was dry and her throat closed up, as if the dirt and dust, the heavy atmosphere in the room had desiccated her. She got to her feet and took one last look around, knowing that she had searched everywhere and found nothing useful – nothing except for the drawings of those bears, drawings that perhaps meant nothing, but were so odd. Then she pulled Danny's door closed and locked it behind her.

55

Colonel Richard Holden-Hough looked from the clock on the wall – 9.30 a.m. – to his office doorway where the young lieutenant was shifting from foot to foot.

Sitting back in his chair, Holden-Hough folded his arms across his chest and eyeballed the lieutenant whose name he was struggling to remember, despite having worked with him for more than a year now.

'I have a meeting with Val Monks, the pathologist, in five minutes. Whatever you need, can you speak to Captain Callan? He is your direct superior.'

Gold shuffled his feet in the doorway, his navy-flecked, royal-blue gaze focused somewhere beyond Holden-Hough's left shoulder.

'I actually want to speak to you about Captain Callan and it's . . . it's a bit sensitive, sir.' He held up a brown A5 envelope.

Holden-Hough could see from its shape that there was more than paper inside. 'Sensitive?' He could already feel his patience, of which he had precious little at the best of times, fraying.

'Yes, sir.' Gold shifted his feet again, nervously. 'I don't normally tell tales, but I do think it's important this issue is brought to your attention.'

What the hell was he talking about? Holden-Hough looked past him to Val Monks, who had appeared behind the lieutenant and was standing in the doorway.

'Come on in, Val. Grab a seat.' And to Gold: 'Leave it on my desk, will you. I'll look at it later.'

'I'd prefer to discuss it now—'

Slapping a flat palm on his desktop, Holden-Hough cut him off. 'On my desk.'

'Right. OK, sir.' Stepping forward, smiling and nodding like one of those spring-necked dogs old folks prop on the parcel shelf of their Nissan Micras, the lieutenant deposited the bulging envelope on the edge of the desk. 'We'll speak when you've had a chance to look at the envelope's contents then, sir.'

With a curt nod, Holden-Hough waved him away.

As Gold left the office, he glanced over his shoulder and saw the pathologist leaning back in her chair, laughing heartily at something that Holden-Hough had said, Holden-Hough's taciturn mouth split into an uncharacteristic grin. In the year he'd been in the Branch, he had never even managed to make the man crack a smile. The sight added another rotation to the fury that had already twisted his gut out of shape.

56

For what felt like the first time in weeks, Marilyn had slept well. The previous night he'd returned to his narrow Georgian terraced house, set inside the city walls of historic Chichester, switched off his mobile and unplugged his land-line, knowing that eight hours in the sack, alone, would be a far more profitable use of the night than either visiting another dubious drinking establishment or mainlining coffee and trawling through the exhausted mess that was his brain for something he had missed, that elusive clue that would lead him straight to the whereabouts of Malcolm Lawson without passing 'Go'.

He woke at eight thirty, his head clear, ready to leap rather than crawl out of bed, get back to the office and get motoring on those tyres – *excuse the pun.*

On the way in he stopped to grab himself a coffee and a blueberry muffin from the coffee shop on South Street, ducking back when he was halfway to his car to grab a second coffee and a raspberry-and-white-chocolate muffin for DS Workman, who he knew would have spent most of the night in front of her computer. Arriving at the office, he broke into an uncharacteristic jog up the stairs to the incident room.

'Americano with milk and two sugars.' He put the coffee on Workman's desk. Retrieving the muffin from his suit jacket pocket, he placed it next to the coffee.

Workman eyed her gifts suspiciously. *Not surprising.* He couldn't recall ever, in the eight years they'd worked together, buying her any kind of gift. Too focused on a result, not enough on the softer side of policing. Not that he was about to change now: *old dog, new tricks and all that.* Everything about this morning – the sleep, the jog up the stairs, the gifted muffin – was an aberration, one that he doubted he'd be repeating in a very long time.

'To what do I owe this pleasure, sir?'

'To a result? The tyres?'

She sighed. 'Ah, yes.'

He raised an eyebrow in query. 'I'm not sure that I like your tone.'

'No.' Workman flipped the lid off her takeaway coffee, took a sip, gave a small satisfied – 'mmm' – took another. Laying the cup down, she reached for the muffin, broke off a small piece and popped it into her mouth. Another 'mmmm'. Then she flipped her notebook open to reveal neat lines of navy-blue cursive script. 'We still have two small independent garages to contact within the search area. Darren's on to it now.' She glanced at her watch. It was nearly 10 a.m., Marilyn realized, shocked. He'd usually have done half a day's work by this time. He could get used to this nine-to-five malarkey.

'And apart from those?'

Another sigh. 'Johnny M was right when he said that these tyres are expensive and infrequently fitted.'

'That's good.' He paused, catching the look on Workman's plain face. 'Isn't it?'

'It should be,' she sighed. 'But—'

She looked tired and dispirited, and Marilyn felt an upswell of guilt for the 'me time' he'd enjoyed, chastising himself a moment later for even using the hideous phrase 'me time'. He'd spent so long dealing with Home Counties crimes that he was beginning to sound like a spoilt Surrey lady-who-lunches.

'I feel as if we've hit a dead end, at least within the search area that we mapped out.' Her gaze dipped to her notebook. 'We have the Surrey area sales rep with a national printing firm. He's recently back from two weeks in Lanzarote.'

'Strike him off the list.'

'Right.'

'And?'

'Tesco Guildford store manager. Vectra. Working the night shift when Malcolm disappeared. It's a twenty-four-hour Tesco.'

'Strike him too.'

'A seventy-year-old man, Mr Derek Porter, and his lovely wife, Barbara. Charming on the phone, she was.'

'And expansive?'

'Very. They put these tyres on their precious twelve-year-old, mint-condition, 5 series BMW because, "You get what you pay for". Then a Mr Felix Peterson with a Mercedes SL. He had his tyres changed to these five weeks ago, his local Kwik Fit told me.'

'Have you spoken with him?'

'Not yet.' A pause. 'Because of what you said about the Porsches, Mercedes, etc, being at the bottom of the list.'

Marilyn gave a listless nod. The good mood that had

kept pace with him since he'd risen this morning was fast dissipating. This whole case felt cursed. Malcolm bloody Lawson felt cursed. He'd had enough of the man the last time they'd had dealings, six months ago; he was buried beyond his eyeballs this time.

'There is something else,' Workman ventured. 'But I'm pretty sure that it's another dead end.'

Marilyn raised an eyebrow. 'What?'

57

Head in his hands, Callan looked down at the open desk drawer in front of him. He'd searched it three times, laying each item out on his desktop the third time, knowing, even as he did so, that he was wasting his time, that he wouldn't find his epilepsy medication. Realizing, with a creeping sense of dread, that someone had broken into his drawer and taken it. Sitting back, he ground his knuckles into his eyeballs, scratched his fingers through his hair. *Fuck.* What the hell was he going to do now?

Spinning on his chair, he scanned the office. The Branch detectives who were at their desks were all heads down, working. A few desks empty, but that was always the case; this wasn't a sedentary job. His gaze tracked along the wall to the windows – the sky still blue, but dull and misty now, bearing the promise of a downpour – continued along the wall. Ed Gold was standing at the door to Holden-Hough's office. He was clutching a brown envelope and seemed, given the way he was dancing from foot to foot, nervous. Nervous and shifty. Callan was his superior officer and he should have no need to speak to Holden-Hough unless it was personal, something he didn't want Callan to know about. And what the hell was in that envelope?

He cast his mind back four months to Wendy Chubb's murder, Marilyn asking him to: *Prise this joker* – Gold, he had meant – *off my crime scene*. Gold standing together with Corporal Kiddie, laughing. Gold's laugh fading to a small, knowing smile as Callan approached. Waiting until he was comfortably within earshot, before turning to Kiddie:

'How can you tell when a drug addict is lying?'

Kiddie looking confused. 'What? A drug addict? I don't know.'

'Come on. A drug addict. How can you tell when he's lying?'

'I don't know. Tell me.'

'He opens his mouth.'

Callan, himself, hissing, 'Jesus, you're at a crime scene. Have a bit of respect.'

Gold, his shoulders still shaking with mirth, saying in a 'fuck you' tone, 'I wasn't joking about the victim.'

Beyond Gold, only Jessie Flynn and Val Monks knew about his epilepsy and he trusted them both implicitly. Looking at Gold now, he realized with cold clarity exactly what was in that envelope that he was proffering to Holden-Hough.

Standing, Callan moved over to the window. Perhaps he should shove it open, drop down and start walking – away from all this shit, away from duplicitous colleagues, from a job that bled you dry, then tossed you out like junk, walk into another life where his epilepsy wouldn't be an issue. But what life? This far, the Redcaps had been his whole life and he didn't know any other.

What choices did he have?

None. He had none. His only option was to confess to Holden-Hough and face the consequences. Whatever happened, he'd lose his job. There was no way that the Army could employ an epileptic. Holden-Hough, however much Callan rated and respected him, would follow the rules. *Better to get it over with.* He turned from the window. Gold was no longer in Holden-Hough's office; Val Monks was. Callan hadn't seen her arrive. Gold was nowhere to be seen. Callan was halfway across the office when Val Monks rose to her feet and shook Holden-Hough's hand across his desk. She came face to face with Callan in the office doorway.

'Callan.'

'Val.' Callan nodded distractedly, his gaze moving past her. 'Have you got a minute, sir?'

Holden-Hough nodded. 'Come on in, Captain.'

Val Monks laid a hand on Callan's chest.

'Sorry, Richard, but I need a quick word with Captain Callan before he speaks to you. It's about Stephen Foster's autopsy. I'd wait, but I'm in a hurry to get back to my bodies.'

'Your bodies are going nowhere, Val, but being the gentleman that I am, I'm happy to let a lady go first.'

Val rolled her eyes. 'Less of the sexist tripe please, Colonel.'

Holden-Hough looked hurt. 'I have no idea how to act around women these days.'

'Just avoid us like the plague,' she said, turning away and ushering Callan to follow with a whispered, 'Let's take a quick walk.'

Callan shook his head. 'I need to speak with him now.'

The soft hand on his chest turned into a firm backwards shove. 'I don't think you do,' she hissed. 'Come with me, *now.*'

She walked past him, her hand moving from his chest to his forearm, fingers gripping with a determination that surprised him. Reluctantly, he allowed himself to be steered along the corridor, Val's heels clicking on the polished lino, the only sound to break the heavy silence, Callan mired in his own morose thoughts. Outside, they turned to face each other. Callan let out a heavy sigh; Val crossed her arms over her ample chest.

'You are not resigning from the Branch – I assume that's why you wanted to see Holden-Hough so urgently, right after Gold had left an envelope containing your epilepsy medication on his desk?' Opening the sheaf of papers she had been clutching, she slipped the brown envelope from between them and held it out to him. 'Holden-Hough didn't see what was in it, and I arrived before Gold had time to tell him.'

Callan didn't smile. 'Thank you for doing that, Val, but it doesn't change the fact that I have a bullet lodged in my brain that gives me seizures. I rely on that medication in order to function. I have to come clean.'

She regarded him carefully, in the same way he'd seen her look into the opened chest cavities of corpses on her dissecting table. Her scrutiny made him feel intensely uncomfortable. Dipping his head to break eye contact, he murmured, 'I should have resigned after Afghanistan, a year ago. I should never have come back to work.'

'The Army needs men like you.'

'The Army needs men who can do their job properly. That's not me, not any more.'

'The Army needs men and women who are committed,

clever, have integrity and are brave. You are all of those things and much more.'

'I've lied all day, every day since I came back. That's not integrity.'

'That's necessity, Callan. You are a fantastic Branch detective and you are right where you should be.'

Callan shook his head. He looked bereft. 'Thank you for your faith in me, Val, but it's over.'

'*No.*' There was no way she was giving in. The Army invalided out young men who had been injured in combat every day, gave them a small pension and tossed them into civilian life, to eat or be eaten. Too many were failing, ending up as alcoholics or drug addicts, homeless vagrants, ending their young lives with suicide because it felt like the easiest option, the only option. Despite what Callan had told her at Stephen Foster's autopsy – to effectively butt out with regard to his health – she had no intention of letting him hang himself. 'You're being self-indulgent, Callan, and it doesn't suit you.'

He looked incredulous. 'What?'

'You heard me.' Her eyes blazed. 'I have been in this job for twenty-five years. I started when you were still running around the playground in short trousers and wetting your bed at night. I have met more soldiers than you have had hot dinners, and many of those I have met have personality flaws far more damaging than your physical flaws.' A slight lift at the corners of her mouth. 'So what if you set off metal detectors at the airport and have the odd fit.'

Callan was still looking, unsmiling, into the distance. Val could almost see the ticker-tape of emotions running through his mind, rolling out behind those jittery amber eyes. She slid the envelope into the pocket of his suit jacket.

'Get back in there and do your job, Captain. Get justice for Stephen Foster. And what I said about Gold being harmless – scratch that. He's a nasty little bastard, excuse my French, and you need to watch your back. You also need to keep that medication somewhere other than your office. The glove compartment of that pimp-mobile of yours might be the best bet, if you need access to it during the day.' Glancing around to make sure that they were still alone, she stood on her tiptoes and gave him a quick, soft kiss on the cheek, feeling his rough stubble against her lips, wishing, as she did so, that she was thirty years younger, that she had more of her life in front than behind. 'Don't let me down, Captain.'

58

Gideon Duursema was waiting for Jessie in her office when she returned to Bradley Court. Pacing in front of the window, his hands clasped behind his back, it was clear from the expression on his usually placid face that he was harbouring bad news.

'Where have you been?'

'Out. Doing my job.' She met his solemn gaze.

'Come and sit,' he said.

'What? No, I don't want to sit.'

Gideon looked exasperated. 'Please.'

'Gideon, it's me. You don't need to go into the "distressed relatives" routine. I can do without the sitting, the glasses of water and the soft-focus voice. Whatever it is, tell me.'

Gideon sighed. He looked towards the window, a delaying tactic, Jessie recognized, the misty sky broken now, raindrops pattering against the glass.

'Ryan Jones tried to commit suicide early this morning. He was found in the shower block at six a.m.'

No.

'What? How?' *Fuck.* 'Where is he now?'

'He's in hospital: Royal Surrey County. He slit his wrists with a shard of glass he'd smashed out from one of the bathroom mirrors. Both wrists. Across, though.' Gideon aped a slicing motion with the edge of his right hand, horizontally across his left wrist. 'Not up. It was the only thing that saved him.'

Lack of knowledge on how to slit his wrists properly, the only reason he was still alive. Great.

'I'm going to see him,' she snatched up her handbag from where she'd dropped it at her feet.

'He lost a lot of blood, he's still unconscious and he may have brain damage.'

Jessie clenched her fists. She wanted to punch something. Herself, preferably. Hard. Really fucking hard.

'It happens, Jessie.'

'No, it doesn't, not with me. I should have seen the signs.' She bit her lip, digging her top teeth hard into the soft pink tissue of her lower lip, relishing the pain. 'I've been so obsessed with Danny Lawson, with the dead, that I neglected the living.'

'You didn't neglect him. You just didn't have enough time.'

Time. Always the issue with their job. Never enough time to reach the people who really needed reaching, to save those who needed saving. It was slowly, slowly catchee monkey with clinical psychology. A disturbed mind, even that of an adult, couldn't be rushed. Although, in the eyes of the law, Ryan wasn't a child, he certainly wasn't an adult. But 'time' felt like too easy an excuse.

'Still, I should have . . . ' What should she have done? Locked him in her office until he bared his soul? She groaned. 'I'm so stupid, so *slow.*'

'Jessie.'

'They're all linked, Gideon: Danny Lawson, Stephen Foster, Ryan Jones—'

'Who is Stephen Foster?'

'Three days ago. The suspicious death at Blackdown.'

'I spoke with Colonel Holden-Hough only yesterday. He said it was most likely murder.'

'No, it was suicide. I saw Captain Callan last night and he thinks Stephen Foster's death is suicide too. Those two deaths and Ryan. Three suicides at Blackdown. They're all linked, they must be.'

'One was twelve months ago. I'll continue to believe that the other was murder until I hear otherwise from Colonel Holden-Hough, whatever your friendly captain thinks.' The emphasis on the word friendly wasn't lost on Jessie. *How the hell did he know about her feelings for Callan? Her unreciprocated feelings.*

'Look, Jessie,' he continued, 'there are hundreds of soldiers at Blackdown, many of them trainees. The footfall of new soldiers through that place – vulnerable young men and women who are not used to the rigid routine, who find the demands on their minds, their bodies and their characters beyond hard – is mindboggling. I think you're seeing links where there aren't any.'

'Young and vulnerable, you said it.'

'Jessie, if I had my way, the minimum age of entry to the Army would be twenty-one.' He threw up his hands. 'This is not a job for vulnerable youngsters, even in the Logistic Corps. Unfortunately, I have no say in the matter. All I – we – can do is clean up the mess created by those who do.'

'I'm going to the hospital.'

321

'Wait. I've asked them to call me when he's conscious.'

She shook her head. 'I'm going now.'

'To do what?' Gideon asked.

'To be there to speak to him when he wakes up.'

'To walk the corridors and wallow in self-recrimination.'

Jessie glared at him. 'That was unnecessary.'

Gideon lifted his shoulders in a resigned shrug. 'Go, but don't make links where there aren't any.'

'I don't believe that I am.'

'I think it might be best if you stop hanging out with that military policeman.'

'I'm not *hanging out* with anyone.'

Gideon raised an eyebrow. 'Very little gets past me, Doctor Flynn.'

Tossing her handbag over her shoulder, she headed for the door, muttering – 'Except for young men being driven to suicide right under your nose' – not sure whether he had heard, not caring if he had or hadn't.

59

Callan watched Val Monks walk away, turned and pushed through the door, back inside, bumping into Sergeant Glynn Morgan on his way out.

'I've been looking for you,' Morgan said. 'Holden-Hough said you'd stepped out for a minute with the lovely Val Monks.' He winked. 'Glad to see you're making the most of a nice sunny morning.'

Callan rolled his eyes. 'Tell me that you have something good for me, Morgan. The Zippo?'

'I do have something good – or bad – for you.' He paused, a shadow crossing his face. 'Very bad, depending on your perspective. I also have the results of the fingerprint analysis on that lighter you half-inched.'

'And? Was it a match for the print we found on the tree?' As soon as he'd voiced the question, Callan knew it was one that he hadn't needed to ask. He could tell from the look on Morgan's face that Jace Harris wasn't responsible for the bloody print that the huge black shepherd had signalled on the tree under which Foster's body had been found.

'Sorry to disappoint, Captain, but Jace Harris is not your man.' He held the Zippo lighter out to Callan. 'You'd better return this to him as subtly as you took it.'

Sliding the lighter into the pocket of his suit jacket, next to the envelope containing his epilepsy medication, Callan said with feeling, 'Fuck. Harris is a scumbag.'

Morgan shrugged. 'He may be a scumbag, but he's not your man.'

Bigoted, sexist, aggressive, but not Batman, not the individual who'd shown up in the woods on Monday night to hold Stephen Foster upright with an arm jammed across his chest and a hand pressed to the gash in his throat. A death that Callan now knew was suicide, the role of Batman still an enigma. It was a conclusion he had yet to share with his Branch colleagues.

Callan sighed. 'Thanks anyway, Glynn.'

A deep furrow of concern had entrenched itself in Morgan's brow. 'There's something else you need to see, Captain.'

'What?'

'Stephen Foster's mobile phone.'

'You accessed the SIM?'

Morgan nodded. 'That guy I told you about, my wife's friend's son who works for Mobile Phone Medic—'

'Your wife's friend's dog's second cousin once removed. Get on with it, Morgan,' Callan interrupted irritably.

'Patience is a virtue, Captain. Anyway, he managed to rescue the data. He sent me the download.'

Callan waited for Morgan to continue. When he didn't, he prompted, 'And?'

'And there were the usual messages from friends.'

Morgan's face had tightened, Callan noticed. He looked tense and unhappy.

'And there are multiple text messages from an unregistered pay-as-you-go mobile.'

'What's in the messages?'

Morgan cleared his throat. 'They are, uh . . . they're dates
and times.'

'Dates and times of what?'

'Just dates and times.' He held out a telephone – a new,
cheap-looking grey plastic smartphone. 'It's all in here. You
can have the phone.'

'You're too kind, Glyn.'

Morgan raised an eyebrow. 'Look after the pennies and
all that.'

'I'm sure that Queen and Country will be grateful for
your thriftiness.' The phone felt feather-light in Callan's
hand and even cheaper than it looked.

'I edited out the benign message from friends, etc – not
that there were many. From his phone, it doesn't look as
if Stephen Foster was Mr Extrovert. I have them stored, if
you want to look through them.'

Callan nodded. He could tell that Morgan was struggling
to get to the point, an affliction that he didn't usually suffer
from.

'Send them to me.'

'Will do.' He met Callan's searching gaze.

'And the ones that are left?' Callan prompted.

'The ones left are all from that unregistered pay-as-
you-go. And no, before you ask, there is no way to find
out who owns it. I've already asked that question. It was
bought from a Phones-4-U in Guildford two years ago –
the CCTV in the shop is wiped clean every month, so no
hope there. The phone's rarely used and has only been
topped up twice – with cash – since it was purchased.'

Morgan paused and blinked a couple of times. Callan could tell that he was trying to think through how best to phrase what he was about to say next. 'The first message is . . . is interesting,' he said eventually.

But Callan had already seen it.

60

Jessie stood by the window in Ryan Jones's hospital room, her heart speeding, a jumble of thoughts careering through her mind, slamming into each other, making no sense.

'*There is no crime . . . Suicide is not a crime.*'

'*Something drove them to it.*'

Callan reaching across the sunlit table, his hand on her arm.

'*Look, Jessie, I know what you went through when you were a kid, with your brother, but you can't let that cloud your judgem—*'

Snatching her arm away. '*Don't you fucking dare do that, Callan. This has nothing to do with my brother.*'

Ryan was number three – and perhaps there were more. More suicides that had featured on neither her nor Callan's radar. Other young men who had been driven to do what her little brother, Jamie, had done. For Jamie, she now had a reason. After turning herself inside-out with guilt and self-hatred for years, she finally had a reason. *The straw that broke the camel's back.* Her father.

The straw.

What was the straw that had made these three sixteen-year-olds want to commit suicide in such determined, brutal ways?

Raising her hands to her face, she pressed them to her temples, squeezing as if she could will inspiration, an answer, into her stultified brain purely with the pressure of her fingertips. But all she saw was the silhouette of a young boy, hanging from a curtain rail, framed against Batman curtains.

Batman.

Someone was with Stephen Foster in that wood. Someone held him up, tried to stem the flow of blood.

It wasn't the chaplain, Callan had said in his voicemail. So who? And why? It didn't make sense.

And who had found Ryan and called an ambulance? Saved his life?

As she dropped her hands, the morning sunlight flooding in through the window blinds caught the letters scratched into her forearm, fainter now, healing. Anne Lawson's bitten nail scraping like the beak of a bird. *Daddy.* Nothing in those blank eyes. *It seems like Malcolm Lawson has a lot to answer for.* She was sure now that Marilyn was wrong. That the assumption he'd made, an assumption she had unquestioningly accepted, was wrong. Anne's scratched word had nothing to do with Malcolm Lawson. Her mind cycled back to the pub garden yesterday evening, Captain Callan. *Daddy? Father? The chaplain?* No, not him either. The chaplain wasn't involved in any of this beyond offering a listening ear, Callan had said.

Moving from the window, she lowered herself on to the chair next to Ryan's bed. His eyes were closed, his body perfectly still under the thin blue hospital blanket, save for the shallow rise and fall of his chest with each breath. His breathing and the regular pips of the heart monitor, the only sound. He looked heartbreakingly young, the deep sleep of the unconscious ironing the worry and fear from his face, returning it to the innocence of childhood.

Her mind sought out the dusty space under a dead boy's bed and the notebook she had found, the bears that Danny had drawn inside it. Had Anne found that notebook too and seen her son's drawings, the captions he had written under each? Had she known what they meant?

Daddy.

'Somebody has been sleeping in my bed,' said Great, Huge Bear in his great, gruff voice.

Daddy.

Daddy Bear?

61

The most recent message on the list – 'sent', not 'received', Callan noticed – had been sent by Foster on the night he died. Half an hour before he had, if Jessie Flynn and his deductions in the pub last night were correct, thrust a screwdriver into his own throat.

The message was only two words long: *Fuck you.*

Callan glanced up; Morgan met his gaze with grave eyes. Exiting that text, he read the next, this one 'received'. As Morgan had said, it consisted of a date and time. Nothing else.

2 April – 2.30 a.m.

The date specified, 2 April, was three days ago, the same night/early morning of Foster's death, the message received a short while before he had killed himself. And Foster's response to that final received text had been: *Fuck you.*

Callan scrolled down.

The third text read: *23 March – 12.15 a.m.*

The fourth: *15 March – 11.30 p.m.*

'Dates and times, like you said.' Callan narrowed his

gaze. 'You've got that look on your face again, Glyn. What's bothering you?'

'Scroll to the bottom.'

Callan did as instructed, scanning the texts as he scrolled, all 'received' except for that last 'fuck you', counting in his head as he did so, clicking every few messages to read the content. There were nineteen 'received' texts in all.

He voiced what he was thinking. 'Nineteen received texts, all specifying a time and a date.'

Morgan shook his head. 'Eighteen received texts specifying time and date.' He looked old suddenly, old and sad, the lines around his mouth tight with pent-up tension.

'What?'

'The last one has an attachment, a photograph. No time and date, just the photograph. I've emailed it to you, too.'

Dropping his gaze to the phone, Callan pressed his thumb to the text message. The screen filled with a photograph: white around the outside, something pale in the middle – a body? – he couldn't see with the sun's glare on the glass. Raising his hand to shade the screen, he studied the picture that had now come into focus. He was silent for a long moment.

'Jesus Christ.'

62

'The Military Police.'

'What about them?'

'Many of their badged service cars are Mondeos and Vectras.'

Marilyn nodded, thinking of Captain Callan in his pimped-up red Golf GTI, realizing that he hadn't seen him for a few weeks, making a mental note to call and arrange a drink. The first time he'd met Callan was a couple of years ago now, at the suicide of a twenty-one-year-old, six months' pregnant wife of a corporal serving in Afghanistan. He had turned up to their modern terraced house, ready for a fight over jurisdiction, bristling at sight of the six-foot-four, absurdly handsome Military Police officer waiting for him in the hallway, next to whom he felt like some aged, wizened little pixie. But despite their disparate outward appearances, he soon found the young Army officer's pragmatic approach was not unlike his own, and they shared a dry sense of humour. Having established that they liked and respected each other, the pair had spent the rest of the evening in a pub. The friendship had been consolidated when they worked together on the Wendy Chubb murder case last November. It was during that investigation that Callan had been shot in the back – a shooting that Marilyn still blamed himself for.

'They took an order of eighty Bridgestone Blizzak LM-32 tyres on the seventh of January for their stores.'

Marilyn refocused. 'Huh?'

'The Military Police, sir. They took an order of eighty Blizzak LM-32 tyres on January seventh. They fit their own tyres, service their own cars.' She paused. 'As I said, another dead end.'

Marilyn sighed and nodded. Despite last night's marathon sleep, he could feel a headache coming on, something to do with continually butting his head against a brick wall with this case.

'So it looks like we're back to square one. We need to expand our search area. I was probably a bit hopeful the first time and made it too small.'

He walked over to the map of Surrey and Sussex that occupied the centre of one wall in the incident room. Workman and DC Darren Cara, who had just got off the phone from the last two garages in the search area, with zero result, followed him.

'This was the search area, wasn't it?' Marilyn drew his index finger from the southern outskirts of Farnham anti-clockwise to take in Guildford in the west, Woking, Camberley and Sandhurst to the north, the circular track linking the villages of Odiham and Long Sutton in the east, returning to Farnham. Workman nodded.

'So extend it to include Wokingham.' He paused, finger-tips of the other hand tapping a tune on the wall, thinking.

'Let's not go as far as Reading yet. That town's a whole other kettle of fish and we'd need to get Thames Valley Police involved. I can't be bothered with the admin headache at this stage.'

His brow furrowing, DC Cara cast Workman a sideways glance, which she ignored. Marilyn's style was careless, but there was nothing careless about his thinking, whatever the impression he revelled in creating.

'Let's include Basingstoke and then down to Hindhead and Haslemere, though again, my gut says that they're way beyond any sphere of influence that Malcolm Lawson would have had—' He broke off, the expression on his face suddenly pure query. 'The CCTV.'

'CCTV of what, sir?'

'The hospital, Workman, the hospital, the night the baby was left.'

'Harry.'

'Harry, Barry, Larry – whatever. We've got a copy?'

'Of course.'

'Get it up, now. Right now.'

63

'Excuse me.'

Jessie almost jumped out of her skin at the voice. A middle-aged nurse was standing in the open doorway. Her gaze met Jessie's shock-widened eyes.

'I'm sorry if I startled you.' The nurse stepped into the room, shutting the door behind her.

'I'm fine. I was . . . daydreaming.'

The nurse frowned. 'Who are you, dear?'

A *work colleague*, Jessie was about to reply, before stopping herself. She knew how medical professionals' minds worked: patient confidentiality, rightly, an obsession. She wouldn't be allowed to stay with Ryan if she told the nurse who she was, and the nurse would certainly answer none of her questions.

'I'm his older sister.' Another lie – who cared now? She'd told so many.

The nurse regarded her solemnly. 'Are you alone?'

'Yes.'

'Where are your parents?'

Jessie's mind filled with the image of a woman with motor neurone disease, whom she had never met, in a home she'd never visited. Did she yet know about her son? Had she been telephoned?

'Our father is dead and our mother is disabled. She can't come. It's only me.'

The nurse nodded. Circling the bed, she squatted in front of Jessie. Something about her manner immediately reminded Jessie of Gideon – *Come and sit down* – except that she was already sitting.

'What is it?' she barely got the words past her dry lips.

The nurse's gaze dipped. Jessie heard the shallow sound of Ryan's breathing, the rhythmic beep of the heart monitor, the wheels of a trolley as it squeaked down the corridor outside.

'I need to let you know that we will have to call the police in to interview your brother when he wakes.'

'Why?'

She felt the nurse's hands close around her own. Her heart rate was through the roof, her breath trapped in her throat, as she waited for the answer.

'The doctor examined your brother on admission. I'm sorry. You need to know that Ryan has been raped.'

64

Angling his computer screen towards the wall, Callan shifted his position so that he could view the screen without anyone else glimpsing it. He didn't want to share the contents of that photograph with his team until he'd had time to mentally process its ramifications.

He had thought, after eight years in the Military Police, that he'd seen it all, that nothing he experienced could touch him, get to him. But as he studied the image of sixteen-year-old Stephen Foster spreadeagled face down on the bed, the man with him slightly out of focus, and masked – *of course, he would be, wouldn't he* – his identity hidden by a cartoon bear mask – *a kids' fairy-tale bear, Christ* – feelings of sadness, disgust and blind fury hit Callan like a freight train. Foster's gentle dark eyes were open, but staring, with that filmy unfocused look Callan had seen before in traumatized soldiers who were trying to fight their demons with barbiturates. And who could blame him?

Sitting back in his seat, Callan's gaze moved from the image on his computer screen to the window. He had the intense desire, for the second time this morning, to shove it open, climb out and run away from all this shit – keep running.

Isolated.

Isolated was what Jessie had said. All these kids had been isolated, and isolation created vulnerability. If he knew nothing else from his years as a Branch detective, the one unalienable truth he had learnt was that predators preyed on the weak. It held true throughout the animal kingdom and it held true for the most vicious and morally corrupt animal of all – the human.

Closing the photograph down, Callan dipped his head to his hands, ground his knuckles into his eyeballs. As Foster's abuser must have done, he understood the weight of machismo. Understood how hard it would have been for Stephen Foster to admit that he was being raped. How he had kept the secret, allowed the abuse to continue for the sake of his pride, his friendships, and his place in this rigid hierarchy, the Army, the only place that he had probably ever thought he would be able to call 'home'. Until he couldn't take any more.

Fuck you.

Had the same thing happened to Danny Lawson? Had he been drugged and raped too? Drugged, raped and then pressurized, by the existence of a debasing photograph, to continue. Was that what had driven him to take a roll of gaffer tape and wrap it around his face? Wrap and wrap until he had blocked all of his airways, suffocating himself to death. Is this what was currently happening to the other kid Jessie had mentioned – Ryan Jones?

'*There is no crime . . . Suicide is not a crime,*' he'd said to her yesterday evening.

'Something drove them to it.'

Reaching across the sunlit table, placing his hand on her arm. Patronizingly, he realized now. Unforgivably patronizingly.

'Look, Jessie, I know what you went through when you were a kid, with your brother, but you can't let that cloud your judgem—'

Jessie – rightly *– snatching her arm away. 'Don't you fucking dare do that, Callan. This has nothing to do with my brother.'*

He was surprised, looking back, that she hadn't slapped his face for good measure. She had been right and he couldn't have been more wrong. It had nothing to do with her childhood. She had an intuition about people that he entirely lacked. But what he needed to do now, and quickly, was to find the man responsible for these rapes. Find the animal.

65

Marilyn stood right behind Workman, right in her personal space, not that he seemed to notice or care if he did, fingers drumming an impatient tune on her desktop while she accessed her list of files, found the digital file that hospital security had sent over and opened it.

'Play it,' he said.

A black-and-white snowstorm filled the screen – *midwinter in Alaska* – shades of jet black, through grey, to murky, then bright white. An empty Accident and Emergency foyer, lit bright white on the screen courtesy of its electric strip lights, black outside the sliding doors, light from streetlamps illuminating misty circular discs in the darkness.

The pram. The man pushing it, the umbrella covering the upper half of his torso, no chance of recognition, but definitely not Malcolm Lawson. They knew that now, about the only thing they did know. Those solid, sensible, thick-soled black shoes. *Clodhoppers*. The man casting one last long look at baby Harry before leaving through the sliding doors, angling right as he crossed the road.

'Pause,' Marilyn said. 'Now. Pause now.'

Workman's index finger flew to the pause key.

The front bumper of the ambulance, the security guard muttering – *Seen enough of those in my time to recognize one from a square inch* – and across the other side of the service road, two wheels, a dirty white stripe of chassis dividing them, alternate blocks of light and dark above the dirty stripe, those blocks navy blue and fluorescent yellow in real life. *One ambulance, one police car. Nothing unusual in either of those being parked on the A & E service road.*

Leaning forward, Marilyn tapped his index finger on Workman's screen. 'Police car. That's what we agreed at the time, wasn't it?'

Workman tilted her head sideways, meeting his gaze from the corner of her eye.

'I know that the quality of the recording is poor, sir, but it's definitely a police car.'

Without acknowledging Workman's comment, Marilyn's gaze moved to DC Darren Cara.

'You've spent the last three years of your life driving a patrol vehicle, haven't you, son?'

The pimply young DC nodded, unsure whether he should be flattered or petrified that those strange mismatched eyes were now focused unwaveringly on him.

'Look carefully, Detective Constable. Is that a Surrey or Sussex badged vehicle?'

A long moment of silence while DC Cara scanned the screen.

Marilyn's fingertips continued to drum. 'There's no rush.' His words at odds with the manic tapping of his fingers, the humming energy that radiated from him. 'Take your time.'

DC Cara shook his head. 'No, sir. That vehicle doesn't belong to either Surrey or Sussex police forces.'

'You're sure?'

'Absolutely, sir.'

'Why, Detective Constable? Why?'

'The colours you can see running down the side of the car – navy blue and neon yellow, they would be, if the film wasn't black and white – those are on our vehicles and Surrey's.'

'And the difference?' The difference was all he cared about.

'Police, sir.'

Police? 'What?'

'The word "Police", sir. All our cars, and Surrey's, have the word "Police" written on both sides of the vehicle, below the blocks.'

'So whose don't?'

The sound of a siren outside, an ambulance, and they all three automatically looked towards the window, saw the windows of the building opposite wash blue for a fraction of a second as the ambulance screamed past, the siren changing in timbre, fading as it continued down the street.

'The Military Police, sir. They have the blue and yellow blocks, same as ours, but no writing underneath. Their cars have "Military Police" written on the bonnet.'

Marilyn knocked the heel of his hand against his fore-head. 'We've spent too long in Surrey and Sussex Major Crimes, Workman. We can't recognize our own bloody police cars any more.'

Grabbing Workman's mouse, he opened Chrome, googled 'UK Military Police Vehicles', clicked 'Images'. The screen filled with photographs, the markings so similar to civilian police cars, but DC Cara was right: the word *Police* was absent.

'Fuck.' The sentiment heartfelt. His good mood dissolved. Gone. Shattered. '*Fuck.*'

66

Raped.

Multiple times, she had added gently. *I'm sorry.*

Jessie's eyes jerked past the nurse. Lieutenant Gold was standing in the doorway.

'Could you give us a moment alone, please, Nurse,' Gold said.

Releasing Jessie's hands, the nurse stood and turned stiffly. 'And you are?'

'Lieutenant Gold, Royal Military Police, Special Investigation Branch. We had a call from the hospital.'

The nurse nodded. She glanced quickly at Jessie. Gold followed her gaze, noting the message contained in her eyes, and gave her a barely perceptible nod. He had picked up on her reluctance to speak in front of Jessie but didn't yet understand why. He hadn't been party to the lie that she had told about being Ryan Jones's sister.

'I'll be back to check on him again in an hour,' the nurse said to Gold. Glancing at Jessie, she added. 'If you need anything else in the meantime, dear, please press the call button.' She indicated the square red button set into the plastic headboard of Ryan's bed.

'Thank you,' Jessie murmured.

The nurse moved towards the door that Gold was holding open for her. Jessie noticed her whisper something into his ear as she passed, saw him nod – 'Will do.' – saw him close the door behind the nurse, heard the metal click as it shut and the sound of her block heels tapping down the corridor into the distance. Jessie stood. She felt close to tears; they were welling right behind her eyes and in the tight, hard wad in her throat.

Raped.

So easy to assume that rape only happened to women.

Gold moved towards Ryan's bed. 'How is he?'

'Fine,' she murmured, meeting his gaze across Ryan's prone form. 'They said that he'd be fine. Physically fine.' But mentally? There was little chance of that.

'I'm glad to hear that he'll be OK.'

'What are you doing here?' Jessie asked.

'Captain Callan asked me to come. I thought Jones would be awake by now. We need to interview him.'

Jessie nodded. Why hadn't Callan come himself? What was he doing that was more important?

Your brother has been raped.

'Where's Callan?'

Ryan. The third victim. Or more. Perhaps there were more that they didn't know about.

'Back at the office.'

'Doing what?'

'Paperwork. You know how it is.'

She nodded. 'Why do you need to interview Ryan?' she tried to keep the edge from her tone.

Raped and he'd said nothing. Felt that the only way out was suicide. Same as the others.

Gold spread his hands in a 'doh' gesture. 'Because he nearly died.'

'Suicide. It was suicide,' she managed.

'Sure. But why? Why did he try to kill himself?'

Who could make these boys feel like that? Feel so trapped that the only way out was suicide.

Jessie held his gaze, her insides twisting, mind churning.

'Often there is no concrete reason,' she said, her voice monotone. 'I spoke with him a couple of times and there didn't seem to be anything specific bothering him. Tough childhood, multiple foster homes, struggling with the rigid Army hierarchy – you know how it is.' She forced a smile, was sure that it looked as twisted and fake as it felt. 'I'll stay. I'll call you when he wakes.'

Tilting his head, Gold smiled back. His navy-flecked royal-blue eyes remained untouched by the smile. 'That nurse you were speaking with. What did she say?'

Someone with the power to control and the power to ensure silence.

Jessie shrugged. 'Oh, chit-chat. I'm a work colleague – not that, even. She didn't tell me anything. She just read the "medical confidentiality" riot act.'

A policeman?

Callan would have come himself. After their discussion in the pub yesterday, he would have come himself, surely?

As nonchalantly as she could manage, she scooped up her bag, hoping that he hadn't noticed her hand trembling. He was between her and the door. They were five storeys up, the concrete car park below the window. There was only one way out of this room and it was right through Gold.

'There's no need for both of us to be here and you look as if you're not going anywhere,' she said casually. 'We've got a stack of patient files ten centimetres high back at the office and Gideon will love me if I come back early and help him out.'

Gold nodded. 'Sure.'

She stepped forward, holding his gaze, though it was an effort, smiling, and as she did so the light from the overhead strip-light found the word grazed on her arm: *Daddy*. Her eyes flicked down, she couldn't help herself; his followed, narrowed a fraction, she hadn't imagined it. A dawning recognition? Understanding?

'Somebody has been sleeping in my bed,' said Great, Huge Bear in *his great, gruff voice.*

Goldilocks and the Three Bears.

Daddy.

Daddy Bear.

Callan wouldn't have sent Gold, he would have come himself. She was certain that he would have come himself.

Seal pup. Ice. Club.

Oh Jesus, she'd been so fucking slow.

67

Callan stepped into Val Monks' office without knocking.

'The autopsy.'

Val looked up from her computer keyboard.

'Oh God, not again. Who is it this time? Ironman? Captain America? Don't make me regret that I saved you, Callan—' She broke off, clocking the look on his face, the knife-edge sense of urgency that pulsed from him. 'What is it? What's wrong?'

There was a spray of white roses in the vase on her desk. *Remembrance and purity.* Funeral flowers.

'Did Stephen Foster have anal sex?'

'What?' Val looked momentarily confused. She moved the vase aside so that she could focus on his face properly.

'The autopsy results. Did the autopsy show that he'd had anal sex?'

Val Monks nodded. 'Yes.'

'Consensual?'

'It was impossible to tell. Gay sex can be rough.'

'He wasn't gay.'

348

'Are you sure about that?'

'Pretty sure.' He rubbed a hand across his eyes. 'Why the hell didn't you tell me, Val?'

'It was in the final autopsy report.'

'You haven't given me the final autopsy report.'

'Excuse me, Captain. I put a copy on your desk yesterday evening. I was going to email you an electronic copy this morning, but I haven't got that far yet.'

'What time?'

'Huh?'

'What time did you put the report on my desk?'

'Seven. Seven thirty—' She broke off.

'I was at Blackdown from six p.m.' *Then in the pub with Jessie Flynn.*

Their gazes met, the same thought running through both their minds.

Callan voiced it.

'Gold.'

Val Monks held up staying hands. 'Steady on there with the accusations, Captain.'

Callan balled his hands into fists. He felt like slamming one of them through Val's metal filing cabinet. 'You don't agree?'

'I'm not saying that I don't agree. But I am saying that you need to be on very solid ground before you accuse a fellow MP of withholding evidence. I know he's a nasty little shit, but what reason would he have to take the autopsy report?'

'To make me look incompet—' He broke off. *Was that likely?* Gold had taken his epilepsy medication last night. Everything Gold had needed to destroy his career had been in that brown envelope; he hadn't needed anything else.

Frowning, Callan shook his head. 'No, not to make me

look incompetent. Taking that autopsy report had nothing to do with me.'

Val raised a hand to her mouth. 'Are you saying what I think you're saying?'

The sudden shrill ring of a phone. Pulling his mobile from his pocket, Callan looked down at the number flashing on its face: DI Simmons. What the hell did he want?

'Yes, Val, that's exactly what I'm saying.' He moved to the door. 'Give me a minute. I should take this call.'

68

Gold.

She'd been so slow.

Somebody has been sleeping in my bed,' said Great, Huge Bear in his great, gruff voice.

Daddy Bear.

Goldilocks and the Three Bears.

Gold.

Someone with the power to control and the power to ensure silence. A policeman. Of course. Simple, now that she knew the answer.

Jesus, she'd been so unforgivably, stupidly slow.

'Goodbye then, Lieutenant.' Giving him another brief, tense smile, Jessie moved towards the door, just as he stepped sideways, mirroring her movement. She breathed in slowly, trying to keep the tension she felt from telegraphing itself straight to her face. His body language was still relaxed; he didn't know that she knew.

'No doubt I'll see you soon,' she said. 'That steak restaurant in Farnham, perhaps?'

He was right in front of her, still chilled, still smiling. A few more seconds and she'd be in the corridor. *Stay calm.* Light from the window reflected off something silver in his hand. It took her brain a second.

A knife.

A hunting knife, the blade jagged, serrated, like shark's teeth, easy to see now that his hand was raised.

'Oh, Jessie, Jessie.' His voice was a singsong.

A freezing cold finger traced down her spine.

'Beautiful Jessie Flynn. You must think that I'm completely fucking stupid.'

Raising her hands, still smiling, a rictus smile now, she backed towards the window, brain computing: keep calm, keep the tension from the situation – ridiculous, given the knife that he was holding out in front of him, lightly in the palm of his hand, like an offering, but the only self-preservation strategy she could think of at the moment. Gold mirrored her movement, stepping forward, maintaining the distance between them.

'Unless you fancy jumping five floors, the only way out is the door, Doctor Flynn.' He held out his other hand. 'So let's go, beautiful.'

Incredulous, Jessie shook her head. What did he expect her to do? Take his hand? Walk out of here like girlfriend and boyfriend? Pop to that restaurant in Farnham for a quick bite, perhaps, before . . . Before what? She took another step back, felt the window frame dig into the small of her back.

'I'm not going anywhere with you.'

Five floors below, through the grimy window, rock-hard tarmac, the cars like Tonka toys from this height. Her gaze returned to Gold, hand still extended, a look of fraying patience on his face.

The red button? The door? Only one choice. If she went for the door, she'd have to go straight through him, straight through that jagged hunting knife. The red button? The emergency signal on an intensive care ward. They should respond to it within seconds.

'Now, Jessie.' Struggling to keep the edge from his voice, keeping up the pretence. *Girlfriend and boyfriend.*

Jessie shook her head. 'Go, Ed.' His Christian name more personal, disarming. 'Get out of here.' Pulling her mobile from her handbag, she laid it on the floor at her feet and kicked it over to him. It was a gesture; there was a landline next to Ryan's bed and the red button above it, but she meant what she said, meant the gesture. If he left now, she would let him go. Preservation for herself and for Ryan. 'Take my mobile. I won't stop you and I won't call anyone. Go. Escape.'

Gold's gaze flicked from hers to Ryan's prone form; she noticed a muscle above his eye twitch.

'Escape? I can't escape.'

'Why? You've got money, surely? Money, a head start and knowledge of how the police think, how they work. You've got a much better chance than most.' *Most criminals. Most rapists, and still over ninety per cent of those reported get away with it.* She didn't say it. 'You'll be fine.'

He shook his head, the movement twitchy, keyed-up. 'I can't escape.' His voice betrayed agitation. 'I can't escape what's in here.' Raising the knife, he tapped the tip of its blade against his temple. 'It's all in here. I can never escape what's in here.'

'I don't understand what you're saying.'

He shrugged, refusing to meet her eye. A flash of intense vulnerability replaced his habitually assured expression, and for a brief moment he looked a decade younger, his face boy-like, brittle, pregnable. 'Much as I'd love to jam this knife into the side of my head and gouge out the memories, I can't.' The hand holding the knife fell back to his side. 'He'll be OK, won't he? Ryan will be OK?'

No, of course he won't. He's broken now. Perhaps too broken ever to fix. You *broke him.* 'Sure. He'll be OK. So go. Go now.'

He nodded but didn't move. 'I didn't mean for that to happen,' he murmured. 'For him to try to take his own life.'

Fear was still curled tight in Jessie's stomach, but a stew of other feelings were sloshing around it: anger, sadness, helplessness and – the most dominant – self-recrimination for being so stupidly slow, for failing Ryan so badly. But despite all those stewing feelings, she knew that she should just keep quiet, bite her lip, continue placating until she had won, until he had left. But she couldn't, because realization had dawned.

'You were raped, too, weren't you? When you were younger?'

Gold shook his head, the movement unconvincing in its fleetingness.

'When?'

'No.'

'Yes. That's what you meant about the memories, wasn't it? You were raped yourself.' She paused, swallowed. 'You were raped and still you did that to him.'

His gaze flicked to the body on the bed. 'He did that to himself.' His voice was strangled.

'No. You did it to him. You raped him multiple times, you broke him and you made him want to die. *You.* You've

354

been through it yourself so you know how what you did to him made him feel. How helpless he would have felt, how he would have hated you for what you were doing to him, but hated himself more, *despised* himself for that helplessness.'

Gold's face twisted in sudden fury. 'Shut up! Shut the fuck up!'

'Perhaps you think you can't help what you are, that you had no choices, but I don't agree with that,' she continued, her voice rising to match his. 'So what the hell did you think would happen to him?'

'Shut the fuck-up, bitch.' Hand raised, he leapt at her, the knife flashing. Swinging her handbag hard into his face, Jessie ducked and spun away from him – *two options, one realistic choice* – and launched herself at the red button. From the corner of her eye, she saw Gold on the other side of the bed, his hand as he swung the knife towards her outstretched arm. Her momentum was pulling her forward, towards the red button, too fast to change direction, and the knife's blade sliced deep into her left palm. A soaking gush of blood and her fingers flopped uselessly like a puppet with severed strings.

Blood arced, painting the wall.

Folding over, she clutched her hand to her stomach, trying to smother the pain, the pulsing blood against her shirt.

Blood everywhere. Had Gold severed her artery? She was constricting the flow from her hand, jamming it hard against her stomach and still the blood sprayed up the walls and soaked the bedclothes. So much blood. Too much blood. It took her a moment to understand where it was all coming from.

Ryan.

Throwing herself across the bed, she jammed her hands to Ryan's throat, feeling the lips of the gash baggy against her sliced palm, the sticky ooze of his blood mixing with her own, her hands coated immediately in hot red gloves. Knowing as she pressed that nothing could be done for him, that he had seconds. Knowing that he was already as good as dead.

Looking up, she met Gold's frozen gaze. 'You fucker,' she hissed.

But what she had expected to see in his face – gloating satisfaction at the life he'd taken – wasn't there. He looked as shocked as she felt. White-faced and gelid, his expression one of naked torment. The hand holding the knife opened, fingers limp.

'Look what you made me do.' His voice so quiet and controlled and yet so insanely uncontrolled at the same time. 'If you'd just come with me like I asked you to, this wouldn't have happened. I wouldn't have slashed him by accident when I tried to stop you reaching that button.'

Streaking her bloody hands across the white sheet, feeling a renewed gush of blood release, a nerve spasm all the way up her arm as the cotton snagged her sliced palm, Jessie slid off the bed. Her hand was throbbing, fingers swollen and unwieldy, the copper stench of Ryan's blood, of her own, unbearably intense. Ryan's body drained now, his face grey-white as the pillow it lay on, his blood pasting the wall above his head and soaking the bedclothes.

'You made me hurt him. Don't make me hurt you,' Gold muttered. 'If you don't come with me now, I will have no choice.'

Jessie nodded meekly. 'I'm sorry. I'll come now.'

She couldn't look at the bed, the horror that it had become.

Gold held out his hand again and Jessie walked towards him, reaching for it placidly. But as their hands touched, she snatched at his wrist and wrenched him forward, tipping him off balance, kicking out at the same time, aiming for just above his kneecap. With proper boots on, it would have been a perfectly targeted kick, would have forced his kneecap backwards, stretching the tendons in the back of his leg, pitching him to the floor in agony, dislocating his kneecap completely if she was lucky. But her loose, slippery ballet pump slid off his leg, and the kick was weak and ineffectual. She hadn't even caught her balance when the handle of the hunting knife cracked down hard on the bridge of her nose. Pain exploded in her face. She stumbled backwards, blood streaming from her nose and running into her mouth. Coughing and gagging, trying to catch her breath, she gritted her teeth against the scream of agony. Grabbing her hair, Gold twisted her head so that she could do nothing but meet his gaze. He moved the cold sliver of metal to her throat, sawed it back and forth, twice, the jagged teeth biting into her skin.

'Stop.'

One word, said quietly, but the menace in his voice cut straight through to the little nugget of self-preservation her dulled brain still retained.

Stop.

His royal-blue eyes with those unusual navy flecks were beautiful, she realized, would have been at least, if they hadn't been so empty.

'Unless you want me to do to you what you made me do to *your brother* Ryan, Doctor Flynn. Stop.'

69

Mid-winter in Alaska.

Marilyn studied the security monitor in front of him, struggling to concentrate on the details lost in the snow-storm, wishing that Callan would stop jittering beside him. He glanced at the security guard.

'Security didn't see anything?'

The guard shook his head. Grey-haired, running to fat, similar in appearance but not the same man who had monitored the bank of CCTV screens three nights ago.

'We're thin on the ground now, sir. Budget cuts.'

Budget cuts. How many times had he heard those words recently? 'We share your pain,' he said.

'There' – Callan's arm shot out – 'there.' He tapped his finger against the screen.

'Please don't tap the screen, sir,' the security guard said.

Giving up all semblance of vanity, Marilyn pulled his glasses from his suit jacket pocket and slipped them on, squinting at the screen through the grubby lenses.

A corridor. Doors to rooms left and right all the way

down it, lift doors to the right close to the camera's lens.

'Where's that?' Callan asked.

'Fifth floor, north side. The corridor that leads from Intensive Care to the lifts.'

Marilyn nodded. They had already seen Ryan Jones's hospital room swarming with doctors and security, the wall above the bed painted in dripping red slashes like a modern art exhibit. Too late for the poor kid. Way too late.

A man and his wife or girlfriend were walking down the corridor towards the CCTV camera. The girl was cupping a wad of tissues to her face with both hands, staggering slightly as if she was drunk. One of the man's arms was wrapped around her shoulders, his hand cupping her neck, the other tucked against her stomach, inside her coat. No, *his* coat, Marilyn realized. The pattern on it a jumble of greys and black.

'DPM,' Callan said. *Disruptive-pattern material.*

'Don't tap the screen, sir.'

'Gold must have changed out of civvies before he went to the hospital. Jessie's wearing his combat jacket,' Callan said, ignoring the security guard.

The couple passed a group of three walking the other way down the corridor, a lone orderly pushing a trolley, a nurse carrying a tray. Each time the man smiled and nodded; his hands remained where they were.

'Why the hell didn't anyone stop them?' Callan snapped.

Marilyn shared his fury and frustration. He'd had the opportunity, six months ago, to stop this animal and all he'd done was to classify Malcolm Lawson as a hysteric and to toe the Military Police line, roll over and wait to have his tummy tickled.

359

Our findings concurred with the Special Investigation Branch: suicide, plain and simple.

But why would anyone have stopped them? A girl who'd had an accident. A caring boyfriend who'd brought her to hospital for treatment. And he was Army, wearing a uniform that, like police, fireman, doctors, instilled trust and confidence. Gold had gambled on the fact that nobody would challenge a soldier looking after his girlfriend, and he had been right.

'Don't tap the screen.'

Marilyn grabbed Callan's arm – 'Direct that anger where it's going to be useful, son' – held it until Callan released his clenched fists.

Pulling his glasses from his nose, sliding them into his pocket, Marilyn looked up a foot and met Callan's seething gaze.

'Where to now, Captain? Where to now?'

70

Jessie lay, curled up tight like a foetus, her arms wrenched behind her back, wrists locked to each other with Gold's handcuffs, and stared into the darkness of the blindfold. Her nose throbbed from where Gold had broken it with the handle of his hunting knife and she felt a dull ache in her head, like a hangover, from where he had punched her in the side of the head when she had tried to break free from him in the hospital car park. It had been raining, another sudden unrelenting spring downpour, and the car park had been deserted – frightening how seamlessly he had been able to march her from the hospital, one arm around her shoulders, hand locked around her neck, the other holding the hunting knife to her heart inside his combat jacket. His grasp of psychology was impressive – he knew exactly how onlookers would interpret what they were seeing: a caring soldier with his girlfriend.

Her first lucid thought had been to kick out one of the tail-lights and shove her leg through to attract the attention of the driver behind, but when she eased off her ballet pump and felt around for the lights with her toe, she realized that Gold had thought of that. What felt like a metal cage was welded across the inside of both tail-lights, immovable, no matter how hard she kicked.

Her second thought had been to try something she had seen in films: follow the undulations of the roads, the lefts and rights, the stops and starts, to listen to the noises outside. But all she could hear was the roar of the engine, the swish of the car's tyres on the wet road, and when those stopped for brief moments of idling, the only sound was the roar of her own pulse as it pumped hard in her ears.

The road was rougher now and she could feel the wheels catching in potholes. They were not in town any more, or on a motorway. A country road then, but that information was meaningless when there were hundreds of miles of country roads in Surrey, thousands more in the surrounding counties, a spider's web of tarmac bordered by fields and woods, all within half an hour's drive of the hospital. They could be anywhere.

The car slowed again, sharply this time, and she was thrown forward, her spine slamming against the back of the boot. Her left hand oozed and throbbed and her nose ached, air whistling to get past the swelling each time she breathed. When she had tentatively raised her fingers to her face a few minutes ago, she had felt a swollen, tender clown's nose. The skin on her hands and forearms was stiff and scaly with her own blood and Ryan's, dried now, its copper tang bitter in the confined space.

Loose stones under the wheels. She could hear them bulleting the chassis, feel the car's traction less certain than when it had been on a metalled road. A gravelled skid as the wheels stopped turning, and a moment later, the engine was cut.

Silence.

Nothing outside. No noises at all. No traffic, no voices, no city sounds. Only the empty, vacuous silence of deep country.

71

Callan braked. 'This can't be right.'

He pulled his Golf to the kerb and cut the engine. They were in a run-down cul-de-sac of small 1930s semi-detached houses, matching bay windows and faux leadlight glass, each set behind a narrow rectangle of lawn. Callan's red Golf GTI entirely out of place amongst the aged black and grey Skoda Octavias and Ford Fiestas parked in driveways.

Marilyn glanced across. 'Why can't it be right?'

'Because it doesn't fit.'

Callan climbed out, slamming the door and walking to the middle of the road, standing with his hands shoved in his pockets, looking irritably up and down the unprepossessing row of houses. Nothing could have been further from the image he had formed of the place where Ed Gold had grown up: a rambling Lutyens manor house at the end of a curved gravel drive, croquet on the lawn and scones with clotted cream for tea, a bottle of Moët permanently on ice. He couldn't conceive of Gold, with that air of entitlement he wore as comfortably as a second skin, his cut-glass accent and his cigarillos, hailing from this faded, pedestrian enclave. If you sliced him in half with a chainsaw – *Callan had thought about it* – he'd have *upper-class twit* carved through his centre like a piece of Brighton Rock.

'Check the address.'

'I don't need to, Captain,' Marilyn said. 'It's there.' He indicated a house two doors down from where they had parked. Net curtains behind the faux leadlight glass. 'Number 10 Heathlands.'

Christ, even the name sounded grand. Callan followed Marilyn up the crazy-paved garden path, lined on either side by spring flowers planted in repeating patterns of mauve and white. Hyacinths, he recognized them, had planted and tended the same in his mother's garden last year when he had been hiding out from the world, fighting a losing battle to reclaim his sanity after being shot in the head in Afghanistan. A matching purple wisteria was growing from a white-glazed cauldron-sized pot on the front step, curling up the porch balustrade. Looking at it, he was transported straight back to Jessie's cottage, to the wisteria he'd had an argument with Ahmose about last year. With thoughts of Jessie came renewed agitation, a weighty awareness of time and a desperate sense of urgency. Stepping past Marilyn, he jammed his finger on the doorbell, held it until he saw the mottled shape of a person materialize on the other side of the stained glass.

The woman who answered the door was as contrary to the impression he had formed in his mind of Gold's mother as the road and the house had been. Where he had envisioned Downton Abbey's Countess of Grantham, this woman was dumpy, mousy, late middle-aged and showing every single one of those years in the lines on her face, a woman you would look at and forget as soon as she was out of eyeshot. The only memorable thing about her was those unusual, questioning royal-blue eyes, flecked with navy – Ed Gold's eyes, he realized, any lingering doubt that they were in the right place vanishing – that flitted from him to Marilyn.

'Janet,' Marilyn spluttered.

Callan stared at him. 'You know her?'

The woman in the hallway was clutching the door handle so hard that her fingers had turned white. 'Detective Inspector . . . '

'Simmons.' Marilyn held up his warrant card. 'Bobby Simmons.'

'Yes, of course. I remember now.' Her voice was stiff, her hold on the door handle vice-like. 'The baby, I presume? You want to talk to me about the baby?'

Marilyn shook his head, knowing now exactly why Ed Gold had deposited baby Harry in the entrance to A & E at Royal Surrey County Hospital.

'It's not about the baby.'

He stepped forward at the same time as Callan, and they did a three-way shuffle, Callan trying to push past her into the hallway, his impatience palpable, Marilyn right behind him, talking, explaining, Gold's mother – the receptionist from Accident and Emergency at the hospital, Callan had gathered that now – still struggling to understand what the detective inspector with the oddly mismatched eyes, who she'd had quite enough of the other day, might want with her now.

'It's about your son, Ed Gold, and it's urgent,' Callan said, cutting through Marilyn's explanation, dispensing with formalities. 'Can we come in?' He jammed his hand against the front door, forcing the handle from her grip, stepped over the threshold and held his other arm out to guide her back down the hallway.

'Yes,' she stuttered. 'Yes, of course.'

She showed them into a room at the front of the house, the formal sitting room it looked to be, hardly ever used: a pale cream carpet, calico walls and two matching floral sofas set at right angles, two sides of a smoky-brown glass coffee table. A neat beige marble fireplace was set into the middle of one wall, its top graced with photographs, the same ubiquitous family snaps that Callan's mother, every mother, had on their mantelpiece. Same photographs, different blond boy, twenty years younger in most, but unmistakably Ed Gold. No sign of any siblings, or a father, for that matter.

'Tea?' her voice rose and cracked.

'No thank you, Miss, uh, Ms—'

'Mrs.'

'Mrs Gold,' Callan heard Marilyn say, as he moved over to the fireplace. 'We're in a bit of a hurry.'

'A hurry?' Her voice was barely audible.

Hands twisting in her lap, she took a seat on the sofa, and Marilyn sank on to the other one, leaning forward, his head tilted confidentially. Callan fought to control his impatience, acutely aware of the minutes ticking past, the image of Ryan Jones's blood painting the hospital wall right at the forefront of his mind. He glanced at his watch: 5 p.m. An hour and a half since they'd watched Gold escort a bleeding Jessie from the hospital on that CCTV screen. They'd made good time, but not good enough to satisfy him. Gold had Jessie and his imagination was happy to supply him with a list of appalling possibilities of what he

367

could be doing to her at this precise moment, while he was standing in Gold's mother's living room discussing tea and looking at family snaps.

Only half-listening to Marilyn's low-voiced questions, Gold's mother's muted answers, his gaze found the photographs again. Gold as a moon-faced toddler on a little wooden trike – he'd had one the same. Gold playing with a toy Army helicopter, a model Chinook – same. Gold building a Lego tank – same. Christ, they had far more in common than he'd ever realized. The middle photograph caught his eye. It showed a Georgian mansion of pale sandstone, twin columns rising up either side of a double-height, double-width front door that sported a massive circular brass knocker, everything about the house magnified, fully deserving of the word 'grand'. A blond boy, thirteen or fourteen, wearing grey trousers, a bottle green blazer and a green-and-grey striped tie stood on the front steps of the house. His body language, his posture said 'assured', but his expression was pensive, sad even, Callan thought, picking up the photograph, his gaze ranging across Ed Gold's delicate, almost feminine teenaged features. This was the house that he had been expecting. This house *fitted*.

'Where's this?' he interrupted, holding out the photograph.

He hadn't expected Marilyn to answer. 'Ashdown House,' he said.

Should I have heard of it? 'Where?'

'Ashdown House,' Gold's mother echoed. 'It's a school. A boys' school in Wiltshire.' She paused and Callan noticed her jaw working nervously under the skin. 'Boarding school. I sent my son there when he was thirteen.'

'Why?'

Mrs Gold looked up at him, her navy-flecked royal-blue eyes narrowed.

'Because that's what parents do for their children, Captain. They scrimp and save and go without so that they can give their children absolutely the best education that they can afford. I only had one child and I wanted to give him the best. I tried to get him into a top independent day school in Guildford, but he wasn't bright enough. Boarding school was the next best option.' Her smile was distant. 'My husband left us when Edward was three. I haven't seen or heard from him since. I wanted my son to have a good life, Captain, not to have to struggle for everything, like I have done. I wanted him to meet the right people, to move in the right circles and I worked very hard to try to make that happen.'

Who the hell are the 'right people'? Callan nodded, his gaze leaving hers, tracking around the room.

'I've told you already: I didn't notice the baby being left, Detective Inspector . . . ' He heard Mrs Gold respond to another of Marilyn's questions. 'If I had done and recognized my son, of course I would have told you at the time.'

Two prints above the sofa. Reproductions of John Constable paintings: *The Hay Wain*, even he knew that one, and a second, featuring a waterwheel. He couldn't recall the name, had probably never known it. A third, smaller painting hung on the wall by the window. Also a country scene, a cottage, the colours matching those of the Constables, shades of muted browns and autumn oranges, but this one was an original. A good amateur effort, but not the work of a master.

'I don't know who his close friends are, Detective Inspector. I'm sorry, but I can't help—'

369

'This? Where is this?' Callan interrupted again.

Mrs Gold looked over, frowning. 'Oh, that's my father's cottage. The cottage I grew up in. I paint . . . used to paint.'

'Does your father still live there?'

She shook her head. 'He died nearly two years ago. I'll sell it as soon as the probate goes through, but you know how long those things take. And in truth, I haven't been so organized about chasing—'

'Where is it?' Callan asked.

'Haslemere.'

'In the town?'

'No.' Pulling a tissue from the sleeve of her jumper, she pressed it to her nose. 'No, it's an old gamekeeper's cottage.'

'In the countryside?'

She nodded. 'Yes. I hated growing up there. It was so isolated, so lonely.'

'What's the address?'

She lowered the tissue to her lap. 'I really don't think you need to know.'

'I'll be the judge of that,' Callan snapped.

Pursing her pale lips, Mrs Gold frowned. 'I'm sorry, but I'm really not sure that I'm comfortable—'

'Just give me the fucking address!'

'OK, OK.' Marilyn held up his hands. 'Let's do this calmly and politely, Captain.'

Lower lip trembling, Mrs Gold inclined her head towards Marilyn gratefully. 'Thank you, Detective Inspector. The address of my father's cottage is Brook Cottage, Hooke Lane, Haslemere, Surrey. It's by a stream – a brook, I suppose you'd call it, hence the name.' The tissue was beginning to shred in her restless fingers. 'Terribly pretty, but very dilapidated now as my father didn't have the money to maintain it. I really can't imagine that my son would be there.'

Callan was already down the corridor; Marilyn felt the gust of air as Callan pulled the front door open. Pushing himself to his feet, Marilyn held out his hand.

'Thank you for your help, Mrs Gold.'

Without meeting his eye, she took it. 'You've heard of Ashdown, Detective Inspector,' she murmured.

Marilyn nodded.

'Are you involved in the . . . the investigation?'

'No, it's Wiltshire Police's jurisdiction.'

'Every Tom, Dick and Harry will hear of Ashdown soon, no doubt.' She raised the shredded tissue to her nose. 'What those poor boys went through at the hands of those house-masters will be in all the papers.'

The sound of a sports engine revving to life in the street.

'We can only do our best, Mrs Gold,' Marilyn said gently. 'And I'm sure that you were doing your best for your son when you sent him there.' He shuffled his feet, embarrassed, unsure how to pose the next question. At times like this, he felt Sarah Workman's absence keenly. 'Do you suspect that he . . . ?'

'Oh, no. No.' She shook her head vehemently, her gaze sliding from his. 'Absolutely not. He would have told me. I would have *known*.'

A blast from a car horn. Marilyn nodded. He felt sorry for this hardworking, caring woman, who had no idea that her world was about to implode because of her son – and not, he suspected, for the first time, whatever she said.

'When was the last time you saw him, Mrs Gold?'

She gave a sad smile. 'I haven't seen Nye for years.'

'Nye?'

She nodded. 'It's the pet form of Aneurin, which is Celtic for "golden". My family are Welsh and my parents gave Edward the nickname "Nye" when he was a baby. His father hated it, but it stuck.'

'Where is his father, Mrs Gold?'

Two more sharp blasts from the car horn; he needed to go.

'He was in the Army, Detective Inspector, and I presume that he still is. That's why Nye joined.'

Tears had formed in her eyes, Marilyn noticed. He kept holding her gaze, pretending that he hadn't.

'But I don't see Nye any more. That's one thing that Ashdown House did for him. It turned him into an angry man, angry at his childhood and angry at me. I think it's shame and embarrassment. I think that rarefied environment taught him to be embarrassed of where he came from and ashamed of the woman who raised him.'

72

The blackness of the blindfold masking her visual sense, Jessie tried to use her other senses to construct a picture of exactly where she was, of what Gold had done to her. Her head ached, a dull persistent throb that became a claw hammer pounding inside her skull each time she moved, but her thought processes, when she really focused, were unimpaired. Just as well: she knew that she needed her clinical, rational mind now more than she had ever needed it before.

The air that touched her skin was cool; not as cool as outside, and there was no wind, but it was chill, the smell musty and slightly damp. A cellar, perhaps? Gold had marched her through a couple of doors and then down a short flight of wooden stairs, so presumably she was now in a basement or cellar.

She was handcuffed, but above her head the chink of metal on metal each time she moved her arms told her that, when he had uncuffed her left wrist for a few seconds, he had passed the chain around a metal bar before cuffing her again. He had bandaged her left hand quickly and efficiently, in silence, refusing to answer though she had talked at him constantly, trying to break through to him, falling silent only when she heard the door swing closed behind him.

She twisted and shifted: underneath her the ground was unexpectedly soft. Shuffling on to her back, she stretched her legs out – nothing; softness still – stretched them to either side, the softness ending in a vertical drop. She was on a bed, she realized, a metal-framed bed, the cover soft, but seams, multiple seams, criss-crossing each other under-neath her; she could feel them digging into her back and thighs. A patchwork cover, perhaps? *Odd.*

Twisting her head, she rubbed her face against her upper arm in an effort to dislodge the blindfold, groaning in pain as the bridge of her broken nose met her arm. She dug her teeth into her bottom lip, diffusing the agony in her nose with self-inflicted pain, and forced herself to continue, twice, three times, before accepting that it was futile: the blindfold was too tight to dislodge in that way. She stopped, waiting for the biting agony in the bridge of her nose to subside, holding her breath to stop herself from sucking into her lungs the fresh gush of blood her efforts to dislodge the blindfold had released from her nose.

And while she was holding her breath, she heard it.

The jerky, sucking sound of laboured breathing coming from somewhere close by. Someone was in the room with her.

Gold – was it Gold? Sitting quietly and watching her? Watching her and waiting, biding his time until . . . until what? What was he going to do with her? He could easily have killed her at the hospital, but he hadn't. His appetite lay in rape; fallout from the abuse she was sure that he

374

had suffered when he was a boy. But murder? Despite his actions having driven Ryan to attempt suicide, he had been as horrified by Ryan's bloody death as she had been. He had taken her because she had worked out that he was Danny, Ryan and Stephen Foster's rapist. But had anyone else arrived at the same conclusion? Had Callan? She had no idea, but at the moment her one certainty was that the only person she could rely on was herself.

Jamming her heels against the bedcover to give herself leverage, she shuffled her way frantically to the top of the bed. Twisting her wrists, tilting her head upwards, she managed to hook the thumb of her right hand underneath the blindfold and prise it over her forehead.

Bright light from a single naked bulb hanging directly overhead. Squinting, blinking to accustom her eyes to the sudden shock of light, she looked around her. Not the crumbling, damp-stained red brick that she had been expecting, or the shabby, jumbled contents of a cellar.

The room was like something out of a fairy tale – a nightmare fairy tale. And she had been right. She was not alone.

73

'So – Ashdown?'

'Eyes on the road, please, Captain,' Marilyn muttered.

They were travelling at ninety miles an hour along a single-lane country road, just wide enough to warrant a white dotted line down its centre, which Callan seemed to be on the wrong side of approaching every corner, thick hedges spinning past on either side. Marilyn consoled himself with the thought that this would afford them a soft crash-landing, should the need arise. He had already called Workman, instructed her to tell the cavalry to meet them at Nye's deceased grandfather's cottage. The National Police Air Service helicopter that covered Surrey and Sussex, call sign NPAS15, would have taken off from Redhill aerodrome by now, would cover the twenty-six miles from Redhill to Haslemere in ten minutes, giving them eyes in the sky. And both of Surrey's two Armed Response Vehicles were on their way from their base in Burpham, Guildford.

'You don't read the paper, I take it?'

Callan shrugged. 'Not often.' He dealt with enough of

the base side of human nature in his job, didn't feel the need to spend his spare time wallowing in more. He swerved sharply, suddenly, back to the correct side of the road as a black Volvo came around the corner towards them.

Marilyn snatched for the door handle. 'Jesus Christ! Let's try and get there in one piece, shall we?'

'So – Ashdown,' Callan repeated, when they had safely rounded the corner.

Marilyn eased his grip on the door handle, but Callan could tell from his breathing that his heart rate was still through the roof.

'Ashdown House is currently under police investigation for historical allegations of child abuse.'

Callan thought of the photograph on Janet Gold's mantelpiece, the one that he had expected to see, the image of the blond boy standing on the steps of that great house. The face, the expression, however, was something he hadn't expected to see. Pensive, sad – not an expression that he associated with the man he had thought, *assumed*, was Ed Gold. *Little Lord Fauntleroy – the upper-class twit.* How wrong he had been.

'A couple of the housemasters from fifteen years or so ago are accused of abusing some of the boys. Putting on masks – masks of frightening characters from fairy tales. The big bad wolf. Bluebeard.' Marilyn's ravaged face had clenched itself into tight lines. 'And letting themselves into the boys' dormitories while they slept. They chose their victims carefully – timid, lonely boys – and took them out quietly. There was a hut in the woods – all part of the twisted, black fairy tale.'

'Why the masks?'

'The masks, the dressing up, the hut in the woods, it was

377

all about tapping into a child's deepest, dormant fears, transporting them back to the time in their childhood when they were tiny and helpless, when they did everything that an adult expected them to do without argument or question. Even though that child is now a teenager, well beyond the age when fairy stories cease to be part of their world, there is still that buried memory, the dormant fear of those dark fairy-tale characters, the propensity to be regressed, to be frightened and controlled.'

The disembodied voice of the satnav: *Turn left in two hundred metres.* Marilyn took hold of the door handle again, braced his feet against the footwell. *One hundred metres.*

When he'd made the turn, the smell of burnt rubber invading the car's interior, Callan glanced over, meeting Marilyn's gaze briefly before transferring his eyes to the road.

'So the housemasters are being investigated?'

'One of them is. The other burned to death eleven years ago in a fire in a hut in the woods.'

'*The* hut?'

Marilyn nodded. 'That's what I've heard.'

'One of the boys? Revenge?'

'It wouldn't be hard to put two and two together and come to that conclusion.'

Callan glanced over again and met Marilyn's sombre gaze for a second.

'Ed Gold?'

'It's a question I'll need to ask Wiltshire Police, but if you work back, based on his age, like I've just done, you'll realize that the housemaster died on Gold's last day at Ashdown.'

'Cleaning out the house before moving on.'

Marilyn raised an eyebrow. 'Eloquently put, Captain.'

'What did Mrs Gold say?'

'She said that Nye . . . Gold wasn't involved.'

'Did you disabuse her?'

'No, I didn't,' Marilyn murmured, his eyes fixed on the view, which had changed from hedges to dense woodland rambling away for what felt like miles on either side of the car. He could hear the intermittent thwack-thwack of a helicopter's rotor blades over the roar of the Golf's engine. They were close now, must be. 'I didn't have the heart to. Wouldn't you want to believe, if it was your child, if you had given everything to send them there, get them the best start in life, that they had remained untouched?'

'She'll find out soon enough.'

Marilyn sighed. 'She will. She will indeed, God help her.'

74

The room was about the size that Jessie had pictured, imagined in her mind's eye, but nothing else about this claustrophobic space met with her expectation.

Her rational mind, her sense of place when Gold had dragged her blindfolded from the boot of his car to here, her sense of smell, told her that she was in a cellar or basement under a house. An isolated house in the country: she had guessed that from the impenetrable silence outside when the car's engine had stopped, and from the rough, untended ground she had been dragged across before reaching the house.

But the room she opened her eyes to was a wooden shed, five metres by five metres, with a pitched corrugated iron roof, from the middle of which hung a single, bare bulb. A lattice of fading light filtered in from one small window set high in the wall to her right, a metal grille covering the glass. Three beds were laid out side by side, their white metal headboards snug up against the wall opposite the shed door, each bed carefully made with a brightly coloured patchwork quilt. The bed to her right was the biggest, a double; the middle bed – the one she was chained to – a standard single; and the one to her left was a toddler's cot.

Goldilocks and the Three Bears.

Insane. He's insane, Jessie.

And folded on to the toddler's cot, barely a metre from her, the broken form of Malcolm Lawson. His arms were folded protectively over his head, his eyes closed, the cheek that she could see hollowed and shadowed with dark purple bruises.

Oh God, is he dead?

No. No, of course not. She had heard his breathing. If she held her breath, she could hear him still, barely. Breathing, but barely.

'Malcolm,' she whispered, not knowing why she was whispering.

Nothing.

'Malcolm.' She shuffled closer to the toddler cot, as far as her handcuffed wrists would allow. 'Malcolm. Can you hear me?'

Twisting sideways, she stretched out her foot and nudged his leg.

Still nothing.

Then one bloodied eye flicked open.

75

Déjà vu.

Standing in the dark with Marilyn, the tree trunks pressing in on them from all sides, shadowy spaces between. Standing, watching, listening to the crackle of the radio, the flak-flak-flak of the police helicopter as it circled in the clear darkness overhead, Marilyn drumming his fingers on the roof of Callan's Golf, the sound maddening. The rain had picked up tempo: it was soaking into Callan's hair, running down the back of his collar.

The windows of the house remained dark. All of them closed.

He studied the house. It was small, benign-looking, a flint-stone and brick cottage, fairy-tale pretty if it hadn't been so decayed. Ivy covered its walls and fingered its roof and grass grew long and untended around the base of its walls. So this was where Nye Gold had made up for his own destroyed life, by destroying others.

If Callan had his way, he would walk right up and kick the patio doors in, but this house was civilian jurisdiction,

Marilyn had made that patently clear on their drive here from Nye's mother's house, and he was purely here on sufferance, as an observer and advisor. Marilyn glanced across, sensing his impotent fury at this standing, waiting, doing nothing.

'Sorry, Captain, but you're going to have to trust me.'

'The last time I trusted you, I took a bullet in the back,' Callan snapped.

Marilyn raised an eyebrow. 'I'll let you off that one. But only the once.'

Callan turned away. He hated feeling so useless. He knew that Jessie and Malcolm Lawson, if he was still alive, were in that cottage at Gold's mercy. He was humming with manic energy and aggression and the only thing he could do with it was to let it circulate inside him. Circulate and fester.

A deafening, pulsing explosion split the night.

Instinctively, Callan threw himself to the ground, his heart rate slamming through the roof, his mind taking him straight back to Afghanistan. An IED?

But his rational brain knew that wasn't the case. Couldn't be – not here in leafy Surrey.

'What the hell was that,' he yelled, straightening in one fluid movement.

The sound of a door smashing, the steel enforcer taking the front door down, the flash of a stun grenade, shouting, the armed response unit going in, their hand forced into immediate action by the explosion.

'Back,' Marilyn yelled, slamming an arm into Callan's chest. 'Get the fuck back or you'll end up getting shot again and this time it won't be my fault.'

'I'm going in with them.'

'No, you are not. This is my jurisdiction and if I have to cuff you to control you, I will.'

Looking back to the house, Callan saw that the patio doors and the windows on this side of the house had blown out. Fire was licking from the gaping space where the glass had been, hot orange and vicious.

76

Déjà vu.

Jessie's chest heaved, panicked by the lack of oxygen getting into her lungs and for a moment she was back in her father's garden, lost in a cloud of black smoke and heat so extreme that she felt as if she'd melt from it, curling into a ball on the pavement, her father screaming in her ear: *What have you done, Jessie. What the hell have you done?*

Beside her, Malcolm Lawson sobbed and pleaded to be allowed to live, to see baby Harry again, his voice fading into a dry croak, muttering words that Jessie tried to tune out. She had to stay calm. Panic only made things worse, made it impossible to think, to make sensible decisions.

But what decisions were there to make? What could she do? She was shackled to the bed in this room, this underground room, this cellar – she knew that it was a cellar from the smell, despite the walls and floor made of planks, the sloping, corrugated-iron ceiling of a shed above her head.

Fucking with your mind – he's fucking with your mind.

One square cast-iron sink between Mummy Bear and Baby Bear's beds; Malcolm folded and cuffed on to Baby Bear's bed. Nothing useful within reaching distance, nothing useful in this sick fairy-tale room at all – Gold had made sure of that.

Something. There had to be something. *Think, Jessie, think.*

Her eyes locked on to the window, up high, covered by a metal grille, but there was no way she could reach it, and even if she could, smashing it would draw in a flood of oxygen which would suck those dancing flames she could see through the crack under the door, straight into the room with them.

The air was heating up, so thick with smoke that her eyeballs were gritted with it, the ceiling lowered to a dense black smog barely a metre above their heads, as if the night sky had filtered in with them, bringing its blackness, solid and impenetrable.

Malcolm muttered and cried next to her.

Shut up! she wanted to scream at him. *Shut up and let me think.*

Digging her toes into the patchwork quilt, scrabbling with her feet, she managed to untuck it from the base and sides of the bed. Kicking and sliding, she bunched it underneath her, shuffled her bottom and legs, writhing, twisting herself into knots until she had bunched it into a ball at the top corner of the bed. Levering herself into a sitting position, the handcuffs snagging tight round her wrists, she hooked a foot into the ball of material, lifted and dropped it into the sink.

She stretched out her leg. Her toes grazed the tap, knocked

it, slipped off the cold metal. Pressing the joints of her bandaged left hand's thumb and little finger together with her right, forcing them so close that they were almost touching, feeling nothing in her sliced hand but a throbbing, dulled pain which sent shivers up the nerve endings of her arm, she managed to slide the handcuff over the bandage to the ball of her thumb. The same with her right hand, the pain this time as if she was clamping the joints of her hand in a vice. It gave her an extra couple of centimetres reach, nothing more. Would it be enough?

Wisps of smoke fingered down towards them from the black ceiling. She coughed, the acrid smoke filling her lungs. Malcolm's breathing was strained, like a pair of bellows with a gash in them.

They had minutes. Less, maybe.

Her plan was futile, she realized, but at least she was doing something, not lying still and waiting – waiting to die.

Stretching, feeling as if her joints would pop from their sockets with the strain, she reached her toes to the tap again.

The water ran. A trickle.

Again.

More this time. A gush.

She lay back on the bed and listened to the water rushing through the pipes, to the sound of glass shattering outside.

77

Movement. A runner. Darting in between the trees, a pale figure, human, disappearing, reappearing, limbs moving in staccato movements, like a character in a flipbook. Young and fit and trained to run, he was moving fast, but Callan was stronger and faster. He sprinted through the under-growth, swift and silent, conserving his energy by not shouting, only the twin sounds of his breath hosing into the night air and his boots slamming into the soft ground. Mud and leaves fountained out behind him as he ran, arms and legs pumping, closing the distance.

Five metres ahead of him, Gold glanced back over his shoulder.

His mistake. Callan flung himself forward, stretching his arm out. He grasped at air, then felt material slide beneath his fingertips, clasped, curling his fingers into a fist, clutching, yanking. The force of Gold's momentum almost ripped the jacket from his hand, but he held on, stumbling, trying to slow his momentum and Gold's and they both slammed forward, landing hard, rolling together. Gold writhed, twisting and kicking out with the heavy rubber sole of his boots, catching Callan in the jaw, snapping his head back. But Callan was stronger and had the advantage of rabid fury on his side.

Spinning Gold on to his back, Callan punched him in the stomach, just once, but hard enough to shock him into motionless. Jamming his knee on to Gold's chest, putting all his weight into the sixteen square centimetres of his kneecap, he listened to the air wheeze from Gold's lungs, watched the colour drain from his face.

'I can't breathe,' Gold managed.

'Tell me something that I give a shit about,' Callan growled.

'Please,' Gold coughed.

Callan transferred more weight on to his kneecap.

'P-p-please,' Gold whimpered. 'I didn't mean for them to die.'

The wide-eyed innocence of his look made Callan want to punch him in the face – punch him until the only thing looking back at him was bloody pulp. But he wasn't going to lose control.

He pushed his face closer to Gold's. 'Them? Malcolm and Jessie?'

Weakly, Gold shook his head. 'Danny, Stephen and Ryan.'

Grasping the collar of Gold's combat jacket, Callan lifted his head up and slammed it back down. 'The boys you raped, you mean? The sixteen-year-old boys you drugged, raped, filmed, blackmailed and then raped all over again, multiple times.'

Gold gasped and his eyeballs rolled back in his head. 'I can't—' His face was white with the effort of drawing in breath.

Shifting his weight, Callan reduced the pressure on Gold's chest.

Gold gulped in air. 'It wasn't my fault. I was taught . . . ' His tongue slid out and wet his lips. 'That's how I was taught to be.'

Above the treetops, the Police helicopter hovered, shifting the leaf canopy with its downdraught, the arc light hanging from its belly scouring the ground around them. It hadn't found them yet. Callan knew that he could do anything he wanted to Gold and nobody would ever know – only his conscience.

'You had a choice. You know right from wrong,' Callan yelled above the noise of the rotor blades. Picking Gold up by the collar, he slammed his head into the ground again. 'You know. You may have convinced yourself that you were helpless to fight your urges, but you still know right from wrong.'

'I couldn't help—'

'Yes, you *fucking* could. But there's one thing I don't understand,' Callan cut in, still shouting to make himself heard. 'Why did you try to save Stephen?' *Why were you Batman?* 'Why did you try to save him when you drove him to kill himself in the first place?'

Gold shook his head again, the movement barely there. 'No . . . not me,' he managed.

'Who then? Who tried to save them?'

The arc light had found them. Gold mewled and screwed up his eyes. Callan resisted the urge to lift and slam Gold's head into the ground again, now that he was being watched from above.

'Who tried to save them?' Callan yelled. 'Who? Tell me who?'

'Wall—' Gold croaked.

'What?'

'Wallisss—'

Wallace? What the fuck was he talking about?

'Wallace?' Callan shouted. 'Colonel Wallace?'

Weakly, Gold nodded. 'My father. Colonel Wallace is my father. He didn't try to save me, his own son, but he tried to save Stephen and Ryan.' A sick-looking smile had crept on to his pale face. 'He tried to save them . . . but he failed. The bastard failed.'

78

Fire and water.

She had watched from the pavement as the firemen had aimed the hose at her father and Diane's house, too late, even she could see that.

Too late for them now?

'Malcolm. Here.'

Gently, she slid the wet patchwork quilt over his head with her foot, eased it as best as she could over the rest of his broken body. Sliding to the floor beneath the sink, huddling as low as her cuffed hands would allow, she pressed her face to the wet wooden slat walls of the shed and let the water from the flooding sink run over her.

'Lie still, Malcolm,' she said. 'And breathe, shallow as you can.'

That incoherent mumbling.

Was sentience still there? Could he understand what she was saying?

'I saw Harry this morning,' she said. Another lie. 'He was in your lounge, sitting in sunlight from the window, playing. Joan bought him a—' *What?* What had Joan bought him? She cast her mind back to four-year-old Sami Scott. 'Joan bought him a farmyard set, with a farmhouse, a tractor and lots of animals. He was laughing, playing with the tractor. You'll have tractor-wheel marks all over your carpet when you get home. He misses you, Malcolm, but he's fine. He's waiting for you to come back, so you need to stay strong. Shallow – breathe shallow and we'll be fine.'

She broke off. She couldn't talk any more. It took too much oxygen. Each breath razored the back of her throat, filled her lungs with rancid black fumes and her head with dizziness.

Voices.

Malcolm.

'Shushhh, Malcolm,' she managed. 'Don't talk.'

A man's voice.

Still Malcolm.

'Shushhh.'

Her head was throbbing and she couldn't breathe and she felt her heart fluttering in her chest like a trapped bird. Curling up into a ball, she pulled her arms over her head and jammed her eyes shut.

Pandy loves you too, Jessie.

79

Colonel Philip Wallace was sitting behind his desk when Callan, accompanied by his superior, Colonel Holden-Hough, entered his office. The sky outside the window was stacked with clouds and though Wallace was wearing those same square, frameless glasses, Callan could see his pale grey eyes. The uncompromising glint was gone, the light in them weary now, his expression resigned. Wallace stood as soon as he saw them in the doorway, stepping around his desk, holding out his hand to Holden-Hough.

'I need you to come with us, Philip,' Holden-Hough said, shaking it.

Wallace gave a dispirited nod. 'Yes,' he murmured. 'Of course.' He unhooked his coat and navy-blue beret from the back of the door.

Callan stepped aside to let him past, but instead of following Holden-Hough into the corridor, Wallace stopped abreast of him.

'The first time we met, here in my office, I asked you to

keep an eye on Lieutenant Gold . . . on my son for me. Do you remember?'

Callan gave a silent nod.

'I'm sure you now know why I did that.' His voice, so controlled and confident the last time that Callan had spoken with him – that time in his office, only four days ago – shook. 'I knew what he was doing and I did nothing to stop him and I will have to live with that knowledge for the rest of my life. I thought that I could convince him to stop, that the . . . the need would work its way out of his system, that it was only a matter of time—' Breaking off, he raised a hand, reaching for Callan's shoulder. Callan tilted back, minutely, but enough to send a clear message. With a despondent sigh, Wallace dropped his hand to his side.

'How did you know that Stephen Foster was going to kill himself in that wood?' Callan asked.

Wallace shrugged. 'Ed . . . my son . . . liked to forward me the text messages he sent to those boys. He forwarded them to me to goad me, to see how far he could push me before I stepped in to stop him. Too far, as it turned out. Far too bloody far.' Tugging off his glasses, he massaged the bridge of his nose with his fingertips. 'It was all part of the, uh, the—' He broke off.

'All part of the game?' Callan finished for him. 'Was that what you were going to say, Colonel?'

He noticed Wallace's Adam's apple rise and fall jerkily as he swallowed, his throat bone-dry.

'I saw that final one,' Wallace said. 'Foster's reply. I'd seen the same from Danny Lawson a year ago and I didn't know then what it meant, what the kid would do to himself. This time, I knew.'

'But you were still too late to save him,' Callan muttered, feeling a perverse satisfaction when Wallace dropped his gaze to the floor, unable to look him in the eye. 'And Ryan?'

'I called the ambulance', Wallace murmured. He gave a dispirited shake of his head. 'I let my boy down, Captain. I walked out on him when he was three, because I was too selfish, too caught up in living my own life to share it with a wife and kid, and I wasn't there to protect him when I should have been. He's a monster, I know that, but he's a monster that I helped to create. I hope you understand, son. I had to put him first. I had to try to save him now, because I wasn't there to save him before.'

Wallace's gaze rose to meet his again and Callan held it, his face expressionless. Did he understand? Not really, not having seen the carnage that Gold had wrought. But then he didn't have children, didn't have that overwhelming, unconditional bond that he had been told a parent had with their child. Would his mother have done the same thing – protected him like that? Probably.

'No child is born a monster. No child. If you ever get the chance to have children, Captain, make a better job of it than I did.'

As they reached the car park at the main gate, Callan caught sight of a familiar figure climbing out of his car, juggling keys in one hand, a polystyrene cup of takeaway coffee in the other as he nudged his car door closed with one softly rounded hip.

'Give me a minute,' Callan said to Holden-Hough.

The chaplain looked up as he jogged over. Laying the keys and his coffee on the roof of the car, he turned his insipid green gaze to meet Callan's.

'Captain Callan, nice to see you again.' His words polite, his tone at odds, prickly – not that Callan could blame him.

'You've heard?'

'Indeed I have. For better or worse, the bush telegraph at Blackdown is highly efficient.'

'I owe you an apology.'

The chaplain blinked pale lashes. 'Yes, I suppose you do, Captain, but I understand the pressure you were under and I'm pleased that you managed to resolve the case so quickly.'

Though it was only four days since he had had that epileptic fit by the side of the A3, since he had joined Gold at the scene of Foster's suicide, having no idea that Gold, *Goldilocks*, was responsible for it all, it felt like ten lifetimes. Each day gruelling, the time stretched thin to breaking.

'Thank you for your understanding, Chaplain.' Callan held out his hand.

After a moment, O'Shaughnessy took it, held it, his grip firmer than his stature or demeanour suggested. 'God, Captain, he's not so bad, you know. I'd be happy to talk it all through with you one day, if you'd like.'

'I'll bear that in mind, Chaplain.'

Lifting a hand, he turned and walked back across the car park to join Holden-Hough and Wallace in the waiting Military Police Mondeo.

80

There was someone in his room, Harry sensed. He opened his eyes. A face was hanging over him – his dad – standing by the side of his cot. In the glow of his nightlight, Harry could see that his father's shoulders were shaking. Rubbing the sleep from his eyes with balled fists, he sat up and reached out his arms to be lifted. His father's strong hands came towards him and Harry felt them folding around his waist, hoisting him, then the warmth of his father's arms as they wrapped around his body and held him tight. Harry nuzzled his face into his father's neck, heard his father's voice breaking on words that he didn't yet understand.

'I'm sorry that I put you at risk, Harry, when I took you along to meet with that animal, but I had no choice. I had to do it for my son – your father, Harry – for Danny, for his memory. If I hadn't thrown him out of the house, out of our family, he would never have joined the Army and he'd still be here with us. I had to try to make amends for my beautiful boy in death, because of how badly I failed him in life.'

But he had failed Danny in death too. Clenching his teeth against the quivering in his jaw, against the tidal wave of sadness, he felt tears run from his eyes, their wetness trailing down his cheeks, cool on the throbbing heat of his skin.

He had agreed to meet Gold in that secluded lane, driven by a righteous fury that he thought would give him unassailable strength, taken the tyre iron from the back of the car and held it on the passenger seat as he drove to the rendezvous, Harry asleep in the back seat, no one to leave him with, knowing, *knowing* only that he had to atone for how he had treated his only son in life, even if that atonement was too little, too late.

Harry felt cool tears wetting his head. Sliding his hand over his father's shoulder, he patted his back as he had seen Nana do.

'They've caught him, Harry,' Malcolm whispered. 'Too late for Danny and those two others, but at least he'll never hurt another boy, never drive another boy to suicide. Thank God they've finally caught him.'

Standing silently, unnoticed in the darkness of the hallway, watching a moment that she had dreamed about, prayed for virtually constantly for the past four days, Joan felt her own eyes fill with salty tears.

'I will never leave you again, Harry.' She heard Malcolm promise as she tiptoed back down the corridor to the sitting room, feeling as if she was intruding on something too personal. 'You're my beautiful Danny's boy and I love you more than anything. I will never put you at risk, I will never let you down and I will never leave you again. Do you hear me? I will never leave you again.'

81

When Jessie woke from the general anaesthetic to repair the severed flexor tendons in her left hand, Callan was sitting by her hospital bed reading a novel, something she had never seen him do. It occurred to her then how little she knew him beyond their working lives. She had slept fitfully for most of the night post-operation, and woken with a jolt several times to find Callan there, his long limbs arranged awkwardly in the plastic chair as he dozed. She thought that she had heard him talking on his mobile once, had heard Gideon's name, but she had drifted back to sleep before she could ask why he was talking with her boss.

When she finally woke fully, daylight was streaming through the window, the sun solidly in the sky – mid-morning then, not early. She lay still for a few moments more, her eyes closed, sensing that Callan was watching her, not wanting to admit yet that she was fully conscious.

She didn't feel any sense of satisfaction or release that it was all over. Only a crushing sense of responsibility at how the final minutes of Ryan's life had played out in that hospital room three floors above her head, at her culpability in his death. She also suspected, from the conversation she'd had with the surgeon before she was put under, that the extent of the trauma to the flexor tendons in her left hand meant that she would never achieve full responsive bend in her fingers, and so would be invalided out of the Army.

Callan dropped her home shortly before lunch, returned at six with bread, pâté, cheese and a bottle of Sauvignon, which they took into the back garden, arranging the impromptu picnic dinner on Jessie's garden table, settling themselves, coatless, in the warmth of the fading evening sun.

'He was a victim too, you know,' she murmured.

Callan looked momentarily confused. 'Who?'

'Ed Gold.'

'He was an adult. He had a choice.'

Jessie shook her head. 'That area of psychology, victims of past sexual abuse abusing others when they themselves are adults is such a complex one, and it's not about choice, not as we understand choice anyway. Most abused children don't go on to abuse, but there *is* a recognized victim-to-victimizer cycle, particularly among males. Boys more often turn the effects of their abuse outwards, while girls tend to turn it inwards, in self-harm, anorexia, bulimia.' She sighed at the sceptical look on his face. 'I know that you think it's all psycho-bullshit, but the connection is real, Callan. Some men become excessively macho, become sex addicts to prove to themselves and others that the rape didn't affect them, that they weren't raped because they were gay. Gold went a different way. He did what was done to him, perpetrated the same crime, but it was effectively learned behaviour, how he was taught to behave.'

'He could have gone a third way and lived a normal life.'

Jessie rolled her eyes. 'Normal? Define normal. Is it you? Is it me? I hardly think so.'

'It's your profession, Jessie. You practise it, so you must believe in it.'

'Yes, it is my profession and I do believe in it, but most of the time when I'm faced with truly damaged patients, I feel as if I'm drowning. The human mind is so multifaceted, people's experiences so individual, there are always going to be more questions than there can ever be answers.' Picking up her glass of Sauvignon, she held it out to Callan.

'Half-full,' he said immediately. 'But I thought you were above lame pop-psychology, Doctor.'

'That wasn't what I was going to ask.'

Callan held up his hands in a mock-defensive gesture, though his face held no apology. 'OK, I'm listening.'

'How heavy is this glass of wine?'

He shrugged. 'Two hundred grams, give or take. Where are you going with this, Jessie?'

She answered his question with a tangential statement. 'The absolute weight doesn't matter. It depends how long I hold it. If I hold it up like this for a minute, it weighs nothing. If I hold it up for an hour, my arm will ache. And if I hold it for a whole day, my arm will feel numb and paralysed.'

The oblique rays of the sinking sun found the raised glass, sending orange stars spiralling across the table and lighting Callan's eyes the colour of warm honey, highlighting the cynicism written in them.

'The weight of the glass is the same in each case, only the longer I hold it the heavier it becomes,' she continued. 'Mental trauma is like that glass. The sooner someone accesses treatment, the greater the chances of a recovery. But the longer a person has buried that trauma, has let it fester, the more damaging the effects.' She set the glass back on the table. 'Gold told no one. A thirteen-year-old boy, abused by a person who had power and control over him and whom he trusted, and he had no one to confide in. His father wasn't around and he felt too much responsibility for his mother to burden her. He lived alone with the horror of what was done to him, had it gnawing away inside him for seventeen years. How do you think that affected him?'

Callan sighed. 'He still knew right from wrong.'

'Yes, of course he knew right from wrong. He knew that what he was doing was wrong, but that knowledge wasn't enough to enable him to stop.' She took a sip of wine, wincing at the bitter taste, her tongue still infused with anaesthetic. 'If I had gone with him when he asked me to, Ryan would still be alive.'

'And you wouldn't be.'

'Maybe I would. Maybe we both would. Gold wasn't a killer, despite the fact that three young men died because of what he did to them.'

'Gold probably was a killer, Jessie. The body of the housemaster who abused him was found in the charred remains of the shed where the abuse took place. He had been burned alive.'

'The housemaster abused other boys too, didn't he?'

Callan nodded. 'A few.'

'So it could have been one of them.'

'It could have been. But the death happened on Gold's last day at Ashdown. He was the only boy leaving school that day. The police concluded suicide at the time, but now that the abuse has come out, they're reopening the case.'

Biting her lip, Jessie fixed her gaze on the blood-orange globe melting into the darkened fields at the end of the garden. Reaching across, Callan laid a hand on her arm, just above the thick bandage that had turned her left hand into a polar bear's paw.

'It wasn't your fault that Ryan died. You made a choice in the moment under huge pressure and the choice that you made was good, sensible. Blaming yourself is pointless and destructive.'

She sensed Callan looking hard at her across the table. Without glancing back from the sinking sun to meet his gaze, she smiled and shrugged.

'I don't. I don't blame myself.'

But she was lying. Yet again, she was lying. She couldn't explain it to Callan. Couldn't explain that everything she had seen since she woke from the anaesthetic made her feel guilty that she had survived Gold and that Ryan, sixteen-year-old Ryan, had died. It had been bad enough in the hospital, her mind's eye painting the wall above her bed with vermilion streaks of arterial blood, knowing that Ryan's chilled, drained body lay storeys below her in the hospital's morgue. But it was worse coming home, everything as she'd left it, life continuing as before. Everything except for her. She blamed herself entirely for Ryan's death and knew that she was right to do so. If she had gone with Gold when he had asked her to, Ryan *would* still be alive. Perhaps she would have died instead, or perhaps they would both have lived and the woman whose image filled the dark space in her mind every time she closed her eyes would still have her only son. Curling her legs to her chest, she slid her arm from under Callan's and wrapped both arms around her knees, her gaze still locked on the shrinking line of orange fire the horizon. The atmosphere between them was strained suddenly, with the truth about what Gold had done, the guilt that she felt for Ryan's death and the reality of her situation, the uncertainty of the new life that she would have to build outside the Army, hanging heavy in the air between them.

'I'd better go,' Callan murmured, draining his glass and pushing himself to his feet. 'I've got lots of paperwork to do for the case and it's easier to get it done with the office quiet.'

Jessie nodded. She stood too and collected both glasses.

'Here, let me take them,' Callan said.

'Oh, OK. Thank you.'

He reached over and fumbled them awkwardly from her grasp. She followed him inside. Setting the glasses in the sink, he switched on the hot tap and rinsed one and then the other.

'It's OK, Callan, I can do them.' She held up her bandaged hand. 'Despite my polar bear's paw.'

His smile didn't touch his eyes. 'What you really mean is, leave them, because you're not doing them properly and I'll have to do them again anyway.'

Jessie raised an eyebrow. 'What are you saying about me, Callan?' Her comment was supposed to have been humorous, but came out sounding edgy, uptight.

'Nothing that isn't true,' he muttered as he walked to the front door.

Unhooking his coat from the rack, shrugging it on in a manner that made her want to reach up and straighten his collar, an urge that she forced herself to resist, he pulled the door open. A breeze billowed into the room, its temperature unexpectedly chill after the warmth of the south-facing garden. It was almost dark outside now, faint stars peppering the royal-blue sky. Ducking his head to get under the lintel, Callan stepped on to the porch.

'I'll, uh, I'll see you soon then, Jessie.'

She nodded. 'That steak restaurant in Farnham, perhaps?'

Callan frowned. 'What?'

'No, nothing. Stupid, bad, bad joke.' *Why the hell had she said that?* Because she was nervous, she realized. Nervous, stressed and sad that he was leaving, that she didn't know what to say to make him stay. He was still the most attractive man she had ever met, and the only one she'd met with whom she thought she might be able to establish a trusting, adult relationship, and now it felt as if that possibility was slipping away from her.

'Take care, Jessie.'

She nodded. 'Stay, Callan.'

He half-turned, then stopped. Stepping on to the doormat, Jessie laid her hand on his chest.

'Stay. I want you to stay the night with me.'

'I think that you should probably get some rest.' His eyes held hers and the seconds passed.

'I can rest with you here.' She gave a tentative smile. 'Or not.' Torn between wanting him so much and feeling ridiculously vulnerable, her feelings laid out for him to stamp on if he chose to, she took his hand in hers, stepped back over the threshold and tugged. 'Come on, quickly, before Ahmose comes out and tells me that I'm too young, naïve, wholesome – delete as appropriate – to spend the night alone with a man.'

Callan smiled. 'You're a bad influence, Jessie Flynn.' Stepping back into the sitting room, he kicked the front door closed behind him. Taking her in his arms, he bent his head and his lips found hers.

'I hope you haven't left a dirty footprint on my door,' Jessie said, her lips moving softly against his.

'Dirty,' he murmured. 'Now there's a word I'd like to try.'

Acknowledgments

My thanks to my amazing agent, Will Francis and also Hellie Ogden, Jessie Botterill and the rest of the Janklow and Nesbit (UK) team. Your support is tremendously important and very much appreciated.

I would also like to thank Julia Wisdom, my Editor at HarperCollins, for her conviction, enthusiasm and commitment, and the whole of the fantastic team at Harper including Finn Cotton, Marion Walker, Hannah Gamon and Felicity Denham. Thanks also to my copy editor Anne O'Brien who has an unrivalled eye for detail.

I was lucky enough to have Mo Hayder as my mentor early on in my writing career and I owe her enormously for helping me get started on this interesting, fun and rewarding journey.

I could not have written this book without my friends and family, who have been so encouraging and supportive over the years. Thank you all. I specifically wanted to mention Ruth and Neil Callan, Bettina Wonsag and Seanie, John Marshall and John's lovely wife Rachel who does her